Jonathan Tulloch has won a K. Blundell Award and the J. B. Priestley Award. *The Times Literary Supplement* listed him as one of the best young British writers. His work has been filmed and translated into five languages.

A WINDING ROAD

Spring 2008. The art world is awash with money. The celebrated art mogul and 'adviser' Piers Guest has a client list which includes the wealthiest of individual collectors and an international merchant bank. A newly discovered masterpiece leads him away from his gallivanting through London's galleries and cafés, and takes him onto altogether different terrain . . . 1933. Under the shadow of the Nazi party, Helga and Ernst Mann bring a disabled child into the world. While Ernst drifts near the baleful influence of the Third Reich, Helga is determined to keep her child safe. 1890. In Auvers-sur-Oise, Vincent Van Gogh lives out his last days. Tormented by illness and regret, he takes up his brush, and paints the picture that will draw many disparate lives together.

JONATHAN TULLOCH

◆

A WINDING ROAD

Complete and Unabridged

CHARNWOOD
Leicester

First published in Great Britain in 2009 by
Jonathan Cape
The Random House Group Limited
London

First Charnwood Edition
published 2010
by arrangement with
The Random House Group Limited
London

British Library CIP Data

Tulloch, Jonathan.
  A winding road.
  1. Painting- -Fiction. 2. Art dealers- -England- -
London- -Fiction. 3. Goch,Vincent van, *1853 – 1890*- -
Fiction. 4. Large type books.
  I. Title
  823.9′2–dc22

ISBN 978–1–44480–163–7

Published by
F. A. Thorpe (Publishing)
Anstey, Leicestershire

Set by Words & Graphics Ltd.
Anstey, Leicestershire
Printed and bound in Great Britain by
T. J. International Ltd., Padstow, Cornwall

This book is printed on acid-free paper

For Shirley and Aidan

Does the road wind up-hill all the way?
Yes, to the very end.
Will the day's journey take the whole long
   day?
From morn to night, my friend.

Christina Rossetti, 'Up-Hill'
— Vincent Van Gogh's favourite poem

Poor fellow, few illusions are left to him now.

Theo Van Gogh

Bloomsbury, May 2008

1

I'm wondering how to introduce the figure that is just about to enter Russell Square Gardens. Place you at the right-hand gate of the Bernard Street entrance where the toilet Tardis stands and he will pass directly in front, close enough for you to reach out and touch the hem of his white Ozwald Boateng jacket. But from there, although you will gain an excellent view of his thick, floppy blond hair — brushed rather than blow-dried — and might even hear a snatch of the jazz riff he is softly scatting, you will miss the full effect of his presence: a swan swimming among the pigeons. To gain this wider perspective I will have to move you to the other side of the gates where a yew tree weeps over a row of red phone boxes. Positioned here, the figure will pass you at a distance of ten yards or so. This standpoint will also allow you to notice the little girl preceding him into the gardens. And her very large chocolate ice cream.

But perhaps I ought to let you see him earlier, as he crosses the busy road of Russell Square itself, say. Rewind sixty seconds from his passing through the gates into the gardens, place you on the kerb with the other pedestrians waiting for the lights to change, and you will see the arresting figure in white, stepping out before the green man shows. As he ambles across, you may notice something of which he is oblivious: the hackney carriage bearing down on him. For an instant it will seem certain that the taxi cab will hit him. Yet to fully appreciate just how close he comes to never making it to the gates of Russell Square Gardens in the first place, I would have to locate you at a window in one of the brown-stone, copper-green corniced hotels lining the square. From this vantage point you will have a clear view of the two destinies colliding like chess pieces: the black rook hurtling towards the careless white knight. There's the taxi gambling with the amber and taking the corner at 37.5 miles per hour; there's the strolling pedestrian, hands behind back, also, as it happens, exactly thirty-seven and a half years old. With the hackney carriage about to reduce the injudicious jaywalker to roadkill you may find yourself averting your eyes. As you hear the screech of swerving tyres, you might picture a white suit splattered red, arms splayed over the tarmac like Icarus. Yet when you do look, the taxi — its driver having fired off a volley of his obligatory abuse — is already slowing down to drop his fare at the next gate, and the stroller, seemingly unruffled, is about to enter the gardens. Such are the margins of fate's measurements. The Angel of Death has swooped down in Bloomsbury and missed by a hair. And people who might have witnessed a horror which they would never forget are passing into the gardens, talking into mobile phones, looking for a bench on which to sit and eat a sandwich. Pigeons land. A small child eats a large chocolate ice cream. The giant plane trees of Russell Square continue to perfect their mastery of t'ai chi.

Yet since we can, why not go even further back? If we were to dig up that skin of tarmac on which the white-suited figure so nearly came to lie, and tunnel deep through the yellow London clay, the rootage of water pipe, gas and cable, we would find the Piccadilly Line, on which, scarcely seven minutes previously, the object of our interest is riding on the tube train drawing into Russell Square station. There he is, sitting opposite you. Having just put away his BlackBerry, he is vacantly scanning the tessellation of the London Underground on the panel above your head.

This encounter will reveal two things that you may not have realised above ground. Firstly, other strangers as well as ourselves are looking at him, a fact he seems used to; secondly, when the train bursts into Russell Square station he alone of the four other passengers getting up to alight keeps his balance at the sudden jolt.

He's decided to take the stairs. There are 177 of them from the platform up to ground level. Everyone else elects for the lift so you two are alone in the steeply winding turret. Round and round you go, the wired bulbs on the low ceiling casting the figure above you in and out of shadow in a play of chiaroscuro effects. His silhouette shortens and then lengthens over you as the height of the ascent begins to seem an absurd piece of London Gothic, as though you are ascending the turret of some towering castle. About two-thirds of the way up he stops for just a moment. Has the sharp, narrow tread of the steps induced a twinge of vertigo? Carrying on, his footfall is as steady and quick as before but it is this half-second, this single pulse of eternity, that separates him from death. Without it, four minutes later the taxi would have hit him, and instead of a live human being following behind a little girl with a big ice cream into the pleasant, spring-tinged gardens, you would now be considering an addition to the countless Ghosts of Bloomsbury: Woolf, Trollope, Dickens, Darwin, Galsworthy, Jonathan Cape. But here he is emerging from the station, and if you are in step with him at the instant when the natural light of the glorious spring day floods over him, you will also know what made him begin to hum his jazz riff, like a bird singing at the hit of dawn.

But let's get back to the gates of the gardens. The figure has just passed through them and the little girl with the ice cream is veering off the path to wander under the plane trees. Our subject watches her with a smile, and for a moment you might wonder if they are connected; if this is his daughter and the young woman with the girl her nanny or his wife. Has the family arranged to meet at the Bernard Street entrance to Russell Square Gardens? An observant eye would quickly deduce that this man's body language expresses none of the defensive readiness of the modern parent. He is not poised to protect the child from either of the twin bogies of urban childhood: the speeding vehicle, or the predatory snatcher. If you are very perceptive you will have noticed that like all good characters in children's literature his smile is in his eyes rather than his mouth; and that as he grins at the sight of the child, he is also taking in the nanny's arse. Here is an individual equally touched by a little girl trying to eat an ice cream before it melts and the body of a young woman.

Why not get even closer to him? Face to face. To engineer this I'll have to make you enter the gardens from the British Museum entrance. Hurry through the square with its granite fountain, its dark-denimed Spanish EFL students, the midnight blues of lunching legal staff blown here from Holborn, the nurses and visitors of the nearby hospitals and the odd recumbent sunbather, and you will reach the object of our interest just as he is looking at the nanny. From this position it might strike you in the gut that here is a person who is likely to score most penalties he takes, and even from a short run up knock out a batsman's middle stump. Bear down on him directly stopping just in time to avoid a collision. With luck you may now find yourself in one of those quirky little rituals urbanites and ants know so well; that peculiar circumspect dance, in which on finding your way blocked you step to one side only to see the other person doing the same. This brief two-step, when a complete stranger becomes your mirror image, can last two or three seconds

5

before it grows threatening, humour piercing the usual city dweller's carapace. If this happens now, you will be able to look directly into the man's eyes, at which point any more description on my part will be unnecessary. As the old saying goes: one taste is enough to tell that the sea is salty. As his blue eyes smile, you shuffle aside and let him pass. That is the essence of this man. A smile that makes you feel privy to the things that matter; invites you to be a fellow conspirator in a world of possibilities. Boyish, disarming, infectiously generous, his smiling eyes seem, for a moment, to have singled you out from the billions.

Now that you've encountered him in all the ways that a stranger may, it's time to let him go. We must surrender our figure in white to the city, allow him to melt into the crowd just as we do every single day to all those other hundreds of thousands of people we meet without ever knowing them. Follow him as far as the flat granite fountain in the centre of the gardens then watch him melt away into London, that vastly complex and permanently unstable compound formed from constantly bonding and breaking molecules. The unfathomable formula of humanity. He disappears in stages, like someone wading into the sea, his bright blond hair showing a final time before the tide of the crowd covers his head, and he is gone, mingling with the other Bloomsbury ghosts as surely as if he *had* been knocked down by the taxi. And indeed an ambulance *is* wailing through Russell Square. Practically everything about this man in the Ozwald Boateng suit shall remain a mystery. We will never know why he likes jazz; what his favourite website is; which foot he leads with when crossing a stile; the reason he has two passports; why from time to time an image of willowherb on a railway embankment comes unbidden into his mind. Likewise the last words his father spoke to him will remain dark. We won't even know that his reoccurring toothache is just about to flare up again, or that his name is Piers Guest.

Unless. Unless we decide to follow him; unless we choose Piers Guest from the teeming millions of strangerdom, and bring him into conception. But we'll have to hurry; he must already be halfway to the British Museum.

It's the little girl who snatches this man from the jaws of oblivion; or rather her ice cream. Seeing her with a cone has put him in the mood for one; and so we are able to catch up with Piers Guest in the queue to the ice-cream van parked at the Montague Street entrance to Russell Square Gardens. We fall in behind him. 'A 99, please,' are the first words we hear him say, then, in reply to a question from the vendor, also dressed in white but not out of Savile Row: 'Yes, I'll have red sauce please. Thanks. Actually, could you put some of the chocolate topping on as well?' And now we can follow him at our leisure as he strolls back among the greenery to eat his ice cream, passes the fountain, and ambles along the gardens' celebrated vine walk.

2

'*Ohmigod*, is that you, Piers? Piers Guest?' Busy with the best bit of the ice cream — when the tube of the cone is pregnant with melting vanilla — Piers Guest looked over at the woman calling from the terrace of the Cafe in the Gardens. Standing up, she began to wave. 'Piers! Piers! It's Lucy; Lucy Short. Lucy Carr when you knew me.' Swallowing the last of his cone, Piers threaded his way over to her table. 'You don't remember me, do you, Piers?'

Piers gave the sheepish grin he always used in these situations; in his line of work it was impossible to remember everyone you met. Indeed, one indication of success was to be recognised more than to recognise; yet in a world where the currency was pegged to slights and flattery, it was essential to *seem* to recognise. 'Of course I do.'

'Don't tell me I've changed *that* much, Piers.'

'I haven't got my contacts in, that's all. You haven't changed in the slightest.'

'How do you know how much I've changed when you don't even know who I am?' The woman was smiling. Piers scanned the table before her for clues: a latte; a mobile phone; a bag whose designer he didn't recognise. 'I bet this happens to you all the time with all those programmes on television,' the woman said. 'There; I can see you thinking. Who's this? Another mad woman accosting me in the middle of Bloomsbury.'

It was the laugh that he recognised first. The

mouth next, the eyes, then: 'Lu! Lu Carr!'

'So you do remember me. How the devil are you, Piers?'

'I'm well. How about you?'

'Just about to get divorced actually. Don't worry, I'll spare you the gory details. Have you got time for a coffee? I think you owe it to me after our last meeting. Still on the strong black coffee?'

'Yes, I'll have an espresso. A *doppio*, please.'

Piers sat down opposite her. Although lines etched her brow underneath the heavily applied make-up and her body had thickened she still wasn't entirely unattractive. Had she been crying? Piers looked about. The cafe terrace was like a scene from a Renoir painting: people chatting as the sun streamed through the foliage of the plane trees. There was a joker at one of the other tables and the laughter of his friends rang out periodically. Lucy's phone rang. 'Are you going to answer that?' Piers asked.

'No. You married Sally, didn't you, Piers? Sally Twentyman.'

'Yes, Lu.'

'Lu? No one's called me that since uni. Are you still together?'

'Fifteen years.'

'Wow. You know, Piers, it's odd, but you look even better in the flesh than you do on television. Maybe it's the white suit. Very dapper.' Having gestured a waiter over, Lucy clamped a hand over her mouth. 'I didn't mean that to sound like it did. I love your programmes, when's the next one?'

'There's one coming out this autumn.'

'The last one about women painters was great. *Impressionists, Expressionists and Feminists*, wasn't it?'

'Yeah.' Or *Impressionists, Expressionists and those with tits* as one drunken production wag put it in the Groucho. 'This one's going to be about modern art.'

'Oh, brilliant.'

The waitress arrived, a girl fresh from Eastern Europe. Piers took in her body without Lu noticing. '*Espresso doppio*, please,' Piers said.

'And I'll have another latte. Why not live dangerously?'

Wings whistling a flock of pigeons flew low over the terrace. At the fountain a down-and-out was distributing bread from a plastic carrier bag. Piers watched the birds seething round their feeder. Smiling at Lu, he tried to remember how things had ended between them. Uncomfortably, he seemed to recall tears. 'I'm sorry to hear about your . . . divorce, Lu.'

'That's all right. We don't have any children. You didn't know him. Lucky you. Listen to me, I'm talking about him as if he was dead. Do you have any kids?'

'Yes. A little girl. Mimi.'

'Bless.'

'Short for Melissa. I suppose she's getting to be not so little. It's her ninth birthday today.'

'Sweet. Is Sally still as beautiful as ever? Come to think of it, I haven't seen her on television recently.'

'Well, she packed all that in to bring up Mimi.'

'Really?'

A brash cacophony of grunts burst out. It was the ringtone on Piers's BlackBerry. He stood up. 'Will you excuse me for a minute?'

Lu finished her first latte watching Piers wander back and forth under the nearby plane tree as he took his call. More pigeons flew overhead to the fountain. A siren waxed and then waned as an ambulance rushed down an adjoining street.

'Like the 'Crazy Frog,' do you?' Lu asked when Piers came back to join her. 'Your ringtone.'

'One of Mimi's pranks. She's always putting things on it. She wants to embarrass me at some glitzy do.'

'Glitzy do? Sounds good.'

'Believe me, they're not. Occupational hazard, I'm afraid. It mainly involves having to listen to old women making passes at you.'

'Really?'

'Of both genders. Charity functions most of the time. Makes it worse. Old women of both genders high on junk money and generosity. When they buy their art they want everything else that goes with it.'

'You're an art dealer as well?'

'Art *adviser*,' Piers said a tad quickly. He brought out a business card. Lu took it.

'You work for a *bank*?'

Again his reply was rapid. 'I've got an office there. As well as being an adviser and all the television work, I'm in charge of the bank's collection.'

'Monets and Picassos in the vaults?'

'Not at all. It's modern art. Actually, the fact is, we've got the largest collection of contemporary artworks in the country.'

'Sharks in formaldehyde?'

'We do have some Damien Hirsts, yes.'

'Well, I don't know much about art, but a lot of the stuff these days — ' She broke off. 'I bet you're sick of people saying that.'

Piers smiled. 'People are always challenged by modern art. I just happen to believe that we're living in the most exciting period as far as art goes. A kind of golden age. A return of the Medicis. A sort of — ' Piers broke off, he couldn't remember what came next on the production notes from the original pitching meeting for the programme. 'Well, you know, the interface of capitalism and culture — it's electrifying.'

The waitress made her way towards them through the other tables, tray balanced on a high wrist. Another confused memory came to Piers. Lu crying in the rain; him eating cake. Lu sighed. 'Look at you in your suit. You've been so successful. I wanted to be an actress. Got as far as *The Tempest* at uni.'

'You were an excellent Miranda.'

'Sally played *that* part. I was servant number 2, or something. It was when you met her. Sally. Anyway, just as well. I would never have made it as an actress; my body succumbed to gravity too quickly.' Piers watched Lu lift her breasts. Other memories stirred. They had performed the play during the second year at university. 'Piers

Guest. I can't believe we've run into each other again.'

'Friends reunited in Russell Square Gardens.'

'I thought we were more than friends.'

★ ★ ★

Recrossing the road on which he had nearly been killed, Piers and Lucy Carr entered the hushed foyer of the brown-stone, copper-green corniced Russell Rooms Hotel. The only witness to their infidelity was the aspidistra and the yawning Ukrainian desk clerk who didn't even bother to watch them walk up the thickly carpeted stairs.

Piers had finished and was wondering how long decency's sake ought to keep him uncomfortably perched on top of Lu when the 'Crazy Frog' called from his jacket. He hauled himself free, and with the condom hanging from him like a choked nestling, took the call in the bathroom. It was his wife. 'Hi, Sal, no I'm still at work. A gallery; somewhere in SW7. Course I remember the party. How many daughters do I have? I won't forget; I'm not a complete spod. Bye. See you soon. Love you.' Piers stared for a moment at the flaccid teat pendulous with sperm. Pulling it off he dropped it into a bin where it slowly oozed onto the nest of tissues left by the previous guests.

The bathroom door was ajar. No bad thing for Lu to have heard his conversation in case she had any ideas about resuming old times.

Filling the basin with cool water, Piers bathed his face. A shower would have been insensitive;

13

he'd get one back at the bank. The water spiralled away as he pulled the plug. Its loud gurgling masked Lu's approach so that Piers started slightly when he felt her behind him. Avoiding her face in the mirror, he reflected on their bodies. The vulnerability of her nudity, offered without the halo of lust, both touched and revolted him like a too persistent beggar. Although they were the same age, his was a body that seemed ten years younger than hers. Piers felt Lu's nipples stiffening against his lower back. Craning his neck round he gave her a chaste kiss, the manoeuvre pulling him free. He did not enquire into why she was crying but in the bedroom as he put his clothes back on he seemed to remember that there had been salt on their last kiss too. 'Have you sold your soul to the Devil, Piers?' she whispered from the bathroom door. 'I mean, you don't look a day older than . . . Don't worry; I don't want anything from you. I know you too well.'

As she sat on the toilet farting the air from her vagina, Piers pulled on his suit jacket and, standing at the window, tied his bright Fairfield Mill tie. Through the plane trees pulsing their spring green, he could see the figure of the down-and-out with his aura of feral pigeons: a brief statue of St Francis of Assisi. On the road, a black hackney carriage was speeding round the corner. 'I meant to ask you,' Lu called from the bathroom, 'do you still paint?'

There was a screech of brakes below. 'No,' he replied.

'You're joking.'

14

'I gave all of that up years ago.'

'Why? I thought you were good. When I knew you, you wanted to revolutionise the world of art. Are you all right?'

'Look, Lu, I'm going to have to shoot. It's been — '

'Yeah.'

Giving one last look to make sure he hadn't left his BlackBerry or wallet, Piers noticed that the bed was almost entirely unrumpled; untouched by their lovemaking save for the slight fault line running down the centre of the duvet: an installation of modern mores.

3

'And where the fuck have you been, Posh Spice?'

'Sorry I'm late.'

'What's that smell? Have you been fucking, Piers?'

'Did you get my email, Mikey?'

'I've got a fucking minging sense of smell, and I distinctly suspect that the odour of woman-fish is clinging to your gills.' As he removed his hand from the table, Piers wondered once again why someone with such a noticeable lisp as Mikey Durrant should choose to spray his speech with so many sibilants. The artist sitting with him outside the Forum Cafe on Great Russell Street often had bad breath but today his liberally dowsing sputum was stinking. 'So who *have* you been fucking then, Posh Spice?'

'I haven't been fucking anyone, Mikey.'

'Well, you should have been; you've got a face on you like a rent boy's arse. Cheer up, man.'

'Did you get my email?'

'Yeah.'

'The client's very, very keen.'

'I still want you to tell him to fuck off.'

'He's *very* prestigious. *And* he *adores* your work.'

'Then why did he put the last piece I let him buy in his downstairs bog?'

'Mikey, Mikey, you don't know that. It's just a piece of gossip. This guy is rich. I mean, he's a Mr Megabucks. And as for being connected! I know for certain that another artist, who shall remain nameless, practically gave him his last piece just so he could be in his collection.'

'I don't give a shimmering dump about that. I'm not serving my soul on a platter for some rich artichoke to shower it with shit.'

'That's some tongue-twister, Mikey.'

'Yeah, well, tell him to fuck himself.'

'Even if he gives you a million for it?' The two men laughed. 'Anyway, don't give me a hard time, Mikey. I'm just the go between. If you'd rather design murals for the local hospital and lead workshops for black, lesbian wheelchair users . . . '

Mikey laughed out a lungful of smoke from his joint. It lolled down the street towards the Quinto bookshop. The artist had dyed his hair black as well as his eyebrows and goatee beard. His bloodshot eyes were ringed with a heavy midnight eyeliner. 'The Nips will always buy it; or the Chinks. What's the matter with the cunt

— has he got constipation or something?' The artist let out an obscene, spraying raspberry. He had also painted his fingernails black for the full daemon effect.

'What's that?' Piers asked. 'On your tongue?'

With a liquid chuckle Mikey Durrant poked out his tongue. On its discoloured fibrous length what looked like a small stone had been pierced. 'I got it on the Net. It comes from fucking Alpha Centauri or somewhere. Piece of asteroid, isn't it? Fucking well minging. Now I really can get spaced, yeah?' He waggled his tongue so loudly that some tourists going to the British Museum hurried past. With a slurping giggle, Mikey took another deep toke on his joint.

'Yeah,' grinned Piers, not too wanly he hoped. 'Very Doctor Who. Anyway Mikey, what have you been up to, apart from mining the universe? In the email I mentioned that lots of other clients have been asking about you.'

'Fucking hell, you sound like a pimp, Piers. Posh Spice the ponce. Actually, I *am* working on something new.'

'Brilliant, I knew it would come back.'

'What?'

'Last time we met you were worried you'd burnt out.'

'Me? No chance. I'm thinking on a big scale, man. I mean, massive. A fucking Olympic-sized swimming-pool installation. Let's just see some fucker trying to put this in their crapper. Big, yeah, but not just in size. It came to me last night. I was watching this programme. About fucking cavemen. What they used to eat. There was that guy on it that lives off the land. Well, he was living like a caveman. Eating the same things. Berries and shit. Spearing fish. They had this way of making stuff that's poisonous edible. I mean, it's fucking poisonous but they could make it edible. You cook the cyanide out or something. They used to preserve hawberries and make them like sweets. Cavemen with sweets. Did you see it?'

'I know the kind of thing.'

'You don't usually think of them like that. Sweets? Cavemen are all raw meat and blood running down the chin. Savage. Pulling their women to bed by the hair, yes; fucking sweets for the kiddies, no. Got me thinking. Food is like the truth. And that's my installation. A fucking history of food. At one end there's, like, cavemen food, then at our end McDonald's and shit. And everything in between. With the cavemen there'll be mounds of hazelnut shells; at our end, bins full of Big Macs. The punters have to follow this path through it all; a path made out of rats. Dead rats. Nailed to the fucking duckboards. I haven't worked it all out but there'll be like animal carcasses rotting away. And the smell won't be hidden in no fucking formaldheyde. *I'm* not scared to confront people with the truth. So what do you think? I'm thinking of calling it *Highway of Progress*. Just to subvert everything.'

'Sounds great.'

'You know, the fucking liberal tradition sees history as leading to the perfectibility of humanity, but really it just leads to . . . '

'A table.'

'Got it in one.'

'Mikey, are you thinking of selling individual items?'

'I'm thinking about dressing up as one of the rats.'

'But for sales — '

'Who gives a fuck? Christ, you've been in that bank too long. It doesn't all just come to *ker-ching*.' Mikey clicked his fingers in a mime of a cash register.

'OK, we'll sell piece by piece. Unless someone wants the lot. In which case we're talking . . . '

'BRGNP.'

'Indeed we are, Mikey, indeed we are! BRGNP. Banana Republic Gross National Product. Actually,' said Piers, trying to hide his surprise, 'this is a good idea. I mean, fuck me, it's a stonker.'

'Yeah. When I was watching the telly I got so excited I had to piss in a mug. Makes you think. If a caveman and his family walked through fucking Bloomsbury, what would they eat? What would they fucking eat here? KnowwhatImean? Know. What. I. Mean?'

'Are you thinking of the Mesolithic period?'

'What?'

'They were hunters and gatherers. Farming only came in the Neolithic.'

'Fuck off. No head-shrinking boffin buggery here, Guest. They're just cavemen. Cavemen.'

'Albert Bresnard.'

'Who?' Mikey sucked so hard on his roach

19

that Piers thought he'd swallowed it.

'Albert Besnard. He did two related pieces. Modern man and prehistoric man.'

'When?'

'Oh, nineteenth century.'

'Fucking hell, Guest. I thought some cunt in London had stolen my idea.'

'In one of the pieces a man is reading; in the other he's fishing. They form a diptych commentating on the different kinds of foraging.'

'A dipstick more like. You and your little uni education. I don't want no archaeological dig here. Art is for the eyes not the brain.'

'Nor the knob.'

'What?'

'I mean, like, yeah. Great idea.'

'Sorted. There's going to be, like, mannequins. One of them dressed modern and ordering food on the Internet from lazyfuckers.co.uk; the others firing bows and arrows.' Mikey, drummed his forehead as he chanted: 'Hey, Mikey, you're so fine, you're so fine you blow my mind, hey, Mikey, hey, Mikey!' He stopped as inspiration visited him again. 'I know, I could do cave drawings in human shit. Some of the shit will be after I've eaten caveman food for a week. Raw meat, berries. Some after fucking McDonald's. The painting could be freshly done every morning from the piles elsewhere in the installation. I could even get the punters to pull down their pants.'

'Yeah. Wicked: a *shit-tych*,' said Piers, wincing.

'What is it?'

'Bloody tooth might be flaring up again.'

20

'Get it taken out; I'll put it in the installation. You know, like on archaeological digs: it's always the teeth that tell them when the artefacts are from.'

A British Museum-bound family walked past the Forum Cafe. The father stepped over to look at the menu. 'Any good?' his wife called.

'They do soup.'

'I thought we said the kids needed something more substantial.'

'You get a bread roll as well.'

'Let's find somewhere else.'

'You might not get anything better.'

'Do they do pasta or something?'

'No, I don't think so. Just soup.'

'Well, I don't call that substantial.'

Piers watched the family move down the road. They stopped a little further along to peer into a cafe window as though investigating a fruit tree. 'I think you've got something here, Mikey. I really do.'

'The only thing about this fucking asteroid,' said the artist, inhaling. 'I keep on knocking it with the roach.'

'How much of that stuff are you smoking?'

'You're obviously not smoking enough. Why are you all on edge?'

'I'm not.' For a moment Piers thought of the taxi that had so nearly hit him. He pictured himself spreadeagled on the road. An instant later he saw a railway embankment blazing with purple willowherb. Blinking the pictures away he stared after the family. They were still strolling at foraging pace. 'You're really onto something here, Mikey. Look at that family; they could be a group of hunters-and-gatherers. *It's somewhere around here that we found the watercress last year*, the father's saying. *And I remember in the winter before she died, the old one singing a song about the deer coming here in a drought.*'

'What the fuck are you on about, Posh Spice?' As he flicked the ash from his joint, the tendons on Mikey's slim wrists tensed like a puppet's pulled strings. His lisping voice was suddenly thick. 'I don't suppose you fancy a cock up your bum, do you?'

'No, not really.'

'Have I asked you that before?'

'Once or twice.'

For a moment Mikey's red eyes smouldered like the end of his joint, then he guffawed. 'You should have seen your face. I love shocking you, Posh Spice.'

The 'Crazy Frog' leapt from Piers's jacket pocket. He answered it with alacrity. 'Hi, Sal. Don't worry, I haven't forgotten. Yes, I'll pick that up. I'm with Mikey. Mikey Durrant. Here, have a word.'

Piers's eyes glinted as he handed the BlackBerry over. 'Hello, love,' shouted Mikey, holding the phone about six inches from his mouth. 'Look, I'm not going to be long 'cos I don't want no egg laying on my head. Cancer, innit? Radiation. Word to the wise, yeah? Give hubby a shag and turn him back into a human being. Otherwise one day you'll end up sleeping next to a wanker. I mean banker.'

Piers took back the phone. 'See you soon, Sal,'

he said over the gales of laughter from across the table. 'Yes, I'll bring it. I know it's important.'

As usual Mikey let Piers pay the bill. 'This asteroid thing, it's a headfuck,' the artist discoursed as they strolled down Bloomsbury Street. 'One minute it's millions of miles away; the next it's in my mouth. It's gone from being far away to — '

'Being in your mouth.'

'Well vamped. Right, come on. Swing by my pad and I'll show you the first sketches of the new piece.'

'I can't. Sorry. Something on.'

'Fuck off. You haven't been to my Chelsea place yet.'

'I can't today, Mikey.'

'What, going to another meeting for Financial Fuckers Anonymous? Snout in the trough. *Oink, oink, oink!* Something's happened to you since you set foot in that bank.'

'You don't mind the money though, do you?'

'Yeah and neither do you. Seriously though, I sometimes wonder what I pay you for.'

'Actually the BBC have been in contact, Mikey; Alan Yentob wants to make a programme.'

'*That*'s more like it. Am I the main artist this time?'

'I think so. I'll tell you later. Look, I'm going to shoot. It's my daughter's birthday party, actually. And seriously, Mikey man, the asteroid's probably not a good idea.'

'Fucking square.'

'No, it's just that they have a habit of being

23

radioactive. They're isotopes. If you're worried about mobile phones, then I'd be *very* worried about that little bit of rock.'

Taking one last pull on his joint, the artist flicked it away. It landed on the bars of a drain where it lay smoking like the Devil's severed finger. 'Taxi!'

The passing cab pulled in. 'Not you again, whitey,' the driver snarled. 'What are you, some sort of fucking ghost?' But Piers was already walking away.

The taxi drove by with its window down. 'That's right,' shouted Mikey, 'get yourself back to your money counter. Go and sit down arse to arse with shit bricks.' Then, plucking the asteroid from his tongue, he threw it out onto the street. It hit Piers lightly on the lobe of his left ear.

4

Piers closed his eyes and luxuriated in the hot, steamy shower. The surging jet and *naturally honey-scented organic shower gel* washed away both the Russell Rooms Hotel and Mikey Durrant. Head directly under the nozzle, Piers felt again that sense of spring he had noticed in the gardens. As he sat on the bench to dry himself, a couple of men came into the changing room. 'Piers, busy as ever, eh?' they grinned.

'Some of us have to work,' he replied, pretending to recognise them.

As they went into the gym, the art adviser glimpsed a tableau of useless toil: the fiercely pedalling, stationary cyclist; the figure labouring on the treadmill; the rower sliding up and down the length of his riveted boat. His BlackBerry beeped. *Don't 4get 2nite lol Sal*. From his capacious locker Piers brought out a fresh shirt and suit. Would there be time for a quick bite before his next appointment?

Crossing the well of the bank's vast interior, Piers stared up at the tiers of the trading floors rising above him. A scale not seen since Babel: over eleven thousand people were employed here. Today more than usual it struck him how much like a prison it was. With the open walkways and cellular glass partitions all it lacked was a safety net and warders; but as the joke went, here they *want* you to die if you jump; nothing more useless than a trader with lost nerve. Piers glanced at the people waiting for the lift. They were young and male too, just like the prison population. He himself was by far the oldest face; in fact he was coming to be something of an old lag. Not being a member of the trading or banking staff he avoided the monthly culls of the ageing staff unable to meet targets. The lift purred down and the doors opened. Young men in midnight-blue suits debouched, young men in midnight-blue suits entered; they were all open-necked these days, keeping their ties just for meetings with clients. Piers tensed as he stepped over the chrome threshold into the glass lift chamber; usually he avoided elevators but there were no stairs in the bank. 'What you doing coming up to the top levels, Piers?'

somebody he did not recognise asked. 'Decided to do some proper work?'

'Slumming it,' Piers replied, hiding his discomfort.

Once Piers had tried to count the computer screens on the main trading floor. He'd given up after two hundred. About the size of a football pitch, the room was ribbed with horizontal metal rows of which each trader was allowed two metres; a small flag representing their nationality, and a photograph of a loved one, were the only concessions to the individuality of the battery hens. As he walked through it all now, heading for the bank's retail mall, some of the traders, clearly in the middle of a deal, clenched their phones; others lolled back examining the markets on their screens, yawning like resting lions.

'We can get that ready for you tomorrow, Mr Guest,' the Filipina in the dry-cleaner's boutique said as he handed over his suit, her pronunciation of *Mr* reaching Piers as *Mirror*.

'I'd better have some new shirts while you're at it. Five. And do you know if they sell ice tea in the delicatessen up here?'

'Yes, they do, Mr Guest.'

'It's my daughter's birthday. For some reason she and her friends have become addicted to ice tea.'

'Better than drugs, Mr Guest.'

'Well, yes.'

'How old is she?'

'Nine. Nine today.'

'A lovely age, Mr Guest.'

Before popping back to his desk, one of the quieter islands in the vast financial archipelago, Piers stopped a moment to look at the new Stephen Chambers he had just hung. He loitered for a while, but none of those passing by even so much as glanced up at it. 'Your wife left a voicemail,' his assistant greeted him.

'Cheers, Cora.'

'She even told me to tell you — '

'Not to forget, I know.' He lifted the bag bulging with ice-tea bottles he had just got from the deli. 'Anything else?'

'Just your usual one million and one messages. Mr X is getting quite aggressive; he says you promised him first refusal on Mikey Durrant's next piece. Oh yeah and you've got that meeting with Roger Bosman at three. You'll have to leave pretty quickly afterwards to get home in time for the party. That reminds me, here are the things you asked for. They came this morning.'

'You're a saint.'

'Cool suit, Piers.'

'Yeah, I feel like frosty the snowman in it.'

Down in the basement, Piers went straight to the Gourmet to Go franchise and ordered a salmon and avocado sandwich, and a bag of Kettle Chips. He sat down in one of the alcoves. Chewing the sandwich, he looked round the space. Although artists didn't like having their work hanging in the food concourse, he felt that he ought to put *something* up here. One of the younger ones; a German maybe; that would keep head office happy. With a vague sinking feeling Piers sensed that it would soon be time for something larger to justify the bank's substantial sinecure. In fact, he would have to begin planning another show for them. The last one, 'Berliners and Bangers', had been a huge success, a perfect mix of German and British art. People had loved the way he'd made the programme like a menu for different types of sausages. And he'd been worried that they'd think he was taking the piss! 'Room for a little one?'

Piers looked up at the young woman standing above him. Her hair was black; she was about twenty-three or-four. 'Zohreh, hi. How are you?'

'Good, thanks. One girl and her herbal tea looking for a temporary home.'

'Yeah, sit down.' Motioning her to the chair at his table, Piers consulted his watch. 'I've got about five minutes.'

'Ah, the Guest charm and flattery again.'

'I mean I've got an appointment in five.'

'Do I know her?'

'Some bloke actually. A trader wanting advice on buying art.'

'An accountant with attitude; lucky you. Watch out, his hormones will be raging. PBT. Pre Bonus Tension. They've all got it at the moment.'

Zohreh sat down and peered at Piers over the rim of her camomile tea. Her long, dark eyelashes were set off by the white of the cup; not for the first time Piers felt a stir within him at the depth of her beauty. 'So how are you doing, Zo? What have you been up to?'

'Thinking about you mostly, old boy.' Piers gasped. Zohreh had reached under the table and put her hand between his thighs. 'Just needed to remind myself it was real after all.' She grinned. 'Look, I need cheering up. Now, I just happen to know that the stateroom isn't being used all afternoon. I could teach you a bit of speed belly dancing from the old country.'

A memory of their last hasty but riotous coupling under the oaken table of the old mercantile stateroom gusted through Piers. Taking out his BlackBerry, he had already begun to email Cora to rearrange the appointment when the more recent taste of Lu interposed itself. 'I can't.'

'Bah, humbug.'

'I tell you what though,' he said. 'We'll have a night together.'

'You're pretty sure of yourself. When?'

'Soon.'

'Yeah, well, me and my remote control might just have a date with a shopping channel.'

'I thought you'd want to, Zo.'

'Of course I do, you wretch.'

He felt her hand reach for his under the table. Taking it briefly, Piers looked around. In the knot of people at the Costa counter he recognised someone from the global markets department. Dropping Zohreh's hand, he raised his own to wave. 'Hi, Piers,' the man called over. 'How's everything in the world of art? When are you going to bring us a shark pickled in urine, or a soiled bed?'

'When I've taught accountants like you to appreciate them.'

'Do you know everyone in this place?' Zohreh asked.

'Not yet,' he replied, opening his bag of crisps.

'What were you thinking about before, Piers?'

'What?'

'I watched you for a little while; you were eating your sandwich and seemed deep in meditation. Haven't taken up yoga, have you?'

'Actually, I was thinking about what Mesolithic man would have made of all of this. You know, the way for some people this bank is their world. Food. Clothes. Warmth. Community. Well. How would Mesolithic man have coped with it?'

'They wouldn't have had nice suits like yours. How did you get the stain out?'

'What do you mean?'

'I saw you before. I was just passing your office. There was a stain on it.'

'Oh, the monkey's blood.'

'Monkey's blood?'

'You know, the red sauce for ice creams.'

'Monkey's blood. I haven't heard it called that before.'

'Well, that's what it's called.'

Zohreh grinned. 'Who by?'

'Don't know; everybody.'

'It's new to me.'

'Maybe because you were born in about the year 2000.'

Zohreh's eyelashes curled over the cup again. They were definitely not fake, Piers decided. 'Piers, you *do* like me, don't you?'

He moved his foot until it was touching hers. 'I think you're fucking brilliant.'

'I mean, I know I'm just a boring old accountant and you're this mystery man, our captive from the wilds of the art world. That's a point — I still haven't worked out just exactly why the bank gives you such an obscene amount of money when you're hardly ever here.'

'How do you know it's obscene? *And* how do you know I'm never here?'

'We girls have our ways of knowing. But what are you doing here, Piers?'

'In the bank? Perfect interface of capitalism and art. The Medicis . . . that sort of thing.'

Scanning the queue, Piers saw someone watching him. He moved his chair back. Sensing the situation, the girl opposite got up and whispered before disappearing down the concourse: 'This little girl hopes you meant it, about the night away.'

The man in the queue was definitely staring. In fifteen years of marriage, Sally had never found out about Piers's women. Why should she? They didn't mean anything; of that Piers was convinced. The man was coming over. He was indistinguishable from the thousands of others like him who worked here. Midnight-blue suit, no tie, hair styled in the manner that Piers described to himself as a *Prince Harry*. 'Piers Guest?' he asked, arriving at the table.

'Yes?'

'I think we've got an appointment. I'm Roger Bosman. I'm interested in buying some art.'

'Oh yes, sorry, Roger. Sit down.' Piers grinned with relief. 'What kind of thing are you interested in?'

31

'Well, nothing way out. No elephant dung.'

'Right. Well, the first thing you need to know,' the art adviser began, 'is that we're at one of the world's most exciting moments in terms of art. You know like with the Medicis . . . ' Piers ran skilfully through his spiel and ended up by recommending a Mikey Durrant drawing. He brought one up on his BlackBerry.

'Oh,' said Roger Bosman.

'It's innovative. At first, granted it might revolt you; but just let it permeate. Did you know that 39 per cent of happy relationships start with mutual dislike?'

'Will it give me a good return on my investment?'

'Oh yes,' Piers said with great certainty. 'How much are you thinking of spending?'

'It depends on my bonus. About ten grand.'

'If you could go up to twenty I could get you something really good.'

'Can I buy it through you?'

'I'm an *adviser*, Roger; not a dealer. But you can go through the bank. There's a credit scheme.'

'I shouldn't need that. Right, well, thanks for your time. I'll think about it.' Roger Bosman stood up; once again Piers felt his scrutiny. 'Oh, that reminds me, Piers. I have to pass a message on. I was at a party the other night and this woman started asking me about you.'

'Really,' Piers replied levelly.

'Yes. Well, we were talking about art. So I told her about where I worked, and the way the bank wants all its employees to appreciate art, that type of thing. And I mentioned you.'

'I see.'

'Course she'd heard of you. Seen you on the telly and things. Ended up with her asking me whether you'd be interested in an undiscovered masterpiece.'

'Well, Roger, I guess the whole art world would be interested in one of those.'

Roger Bosman's prominent eyebrows thickened. 'I mean, she said it was an Impressionist or something. Or a neo-Impressionist. I'm no expert. But she seemed to think that it was big.'

Piers grinned. 'If you took all the undiscovered Impressionist masterpieces discovered in the past ten years and put them in this bank, there wouldn't be an inch of wall space left.'

'Does that include the neo-Impressionists as well?'

'No, you'd have to let them have the floor space. Trouble is, they have an irksome habit of not being genuine.'

'This woman, she seemed certain that you'd be interested. A foreign woman. She said she was an old friend of yours. Said she wanted to keep it hush-hush until you'd talked. Anyway, she asked me to give you this.'

Roger Bosman brought out the woman's card and placed it in the art adviser's breast pocket; it wasn't until Piers was on the tube going home that he found the photographs in his waist pocket. He recognised one of them instantly. A copy of an old black-and-white exposure, its composition had been as carefully constructed as any old master. Two friends were sitting at a

33

riverside cafe deep in discussion. Around them the world arranged itself as though through a perspective frame: the vertical parallels of the roads, the crisp horizontal bars of a railway bridge, the vanishing point formed by the converging of the river and the roof of the café. A single emaciated tree stood over the two friends, only one of whom faced out of the photograph. The man with his back to the photographer, Piers knew, was Vincent Van Gogh. It was his last known photograph; taken in Paris in 1882, the year the artist discovered colour. The second photograph was not familiar to Piers. It contained only one figure. Again, in black and white, it showed the back of a man. He was standing in tall corn before an easel. As the tube began to slow to his stop, Piers took out the business card. It belonged to a woman from the Van Gogh Museum in Amsterdam.

5

The birthday party had already begun when Piers walked down the four-wheel-drive-lined street and drew nigh his own house. Ascending the flight of seven stone steps that swept up from street level to his front door, he peered through the pane of art deco stained glass. The hall was swollen with the impedimenta of young schoolchildren, their bags, violin cases, lunch boxes, along with pushchairs and a couple of bikes. Sinking down onto the top step, Piers contemplated the thrum of the London traffic in the middle distance. He had always found it a comforting sound, like the creaking of a hammock. From closer at hand, in the canopy of the tree of heaven that rose above him, came the hum of bees. Rooted in the cellar well, the tree lifted its nectariferous leaves to the first-floor window, its cream blossom and matt-green foliage thrown into relief by the house's white façade. The branches were bathed in sunlight; the bees drifted like motes of honeyed dust. A burglar alarm wailed from the next street, then shut down abruptly, leaving the air almost peaceful before the next distant siren took up the baton of woe.

Piers had been sitting there for about five minutes when he heard the familiar, erratic banging of a tambourine. He watched its player being pushed slowly into view: a wizened, grey, wheelchair-bound woman with a loose jaw and lolling head. Moving past the four-wheel drives, she banged her tambourine, groaning with joy. 'Hello, Marg,' Piers greeted her. 'Having a good old play?' Throwing her head back the woman drooled with laughter. Piers came down the steps and beat out a rhythm on her tambourine.

'Going far today, Ralph?' he asked the wheelchair pusher, a fat, down-at-heel man with a greasy ponytail.

'Yeah, spring, innit?' Ralph glanced up at the tree of heaven. 'Look at the bees. Marg, look at all them bees. You'd think you was in the countryside.'

Marg laughed and beat a tattoo on the skin of

her tambourine. 'That's jazzy,' said Piers. 'I like that.'

Piers watched the couple continue along the road. Where did they come from? Where were they going? Another one of the capital's ordinary mysteries. The last thing he could hear before they were subsumed into the sound of London's growling belly was the little rumble of Marg's cries of delight and the cymbals ringing on the edge of her instrument. Going back up his steps, Piers opened the front door.

'Where have you been, buster?' Sally asked as he tried to sneak into the kitchen without being noticed.

'I was abducted by aliens. I told them I wanted SW7 but they took me all the way to heaven.'

'Have you got the ice tea?'

Piers lifted up the carrier bag. 'Something smells nice.'

'Just a few organic pastries.' Sally opened the oven and rode the rush of heat. 'Oh . . . bloody hell. Some of them are getting burnt.' Piers looked at his wife. Sally swore so rarely, and when she did it always accentuated the northern accent which had been quite marked when he had first met her, but had slowly eroded like a peninsula. As she straightened up, Piers saw a coronet of sweat on her brow. A lock of blonde hair fell across her face. Taking the pastries over to the kitchen surface, she passed through a beam of sunlight that exposed the first few wrinkles on her face; the slight speed bumps beneath each eye. Piers felt a surge of love.

'Don't just stand there staring like a cow in clover, Piers — serve the ice tea.'

'Can I just say something first, Sal?'

'No, get that ice tea through there.'

'I love you.'

'Take the ice tea. We have to leave soon.'

When Piers backed into the room with the tray there was no sign of Mimi and her friends. He looked at the adults. Those his age and over were mothers, they were sitting on the comfortable seats and sofa; the younger ones perched on dining-room chairs were nannies. 'Oh yes, Piers,' said one of the mothers. 'The tray suits you. I see you've got a new vocation. Can we have you as a waiter for our next bash?'

'I'm too expensive. Where are the girls?'

'They're upstairs getting changed. At least we *think* that's what they're doing. We keep on hearing great gales of laughter.'

'This is a serious business, Piers,' said another mother, who was breastfeeding a tiny baby. 'A trip to the theatre.'

Piers grinned. '*High School Musical.*'

'Well, it's not quite *Die Zauberflöte*,' the breastfeeder admitted, handing the baby over to her nanny for winding before it could posset on her shoulder. 'But it's a start. Is that a German Expressionist piece on the wall, Piers?'

Piers looked at the lavishly coloured canvas hanging on the wall. 'It's Sally's.'

'I thought *you* were the art dealer.'

'Art *adviser* actually.'

'Wheels within wheels,' winked the mother.

'Organic pastries anyone?' said Sally, coming into the room.

Piers grinned. 'Your Georgiana Fairbanks is causing a bit of a stir, Sal.'

'It's very . . . vivid,' the mother said.

'Actually, she's probably Britain's greatest Expressionist. *Only* Expressionist come to think of it,' said Piers.

'Georgiana Fairbanks?' mused the mother.

Piers nodded. 'She was a bit of a one-off, a wild woman. Just ask Sal about her. She was born in Cumbria.'

'In the rectory beside our farm,' said Sally. 'When I was growing up, there were all sorts of stories about her. People said that she was kept a virtual prisoner.'

The mother sighed wistfully. 'Artists are such interesting people. I bet you meet some wonderful individuals, Piers.'

'Not many that I'd want to take to *High School Musical*.'

'Well, you can't start them on opera too young,' another mum put in. 'But I think anything's good if it gets them in a theatre. Tara was really keen on seeing *High School Musical*. She didn't even mind missing her yoga class.'

'What a sacrifice,' said Piers.

'We were double-booked too,' said a third mum. 'But it seems for Olivia that *High School Musical* easily wins out over her Cantonese lesson.' She gestured at the toddler drawing with a crayon on the wall. 'Pixie, don't do that please.'

'Where does Olivia go for her Cantonese class?' the first mum asked.

'Just the Language Centre. But you know they're thinking of starting lessons at school. Give them a good head start.'

The third mum nodded. 'They do Mandarin as well as Cantonese after school hours at JAGS. We're almost certainly sending Tara there when she's eleven. Pixie, Mummy said *don't*.'

'Really? We'd thought of JAGS for Olivia. We were both very impressed. I knew they did Critical Thinking and Latin. I didn't know about Mandarin. Excellent.'

'Ya, perfect. *Just* what Oxbridge is looking for these days.'

'What do you have to do to get a drink in this house?' demanded a man coming into the room from the hall. 'And you need a plumber, Piers. Your downstairs loo's blocked.'

'The bearer of good news as ever, Gav,' Piers replied.

'And judging by the noise that's coming from upstairs, you might need a builder as well.'

'What do you think, Gav?' Pixie's mother asked. 'The BBC will be needing people with Cantonese and Mandarin, won't they? Or will it be Arabic?'

Gav nodded sententiously. 'Ten, fifteen years, China will be on the ten o'clock news more than America. Arabic? It's too carbon-based.'

'I think this one's already learnt how to write the Chinese characters,' said Piers, wresting the crayon from Pixie's tight little fist. There was an angry sob as Pixie swung a punch. Gav drew Piers into the kitchen. Sally was coming the other way with a huge cafetière.

'Don't go sloping off,' she whispered.

'Christ, Piers,' said Gav. 'The mums' army's enough to drive you up the wall. Did you see all the Chelsea tractors outside? More tanks than the Battle of Kursk. Your house has been turned into an oestrogen-on-the-make zone.'

'So what are you doing here, Gav?'

'Party? Group of nine-year-old girls celebrating your daughter's birthday? Trip to the theatre? My daughter Emily goes to school with your daughter Mimi? They're best friends? You savvy now, big white fella?'

'You should lay off the autocue, Gav. It's playing havoc with your conversational skills. Have you been auditioning for a part in some Australian soap opera? I thought the BBC frowned on its broadcasters raising their inflection at the end of a sentence.'

'Nice suit, Piers. I didn't realise Top Shop had opened a new gay branch.'

Piers seemed to scrutinise his friend. 'Clucking bell, Gav, are you wearing make-up? I know you have to put it on for Auntie Beeb but I didn't know you'd taken to wearing it on the streets.'

'Hilarious. I hear you've got the brain of an octogenarian, Piers. Mimi told me you tried her new brain gym exercises this morning.'

'Anyway, what are you doing here? Aren't you supposed to be in some far-flung corner of the globe bringing truth and enlightenment to your poor benighted audience?'

Gavin sighed dramatically. 'Actually, you're not wrong. Things are coming to a head at the

Beeb. It's the big Z. The feeling is that it's going be another Rwanda.'

'The big Z?'

'Zimbabwe. You know, hot country north of Cape Town? They want someone to go down there and do a full exposé. Five ten-minute reports for the ten o'clock news, a week of *Newsnight* and a *Panorama*. That's unprecedented coverage. Did I say *someone*? Actually it's me they want to — '

'To save the world again? How tiresome for you.'

'It's all right for you to be a cynical bastard, but if somebody doesn't do something they're all going to die. It's actually an obligation. A question of morality. Don't you know the poor fuckers are dropping like flies, or aren't there any windows on the world in London's art galleries?'

'What are you getting so uptight about, Gav? It's perfect for you. Go out there and save the world.'

'Christ, Piers, do you really know so little?'

'I thought it would be just up your street. You could do a John Simpson and liberate Harare.'

'Don't talk to me about John Simpson. Anyway, the BBC is banned from Zimbabwe. With my profile they'd arrest me the moment I crossed the border. And if everyone's starving what the hell do you think the jails will be like? I don't mind reporting on the ravages of Aids but I'd rather not catch it myself.'

'Especially if you go in wearing make-up. Gav, I've got to ask you this as your oldest friend: are you on the turn?'

From upstairs came a clatter of girlish laughter. The espresso machine punkahed the kitchen with the aroma of coffee. Sally swept in to collect the cake. It was iced with a picture of a three-year-old Mimi on a slide.

'The domestic goddess,' said Gav. 'Seriously, Sal, a production company I know is looking for someone to present a new cookery programme. A kind of antidote to Nigella Lawson. Do you want me to arrange a meeting?'

Piers nodded as his wife folded the serviettes and brought out the cake forks. 'You could call it *Cumbrian Kitchen*. You'd only use local northern produce, and there'd always be a cow in the garden.'

'Nice idea,' Gav said.

'And she could present the programme wearing wellies, which she can then use to throw at the cow. Jesus, Gav, I'm winding you up.'

'Think about it, Sal. People are often asking me about you. Just the other day I was at the Sky offices and they were putting out feelers.'

Music blasted down through the ceiling. 'I told her not to play it so loud,' Sally said. 'We'll have the Huffingtons next door complaining again.'

'Oh let them,' said Piers. 'It's only half five for God's sake. Bloody *Honourable* Huffington thinks he owns the world.'

'Well, he does,' put in Gav. 'Half of Chelsea anyway.'

'It's all right for you, Piers,' Sally said, gathering up the plates. 'But I'm the one who has to sweet-talk them round. It took me weeks of diplomacy to smooth out that jazz quintet you insisted on hiring. Now don't slope off, we'll be singing 'Happy Birthday' in a few minutes.'

'Why do you keep on using the word *slope*?'

'Think about it, Piers.'

'And you think about what I said, Sal,' Gav said as he held the door open for her. 'Mimi's nine now. You don't need to play the little hausfrau any more. Do what we've done: get a live-in nanny. She's brilliant, and she's got a sister, if you're interested. Polish. Doubles up as a plumber too. Looks after the brats, unblocks the crap. What more do you want?'

As Piers steamed the milk for Gav's latte, he felt the familiar, fluid rhythm of his wife going up the stairs followed by the quietening of the music. 'How's the garden bench weathering?' Gav asked.

'For pity's sake, Gav, if you want to have a fag just go outside and have one.'

It was still warm. They sat on the bench beneath the hawthorn. From time to time its blossom fell. As Gav lit up his cigarette, Piers stared through the French windows. Sally had come downstairs and was talking to the adult guests. In the days when they had been falling in love Piers had frequently felt sick with the strength not only of his desire for her but of his tenderness. Even now the flash of her golden hair in the distance, or the sudden perfection of her philtrum could thrust him off balance. Glancing at Gav, Piers realised that he too was studying his wife. 'You bastard, you lucky, lucky bastard. You've got it all, haven't you?'

'What are you rabbiting on about now, Gav?'

'Who else has got a back garden like yours in the whole of west London?'

'Not the Honourable Huffington, and that's what galls him.'

'Ah yes, trouble with the neighbours in SW7. You spend a million and all you get is a lousy terrace. Watch out, Huffers'll slap an asbo on you.'

'I bet he's considered that. No, really. These judges think they own the place. In fact, I'd be careful with that fag if I were you, Gav. He might fine you for smoking in public. That wouldn't go down well at the Beeb. They'd be looking for a new poster boy to join their elite news team.'

Gav gestured at the garden. 'She's made it lovely out here. Actually, maybe it's a gardening programme she should be doing.'

'Will you fuck off, Gav? It's getting a tad tedious. Every time you put your nose round the door you're offering to fix her up with a different television crew. What are you going to suggest next, the lead role in an Andrex advert?'

Gav blew out his smoke evenly. 'Why do you insist on stifling her creativity, Piers?'

'I didn't know I was.'

'Well, you are. She'd be the anchor on News 24 now if it wasn't for you.'

'Oh God, what a gilded Olympus that must be! What a Mount Parnassus Top! Not everybody wants to chase the wind, you know; some people are more at home with the

44

important things of life. What's that snort for?'

'Like you, you mean?'

'I know when I'm lucky.'

'Do you?'

'What's that supposed to mean?'

For a moment Gav seemed about to reply, then he shook his head. 'Leave it.'

'Leave it? What's got into you? You've been a pain in the arse ever since you got here.' Piers gurned at his old school friend. But there wasn't the usual bantering glint in his eyes. 'So what's the Polish nanny like, Gav?'

'Brilliant with Emily and blocked toilets. Ugly as sin. That was one of the required skills Rochelle put on the unofficial application form. Must be unable to inspire erection in man of the house.'

The two friends' laughter rang round the garden. The hawthorn blossom shimmered in the gentle breeze. 'Actually, I don't think I *can* leave it,' Gav said, inhaling deeply. 'Piers, look, something's happened. Well, it might not have but . . . Shit, this is difficult.'

Through the French windows, Piers could see that the girls had come downstairs. Sally was adjusting something on Mimi's dress. Their daughter didn't have her parents' grace. She was destined to be a plain woman. Seeing her now, beside Sally, Piers felt a fierce desire to keep her safe from the world.

'Look,' said Gav, 'there's no easy way of saying this; I'm going to just come straight out with it.'

'I wish you would.'

'Are you having an affair, Piers?'

'What?'

'There's a rumour.'

Piers swallowed. 'What a fucking load of rubbish.'

'So it's not true?' Gavin sighed with relief. 'Don't look at me like that, Guest, old mucker, I'm only telling you what a little birdie told me.'

'Little birdie? You mean a bloody great vulture. Who?'

'It doesn't matter.'

'Doesn't matter? Someone's spreading muck about me and you say it doesn't matter. I want to know who it is so I can go and have it out with them.'

'I've already done that. I told her to fuck off. Said you might be a pain in the arse but you weren't a bastard.'

'Cheers, Gav, cheers.' As Piers put his cup and saucer on the armrest of the bench, his mind raced. He'd always been so good at covering his tracks; even from his best friend. That was what made the bank such perfect terrain: it was completely separate from the rest of his world. Who had he been seen with? It couldn't have been Lu; even in London a forest fire takes longer to rage. The two men peered over at the French windows. Sally was helping another one of the girls with her dress. The idea of hurting her hit the art adviser like a blow. 'Let me ask you something, Gav. Do you think I'd ever, I mean *ever*, do anything to risk losing her?'

'Course you wouldn't. I mean, you might be ugly but you're not stupid. Look, forget it, Piers. I just thought I should mention it, that's all.

Thought you had a right to know.'

At the French windows Sally was holding up a BlackBerry. She opened the doors so that the two men could hear it ringing. 'Not mine,' said Piers. 'I've got the 'Crazy Frog'.'

'Shit,' said Gav, checking his pockets. 'Mine.'

'It was in the loo,' Sally called.

Gav came over and scrolled through the missed calls. 'Oh-oh. Got to go.'

'The world collapsing without you again, Gav?' Piers enquired.

'Look, Sal,' said Gav, 'can you ring Katya and tell her to meet you at the theatre?'

'Katya? Oh right, your new nanny-plumber. Have we got her number?'

'I keyed it in for you under GP: Gav's Pole. Bye.'

Piers lit the candles on Mimi's organic, artisan-baked cake; his rousing rendition of 'Happy Birthday' was not taken up by the others. 'Put the brain gym away,' he said to his daughter who with a tight group of her friends was crowded round the Nintendo DS Lite.

'Just because you're eighty,' Mimi replied.

'Blow your candles out and make a wish, munchkin.'

'Now I'll have to start again.' Mimi blew on the candles half-heartedly.

'And the rest,' laughed Piers. 'Daddy wants his kiss.'

'Don't embarrass her, Piers,' Sally put in.

'Embarrass her? I'll get the rest of her baby pictures out in a moment. But seriously, gis a kiss, love. Otherwise you won't get what I've got in here.' Piers brought out the carrier bag Cora had given him. From it he produced a book by Beatrix Potter. All the girls laughed. A phalanx of phone cameras snapped Mimi holding up the book.

'Daddy's lost count,' Mimi grinned. 'He still thinks I'm six.' She turned to her friends. 'I apologise for my father's rather feeble sense of humour.'

'So I don't get my kiss. How about this?' With a flourish he brought out another object from the carrier bag.

'That is so cool!' Mimi whooped. 'A signed Chelsea top.'

'The whole squad.'

Again the camera phones came out. 'You've redeemed yourself, Daddy.' Mimi threw her arms round her father. For one brief instant, he closed his eyes; but already she was pulling away. 'Come on, let's get everyone in the picture.' Holding out the shirt, the girls formed a tight group, snapping themselves with their camera phones held at arm's length.

Sally was stacking the dishwasher when Piers came into the kitchen. She'd put her hair into a ponytail and he felt the fine tips tickle his nose as he came up behind her. 'Maybe Gav's got a point,' he whispered. 'We could do *Sally's Kitchen*. Make it a porno. *Sally Does It in the Kitchen*. Have you dressed in only your grandmother's apron.'

'I think the shirt was a bit excessive, don't you?' she said, continuing to load the dirty dishes. 'I mean, the theatre trip and meal and everything else is costing practically a grand.'

'An art collector got me the shirt, Sal.'

'And remember the drawing party at the V&A tomorrow morning.'

'That's another freebie.'

'And thanks a bunch for putting Mikey Durrant on your phone.'

'Hey, Mikey, you're so fine, you're so fine you blow my mind, hey, Mikey!'

'I could hear you sniggering in the background,' grinned Sally as she turned into Piers's arms.

'I just wanted to remind you of the kind of people I have to work with. Actually, Mikey had quite an interesting idea today. His first.'

The dishwasher began to throb against Sally's buttocks. Piers placed an exploratory palm on them but was relieved when she twisted free. The taste of Lu repeated on him like a ring of raw onion eaten at breakfast. 'Piers, there's a whole squadron of Chelsea tractor drivers and their cherished offspring in the next room.'

'Not to mention the nannies. It's a bit weird though, isn't it?'

'What?'

'I was thinking about it in the garden. How different the parties are to when you and I were that age. Maybe oop north you were all sent scavenging on the coal tip on your ninth birthday but in the soppy south I seem to remember party games. You know, Blind Man's Buff, Grandmother's Footsteps, What's The Time, Mr Wolf.'

'Times change.'

'Then when I saw Mimi and her mates all together I thought, nine going on nineteen. They're going to start talking about boys in a minute. Since when did you become a teenager at nine?'

'Grandmother's footsteps *is* What's The Time, Mr Wolf. Anyway, help me tidy up, the stretch limo will be here soon.'

'Tidy up. What about Raquel?'

'It's her day off.'

'Day off! That's what comes of having a Spanish nanny. I knew we should have gone for a Filipina. Gav's sorted it all by getting a live-in Pole. Plumber *and* nanny. Two for the price of half.'

'What was the matter with Gav?'

'How do you mean?'

'I saw you arguing in the garden.'

'We weren't arguing.'

'Looked like it. Anyway, I thought he was acting a bit oddly. He was early too. *Very* un-Gavlike behaviour. He was a bit annoying actually. Kept following me.'

'Oh, you know how it is, he fancies you.'

'Don't be ridiculous, and keep your voice down. That lot in there' — she pointed at the door — 'have a hot wire to the whole of London. Don't you need to get changed?'

'You think I need to?'

'Your Ozwald Boateng might be a tad fluorescent under lights.'

'Oh damn, that reminds me — I'm going to have to leave at the interval.'

'Why?'

Piers grimaced. 'I've got to go somewhere tonight.'

'Oh Piers, you promised Mimi.'

'I'll be back tomorrow evening. Noon the day after at the latest.'

'But the painting party is in the morning.'

'I can't help it.'

'And what's so important that you have to miss your daughter's birthday celebration?'

'The usual thing. Some idiot with a million pounds to waste.'

'Well, if you have to, you have to.'

'Believe me, it's the last bloody thing I *want*. I mean, do you think I like having the carbon footprint of an elephant just because some tycoon with piles wants the most recent piece of mindlessness from some pampered, pretentious idiot like Mikey Durrant?'

'Someone will hear you speaking like that one day.' Sally pointed at the clock. 'You've got ten minutes before the limo comes. I hope next door doesn't complain. I told you when you hired it he wouldn't like it.'

'Even Chelsea has to have its Streatham moments.'

'By the way, you surprise me.'

'How so?'

'Grandmother's Footsteps. I can't imagine your mother leading party games.'

Upstairs Piers put on a jazz CD and, undressing, scrolled through his phone numbers. He selected one marked 'Phil Bacon, asset management'. A strange woman answered. 'Is Zohreh there?' Piers asked.

51

'Who's calling?'

'Mikey Durrant.'

There was only a short pause during which Piers could hear some bass-heavy music thumping. Piers turned up his own music. 'I've been waiting for you to call,' said Zohreh.

'Who answered?'

'My flatmate. But I knew it was you; sex with you has woken my latent telepathy.'

'It's short notice but can you meet me at Heathrow?'

'Tonight?'

'If you can't it doesn't matter.'

'Try and stop me. Where are we going?'

'Surprise.' Fiddling in his pocket, Piers brought out the afternoon's accumulation of business cards. 'We'll decide when we get there.' One of the cards was from a gallerista he'd met on the tube, another from one of the mums who'd just started a catering business called Simply Natural and was keen to get into the art scene, and then there was the card Roger Bosman had given him, nestling between the two photographs. 'I'll see you at Costa's in Terminal 4 at nine.'

With the black-and-white photographs in hand, Piers stood at the window. A third of the garden, about the area of a tennis court, had been made into a wild-flower meadow. In it, the bluebells were fading. They had moved here just after Mimi had been born, when the success of his second TV series and the accompanying book had made them decide to risk a house way beyond their budget. With the exponential bull charge of the art market, the gamble had paid off. Piers could only remember it vaguely but on purchase the garden had been a place of patios and pergolas around a carefully manicured lawn. Brick by brick, stone by stone, concrete wedge by concrete wedge, Sally had cleared it all, bringing in their place, from her parents' farm, saplings, seeds and newts. With Mimi sleeping close by in her pram, Sally had patiently conjured a piece of her native Cumbria in west London. Once, Piers had come home from work early and had watched from this window as Sally fed Mimi at the breast. As a toddler Mimi had loved nothing more than flying down the slide to her mother waiting at the bottom. For a moment Piers half heard the sound of his daughter's laughter, a child of three again. 'What are those?' Sally asked. He hadn't heard her come into the room. She was looking over his shoulder at the photos.

'Oh, nothing. Some artist or other trying to get me to promote his work. You wouldn't believe the scams they pull to get your attention. That one's a photo of Van Gogh, the other's obviously a mock-up of him. Oh Christ, I bet it's an installation called *Dead Sunflowers* or *Wheatfield Growing Dead Artist*. But where is it, Sal?'

'Where's what?'

'Mimi's slide; it's gone from the garden.'

'It hasn't been here since last summer. Piers, haven't you noticed your little girl is growing up?'

'Oh, look.' Piers turned abruptly from the

window. 'I'm not going. I mean, I'm *going* to the theatre with you and Mimi, and I'm *not* going to meet that buyer. I'm sick of all that. It's her ninth birthday for God's sake. That won't ever happen again, will it? I'm going to ring up and cancel.'

'Is that the stretch limo? Come on, Piers.'

The University of Freiburg im Breisgau, November 1953

1

According to the label on its tin, this is the oldest film reel he has looked at so far. The numbers count themselves down on the makeshift screen, and the grey snowstorm eases to reveal an aged woman sitting in a ladder-back rocking chair. With a pointed nose and chin, and a forehead as fissured as the bark of a black poplar, she is a figure straight from the pages of a Jacob and Wilhelm Grimm tale. Despite the jerky footage, her rocking motion remains smooth. A cat crouches on her shoulder; a ball of wool dances on her lap. As she tells her story, she knits; the large needles agile as wands in her tree-root hands. And it is these hands that draw the eye of the viewer into the grainy movie; they are the silent film's centre of gravity, a pulsing, pumping heart that functions far better than the watching professor's own failing organ.

It is towards the end of the short film that he sees again what took him so utterly by surprise the first time. Even a second viewing makes him feel the shock, a blow to the base of his spine like an axe at the root of a fir. The crone gets up and the camera follows her over a rush-strewn floor to where a group of children are sitting listening to her story. They must have been misbehaving and she dispenses the summary justice of a few blows. Returning with her to the still-rocking chair, the camera momentarily picks out a figure standing in the corner of the kitchen. His face is in shadow, a hair on the lens divides his face, but the professor recognises him. Of course this had always been a possibility; viewing so many hundreds of hours of his films there was always the chance that he would catch a glimpse of the film-maker himself; yet the old man could not be more shaken if the crone had stepped down from the screen. The reel ends; and the makeshift screen, a sheet draped over a tall bookcase, becomes a brilliant blank again. In that single instant of footage, that moment of a man peering from the shadows, the professor has remembered exactly what it was like to be in the company of Ernst Mann.

Having spent his life exploring the superstitions and fantasies of others, Professor Dietrich Gruber is himself obdurately empirical, but as he stands there by the heat of the projector, the tail of film still flapping around the spool, he feels a curious reluctance to look in the corner of the room where his former student's desk used to stand. The hair on the back of his neck crackles. Of course, nobody is there; even the desk is long gone. But the moment he turns his back on it, the sense of Ernst's presence grows once more, taking shape in the place where he sat so often, especially in the beginning. Amputees talk of the pain that persists in missing limbs; the old man knows that the human heart has its own version of this syndrome.

Leaning heavily on his stick, Professor Gruber sets off across the dusty room. He cannot allow emotion to enter the matter; nor ghosts either, although it is his task to descend among them. As he passes through the projector beam his own silhouette looms on the screen.

The long oaken table is stacked high with an array of neatly piled objects. Film reels, photographs, manuscripts, typescripts, letters, Magnetophone Sound-writer tapes, everything pertaining to the work of Ernst Mann: a meticulously arranged archive. It has taken the professor a month just to collate and assemble this, and his job has hardly even begun. He searches through the Sound-writer tapes. Holding up each one in the light of the projector, he tries to read the barely legible letters. For all the undoubted brilliance of his fieldwork, Ernst Mann never mastered the etiquette of clear labelling. Dietrich Gruber screws up his eyes. This one seems to tally with the date on the film tin: *May 1936*; and he feels fairly certain that the woodworm scrawl of his student's handwriting also seems to specify *GE. Aarne-Thompson Tale Type no. 130. Travelling Animals. Variation LXX*. But even he, who knows this handwriting probably as well as anyone on earth, cannot decipher whether the tangle of letters denoting place form *Engenlund*, or *England*. England most likely. He remembers the trips Ernst made across the North Sea; recalls his love for that cousin nation's down-to-earth yet fantastical stories.

The old man makes his selection from the heap of transcripts more easily. He has already catalogued them, attaching his labels with strong paper clips. The notes, however, still form a bulge in the hessian sack. He hasn't even begun to sort through them, knowing that for all their chaotic disorganisation they will reveal the full brilliance of his friend's mind in a thousand fresh ways. Gruber leans heavily against the table. Before carrying the Sound-writer tapes and papers on the short journey to his chair, he must regain his strength. These days the simplest of things loom over him like the Herculean errands of a task tale.

Even though he has shrunk with age the chair fits him as well as it ever did. The headrest seems to reach out to cradle his stiff neck; the seat ripples in accommodation of his withered buttocks. Just to sit here is a far more effective palliative than the doctor's pills he pretends to take for his niece Helga's sake. The chair's maple wood shows no wear, except for the shiny ellipses where he was wont to rest the points of his elbows when deep in thought, a habit older than the century. Yet as soon as he looks at the transcript, written in the graceless hand of his student, the comfort evaporates. Once again the figure seen on the film seems to be watching from his desk. *Travelling Animals*, most commonly known in the form collected by the Brothers Grimm as *The Musicians of Bremen*, was Ernst's favourite story.

How bad the ache is this afternoon. If only he could get up and walk away as he did fifteen years before. Why should he be the one to conduct this inquest? After all, it's only a self-imposed task; no one else would know if he returned all these papers, films, tapes and photographs to the damp and cold of the deep cellar where they'd been since the end of the war; who would care if he left the memory of Ernst Mann to fade like his bones mouldering away into a kilo of slime compressed beneath the new buildings of Berlin?

The squeak of trolley wheels coming down the long corridor breaks into the old man's despair. 'That's the last load I'm bringing.' As ever the sub-archivist enters without knocking. His voice is sharp with the usual sense of grievance. 'If you want the rest of that junk you'll have to go and get it yourself. I'm not a porter, you know.' The trolley grates as he upends its contents, spilling them over the dusty floor. A dander of must rises from the scattered artefacts. 'What do you want all this rubbish for? And you've left the projector on. I've warned you about that before. It's expensive as well as being a fire hazard.'

Professor Gruber does not reply. He has found it easier to say as little as possible to this abrasive young man, although there is so much he *might* say; after all, the records of other academic disciplines are far worse than that of his own. Responding to the sub-archivist's jibes will only antagonise him, and the old man lacks the strength to carry up the countless pieces of the archive from the cellars himself. He can't ask

Helga to help; it's hard enough for her to have to bring him here every day. Besides, this boy's contempt is only a reflection of that felt by the greater world: a thimbleful of an ocean's contempt. What can this young man understand? What can anyone know who didn't live through it?

'What are you doing here anyway, old man, salvaging your tales from the master race storybook? People like you.'

This is not the first time that the professor has been on the receiving end of a stranger's casual cruelty. Fifteen years ago another young man stood before him in this very room stripping him of his professorial chair and doctorate. That one had been a Nazi, but the sub-archivist is no different. If the professor has learnt anything then it is this: evil is a matter of opportunity. The greatest mischief is done by those who create the opportunity in the first place. People like Ernst Mann. The projector beam dies; the sub-archivist has pulled the plug. 'Please,' begs the old man, 'let me have it for just one more day.'

'People like you.' The sub-archivist does not close the door behind him and Dietrich Gruber listens to the fractious squeak of the trolley fading down the long corridor. Easy enough to see how a bully like this would become a Nazi, but how did Ernst become evil? Opportunity? No, that's not explanation enough. Through the open door, the cuckoo clock calls just as it did thirty years ago when Ernst Mann walked down that corridor for the first time to the Department of Folk Narrative and Customs. A meeting that

60

would change so many lives.

It had been during the leanest of the Versailles years when the university begrudged the department even the candles to read by. One late afternoon the professor had been deep in a compendium of folk curses when a knock as insistent as the spring drumming of a wood-pecker had interrupted him. Rising with a tweak of annoyance, the professor had found a young man, no more than a boy, at the door. Barefoot and so thin that his ribs marked the fabric of his homespun shirt like the scours on a rune stone, Ernst was about to become the first student to enrol on the professor's Folk Narrative course for a decade. Small and wiry as a gymnast, his red hair flaming on a head that seemed too large for his shoulders, Dietrich Gruber had instantly been put in mind of one of the little people of the Celtic twilight. An impression that was to grow with each passing year.

2

Theoretically portable the Magnetophone Sound-writer is a formidable machine. Professor Gruber lifts its lid onto the workaday mystery of rubber and metal. The sharp, familiar tang of mechanical intestines coils up through his nostrils. Ernst, a great believer in utilising technology, used to call it his 'story net'. *If the Brothers Grimm had had one*, he would joke, *it might have curbed their excesses*. Controversial enough territory, although of course nothing like what was to

61

come. *Listen to this, Professor,* his student would say, switching the machine on to play his latest field recording. *Can you hear the log crackling on the fire? Well, is it pine or fir? That grunting is the family hog at the door. Professor, we no longer need to read the past like a document, we're sitting down with it by the fire. We can scent the woodsmoke of years gone by, smell the pig shit of history.* Retaining a memory that his mind has lost, the old man's brittle fingers fit the Sound-writer tape in the machine: *GE. Aarne-Thompson Tale Type no. 130. Travelling Animals. Variation LXX.*

The Magnetophone begins to wheeze. It takes time for it to warm up. Long enough for Professor Gruber to grope his way back to the projector, plug it back into the wall and begin to refit the reel. He must synchronise the images with the sound.

But it is no easy matter threading the film and fitting the celluloid tongue on the spool's metal palate, and he has only just managed as the Sound-writer tape hisses into life, filling the room with his student's voice. No matter how many times the professor has heard it over the past few weeks, once again it jolts him to the core. 'GE. Aarne-Thompson Tale Type no. 130,' Ernst announces. 'Travelling Animals. Variation seventy.' Even reading the blandest of words, Ernst's voice twinkled like his eyes, when he spoke of wonderments he seemed to cast a spell over the listener. A strange accent; no one ever did find out where he came from. 'Sixth of May 1936. Cumberland, England. We are in the kitchen of Jessie Twentyman. She is sitting on a ladder-back rocking chair knitting. She is eighty-three years of age. Listening to her are her grandchildren and great-grandchild. The cat is called Jemima.' The reel wheel spins the flat monochrome of the celluloid into an old woman, a rocking chair, a cat and a tale. The knitting hands pulse. Ernst seems to fall into a crackling void out of which the voice of Jessie Twentyman emerges:

'Yance upon a time when hogs spake in
  rhyme
And donkeys chewed 'bacca
And hens snorted snuff to make them tough
And ate pease pudding to make them
  fatter . . . '

Dietrich Gruber has difficulty in understanding; she seems to be speaking in a dialect. The English equivalent of Alemannic perhaps, the language of the professor's native Black Forest. The transcript is no help either; Ernst, an expert in all Germanic languages, especially English, has transcribed the dialect phonetically. The crone's voice is thin but expressive like a stream in the low water of summer:

'In them days when wishing was having, there were a farmer living up on the fell. He had a donkey what had served him for many a half-year never once gannin' noughty even when he had to carry them heavy sacks of corn up top. And that's a queer lang way to gan. Came the day when cuddy was awer auld for sacks of corn.

63

Came the day when cuddy heard his master sharpening his gully knife . . . '

The old man feels his chest tightening. The doctor has given him only weeks. He has kept it from Helga; his niece's hope is another one of his palliatives. But there's no time to think of this; once more the ancient narrator is knitting Ernst from the shadows. She rises from her rocking chair, the young audience ducks under her blows. The Magnetophone plays an incomprehensible snarl of northern English, and there on the screen Ernst Mann is again standing in the twilight of the old rush-strewn kitchen. Of course, the monochrome cannot show the full flare of his red hair, but it emphasises his size so that he seems like one of the children. Like a conjuror at a party, Ernst Mann had the face of one barely able to conceal the coming fun, and the old man is asking himself the same question: how could someone so good, so kind, so funny, so brilliant, so full of life end up serving the Nazi black death? Although this is the third time the old man has seen the footage of Ernst listening at Jessie Twentyman's rocking chair, it still takes the breath from him. Even in death Ernst Mann has preserved his habit of surprise. And the last time the old man saw his former student and friend had been the most surprising of all.

It had been late in 1943 when the professor had found himself on trial at the People's Court. He can no longer remember the exact wording of the charge brought against him, there was never much variation in such matters, but the tone had been set right from the start when his

64

own lawyer had begged to be relieved of defending him. 'How can I face my children tonight,' the old man's counsel had pleaded with the court, 'if I've been handling this toxic weed of arcane academia?' Other things Dietrich remembers from the proceedings against him are the judge's sputum caught in the morning sun as he roared abuse; the prosecution's mocking him as a *broken cuckoo clock* on account of his Black Forest accent and the slight stammer that became catastrophic under stress; the blue flower drooping in the vase beside the rigid back of the stenographer. His only guilt had been a refusal to prostitute himself to the Nazi Party's pseudo-intellectuals, more than enough reason for execution in those days when you could catch death like a cold. The old man had long abandoned hope when he heard the court call the name of Ernst Mann. It was the first and only time that Dietrich was actually to see Ernst in his SS uniform — black except for the red area around the swastika on his arm: a crow with a gaping palate. At the sight, he had felt the first onslaught of the physical pain which was now killing him; as though at that moment, like Faithful Heinrich in *The Frog Prince*, an iron band had been placed round his chest.

Last week the old man came across the transcript of this trial; a curious thing for Ernst to have preserved. The professor filed it along with the other legal documents in the archive: proceedings of an eighteenth-century werewolf trial; a medieval tribunal investigating an accusation of witchcraft and cannibalism. All

65

three of a piece. Yet what had struck the professor most forcibly during the trial itself was not its monstrosity but Ernst's utter vulnerability before the full fascist panoply: a pixie standing beneath the Nazi eagle soaring on the wall behind the judge. Was it at this moment that Ernst realised, like a character from the *Sorcerer's Apprentice* genre, the real nature of the forces he had flirted with? Was it then that he had begun to understand his side of the bargain in the sale of his soul? Dietrich felt no anger then nor does he now. A father betrayed by his son knows only the agony of sorrow.

From the corridor, the cuckoo clock calls the old man back to the present. Jessie Twentyman has disappeared; the screen is blank. Going to the door left open by the sub-archivist, the professor looks down the corridor. Even during the brief heyday of the Department of Folk Narrative and Customs this was never a busy thoroughfare. Now its silence is troubled only by the sparrows in the gables outside, and twice a day by his niece Helga who accompanies him down its length each morning and returns for him in the evening. Mullioned windows overlook an overgrown cloister from the middle of which a thorn bush is spreading its tentacles. All it lacks is a sleeping beauty. But of course there are none of those in this story. If the past has taught the old man anything it is that death does not deal in counterfeit. Cold draughts squeeze through the leads of the windows and ghost down the parquet floor. From the wall, portraits of eminent academics peer down myopically. There is a gap where the professor's portrait used to hang. The faintest of shadows remains on the wooden panelling. Helga will be here soon. Dietrich sighs. His niece is often on his conscience. Wasn't it his fault that she fell in love with Ernst Mann in the first place? Helga's task is far harder than his own. He lost only a brilliant student, a friend.

Even more careless than usual, the sub-archivist has left a wake of documents winding up the corridor. Weariness fills the old man. If only birds could scoop up the crumbs of *this* trail; if only he didn't have to follow them to the dark eaves where they lead. Bending stiffly he begins to take them up, aware that he is not only picking up the work that breathed new life into an entire academic discipline, but also the shards of his niece's life, and the pieces of her children's childhoods. How strange that in so many ways a Nazi could make such a wonderful father.

So tired. Clutching the papers the old man stumbles back to the chair; his breathing slowly stabilises as he reads through the salvaged papers. Each page is a reminder not only of the brilliance of his former student's insight but his lightness of touch. Not for him the heavy hand of the expert: he wrote about stories with all the skill and nuance and caprice of the best tale-tellers. But the professor is not here to admire Ernst's undisputed genius. His is the role of a detective sifting through evidence in order to pinpoint the moment when flirtation becomes crime; to catch the clink of Mephistopheles's coins. Mustering as much strength as remains, the professor jams his swollen knuckles down on the arms of his chair. Experience has taught him that pain is the only sure way of keeping himself awake.

Yet for all his efforts the professor must have drifted off because he comes round from his dream of the People's Court to feel the worm of sleep escaping from his mouth, and to hear the squeak of the sub-archivist's trolley coming down the corridor once more. Too late to switch off the projector, he snatches up a leaf from the concertina of pages spread on his lap. It's easier to bear the sub-archivist's hectoring if he doesn't look at him; and unlike the Gestapo *this* young man lacks the power to compel him. The page he reads is a discourse on a strange variation of the *Travelling Animals*. He remembers Ernst bringing it back from a wedding in Schleswig-Holstein; an old, old version in which the robbers in the house are demons and instead of driving them away the animals beguile them with their music for which they receive rewards of gold and maidens.

Lost in Ernst's reading of the story — his commentary on the donkey playing a squeeze box is so simple yet so beguiling, his ideas on the pre-Christian persistence of materials still truly fascinating — the professor has forgotten the presence of the other man. When he looks up he sees that it is not the sub-archivist at all. 'Can I help you?' Dietrich asks.

'I'm sorry,' the other replies. 'I didn't mean to frighten you.' His speech is that of a local; vowels high-reaching and steeply plunging as the precipitous sides of the Black Forest valleys: a janitor.

'The mops are over there with the brooms.' Gruber points to the corner of the room where the cleaning stores are kept. 'And would you mind turning the projector off for me?'

'Certainly.'

After the sub-archivist's hostility, the janitor's courtesy is a welcome relief. The projector dies and the room is immediately plunged into dusk. It is later than the old man had thought. The janitor clicks on the light switch, but nothing happens.

'The university sees fit to keep us in the dark,' the old man says, not entirely able to keep the bitterness from his voice. 'Would you pass me a candle? They're in a box under the dusters.'

Returning to the manuscript, Dietrich hears glass chinking; a chair being dragged across the floor. All at once the room is bathed in light. 'The bulbs were dead, that's all,' the janitor says. 'But, Prof, when did they turn your department into a store cupboard?'

The professor looks up. The janitor is still standing on the chair. Large and dishevelled, he is a bear of a man. Dietrich purses his lips warily. Not a janitor; a journalist perhaps? Have the vultures got wind of what he is doing? Yet he seems too down at heel even to be a gentleman of the press. His suit is ill-fitting, the buttons round his middle clearly unfixed; his tie is feathered and stained. A smell of goats infiltrates the scent of disinfectant and books. Sour alcohol too; the local *Blutwurz* if he's not mistaken. His fingernails are encrusted with grease. 'I'm down on my luck, boss,' the bear says, as though reading the old man's thoughts. 'What can I do? People just don't want cuckoo clocks any more. All the same, don't you recognise me? Have I changed that much?'

'Hans,' Dietrich whispers. 'Is it really you?'

As he steps down from the chair, a sad smile sets Hans's grey moustache quivering. 'Larger than life, *Herr Professor*.' He surveys the room with a heavy melancholy. 'Funny to see the old place again.'

'Hans, can it really be you?'

Hans knocks his head with a large fist. 'Sounds like me all right.'

Professor Gruber feels his heart lurch. Is he hallucinating, or has the man who accompanied Ernst on all those field trips really materialised before him? Back from the dead, Ernst Mann's cameraman, sound recordist, driver through all the corners of war-torn Europe, general factotum. The empiricism that has so long been the characteristic of the professor's life feels as insubstantial as a fairy's whim. 'I thought you were dead, Hans.'

'You too, Dietrich?'

The professor tries to rise. His limbs have stiffened; he forces himself upwards through the pain. Shuffling halfway to the dishevelled visitor he stops abruptly. An animal terror has seized him. Not even the dock in the People's Court made him feel like this. Has he indeed descended among the ghosts? 'You've come back?' he asks, his lips trembling.

'That's right, boss.' Gently placing a huge arm round the frail old man's shoulder, Hans takes him back to his chair, and lowers him into it.

'Where have you been all these years, Hans?'

'After the war, I drifted. South America, Africa. Settled in Switzerland. As you can see, nobody could accuse me of prospering. I make cuckoo clocks that nobody wants; every now and again someone might trust me to repair one. Those Swiss. They think they invented the cuckoo clock. And that's my life. Since, you know.'

With the projector turned off, the chill is quickly gathering in the room. The old man gazes in wonder at Ernst's faithful friend, his *fidus Achates*. 'I never thought I'd see you again.'

'Likewise, boss.'

'How did you know I was here?'

'I didn't.' Hans rubs his hands together. 'Do they insist on the room being so cold?'

'I don't like to use the stove.'

Hans disappears down the corridor, and although he has changed almost beyond recognition, his footfall is as comforting as ever. The man that comes back into the room with a huge armful of logs is no ghost. In no time at all the stove is roaring. The scent of resin and wood smoke ousts the disinfectant. 'Hans,' the professor says, then gestures at the archive on the table.

Going over to the table Hans blows through puffed cheeks: a mannerism Dietrich remembers. He peers into the Magnetophone. 'The

71

story net. I bet it still works.' The professor nods as with an oily forefinger Hans caresses one of the red, iron oxide coils, cajoling a ball of fluff from the vinylite recording head. 'It's the best machine of its type ever made. Look: rubber pulley as tight as the day of our first recording. We must have recorded thousands of hours but not a sign of wear and tear. I worked it out once, boss, six months of real time. Almost as good as one of my grandfather's cuckoo clocks.' Still gazing into the Magnetophone Hans speaks quietly: 'Ernst Mann was never a Nazi.' He picks up a reel of film. 'Now if only the camera had been as good as the Magnetophone. The trouble I had with it. Say it jammed once, it jammed a thousand times. Of course working with cuckoo clocks put me in good stead. As Ernst said, each machine speaks the same language, though the dialects vary wildly.'

The old man can barely trust his voice as he asks: 'Hans, how did he die?'

Hans belches softly; and Dietrich definitely detects the blur of *Blutwurz* alcohol on his breath. 'I think you know, Herr Professor.'

'It's never been confirmed.'

'Well then, he was killed in action.'

'Were you with him?'

'No.'

Although each passing moment revives the old man's affection for Hans, he must still stick to his task. He selects an item from the archive and hands it to the bear-like man. It is a photograph of Ernst in SS uniform. 'Boss,' says Hans, 'if you think Ernst Mann was a black crow then you can't have known him.'

The question that the professor must ask now catches in his throat. Nevertheless he rips it out. '*Is* he dead?' Without replying, Hans picks up another log and opens the stove door. 'It's just that one hears of people resurfacing. Argentina, Brazil, South Africa.'

A flurry of sparks flares from the stove as the fuel is thrown in. Licking his fingers, Hans bends down to pick up a burning chip. He flicks it back onto the fire. 'Tell me something, *Herr Professor*. Did you find out where he came from?' The old man shakes his head. 'Me neither; even though we spent all those years working together I never ever knew where he hailed from. Well, at least we know where he's gone. He died defending Berlin.'

'In the uniform of the Waffen SS.'

Again the belch. Dietrich pretends not to notice as Hans takes out a bottle and, turning his back, puts it to his lips like a bugler. 'Prof, don't you remember what it was like in those days?'

'How could I forget?'

'There were very few choices. In fact just one. Either you lived or you died. And even to live, you had to let part of you die. Ernst chose to live.'

'No. That's not enough.' The old man's raised voice rings out reedily. His hands flutter as he fumbles at the archive and snatches up an illustrated periodical. He flicks through it. 'Page after page of rubbish, perversion, poison: articles on sun altars with swastikas, calendar costumes, the tale of Germanic blood . . . '

'Did he write those things? I don't think so.'

'He allowed them to be published in his periodical.'

'He didn't even read them.'

'He was the editor. Look, *Dawn of Destiny*, edited by Ernst Mann.'

'A figurehead.'

'He let them use him. Let them take everything we held sacred and then watched as they twisted it to their own ends.'

'And what else could he have done?'

The bewildered look on Hans's face touches the professor, the intervening years seem to have been equally as cruel to him, but he cannot stop now. 'Tell me something, Hans. Is this why you've come here, to tell me he's innocent?'

'And you, Professor, have you come to prove his guilt?'

'It doesn't need me to prove anything. He damned himself.'

The wood roars behind the glass, a generous heat spreads itself between the two men. 'As for me, Prof, I'm only a simple man. The village idiot, if you like. When I want to know what someone has done I look at his hands. If he's been mending the engine of a car, there will be oil; if he's been killing people there will be blood. I saw no blood on Ernst Mann's hands; except for his own. And I was with him through it all.' As Hans rubs his hands before the stove, the old man notices them shake.

'There's more than one way of taking life.'

'If a crown of pine needles falls on a hare's back, does that make him a hedgehog? A man walks through the forest during a storm; do you blame him for the timber that gets uprooted? And if one of the trees kills him too?'

'Don't you see what he did, Hans? What were those Nazis but a group of thugs? Who would believe what such rogues said? Ernst lent them credibility. He helped them disguise their lies; turn their propaganda into a story.' These are things Dietrich Gruber has told himself so often that they have acquired the ring of a litany. 'You say he did nothing, but he helped justify murder, even made it seem necessary, and once that's been done mass murder becomes just a matter of timetables and distribution.'

'You think that by collecting a few stories he built Auschwitz?'

'He helped create the opportunity. Any fool can light a fire, but it takes someone pretty persuasive to convince people that books should be burnt. Get the heart and the mind and there will be plenty of willing hands. What Ernst Mann did was to help reduce genocide to a question of logistics.' The old man leans heavily against his stick.

Hans's voice is a murmur. 'If Ernst Mann is guilty then so are we.' They look at each other in silence. 'Just like old times, boss,' Hans says at last. 'I never did understand anything that was said in this room. And after all that has happened, it's strange but I'm half expecting him to come walking in that door.'

Dietrich nods. 'With a new trick or a joke.' For an instant he rests a hand on one of Hans's. 'I miss him too.'

'You didn't meet an Ernst Mann every day and that's the truth. Sometimes I used to think he'd wandered our way from the pages of his stories. But, Prof, I haven't come here to argue or rake over the past. When embers are cold they're good only for strawberries.'

'So why *have* you come, Hans?'

'To bring this.' Hans wheels over the sub-archivist's trolley. 'Manners have taken a bit of a dive round here. Your friend didn't seem keen on lending me this means of transportation. Still, here it is. Where do you want it?'

Professor Gruber immediately recognises the heavy trunk Hans is lifting from the trolley. It was one of the wedding presents he gave Ernst and Helga. Once it was his. Hans's grandfather, also Hans Rosenbaum, the greatest craftsman and clockmaker in their area, made it for him. He'd dearly hoped never to see it again. The smell of the boxwood is almost too much for both men to bear. As Black Foresters they know the long memory of wood. 'I wondered where it had gone,' Dietrich whispers.

'I brought it back, at the end, when Ernst stayed in Berlin. Helga refused to have it, so I've kept it all these years, waiting for the right moment to return it, say when one of the children wanted to find out about their father. Who knows, I thought, in time maybe even Helga might want to look inside this trunk. But the right moment never came so I decided to bring it back here. I didn't know what else to do.'

'Then it's a coincidence.'

'If you like, boss.'

'Hans, come and stay the night with us. Helga will be here soon. She'd love to see you. She doesn't blame you. Nobody does. And you can see the children too. You haven't seen them for years. Of course, they're grown up now.'

'How are they all?'

'Didn't you know?'

'Know what?'

'Peter died. He was killed by the Russians.'

'But he can't have been fourteen years old.'

'Gustav qualifies as a doctor this year.'

'And Lotte; how is little Lotte?'

'Lotte is . . . ' The old man breaks off. 'After the war, she had the operation again. And this time it was successful, but she still doesn't talk. You remember her sign language? Helga seems to be able to understand it the best. A kind of *hand-Alemannic*. She'd love to teach you some of it.'

'Lotte won't remember me.'

'I don't think she forgets things.' Dietrich sighs. 'It might be easier for her if she did. And Helga too. Things seem to get harder with time.'

'And seeing me will only remind them all. You thought I was dead? Well, let the dead stay dead. Maybe I am dead after all, and they've let me return for a day to deliver this. That's all. Goodbye; it's been good to see you, even for so short a time. But forgive me, it reminds me of too much.' Hans pauses at the door. 'You call him a murderer, boss, but he saved lives. You know what I mean, don't you? He saved yours. The People's Court. They were ready to string you up. Until Ernst intervened. And another

77

thing, he loved Helga right to the end. The children too.' The old man does not look up from the trunk. He hears the sad reveille of the *Blutwurz* bugle and then Hans has gone, like a ghost.

3

The moment that Dietrich Gruber had hoped never to face has arrived. The scholarly items of the archive have been difficult enough; how will he cope with his friend's personal artefacts? The curtainless window is darkening with the falling night; the polished sides of the boxwood trunk dance with light from the stove. The instant the professor opens the lid his fears are confirmed. It contains Ernst Mann's private possessions. He reaches inside, bringing out the first thing his fingers encounter. A thick wad of letters.

Most are from Helga and the children. The rubber band snaps as he undoes the bundle. The letters fall into his lap. There are a lot of them — Ernst was often away from home on field trips. The old man recognises his own writing too and selecting those begins to read. In contrast to his usual standards, Ernst has ordered his personal correspondence with immaculate care, arranging them chronologically. Dietrich's epistles start warmly enough, full of shared jokes and passionate discussion of the subject they both loved; pages filled with quips about donkeys playing squeeze boxes, and birds debating the destinies of men: a cruel reminder of what was lost, of how the professor might have been here organising this archive for an entirely different purpose. It is not until Dietrich sees the year 1937 franked on the envelopes that the first warning note is sounded, and that is merely the mildest of jibes about the danger of his former student's work being misinterpreted. Even at the outbreak of war Professor Gruber is warning Ernst only to safeguard himself against pernicious influences. Sifting through the correspondence, the old man is dismayed to see how slowly his scale of remonstration with his former student rose to the final, unequivocal denunciation. It is at as late a date as autumn 1941 that he finds himself openly chiding Ernst for the first time; too late, since in the next letter he is pleading with him about his decision to bring the Folklore Department under the auspices of the Office of Ancestral Inheritance.

The heat of the stove has woken a fly in its winter quarters high in the bookshelf between the pages of *The Jew in the Thorns*; the insect buzzes drunkenly about the room. Dietrich Gruber watches it dumbly. Just to see those words again is almost enough to make him despair: *Office of Ancestral Inheritance*. That monstrous mockery! A sense of his own culpability buzzes around the professor's head like the fly. Couldn't he have done so much more to persuade Ernst against the path he was taking? Of all people, his protégé ought to have been made to see that every bargain-story ends with the moment of reckoning.

After his own letters, the old man takes out those written by Helga. They're even harder to read. At first the correspondence is full of the simple strength of their uncomplicated love: Helga reminding her young husband of their special place in the forest; telling him that the Kaiser beech, the oldest tree in their valley, is missing him; begging him to hurry back so that they can watch the dawn together as it creeps like a doe from the forest. Feeling as though he is eavesdropping, he reads Helga's hopes for the future, her dreams for the child taking shape in her womb. With the birth of their first son, Gustav, Helga's correspondence takes a new direction: first steps, first bruises, and the spendthrift currency of little hugs. A lost world made unbearably poignant by seeing it through a new mother's eyes. Professor Gruber too had believed in life then. How proud he had been when Gustav was born and not long after, Peter. Then Lotte! Lotte! Up until then the professor's work had been everything to him; with the birth of the little girl that changed. Instead of sitting in the library day after day like a frog on a lily pad, at the least excuse he would come out to Keilburg, the remote valley with its thatched two-tiered *Schwarzwaldhaus* in which Ernst and Helga were rearing their family. Accustomed to apportioning his hours as strictly as any cuckoo clock, he willingly frittered away whole after-noons carrying and then walking the little girl round the pond, watching the mill wheel turn, throwing scraps of bread for the wild ducks, laughing at the storks on the roof. Instead of dusty books, the professor filled his days with Lotte's birdlike chatter. For to start with, she was such a chatty little thing.

Ah, if only the prick of a spindle had sent them all to sleep when Lotte was three years old, allowing them to wake in safety after the war. Instead they found themselves being roused to a reality that increasingly became a nightmare. And from a babbling, happy little girl, Lotte withdrew into silence.

The pile of letters spills to the ground. The old man can hear Helga's step in the corridor. He has lost track of the time. Quickly he scoops up the correspondence. But how to hide the trunk? She will recognise it instantly. His mouth trembles with panic. Tearing down the sheet he has been using as a screen he casts it over Ernst's luggage only just in time. His niece is at the door. 'So they've finally lit the stove for you, Uncle. And the light too. After all you did for the university it's the least they can do.'

'Yes,' he replies. Helga's hair is grey now, her face prematurely lined; nothing remains of the beautiful young mother who wrote those letters.

'Oh, you've taken another sheet. I won't have any bedding left at this rate.' For a moment the professor thinks his niece is going to take the cover and reveal the trunk beneath. 'Uncle, are you all right?'

He waves away her concern; steels himself to hide the pain. 'I just wish you wouldn't come up here. There's no need.'

'And who would take you home?'

'I mean, I could come down to the car; save you . . .'

'Why are you doing this, Uncle? It's only making you ill.'

'I'm ill already.' They look at each other; as much father and daughter as uncle and niece, Dietrich raised her as his own after his brother was killed in the first war. 'Helga, do you really have no love left for him in your heart?' As soon as he has spoken the old man regrets his words. The breathless innocence of her early letters is belied in her narrowed, cold eyes. A princess turned into a frog. 'I'm sorry, Helga. I'm old; I'm confused.'

'Come on, Uncle; Gustav and Lotte are waiting downstairs in the car. They say it's going to snow. Some of the valleys are already covered.'

'Snow?' The professor crosses to the window. It is fully dark now but the light is on in the small Volkswagen below. Gustav's car radio drifts up: some American big band. The sudden parp of the horn reverberates around the neglected college building. Gustav has seen him. A hand emerges from the lowered window to wave. There is something of Ernst's flamboyance in the gesture. Gustav is not much older than Ernst was when he walked barefoot down the corridor for the first time. Father and son share a similar physicality, red hair burning on a large head; but Gustav's eye does not twinkle half as frequently, as though the body remains but the magic has departed. Extinguished by having seen too much, too young? After all, Gustav made that journey across Germany in 1945 with his mother

82

and Lotte; the one from which Peter never returned. A snowflake falls past the window. 'Please, Uncle, we must be going.'

'I haven't finished.'

'I'll wait.'

'I mean, I'm not coming home tonight. So much to do. And what do I want with sleep?'

Uncle and niece stare out of the ancient window of the onetime Department of Folk Narrative and Customs. The draught is bitterly cold. Helga does not argue. Despite the old man's wishes, the doctor has spoken to her. She knows her uncle is living on borrowed time. She also knows, putting her own pain to one side, that this is the best place for him to die. She throws more logs in the fire from Hans's large pile; there is enough here for the coldest of nights. They embrace. Dietrich closes his eyes; when he opens them again Lotte is standing at the door. She has not been up here since she was a little girl. The old man feels another stab of pain.

He forces himself to smile. Her hair too is red; her eyes blue as a mountain glacier. When did she become such a fine young woman? Before Helga turns and realises that her daughter is there, Lotte raises finger and thumb together to her mouth, blows gently as though blowing a dandelion clock, and then is gone. The old man has never got to grips with the full subtlety of her language, but he knows that this is Lotte's most tender way of saying goodbye. He wonders for the thousandth time what it must be like to have a father who believed in your destruction.

'Goodbye, Uncle.' Although she has told herself not to, Helga can feel her tears beginning to fall. Unable to trust her voice she too uses Lotte's gesture of farewell, displaying the missing finger lost on that desperate journey across Germany near the end of the war.

'Helga, I . . . ' Faltering, he also blows the hours of the imaginary dandelion clock.

And he is alone again with the drifting seeds of the past. At the window he waits until the headlights of Gustav's car scour the side of the university then split the night as the young man drives his mother and sister away.

4

Why didn't he do more; speak out earlier, more forcibly? Why didn't he tear down his student's endless, all too plausible excuses, with the rigour he used to show in academic disputes? Perhaps he ought even to have turned that barefoot boy away when he knocked at the door for the first time, reviled him as a malicious Rumpelstiltskin.

As the fire in the red stove glows warmly and the black window writhes with snow, the professor returns to the letters that Ernst wrote but never sent. The old man then lifts out a small pile of photographs from the chest. None of them shows the merest inkling of what was to come; what business do family snaps have in becoming part of this kind of investigation? Helga as a beautiful young woman; Helga and Ernst on their wedding day; Dietrich himself holding baby Lotte; Ernst pushing the boys in the swing he made for them on the Kaiser beech; the old thatched *Schwarzwaldhaus* in Keilburg; the lake. After the photographs the professor brings out his student's wallet. It contains a roll of old Reichsmarks, and in the document partition, official papers bearing the baleful stamp of the eagle and the signature recognised by every German. It is Ernst's pass from the Office of Ancestral Inheritance endorsed by its chief, Heinrich Himmler. The old man shudders as though he has fingered a coiled snake.

At last the trunk is empty. But Dietrich knows the worst is still to come, for the trunk has an ingeniously disguised false bottom.

Hans's grandfather had fitted it at the end of the last century when Professor Gruber found himself embroiled in the near hysterical controversy that was his own most lasting contribution to the subject of Folklore. Not only had he cast aspersions on the legendary collecting methods of the Brothers Grimm, who, far from gathering their treasury of stories from the spinning wheels and firesides of primitive Germany, had often used literate, urban middle-class sources, he had also accused the holy brethren of neutering the true narratives. He had proved this adulteration through his discovery of early manuscripts containing forms of many of the Grimm stories which greatly pre-dated the brothers' collection. The early version of *Rapunzel* was the most damning, showing beyond doubt that the brothers had purged blatant references to the sexual relations between the girl in the tower and the passing prince, and entirely omitted the description of her growing pregnancy. When rivals broke into this very room to destroy the evidence, the professor had called on Hans Rosenbaum's help.

Dietrich's knock against the bottom of the trunk produces a convincingly dead sound, but when his knuckles rap a few centimetres to the left his practised ear picks up the hollow note. The professor hesitates. What he is going to see now will be as close to the matter as he can get. It will be a glimpse into the squandered soul of his friend and brilliant colleague.

The light bulb flickers and then dies. Another power cut? Bending down, the old man puts more wood in the stove and, leaving the door open to fan the flames, waits for the firelight to grow strong.

The first object he brings out from the hidden compartment is a brown-paper parcel. He knows instantly what it contains. Untying the strings, he finds himself holding Ernst's side of his bargain with the Devil: his SS uniform. The old man takes the tunic over to the window and holds it beneath his chin. Black with a red armband, it is the colour of the woodpecker so common in the trees round Keilburg, Ernst's little valley. He gazes for a long time at his reflection then goes back for the trousers. He is holding them against himself when he feels the lumps. Both legs have been stuffed with something, as though the uniform had been plucked from the battlefield, the pulp of the shattered thighs still within. He extracts the blockages: two tight tubes of coarse material. Why has Ernst placed these rolls of rags in his inner sanctum? One after the other he unrolls the tight tubes over a pile of Soundwriter tapes. They are not only rags. Among the dun pieces of sacking and torn vests, the growing stove light catches colour. Dietrich finds himself looking at a pair of paintings.

Twice as long as they are high, a metre by half a metre perhaps, both canvases are about the size of a stillborn's shroud. They show the same thing, a garden scene; but the old man is not taking in any of the verdant details. This is an even crueller blow than he had expected. Could this really lie at the heart of his former student's collaboration with Himmler's Office of Ancestral Inheritance? It is common knowledge that all the Nazis' high talk of Germanic mission and recovering cultural goods was just a euphemism for theft, loot, in particular rifled artworks. Was his friend no different to all the other grubby little opportunists fighting over their cut of the corpse?

He turns from the looted pictures back to the cavity and brings out a bundle of sealed letters: one each for Helga and the children; also one for Hans; and one for Dietrich himself. The third item in the secret cavity makes the professor gasp. He remembers it so well that to touch it once more is like clasping the dead man's hand. It is the book Ernst wrote for his daughter, an illustrated version of the *Travelling Animals*, which he called *The Musicians of Keilburg*, after their little house by the mill. How many times did Dietrich sit reading this book with the little girl? It is marked indelibly in his mind. The wonderful illustrations that Ernst drew with the Staedtler coloured pencils; and the writing itself, which Ernst laboured endlessly over as he struggled to render his scrawling hand into a legible print: he once told the old man he wrote it out a hundred times before he was satisfied. As Lotte withdrew into her silence, the only sure way to reach her was through this book. How she had loved that donkey. On the bottom corner of each page Ernst had sketched an ass in a slightly different pose so that when the pages were flicked they showed an animated scene. Even after she had stopped talking she still laughed at the moving donkey. *Again, again,* she would gesture to Dietrich, begging him to reactivate the little thumb-cinema. *Again, again.* In fact, her sign for *more* is still the pincer of thumb and finger needed to flick pages quickly. With his stiff fingers Dietrich flicks the pages. The donkey comes to life; its hooves romp a squeeze box; its eyes close with pleasure; its ears flatten in the ecstasy of tune.

As he comes to the last object, a reel of film, the professor's hands are shaking so badly that he can barely fit the celluloid tongue on the projector. There is no date or description on its tin but the footage he is about to see, he feels certain, will reveal Ernst Mann. It is the mirror that still holds his most brilliant colleague's reflection.

With no more energy to fix the sheet back up, Dietrich views the film against the wall. Fretted with long vertical lines, clustered dots scintillate in and out of focus. Is the film damaged? As his eyes grow accustomed, the old man realises that what he is seeing are trees, upside down. He checks the projector; has he fitted the reel the wrong way? It is the sudden thrust of a bare foot right at the top of the shot that reveals the truth. He would recognise that foot anywhere. Slender and with toes so prehensile that they might draw with a colouring pencil, this foot can belong only to Ernst Mann. He often walked unshod, to read, as he said, the Braille of the earth. But he is not walking here, he is hurrying through trees, the camera dangling forgotten at his thigh. Where is he? In the forest around Keilburg, or further afield, in one of the tortured corners of the wartime world that Ernst and Hans visited? The bark of the trees is white: birches. There are few birches around Keilburg. Their ragged leaves reveal late summer or early autumn; birch leaves fade early. All at once the trees give way; Ernst must have entered a clearing. There is something standing in the clearing. Dietrich tilts his head as far as he can and sees that it is a table. It is set with a number of bottles and a pyramid of champagne glasses. Panning haphazardly round the birch clearing, the camera sweeps past a group of men. Some are stripped to the waist, a number wear swimming trunks. All at once the camera is lifted; a figure in the uniform that the whole world has come to recognise fills the shot. The old man looks in horror at the death's head on his hat. What's happening now? For a few moments the professor thinks that the woods beyond the clearing are moving, approaching, then he realises that what he had mistaken for the white bark of birch trees is in fact human skin. The woods are swarming with naked women; they are being driven towards the clearing. The man wearing the death's head hat grins.

5

Excerpts from:

The archive of Ernst Mann. Edited (unfinished) by Professor Dietrich Gruber, November 1953, former Chair of Germanic Folk Narrative and Customs. Further annotated by an intercollegiate group of folk-lorists in 2002, who found the archive dumped in a cellar among old chairs and other furniture; little more than a storage room, there was not even a lock on the door.

a. GE (Germanic English). Aarne-Thompson Tale Type no. 130. Travelling Animals. Variation LXX. Matching Magnetophone Soundwriter field recording no. 28. May 1936. *Location*: Cumberland, England. *Location particulars*: Kitchen. A flag floor strewn with rushes; a common floor covering in poor houses in the area. *Narrator*: Mrs

Jessie Twentyman. *Narrator details*: Known as Nana Jess, she speaks with a strong regional dialect, which has a hint of Scots. *Points of interest*: Lengthy opening formula, use of local place names to indicate preliterate tale, the musical instruments are also valuable time indicators especially the cat playing the so-called *Paddy-man pipes*, a name for the local type of bagpipe, the last-known player of which died in the eighteenth century.

Further notes: Translations into High German of this tale can be found on p. 69 of the translation supplement; for the Alemannic version, see p. 65.

. . . And this was the plan. Hound jumped on cuddy's back, cat leapt on hound and cockerel flew on top of puss. The moment cuddy donkey smashed open the window, they all began to play their instruments at once. What a queer din. Them reivers thought a ghost was under the eaves, so up they upped and gnashed away into the woods. The four musicians sat down in their places and noshed till there wasn't room in their bellies for the space of a fart.

There wasn't a bite left. So they put the light out and went to bed, each one choosing the most comfortable place. Pussy on a rocking chair by the fire, dog curled under the table, cockerel on a beam. 'And me,' says cuddy donkey, 'I've always fancied sleeping upstairs on a feather bed.'

They were all fast asleep when Black Jack, the Kinmont Willie, the chief thief, the king of all the reivers crept back along the river to the house; and if you'd seen him you would have wished you hadn't. His face was that angry it would have turned milk. 'I should never have been frightened off,' raves he. 'The shame of it. And it was only the wind.'

At first he thinks everything is all right so he shouts to his men, who were still hiding, to come back. But looking to light a tallow candle so he can sit in his chair he stands on pussy's tail. She flies at him biting and scratching for all she's worth. Clawing her from his shoulders he knocks against the table, standing on dog's paw. Dog sinks his teeth into Black Jack's ankle. With a scream the rogue pegs it up upstairs, but who should he meet at the top but cuddy who kicks him back down again. As he runs to the door, the cockerel flaps screaming in his face: 'Cock-a-doodle-do!'

Well, what a to-do. Black Jack meets his fellow robbers coming in. 'Don't go in there,' he cries. 'There's a horrible witch sitting in my chair, she scratched me with her long fingernails; then a man slashed at me with his knife; I tried to get away but a giant kicked me down the stairs, but the worst of it is the bogle sitting on the rafter shouting: 'Cook-him-in-a-stew!''

b. (i) *Dawn of Destiny*, ed. Ernst Mann. Issue 1. 1938. Page 5, paragraph 3. 'THE TRUTH IN STONE: The sun altar of Mazuria.'

. . . there can be no proper ethnography, no authentic folklore whatsoever unless it is bound to a concept of *Volk* or race. Blood must be our essential rationale and method. The ancient sun altar recently discovered in Mazuria proves the point most tellingly that our folk must be listened to at its life source, in the blood and the soil which is its essence. On the sun altar, believed to be at least three thousand years old, swastikas are clearly discernible in the stonework. Even then the German folk were aware of our destiny . . .

(ii) *Dawn of Destiny*, ed. Ernst Mann. Issue 3. 1938. Page 1, paragraph 1. 'THE FONT OF BLOOD: A racially hygienic folklore.'

By requiring folkloric fieldwork to concentrate only on what is racially pure, on what is in our blood, we can separate away any impurities and snap off the suffocating tendrils of anything racially alien, or parasitical. In this way a racially hygienic folklore is also a branch of surgical medicine removing the cancer that has poisoned our blood for too long.

(iii) *Dawn of Destiny*, ed. Ernst Mann. Issue 15. 1941. Page 67, paragraph 3. 'BUILDING THE THOUSAND-YEAR-OLD HOMESTEADS.'

What is this, a folklore organ dispensing construction tips? Put simply: yes! When it comes to constructing the new homesteads in the east, our building principles will come from the research done on our peasant building methods. Basically all construction will show a Nordic rather than a Celtic-Romano or indeed Slavic style. For example, the hearth should be placed centrally so that the good wife can see the whole house . . .

(iv) *Dawn of Destiny*, ed. Ernst Mann. Issue 16. 1941. Page 21, paragraph 2. 'SOWING THE BLOOD-WHEAT: Guidelines for Folklorists in occupied territories.'

The recent glorious successes in the former Soviet territories make it a priority for folklorists to collect as many calendar customs as possible so that our pioneer soldier-farmers will not go into the reclaimed, Slavonic Jew-tainted soil empty-handed, but carry with them the most profound spring of their German blood. We have in mind such things as Sleipner's crop circles, the phenomenon of leaving corn standing for Odin's eight-footed stallion discovered in Lower Saxony recently, and the spring incantations to the ash tree, which of course is a reference to the ancient Germanic Yggrdassil, the tree of life, and one of Nordic man's most sacred totems. These will be at the cultural heart of our new territories . . .

c. Two paintings. Size: 100cm by 50cm. Medium: Oil on canvas.

Note from annotator: Although catalogued by Professor Gruber these items were missing from the archive when we came to annotate it in spring 2002. It has not been possible to trace them. All that exists is the professor's description of the paintings. Nothing is known about their provenance. Professor Gruber's unequivocal opinion was that they were looted by Ernst Mann as part of the Nazi wholesale theft of artworks.

These are two equally stunning artworks that to my eye differ only in a single aspect: one alone of these garden scenes includes the figure of an artist at his easel. Although I claim no connoisseurship, the robust brushstrokes and sloping camber of the compositions put one in mind of the German Expressionists, Wassily Kandinsky perhaps or Ernst Ludwig Kirchner. But they are more accessible; and both, I would say, executed by the same hand: in these sumptuous spring gardens we have massed flowers; a golden laburnum tree burning like the sun; a black cat; a green bench inviting the viewer to sit; and in one of the pictures the figure of an artist painted from behind. The artist seems to be toiling heavily. Yet no matter how beautiful these pieces are, they are the cancer at the heart of Ernst Mann . . .

d. (i) Note 73 from the uncatalogued miscellany of Ernst Mann's sack of notes.

The woman in her ladder-back rocking chair, the woman who tasks as she tales, is the paradigm of preliterate Europe, the shadow spinner, the human bridge we need to bear us over our fears of the night, to hold us safe, to console us for the disaster of twilight.

(ii) Note 134, ibid.

Story belongs to the firelight. It's there that it began and it is there that it flourishes. The gods punished Prometheus for stealing the spark, but they left unchecked his greater theft, that of story, the bowl of greatness, the seeds of discourse and harmony, the ability to imagine yourself in place of any man or any god. A gift but is it also a curse?

(iii) Note 321, ibid.

I don't know why it should be, but one of the fundamental strengths of the human soul is to be able to imagine a donkey playing a squeeze box with his hooves.

(iv) Note 341, ibid

How dangerous it is to be fashionable.

(v) Note 350, ibid

I have found many, many times that the storyteller's initial sober profession as not to believe in the incidents she is narrating disappears as she tells her tale.

(vi) Note 370, ibid

What does a story mean? Everything and nothing. The literal words are magic beans. Inconsequential as it may seem, a tale is the only thing simultaneously big enough and small enough for the human soul. Both have vast forests, good and evil characters, and quiet, inhabited millponds. And finally: trust the story; never the storyteller.

(vii) Note 500, ibid

I would give everything for my life to have been different.

e. Excerpt from *Hitler Youth Handbook owned by Peter Mann, second son of Ernst Mann.* (Annotators' note: this is a single page which seems to have been torn out of the book.)

From the study of genetics we have learnt

that the individual human being is inextricably linked to his ancestors through birth and inheritance. But the great genetic river of a people can suffer many impurities and injuries along the way. These can occur in two ways: first, diseased genes can develop within the bloodstream of a people. If a people is to remain strong and healthy, these cannot be allowed to be passed on. The purpose of our current genetic policy is to prevent the passing on of such diseased genes and to promote healthy blood. A people's bloodstream, however, can also be injured by mixing it with alien blood from foreign races. Our racial policy is designed to prevent this from happening.

. . . The worst inherited diseases are: feeble-mindedness, schizophrenia, insanity, inherited epilepsy, inherited St Vitus's dance, inherited blindness and deafness, and inherited physical impairments, including, among others, bone disorders, club foot, harelip with cleft palate . . .

. . . There are inherited diseases whose external effects can be treated by the art of medicine, but do not lose their genetic nature. Even, for example, if someone with a bone disease or a harelip with cleft palate undergoes surgery, the problem will still reappear in their descendants.

f. Personal letter: Helga Mann to Ernst Mann, ?1933.

. . . and Dr Wolff says that if the operation is successful Lotte will look just like any other little girl. In her medical notes he says he will write down that the scar left on her lip was a wasp sting. Dr Wolff thinks that the only effect of the repair work might be a slight speech impediment. He has assured me over and over that she has no mental abnormality. So even if the new government really does bring in these terrible new measures, Lotte will be safe . . .

g. Document no. I from the Office of Ancestral Inheritance.

These papers allow the bearer, Ernst Mann, and his assistant, Hans Rosenbaum, unrestricted travel within the Reich and all theatres of war and occupied zones. They are on essential work for the party. Reichsführer Heinrich Himmler.

Heathrow, May 2008

1

For Piers there was something enduringly exciting about airports. He had shown his passport on perhaps five hundred occasions in his adult life and still felt a frisson passing through customs. The sudden shuffling of the destinations board felt like a lottery for which he owned a ticket.

He spotted Zohreh before she saw him: a distant figure on the far side of the concourse. He watched her pick her way across the wide open space like someone crossing an estuary at low tide. Obscured by the traffic of trolleys, shouldered travel bags, cleaners and the loose herd of waiting passengers, she passed in and out of his ken. A luggage train lumbered between them and at last she was waving her hand with childish enthusiasm. He waved back and waited.

'I've brought them both.' Zohreh was holding up a scarf and suncream. 'Where are we going?'

'A magical mystery tour.'

'Oh good!'

'Well, not that magical really.'

'Oh bad.' As Zohreh briefly hugged him Piers felt the lobes of her iPod earphones dig into his neck.

'We're going to Amsterdam.'

'Hamsterjam? Fab. I've never been there before.'

'Are you joking? I thought people of your age were never away from the place.'

'Not guilty, Me Ludd. I think that's more people of *your* age. When do we check in?'

He allowed himself a smile. 'Darling, we're going club class.'

'Now you're spoiling me big style. Do we get to use the posh lounge as well?'

'I thought we'd slum it out here first,' said Piers, who often met acquaintances in the club-class lounge. 'Here, have a coffee.'

'As if the girl's heart isn't thumping enough. I can see that there's no need to dress for an upgrade when I'm with you.'

Piers turned to watch the destinations boards spinning like a roulette wheel.

The plane was virtually empty. A small group of exhausted football fans clustered the back seats. Piers and Zohreh were alone at the front. Once airborne, a stewardess drew a curtain across the aisle. 'Club class,' Piers grinned. 'Charter-style. At least we won't have to smell the plebs' breath.'

'Piers,' Zohreh whispered undoing his seat belt, 'does your BA gold card also entitle you to use the mile-high club lounge?'

The art adviser spluttered with laughter.

The face of one of the soccer fans pierced the curtains. Tumbling through them he tottered towards the toilet. He was six foot four and wore a horned Viking helmet. 'Technically he's not supposed to use the privilege loo,' Piers said. 'But I don't think we'll insist.'

They waited until the Viking had finished and then, without another word, both rose from their seats.

No matter how unchanged by the passage of time, or how much of a Peter Pan figure one might cut, it's difficult for a middle-aged man to maintain his dignity when getting undressed in front of a twenty-three-year-old girl. Particularly in a smelly confined space. Under the unforgiving probe of the toilet light, Piers's erection leapt forth from his underpants absurd as the loo brush bristling in the corner. He sucked in his stomach muscles only to blow them out again at the cold caress of the toilet handle. The mirror seemed hell-bent on counting the individual hairs on his arse. 'Sit on the loo,' urged Zohreh, already effortlessly naked, a single tattoo etched on her hip bone. Trousers round his ankles, Piers slipped on a patch of wet floor. For one nightmarish second he suspected he'd torn a hamstring.

'We'll have to be quick,' he said. 'We're already over the North Sea.'

The thin red line of her knicker elastic faded under his fingers as he eased her towards him. With relief he felt the touch compensating his senses for the acrid honk of Viking shit and industrial detergent. He closed his eyes with pleasure. Recently he'd read on one of his favourite websites — miscellany.com — that the most common male deathbed regret was not having had enough sex. Piers's hands described ever decreasing circles.

The turbulence hit just as she was mounting him. She fell awkwardly; he yelped with pain, the sudden movement chafing the condom. As she yanked the contraceptive back into position he found himself picturing the too-small Marigold gloves which lived on the kitchen taps at home; he had put them on once when their cleaning lady had had the flu, and his wrists had gone white.

'Sit back on the seat,' she breathed.

No sooner had he complied she was on top of him once more. Mustering his resources for a speedy conclusion, he caught himself picturing the down on the small of Sally's back. To rid himself of this troubling image, he began kissing Zohreh's breasts, breathing in her cool moist skin. Then — 'Aagh.'

'What's the matter, Piers?'

For a moment he thought a filling had fallen out: the unmistakable invasion of metal against the softness of the palate. But it was too solid and jagged. He continued to kiss Zohreh's breasts but the metallic entity hooped round his tooth, sawing the gum. 'Christ on a bike!' Yelping, he spat violently. A tiny torque was deposited on Zohreh's shoulder.

'You beast,' she giggled. 'My nipple ring.'

She began to jounce. Her hair dowsing him with pheromones, he cupped his hands beneath her to catch his ebbing lust. There were some things favoured by Zohreh's generation of which he heartily approved: their Cleopatraesque make-up, their habit of displaying a visible strip of underwear, but not their propensity to quill the body with metal. Although it did little to disguise the last bodily transaction enacted here, the strong essence of detergent was beginning to claw his eyes. In the heat, this combination of chemical and biological was overpowering. As Zohreh began to moan, Piers recalled that miscellany.com also recorded claims that eunuchs never get prostate cancer; as well as pointing out that there were more microbes on the seat of a public toilet than the number of human beings that have ever lived on earth. *When,* he wondered, *did I become able to remain this detached during moments of supposed passion?* Crying out, Zohreh's shunting movements screwed his hairy arse nearer and nearer to the blue tongue of the chemi-toilet. Back still creaking, Piers leant away so that she couldn't mark his neck. He'd made that mistake before and had had to wear a cravat for a week. The cravat's designer had insisted it was the coming thing, but Piers had felt like a predatory character from a Somerset Maugham novel. 'Are you all right?' Zohreh asked.

Closing his eyes to the floor with its empty condom packet and the sodden tube of pink knickers, Piers desperately tried to bolster himself. What was the matter with him? miscellany.com said that 19 per cent of middle-aged men would actually give a little finger to have sex with a beautiful girl in her twenties. And how beautiful she was. Firm and supple, with just a hint of the doe-eyed: the epitome of youth. He was hardening again when Zohreh arched like a salmon and exposed the mirror to Piers's view. For a febrile, shocking moment he thought the worn, suspicious face staring back at him belonged to another: a third person standing in the cubicle watching them. 'Sorry, Zo,' he whispered. There was an audible flup-fart! as he withdrew.

Zohreh continued to thrust for a while, mercilessly throwing into Piers's mind an image of the water boatman Mimi once caught in the garden pond; she had dropped the hapless insect on the grass where it bucked and gyrated against the strange new element. Slowing to a halt, Zohreh collapsed against his chest. When she gazed up at him through a tangle of dark hair, he had never seen her look so young. 'I love you,' she whispered. Still panting, she yanked off the condom and knelt on the floor before him. 'Do you want me to blow, babe?'

'Actually, I think there's someone waiting to get in.'

When they came out of the cubicle, the Viking was indeed waiting. He beamed in beery approval.

Back in their seats, Zohreh took his hand. On miscellany.com Piers had read that once a man begins to ejaculate he can be shot in the back and his orgasm will be entirely unimpaired. That seemed more plausible than the 19 per cent giving a little finger. *Nine* per cent, he could perhaps believe. Piers shifted position, his underpants were wet; his skin itched with toilet chemicals. The unpalatable image of his face puckered with weary lust in the mirror repeated on him like the smell of the football supporter's squits. He drank a gin and tonic with Zohreh, while the malodour of burgers drifted from the *Burger King* trolley on the other side of the curtain. Perking up momentarily, the fans chanted the name of their team a few times then fell back into bleary silence. Zohreh laid her head on his shoulder and gently gripped his upper arm. The manoeuvre was so tender that he was almost lulled into explaining that he had already made love once that day. 'Zohreh,' he said instead, 'did you have a slide when you were a little girl?'

'There was one in the park Dad took me to.'

'When did you stop playing on it?'

'When I got too long, or the slide too short, I can't remember which.'

'But how old were you?'

'I'll let you into a secret, girls never grow out of slides. But why the interest?'

'No reason. I suppose I've just got an eclectic brain.'

'So why Amsterdam?'

'Well, I've got a little work to do there. I thought we could make a mini-break of it.'

* * *

The tram took them through a leafy suburb of tall chocolate-brown buildings and graceful trees. They alighted into a night that seemed to be falling softly from the thick canopies of chestnut and sycamore. Bell ringing, the tram clattered away, throwing handfuls of electric stars onto the warm night air. 'The bank has a small pied-à-terre just round the corner,' Piers explained. 'It's a nice quarter. Little galleries, street cafes.' Walking past one of the cafes whose outside tables, filled with chattering customers, spilt onto the pavement, Piers felt the BlackBerry in his top pocket vibrate against his heart. It would be Sally or Mimi telling him about the show. He did not look.

That night Zohreh fell asleep in his arms. Piers stayed awake long after the bell of the last tram. The tooth sawn by the nipple ring was growling. He took three paracetamol then fell into a dreamless sleep.

2

They breakfasted at one of the cafes: croissants warm in the basket; morning sunlight playing on knives glistening with jam and butter. A bird with scimitar wings shrieked overhead into one of the chestnut trees. 'Parakeets,' Piers said. 'The jungle's encroaching on Amsterdam. No one knows where they came from, now they're everywhere.'

'What are those hooks?' Zohreh pointed to the metal stake protruding from under the eaves of the building above them. 'There's one on the side of our apartment too.'

The waiter who had been hovering said: 'For deliveries.' He mimed hauling on a rope. 'So you don't have to carry your grand piano up all those stairs.'

He fancies her, Piers thought. 'I'll have another espresso, please,' he ordered, almost curtly. 'Who are you texting?' Piers asked Zohreh.

'Cora. She's green with envy.'

'Cora, my assistant?'

Zohreh nodded.

'Cora, my assistant, knows you're here?'

'Don't worry; she doesn't know I'm with you. We're flatmates now. She moved in with me last week. Boyfriend trouble!'

'Oh.' Piers considered the girl across the table from him as she finished her messaging. It was always difficult to know when to end things. Without some degree of intimacy, it was simply like humping a stranger; but nothing too deep could be permitted to take root. They'd been seeing each other for two months now; ordinarily there would still be a while to go yet but he didn't like this new development, the Cora link. Then there'd been the whispered declaration of love during their toilet cubicle coitus interruptus. He liked Zohreh, but he couldn't afford to let it carry on much longer. Still, there was Amsterdam to enjoy first.

The waiter arrived with the single espresso. 'There's a story about the metal hooks,' he said to Zohreh. 'During the war when the Nazis marched into Amsterdam, a beautiful young woman went from roof to roof throwing the spikes down. She'd killed ten of them before they got her.'

'Wow, what a story,' said Zohreh.

'Yeah,' said Piers. 'The Dutch are always heroes of course. Great record in both world wars. We'll have the bill.' *The waiter definitely fancies her*, he thought. *Of course he does, everybody does*. Sipping his espresso he felt a shiver of pleasure. 'So you live with Cora?'

'Relax, Piers. She's in the dark. There's only you and me in this loop.' He pictured her flat, a tiny box in Acton Town. He'd only been there once. Posters on the wall, the single bed from whose foot an array of cuddly toys dropped one by one as they made love. Her teddy bear had even mewled as it hit the ground, a queasy reminder that Zohreh was closer to Mimi's age than his own. 'Would it bother you?'

'What?'

'If Cora knew. Don't worry, I haven't even told Daddy.'

'Daddy?' One of the few details that Piers knew about this young woman was that her father was some kind of dissident writer who had fled the Ayatollah Khomeini's Iran. 'What's he like?'

'Daddy?'

'It's just that I've known a few writers in my time and I can't imagine any of them being good parents. There's one who keeps a book with the names of anyone who's ever given her a bad review. There's a punishment allotted to each entry. She showed it to me; told me she's just waiting to contract a fatal disease before carrying the punishments out.'

'Daddy's not like that; not after what he's been through.'

'Sorry; yes of course. I was being facetious.'

'As long as you don't ask me to spell that.'

'Another author told me that when he's writing he can't talk to another soul in case it disturbs the voices of his characters. His last book took him three years to write. Has to have the window shut too, in case they escape.'

Zohreh grinned. 'So what's your secret madness?'

'What d'you mean?'

'Well, *you're* a writer.'

'Me? I just bash out a few words here and there.'

'Mr Modest. I think your books are brilliant.'

Although the Cora development made Piers feel chary about encouraging any deeper intimacy, the soft brown eyes with their long lashes, and the gentle breeze stirring the last few blossom candles of the chestnuts above the street cafe, made him say: 'Zo, do you think of yourself as English or Iranian?'

'My mum was born in Bournemouth; and I've never been to Tehran. But Daddy's told me stories about the old country since I was a little girl so I feel as though my heart belongs there. But what about you, what's your dad like?'

'He was a doctor. A surgeon. He died when I was young. My mum's South African.'

'So how do you think of yourself then?'

'What do you mean?'

'Are you English or African?'

'I've never thought of it like that before. Well,

110

I've got two passports. Or used to.'

'Do you miss him?'

'Who?'

'Your father.'

'Oh, I can't really remember him. Well, I think we'd better vamoose before that waiter proposes to you. He's been looking at you ever since we got here.'

'Jealous?'

It was a perfect morning. The sun shone brightly on the thick foliage of the Amsterdam trees. Hiring bikes, they rode into the old town, laughingly dodging pedestrians and trams. They took a pedalo up the canals, meandering along the waterways and under bridges where the bright spring light would suddenly darken to an aqueous green and the fronds of hart's tongue ferns reached down to them from the arching stonework. *God*, Piers laughed to himself, *I feel as though I'm twenty again.* When they stopped for lunch, he went to the toilets and took out his BlackBerry. As well as a raft of seven-figure offers for Mikey Durrant's work, a message from Mimi was waiting. She'd sent him photos of herself wearing the Chelsea top. 'I've been thinking, Sally,' Piers said into his wife's voicemail. 'Why don't you come on my next trip? Both of you. We'd have such fun.' As he spoke, once again he caught a glimpse of himself in the mirror. Turning abruptly from the corrugated brow, he put his BlackBerry away, and returned to the table.

'So he was a surgeon?' Zohreh began when the first course came.

'Who?'

'Your dad.'

'Yes, and my mum was a nurse. They met in the hospital where they were working. Nowhere near as interesting as your dad.'

'*I'm* interested.'

'As I say, I can't really remember him.'

'How old were you when he died?'

'I don't know, nine or ten. He was quite a bit older than Mum. He'd been in the war or something. Now, I thought after lunch we'd go to the Van Gogh Museum.'

Zohreh clapped her hands together. 'I was hoping you were going to say that.'

'Well, when in Rome, old girl.'

After lunch they wandered onto the Museumplein. The sweeping public square was full of people enjoying the late-spring sunshine. The flags from the concession stalls feathered slightly in the wind, rippling the sun-faded images of Van Gogh's sowers, sunflowers and self-portraits. Piers bought a pair of sunglasses. 'Such a bore being recognised.'

Zohreh laughed and then kissed him lightly, almost solemnly, on the cheek. Piers felt a troubling sense of intimacy. They walked to the head of the queue at the Van Gogh Museum and Piers handed over a piece of paper. 'The BA gold card again?' Zohreh grinned.

Having been frisked, they passed through the security turnstiles and entered a wide, bustling atrium above which the gallery's balustraded upper tiers could be seen rising like the interior of a beehive. The excited buzz of voices, mixing with the bleep of retail points and the clink of cutlery from the restaurants, filled the high air like insects swarming in a wood. The open stairway cascaded with visitors. 'All this for just one artist,' Zohreh said. 'I mean, nuff respect, he deserves it, but isn't it just a bit ironic?'

'What do you mean?'

She gestured at the walls of the retail well where the prints of his self-portraits were quartered with Sold Out signs. 'When he didn't actually ever sell a single painting?'

'Well, he did actually; and a number of drawings as well. But I suppose the facts don't always sit well with the myth.'

'Now, now, no snobby artiness. Just because I work with numbers doesn't mean that I can't appreciate good art. I happen to *adore* Van Gogh. To think he cut off his ear because he loved Gauguin.'

'Yeah and when we're finished I'll pop to the shop and buy you a special painting-by-number set of *Wheatfield with Crows*.'

'That's like so not funny! You culture bully.'

'I'm just waiting for the action doll, complete with detachable ear and syphilis spores. Christ on a trike, it's jam-packed in here.'

'Not used to rubbing shoulders with the *hoi polloi*, eh? I bet you lot usually have these places to yourself. Have you ever dealt in a Van Gogh?'

'Zohreh, I don't deal in any art. And these days nobody *deals* in Van Goghs unless they're a member of the Chinese mafia or have got about a billion pounds to risk. Now come on, it's my duty to educate a rather starry-eyed accountant on the not so starry reality of the painter of *Starry Night*. And remind me *not* to use that if I ever make another programme about him. Shall I get you an audio tour?'

'When I'm with the world's premier expert?'

'An expert is someone who knows more and more about less and less.' They began among the sombre twilights of the Dutchman's early work. Lonely dwellings set on featureless plains; twilight figures toiling beneath punishing skies; a soil-bound world from which only smoke rose and the sun always seemed to be sinking. They stopped before *Potato Eaters* to eavesdrop on the family of five Brabant peasants sitting down to share their meal in a dusty hovel lit only by the kerosene lamp brooding from a rafter.

'Personally I've always found this one slightly farcical,' Piers whispered. 'Don't you think the laddo with the big lips and ears is a dead ringer for Plug?'

'Plug from the 'Bash Street Kids' in the *Beano*? That's rather shallow for an art expert, isn't it? It says on the wall that it's his first masterpiece.'

'Firstly, I'm really not an expert; secondly, there are no experts when it comes to Van Gogh: just big mouths. Thirdly, how have you heard of Plug?'

'They still do the *Beano*, you know. I sometimes get it. Seriously!'

'So. Back to the Bash Street potato family. Van Gogh was obsessed with showing the dubious profundity that those eating the spuds are the ones who planted them. As he said about a million times in his letters to his personal banker.'

'Banker?'

'His brother; which in his case came to the same thing.'

'You don't seem to like him very much.'

'I don't like the myth; or theme parks like this one. It's art, not artists that interests me. I've known too many artists. Besides, this whole place, this cathedral, what does it really show us about Vincent Van Gogh?'

'That he might have been a PSV fan.'

'What?'

'It says on that panel that he was born and bred in Zundert, near Eindhoven. That's PSV Eindhoven.' Piers's laughter bounced up from the wooden floor and hitting the anti-glare aluminium coloured ceiling bounced back down again. 'Anyway, *I* like *Potato Eaters*,' Zohreh said. 'I feel as though I'm squinting through a knot in one of the cabin's walls.'

'Yeah,' drawled Piers. 'The light inside the cottage is just like soil. And now you come to mention it, don't you think the family themselves look a bit like potatoes?'

They followed the chronology laid down by the museum so that the dusky kerosene-lit interiors of the Dutch Brabant gave way to the artist's discovery of colour in Paris like the breaking of dawn at the window of a weaver's hovel. After the fresh morning parks and windmills of his French Impressionism and his flirtation with pointillism, came the artist's sojourn in the Midi. Each canvas from Arles, baked sharp as a ceramic, glinted like the midday sun. Then, after his noontime collapse came the half-sickbed, half-siesta of the mental hospital in Saint-Rémy, in which drowsy afternoon peace alternated with nightmares. And finally to sodden, green Auvers-sur-Oise where night fell so abruptly, drawn down by the Dutchman's own hand. 'You're disappointed that they haven't got the sunflowers, aren't you?' Piers grinned.

'What a life.' Zohreh's voice was hushed. 'He was a kind of martyr.'

'A murderer too. His brother Theo died six months after him, picked clean by his brother, emotionally, mentally and financially.'

'You're very cynical behind that pretty smile of yours, Mr Guest. Anyway, I was watching the DVD of your programme about Van Gogh last week. You didn't say any of that then. You seemed to be a fan.'

'I was young and foolish.'

'Now I really *love* this one.' Zohreh pulled him to a canvas containing a tempestuous swirl of storm clouds and billowing wheat. Crow silhouettes flecked the piece like black spindrift.

'You'll have to buy the poster, Zo.'

'I will,' she said, missing his irony. 'What a picture; look how thick the paint is. Isn't this the last one he ever did?'

'So runneth the Hollywood text. Truth is, nobody knows. *Wheatfield with Crows?* You can see why people would want it to be his last one. Bleak isn't the word. Funny thing is, in his letters of the time he was waxing lyrical to his brother about the health-giving properties of the

116

countryside; you see, he was trying to persuade him to bring his wife and child to live with him in a kind of artists' colony. Doesn't look too healthy, does it? Then he goes and puts a bullet in his chest.'

'Piers, you're the same age as Van Gogh when he painted it!'

Again the laughter rose up to the anti-glare ceiling.

They gazed at the long, troubled stormscape. As always, whenever he looked at a Van Gogh original, what struck Piers most powerfully was the physicality. Great peaks and troughs of paint gave the pictures their own topography. In *Wheatfield with Crows* the thick, relentless brushstrokes were as much a part of the encroaching storm as the lashed wheat, each one separately identifiable as a flick of the artist's wrist. 'Was Auvers by the sea?' Zohreh asked.

'No, the River Oise is a tributary of the Seine. It's about twenty kilometres from Paris. There was a nice little train service to the capital. A kind of *fin-de-siècle* Surbiton.'

'It's just that it looks more like the sea than land. Don't look at me like that, Mr Arty-party. Everything's billowing like in a sea.'

'Perhaps Miss Accountancy 2008 has missed the three paths at the centre of the piece?'

'Paths? They're more like causeways being covered by the tide, aren't they? Actually, that middle one is like a pier. See, it doesn't go anywhere. It's a pier falling into the sea. A pier, my dear Piers.'

From behind the earphones of their audio

117

tours, the other visitors frowned at their laughter. 'And the wheat itself is presumably code for seaweed?' Piers added quietly.

'Yes, when it dandles in the undertow.'

'*Dandles*? You know, Zo, you're the one who should be making art programmes. You'd be brilliant. Actually, I think you're on to something. That white bit there, that smudge, do you think it's a reference to a seagull? Hold on, hold on. It's more like an ear. As though he's sending a message: *I've taken off an ear, now I'm going to sever the lot*. Half-ear, half-seagull; you know, this painting is really a postcard from the seaside; a postcard doubling up as . . . a suicide note.'

'Don't laugh at me, Piers.'

'I'm not. That was a genuine theory by one of the so-called experts. Honestly, Zo, I'm not joshing.'

'Promise you're not laughing? Take your glasses off so I can see if you really mean it.'

When he lifted his shades and Zohreh saw his eyes in the gallery's pristine light she knew that there was no point in continuing to deceive herself. She loved Piers Guest. She loved the way his hair fell in an unruly flop over his face; she loved the way he smiled with his eyes; she loved his sudden laughter. She loved him even though she knew she shouldn't. She'd told herself countless times that it was only a bit of fun, but when he'd rung her up last night she'd almost passed out with excitement. She very nearly hadn't come; not because she didn't want to, but because she wanted to so much. Cora had told

118

her about his wife, Sally, that impossible combination of nice *and* beautiful; and about Mimi too. According to Cora she was a bit of a brat, like the way she'd demanded that Chelsea shirt from her dad. But what did *that* matter? Even as the taxi had pulled up at Terminal 4 Zohreh had not got out immediately. Her father had sacrificed everything for the truth, and here was she playing with the life of a family. Except she wasn't playing. 'So tell me this,' she said, putting these thoughts to one side. 'How come if the experts know so little about him Mr Guest does?'

'Actually, not that much *is* known about him. And practically nothing about his time in Auvers. You see, he stopped writing to Theo about his work; of course he still asked for cash. All we know for certain about Van Gogh in Auvers-sur-Oise is that he was completely fucked both mentally and physically: alcoholism, syphilis, schizophrenia, dyspepsia, acute intermittent porphyria induced by absinthe, take your pick. For which cocktail of illnesses his doctor prescribed foxgloves. Hence the portrait of wacky old Dr Gachet and its bunch of foxgloves. Incidentally, taken in the wrong way foxgloves, digitalis purpurea, are highly toxic. Look, the only thing I can tell you about Vincent Van Gogh with any certainty is that if he walked in here now most of these people slobbering over his paintings would run a mile. It would be like a dog with rabies coming in; or a snake dropping from that air vent. The whole lot of us would scatter.'

'Why do you think he killed himself, Piers?'

'Oh, who the fuck knows. Why does anybody?'

'Maybe we should do it together,' Zohreh said, coming so close that Piers could feel their bodies together like the ball and socket of a hip bone. 'I mean, maybe we should make your next programme together.'

'Good idea. Lauren and Hardy.'

'No, I'm being serious. A reappraisal of the life of Vincent Van Gogh. You know, make it iconoclastic. We could spend more time together. Go on location. We could . . . get to know each other properly.'

Christ on a bike, Piers thought, *I really am going to have to cool things down here.*

'Oh, he's been done to death. Actually, Zo, a lot of these paintings might not be authentic.'

'You mean they're fakes?'

'Fakes, acts of homage. The fact is Van Gogh has been credited with churning out over seventy canvases during his time in Auvers. Practically one a day. How could anyone manage that?'

'Piers,' said Zohreh, 'I would like to make an announcement. As Vincent Van Gogh is my witness, I want you to know that, among many other random things, I love you.'

3

I'm spending far too much time in toilet cubicles, Piers thought as he stood leaning against the locked door. He was going to have to proceed with great care. Zohreh was in far deeper than he had thought. His tooth had begun to nag. Ripping open the silver foil on his packet of paracetamol, he swallowed three down. The taste of the medication sharp on his palate, he racked his brain for an escape plan.

Coming out onto the atrium he spotted Zohreh in the retail area, and felt a pang. He knew that she deserved better than this. A fucking cliché but there must be some boy her own age somewhere with whom she could have quasi-mystical chats about Vincent Van Gogh. She was speaking to a shop assistant and pointing at one of the posters on the wall.

Piers was halfway across the atrium when he heard someone speak his name. He turned and found a woman with long black hair and shades like his own standing there. 'It *is* you, isn't it, Piers?'

'Yes,' he said warily.

'It's Maria Hertz. From the Van Gogh Museum.'

'Oh, Maria, hi.' Gaining his balance, Piers faultlessly performed the little air-kiss dance. 'Well, I got your card.'

'How's London's second stock exchange? Suffering from the credit crunch?'

'*Au contraire.* Going through the roof. You wouldn't believe what people are offering for Mikey Durrant.'

'I apologise for the cloaks and daggers, Piers,' Maria said in her non-identifiable European American-English.

'You're referring to Roger Bosman.'

'Exactly. As you'll see, there's reason for

caution. I'm so glad you've come. I knew you would.' Piers looked over to the retail well where the shop assistant was wrapping Zohreh's poster. 'Can we go somewhere a little more appropriate? And perhaps you might arrange to meet your companion later? I think perhaps it would be better if you came alone. We have something rather important to discuss.'

'Don't tell me, you've unearthed an unknown masterpiece.' Piers's smile could not entirely hide his weariness.

'I'll be waiting in the cafe.'

Piers gazed over to where Zohreh, poster secured under her arm, was browsing through a book of the artist's prints. It was a pity to spoil the moment, but the perfect opportunity to break off had presented itself. The next few minutes might be unpleasant, but they'd both be better for them in the long run. He took out his BlackBerry and accessed his travel account.

'How's the tooth?' she said when he came over a few minutes later.

'I've taken some painkillers.'

'Look at this, Piers. You know you were saying about them not knowing what Van Gogh's last picture was? This book says that his picture of *Daubigny's Garden* was. Or one called *Tree Roots*.'

'Look, Zohreh, I'm afraid something's come up. I'm going to have to leave you. I mean, it's work. I thought it was only going to take five minutes or so but apparently not.'

'So was that why you were talking to the

122

ageing Yoko Ono? I was watching you. I don't mind waiting.'

'Yes, well, it's going to take a while.'

'I'll look round again; I haven't been able to take it all in yet.'

'I mean, it's going to be the rest of the day.'

'I'll go and come back.'

'Sorry, it'll go into the night as well. Look, I feel terrible but it can't be helped. I think you should just fly home.'

'No, really, I'll — '

'I've booked you a flight already. I've emailed you the details.'

At that moment Zohreh's phone bleeped with Piers's incoming mail. She read it. 'Oh bump. The girl falls from the stars.'

'See you.' Piers took a step away. Then, the girl's abject look touching him, he took out his wallet. 'Here, have a few euros.'

She looked at the fistful of cash.

Piers had already walked ten paces when he heard her call him. He debated whether simply to walk on, but decided not to. Softly-softly catchee monkee; or in this case, let monkee go. 'I bought this for you,' Zohreh said. 'It's *Wheatfield with Crows*.'

'You didn't need to do that.'

'I know.'

And before he could avoid it, she'd put the poster tube into his hands and was walking away across the atrium.

Maria Hertz was in the cafe. 'I've got you an espresso, Piers.'

'You must have a long memory.'

'For some things, yes.'

Piers felt a twist inside. Had he slept with this woman as well? No; it had been his policy right from the beginning not to see anyone even remotely connected with the art world, and Maria Hertz was quite an important name there. He'd met Maria a number of times — how small was the international art community — and she'd done a talking heads spot on one of his TV programmes, including one memorable quote, which they'd finally decided to edit out, when she'd claimed that to the Victorians *a painter's brush* was a well-known euphemism for a fully erect phallus. The art adviser drained his coffee in one go. It had been harder than he thought to make the break with Zohreh, but now he felt relief. He would have to ride the inevitable scene with her at work but if all was handled satisfactorily then in a week's time it would blow over. 'So what's all this about then, Maria?' he asked, trying to squelch a yawn.

'When you are ready I will show you.'

'I'm ready.'

He followed Maria into a disguised entry that led off from the public gallery and through the intestines of the huge building until a side door took them abruptly outside. Piers lifted his sunglasses and felt the bright sunlight strike the back of his eyes. A passenger jet was passing through the slipstream way above Amsterdam. Beneath his feet he felt a smooth level of paving stones, caught the blue of flowers, and then he was entering another building. Maria took him past a library where a scholarly pair

124

of shoulders were hunched over a table covered with large exhibition catalogues and monographs, and then passing the untenanted reception desk descended some stairs to a complex of cellars. With a reading of her thumbprint she gained entrance to one of the vaults. 'We won't be disturbed.' Like clocks on a jeweller's wall, the array of air-moisture modifiers clicked on one after the other. Maria took off her dark glasses. 'This is where we keep documents and letters from the Auvers period.'

'I may have been down here once or twice before.'

Opening one of the metallic dockets bracketed on a rail, she brought out a Perspex tray and placed it within a viewing device. It contained a letter. The ink was brown with age, the handwriting neat but somewhat meandering. The language, French. 'Vincent Van Gogh's last letter to his brother,' Piers said.

'You recognise it?'

'*My dear brother,*' Piers translated. '*Thanks for your kind letter and for the fifty francs it contained.*'

'You find Vincent Van Gogh's last epistle a subject for funny?'

'I was just having a conversation about the brother-banker scenario, that's all.'

'With your beautiful young friend? I hope she hasn't been too inconvenienced.'

'Maria, can we just cut to the chase?'

'As I turn up the magnification, please recognise all the physical features of this letter.

125

The quality of the paper, the handwriting, the ink. Now compare it to this.' From her briefcase she brought out another Perspex tray and placed it in the viewing device beside the first. As well as words, this letter contained a rough sketch. The same handwriting skeined the page like a gaggle of geese, its formation parting for the drawing. 'What do you notice about the weave of the paper and the ink in this second letter?'

'Identical to the first.'

'The handwriting? In particular the capital Is and the loops on the Ds and Zs.'

'The same.'

'Look at the dip-to-word ratio.'

'What?'

'On average how many words the writer manages between dipping his nib in the inkwell. The first few words after a fresh immersion are thicker, and those before are the thinnest. It basically shows how hard the writer presses with his pen.'

'Just looking with the naked eye, they seem the same on both.'

'We've had it verified scientifically. This letter is also by Vincent Van Gogh to his brother Theo. One that doesn't appear in the current volumes of his collected correspondence. And never has.'

'Bloody hell.'

'Piers, do you read Dutch?'

'Yes.'

'Then perhaps you'll recognise the period to which this is relating.' But before he could read anything more than the words *Auvers-sur-Oise*, she had taken the letter away. 'We have every reason to believe that what you have just seen is Van Gogh's last ever letter. In fact, I would stake my professional reputation on it.'

'Congratulations, Maria. You're made for life.'

On the wall the air-moisture modifiers clicked. 'What is that English saying?'

'In a situation like this? Fuck me sideways, probably.'

'*We have larger fish to fry.*'

'Larger than the discovery of Van Gogh's last letter? It must be a whale.'

'Leviathan would be more appropriate.' She stared at Piers.

'Oh, come off it.' Piers waved a dismissive hand. 'You can't mean that. There are more undiscovered Van Gogh masterpieces than splinters of the one true cross.'

'The celebrated British sense of irony? Tell me, Piers, what do you know about the paintings from his Auvers period?'

'Mainly that Money hasn't believed in them for years. Auvers-sur-Oise is one of the most uncertain times of all. I would say that nobody believes Van Gogh did even half of those pictures any more. Remember when *Daubigny's Garden* was on the market? It couldn't get a buyer. It had to be withdrawn. And then there's the trouble they've had authenticating the portrait of Dr Dolittle.'

'Who?'

'I mean Dr Gachet.'

'And what if there was a new *authenticated* Auvers canvas?'

'Yeah, and they've just authenticated the Shroud of Turin. I've got a toothache coming on, Maria, and I'm not in the mood for jokes.'

'Piers, do you still deal in Georgiana Fairbanks?'

'What?'

'Personally I've always thought she was criminally underrated. But the British have only just begun to appreciate their artists. Yet I think even they know the value of Vincent Van Gogh.'

'What's Georgiana Fairbanks got to do with anything? Look, Maria, if you've got something to show me then let me see it.'

'Now it's you I think that must be joking. You think I've got it here? Have you any idea the value on something like this? Look, let's just call this a first meeting. If you're interested we can take it a step further. Only I must insist you keep our little conversation to yourself. You know the form, Piers.'

'And what happens if I'm not interested?'

'A man of your reputation missing the art story of the century? Besides, do you think I haven't seen my own fair share of so-called 'undiscovered masterpieces' not to understand what I'm talking about? Anyway, I've always looked on you as a cat. Curiosity.' The two senior members of the international art world looked at each other; they both put their dark glasses back on at the same time. 'I almost forgot,' Maria Hertz said as they came back out into the light of day. Having handed Piers an envelope she walked away. He opened it. Inside was a cheque for €100,000.

4

Sally and Mimi were in the garden when Piers got home the next morning. He watched them from the kitchen. Mother and daughter were painting. 'Hello, you two,' he called, coming out through the open French windows.

'Hi, *Pater*,' Mimi replied without looking up from her canvas, a portrait of Sally.

'You've come at a delicate moment, Piers,' Sally explained. 'I'm under strict instructions not to move. Will you be much longer, Mimi?'

'I'm trying to capture your lovely hair, Mummy.'

Piers was at Mimi's shoulder looking at her picture when he realised that he hadn't brought her a present back from Amsterdam. 'I've brought you this,' he said, lowering the poster tube that Zohreh had given him into his daughter's eyeline.

Mimi opened it up and unrolled the poster. '*Wheatfield with Crows*. Cool!'

'Well, it's for you *and* Mummy, since you've both embarked on artistic careers.'

'So you went to Amsterdam, darling?' Sally asked, flexing herself. She looked at her daughter's canvas. 'Not bad, Mimi. In fact, it's good. Don't you think, Piers?'

'Definite touches of German Expressionism,' said Piers.

'I'm doing it in the style of Georgiana Fairbanks,' his daughter admonished. 'Oh Daddy, it was brilliant at the Painting Party at the V&A. We learnt how to do portraits and everything.'

Piers looked at his wife's canvas: a portrait of their daughter. The girl was already recognisable on the canvas; the background was the green fire of the meadow.

'Why don't you get a canvas and have a go, Daddy?' Mimi said.

Piers was leaning down to kiss his wife when the doorbell sounded from the house. 'That'll be Gav,' Sally said.

'Gav?'

'Yes, Piers: Gav. You know; Gav, your best friend.'

'Again? To what do we owe the privilege of such attention from the busiest man in London?'

'He's bringing Emily over to see Mimi,' Sally said.

'Emily and I have decided to become artists,' Mimi said. 'We're going to smash the male-dominated art world.' She beamed at her father. 'And if you won't be part of our school then you'll just have to be our dealer.'

'I'm an *adviser*, darling; not a dealer. Anyway, I'd better let Gav in before he has to waste another ten seconds of his precious time. What's happened to his live-in Pole, or doesn't she stretch to escorting a child over five hundred yards of Chelsea?'

'It's Sunday, Piers,' Sally said.

'Even immigrant labour is entitled to Sunday off, Daddy.'

'Don't say things like that, sweetheart.'

'But it's true, Mummy. Emily's Pole has Sunday off. She goes to church.'

'I take it Emily's Pole has a name?'

130

The bell rang again just as Piers was coming down the hall. 'They're out the back,' Piers told Gav and his daughter as he opened the door. 'Emily, I hear you're becoming an artist.'

'You're either *born* an artist or not,' Gav's daughter explained wearily. 'You can't just become one.'

'Mimi and Emi,' Piers replied. 'Don't you think it's got a ring?'

Emily strode proprietorially down the hall then stopped. 'Oh Daddy, you left my easel. Go and get it.'

'I'm sure Sally will have a spare one,' Gav said.

'But it's my special one; I got it yesterday at the V&A. Mimi will be upset if I haven't brought it. She has an artistic temperament.'

'Off you go, slave,' cackled Piers as he bounded up the stairs.

The morning was growing warm. The tooth seemed to have settled. After his shower Piers stood at the open bedroom window watching Sally and the girls painting. What a subject for an artist: *The Painting Party*. As a boy he too was always drawing and painting. When he had got dressed he came back to the window. Zohreh was standing at the easels talking to Sally.

'Piers, how ungallant of you,' his wife called to him as he came out through the French windows. 'Leaving this poor girl in the lurch.' Sally turned to Zohreh. 'It's Zohreh, isn't it?'

'Yes,' said Zohreh. 'Hello, Piers.'

'Ah,' said Piers arriving.

'Zohreh's been telling us how you walked out of the meeting.'

131

'I'm afraid they weren't very happy, Piers,' Zohreh said. 'The Dutch production team. You see, we're making a film about Van Gogh. I'm sure Piers has told you about it.'

'Piers doesn't really tell anyone anything, do you?'

'Not guilty,' returned Piers, trying to regulate his breathing.

'Oh. Well, it's at a bit of a delicate stage actually,' Zohreh said. 'So sorry, for barging in at the weekend. But if I could just borrow him for a couple of hours. It's pretty crucial. I need to put Piers in the loop.'

'Of course. Would you like a drink before you go, Zohreh?'

'That would be lovely.'

'Are you an artist or just a dealer like Daddy?' Mimi asked. 'If you're an artist you can have some ice tea.'

'We'd better be going actually,' said Piers. 'Better not keep them waiting. You know what the Dutch are like. Pretend to be laid-back and rip you to shreds if you're half a minute late. See you later.'

'Bye,' said Zohreh, 'it's been lovely meeting you all.'

As Piers guided Zohreh back through the garden he tried to work out a strategy. The first thing was to get her away from the house. Opening the front door, he led her down the steps. 'I'm so, so sorry,' said Zohreh. 'I can't believe I've just done that.' Piers did not reply. He was still too near the house to begin. 'This isn't me, Piers,' Zohreh said, hurrying after him.

'Then who the hell is it?' he hissed. 'Madame Fucking Bovary?'

'I couldn't stop myself. I had to see you again.' Not trusting himself to answer, Piers flagged a passing taxi. 'It meant so much being with you in Amsterdam,' Zohreh continued. 'I didn't realise how deeply I felt until we got there. I wasn't joking when I said I loved you.'

'Madame Tussaud's,' Piers said, thinking it the place he was least likely to meet anyone he knew.

'I just can't believe I went to your house.'

'*You* can't believe it?'

'But I *had* to.'

'Zohreh, this isn't going to work.' Piers took a deep breath. Experience had taught him that although anger had its effect in these situations, it also had a worrying tendency to breed acts of revenge. 'You're twenty-three years old.'

'Lots of people have been happy with an age difference much bigger than ours.'

'I'm happily married.'

'Sally and Mimi?'

'Don't say their names.'

'Piers.' She reached out for him.

'For pity's sake, I — ' He stopped himself. Attempting a half-smile, he tried to keep it light. 'When you were being born I was probably having a wank.' Piers caught the driver's eye in the mirror. 'We belong to a different generation. You wear green eye-shadow, for pity's sake. I had a great-auntie who wore green eyeshadow.'

133

Zohreh's face crumpled. 'You said you liked the way I look.'

'I do. I mean, who couldn't? And that's why we've got to stop seeing each other. You deserve better than this. You're wonderful, beautiful and funny; and you should get someone who can give themselves fully to you. Not some old man like me.'

'Please stop the cab.' The tears she had sworn to keep hidden whatever happened filled her eyes. Piers felt the splash of their warmth on his hand. How stupid he'd been. Surely he ought to have realised that she was getting too serious?

'Can you pull over, mate?' he said to the driver.

The taxi stopped. Zohreh staggered out.

'That's eight pounds — ' the cabby said.

'I won't be a minute.'

'I'll have to keep the meter running.'

Piers caught up with Zohreh outside an antiques shop. 'Did I really walk into your garden?' she agonised. 'As if I didn't hate myself enough.'

'There's nothing to hate yourself for.'

'In Iran I'd be stoned to death for this.' Turning from him with a sob she ran up the side street.

'Where are you going?' he called, but when she turned a corner, he did not pursue her. 'Where to now, guv?' the taxi driver asked as Piers climbed back in.

On the way home Piers kept catching the driver's eye in the mirror: one of the 9 per cent?

The hands spanning the wheel retained all ten of their digits.

Gav was sitting on the steps beneath the tree of heaven when Piers returned. 'How could you?' the media man demanded. 'Not content with shagging a sixth-former you actually bring her round here.'

'What the hell are you on about, Gav?'

'I was sitting in my car when I heard the pair of you. *It meant so much being with you in Amsterdam. I didn't realise how deeply I felt until we got there. I wasn't joking when I said I loved you.*'

For a moment Piers seemed to be peering at the bees in the tree of heaven, then he heaved a theatrical sigh of relief. 'Thank fuck you know about it at last. I've kept meaning to tell you about it, Gav. What a nightmare. I just didn't know what to do. Look. We work together and she got keen, that's all.'

'That's all.'

'I suppose I should have spotted it. OK, maybe I flirted with her; who wouldn't? She's stunning. You would yourself. Only before I'm wise to it, she's turning up here telling me, of all things, she loves me!'

'*Of all things.*' Gav took out a cigarette. 'And to think, *of all things*, that all these years I've believed you. The times I've defended you. She's not the first, is she? No, no, don't say anything, Piers.' Gav's BlackBerry rang. Angrily, he pressed the cancel-call button.

'Christ on a troika,' said Piers. 'Gavin Henchard not taking his calls; it must be serious.'

'Finish it or I'll tell Sally,' said Gav levelly.

Piers's tooth twinged. 'It's finished,' he said. 'I've just finished it.'

'Do you really expect me to believe that?'

'It was nothing. Nothing, nothing. Just nothing.'

'For fuck's sake, I won't see her treated so shittily.'

'Who?'

'Sally! Finish it or I'll tell her.' Gav exhaled smoke. 'You've got everything anyone could ever possibly want, Guest, and you blow it all for a quick shag.'

When Gav was gone, Piers leant back and stared up at the tree above. From the garden drifted the occasional voice from the painting party. Into his mind came a blurred expanse of purple. The focus sharpened. It was a railway cutting blooming with willowherb. And his father was standing in the midst of it.

Keilburg im Schwarzwald,
June 1936

1

'We're lost.' There was a wobble in the younger brother's voice. 'You've got us lost.'

The older brother frowned at the fork in the path. Both ways looked identical. Although it was still early afternoon, in the forest it felt as though night was already falling. The silver firs rose high above them, their huge branches locked in tussle like wrestling giants. ''Course we're not lost,' he retorted with a conviction he did not feel.

'Then what are we waiting here for, Gustav?' The younger brother's voice had become a whine. 'I knew we should have stayed at school.'

'You didn't have to come, Peter. Nobody asked you to.'

'But *I* wanted to see Papa too.'

Gustav narrowed his eyes. Was it his imagination or did the path to the left feel slightly darker, as though it led deeper into the forest, and the path to the right smaller, a deer trail perhaps, or a wolf track? What was worse, to be lost forever or eaten quickly by a wolf? A little circle of sky was just visible through the canopy of the forest. It was like staring up at the world from the bottom of a well. 'Gustav?'

'What now?' With a surge of annoyance Gustav realised his brother was close to tears.

'Are witches true?'

''Course not.'

'So *you* don't believe in them?'

'Only babies do.'

'Papa does. And he's not a baby.'

''Course he doesn't.' Gustav turned to Peter. Underneath the family red hair, his little brother's face was crumpled. 'I know he doesn't,' he said more kindly.

'How do you know?'

'Because he told me.'

'When?'

'Last time he was at home.'

'I don't remember him saying that.'

Gustav paused. Lying was wrong but it was better than his brother crying. 'You were in bed. There are no such things as witches. That's exactly what he said. There are no such things as witches.'

'Then why do his stories have them?'

'Well, a story's a story, and the truth's the truth.'

'So is the Bible just a story?'

'Well, *that's* a true story.'

'Then how do you know all the other stories aren't true? Why would someone lie like that? And if they'd never seen a witch how come they could just invent one?'

'Shh, I'm thinking.' Gustav pretended to study the two paths ahead of them, whispering to himself as though debating the merits of each. Sometimes it was hard being nine years old with a younger brother. By himself it wouldn't be so bad but with Peter set to blubber at any moment he couldn't concentrate. He didn't fancy their chances of survival if they blundered into a wolf's lair. He only had a catapult, and Peter would be too terrified to put up much of a fight. He should never have let him come. Not only that but with them both gone from school at the same time their absence was more likely to be missed.

'We should have gone by the road,' Peter said.

'We couldn't.'

'Why couldn't we?'

'Because someone would have seen us.'

'Better that than being lost in the forest.'

'Go back then.'

Gustav heard his brother whimper. 'Did you really see Papa, Gusti? Maybe he's still away on a field trip.'

'How many times do I have to tell you? Thomas Hermann said he saw him driving by when he was out straightening the flag. So he must have come back. Now let me think.'

Gustav narrowed his eyes again. No wonder so few people walked this way. Papa called it the huntsman's path, and said these days it was only used by the elves. Gustav had thought he was joking but now he wasn't so sure. A favourite trick of the elves was to lead mortals deeper into the forest. 'Come on,' he decided at last, 'we'll go this way.' And lifting a fir bough aside he stepped out on the left-hand track.

After a few hundred metres he looked over his shoulder. His brother was not with him. A feeling of sickness gripped his throat. Taking out his catapult and fitting a stone, he retraced his steps. Disturbed from its perch in a dark silver fir, a nutcracker flew across his path. Giving a little shriek, Gustav began to sprint. What would he say to Mama and Papa if he lost Peter?

He found his brother back at the fork calmly sitting on an old stump among the brightly coloured toadstools. Enraged, Gustav pulled back the elastic on his catapult. But something he saw stopped him in his tracks. 'What are you doing?' he demanded.

'Reading,' Peter replied without looking up from his book.

'Reading what?'

'About how to survive the night outside. It shows you how to build a shelter. And get water too.'

'You can't read.'

'I can. There are pictures too.'

Gustav's voice boomed down the dark corridors between the trees. 'Give me that book.'

'Why should I?'

'Because I say so.'

'Well, I'm saying no.'

'Give it to me, Peter.'

'You're not in charge.' Peter's habitual defiance weakened when he saw the look in his brother's eyes. 'What is it, Gusti?'

'That book.' Gustav's words were a guttural growl as he slowly approached the tree stump. 'Give it to me. Papa would say you had to.'

140

'How do you know?'

'Do you know what that book is?'

With a sudden rush, Gustav snatched the *Hitler Youth Handbook* from his brother. 'Give it back!' Peter cried, but Gustav held the book out of his reach. When kicking and elbowing didn't work Peter bit Gustav's arm. With a howl of pain, the older brother swung a fist. For a while, their chests heaving, the two brothers stared at each other, the book between them. Peter was too shocked to cry.

'Don't you understand, Peterli?'

''Course I do. We're lost. *You* don't know where we're going. So we need to build a shelter, *and* light a fire. That's all in the book.'

'Peter, it's a Nazi book.'

'So?'

'Don't you know anything? It's because of the Nazis that we're not allowed to talk about Lotte to anyone.'

'No it isn't. It's because of her mouth and because she can't talk properly.'

Gustav shook his head in utter exasperation. He pictured their young sister: the mark of the wasp sting on her lip, that strange rift cleaving the roof of her mouth, her clumsy babble of speech. 'If Papa saw you with this book, he'd beat you.'

'No he wouldn't. He didn't even beat me the time I cut the well rope.'

'*That's* nothing beside this. Don't you know what the Nazis would do to Lotte if they found her?' Gustav sighed. It wasn't his brother's fault; after all Peter *really* didn't know anything.

141

Sometimes he wished that he didn't know anything either. June now, it had been Christmas when Gustav had first begun to know things. How he regretted ever discovering that the knot in the floorboard beneath his bed could be removed. Since then he had seen and heard many of the whispered conversations between his parents in the room downstairs. Much of what they said about Lotte he didn't understand, but he knew enough to realise the dangers. Their talk always came back to the Nazis. Gustav could hear the words of his mother now: *If a Nazi ever come anywhere near this house, they'll see Lotte and they'll take her away.* 'Peterli,' Gustav said to his brother, 'if the Nazis ever come anywhere near our house, they'll see Lotte and they'll take her away.'

'You're just saying that so I'll give you the book.'

'No, I'm not.'

Gustav looked at his brother. He was no longer angry; Peter's vast incomprehension just made him feel lonely. Gustav didn't really understand the Nazis either, but you don't need to understand something to fear it. When he was younger he was terrified of the nixie he thought lived in the millpond. Now that he was nine years old and grown up, he realised nixies were not true, but Nazis had taken their place. At least nixies had to stay in their millponds. How terrible it was that real things were worse than nightmares. With a cry, Gustav began ripping pages from the *Hitler Youth Handbook*; he scrunched them into balls and threw them into the dark shadows between the trees.

Peter gasped in horror. 'Teacher gave me that. She said it was the most important book in the school. And now you've gone and ripped it.'

All the long months of frustration since he'd discovered the knot in the floorboard seemed to explode at once in Gustav's throat. 'The Hitler Youth is stupid!'

'No it isn't,' Peter barked wildly. 'It's fun.'

'How do you know?'

'Everybody says.'

'Well, *you* can't be in it anyway.'

'Yes I can.'

'You've got a doctor's note.'

'*You* can't be in it either.'

'I don't want to be.'

'Don't you?' Peter looked beseechingly at his elder brother. 'Everybody else says it's brilliant. You get to go camping.'

'Last year our old teacher said it was a load of rubbish.'

Peter's eyes narrowed. 'New teacher said old teacher is in prison.'

'That's rubbish,' said Gustav, his fists tightening. He'd heard the same rumour. 'Say it's rubbish.'

'I won't.'

'Say it.'

'It's true. It's not something in a story; it's true. Everybody knows she's in prison.'

'Shut up, you little idiot.'

Knocking him to the ground, Gustav pinioned Peter with a knee across his throat so that as he screamed he could feel the vibration of his

Adam's apple. 'It's true, it's true,' the younger boy insisted desperately. 'She's in prison.'

'You're lying! Admit you're lying!' Gustav suspended a long line of drool over Peter's face, sucking it back just moments before it broke under its own weight.

'New teacher says old teacher is a communist, and a Jew!'

The string of gob broke. The younger brother bucked wildly but Gustav held him firm. 'Lying is what makes witches come; they hear you and jump out!' Gustav regretted his words while they were still echoing back to him from the steep fir-clad mountainside. 'Anyway,' he said, releasing Peter, 'I know for certain she hasn't gone to prison.'

'How?'

'Papa told me.'

Peter sighed. 'I wish he'd tell *me* nice things.'

Gustav looked at his brother's grubby face. Even when he annoyed him there was something in his little-kid eyes — still like a baby really — that made him feel sorry for him. '*He does.* He told you that you were a good runner. Remember? When he raced us round the millpond. And Papa's always right.' A downy feather from the breast of a nutcracker spiralled down; both tried to catch it. They smiled their truce. Gustav looked at Peter. He had to get him moving otherwise they'd never reach home. 'I know,' he said brightly, 'I'll give you a comrade's lift; just imagine I'm rescuing you from the battlefield.' Peter laughed for joy as he felt himself being lifted over his brother's shoulder.

'I've just picked you up from the trench,' Gustav announced, heading back down the left-hand path with his brother over his shoulder. 'And I've got to get you back to headquarters for your Iron Cross.'

'What have I done?'

'Killed ten enemies.'

'Jews?'

'No, other soldiers.'

'An Iron Cross; promise?'

'Promise,' said Gustav airily. 'I'll make you one like mine. And each time a branch knocks against you, it's a bullet. But don't worry, you can't die.' Closing his eyes Peter imagined himself bleeding profusely while the bombs fell all around. He would show Papa his Iron Cross, and he'd be so proud. 'You're getting heavy,' said Gustav, hoping to cheer his brother up. 'In fact, I don't think you're the smallest in the school any more.'

'Who's smaller?' Peter demanded.

'Well . . . Thomas Hermann.'

'You really think so?'

'I know it scientifically. When you were learning your letters, we older ones were measuring. I measured Thomas Hermann and made a mental note of his height.'

'Honest?'

'Honest. *He* would never win an Iron Cross.'

'Thanks, Gusti.'

For a while Gustav felt his spirits lifting but it wasn't long before his brother really did begin to feel heavy. The ripped book he'd stuffed down his shirt pressed against his sternum. He tried to imagine it was a field dressing over a near fatal wound he'd sustained through heavy enemy fire. 'Pull me up higher,' the younger boy demanded.

'Don't elbow me like that.'

'Well, don't drag me along the ground.'

By imagining that he really was a soldier bearing a wounded comrade, Gustav was able to stumble on a little further, but at last he sank to his knees and deposited his brother. Despairingly, he brought out the book. Peter's voice seemed tiny in the vast corridors of the forest: 'What am I going to do tomorrow when I have to show it to teacher?'

'Look, a stag!' Gustav cried and pointed. As Peter looked down the path, Gustav hurled the book up into the boughs of a fir. 'Oh, it must have darted away,' he said when his brother turned back questioningly. 'You'll have to be quicker next time there's an order. You'll never earn an Iron Cross being that slow.'

But before he could get Peter moving, the book tumbled down through the branches to the ground. He stuffed it back in his shirt. 'I know,' Peter said, sensing his brother's desolation. 'We'll say that we met a witch and she took the book from us and tried to burn it.'

'Where are the burn marks?'

'We got it back before she could set it alight. That's how the pages got ripped. I'll let you say you did it, if you want; then you can be a hero of the *Volk*. Maybe earn a real Iron Cross.'

'You have to kill people to get that. Anyway, she'll never believe that story.'

'We can say it was a dwarf; Rumpelstiltskin!'

'I've told you before — *Rumpelstiltskin*'s just a story. Evil things like that don't really exist. We *could* say a wolf did it.' He picked up the book. 'It could easily have ripped it with his teeth.'

'I know,' Peter declared. 'We'll say it was a Jew. They'd *definitely* believe that. A Jew came out of the trees and crept up behind us. He punched me, and you could say he bit you. Anyway, we don't need a book. We can gather mushrooms and berries without it. We've already built lean-tos. Yours are quite good.' Peter waited. 'Do you think mine are all right as well?'

'Yes,' Gustav lied. 'Now come on; otherwise we will have to spend the night here.'

They had gone another two kilometres or so when Peter stopped. 'I'm hungry.'

'We're nearly home.'

'You said that before.'

'If you carry on you can have my Iron Cross as well.'

They came to a stream. It cut deep into the stone of the mountainside. The only way across was by a dilapidated bridge from which a number of the wooden slats were missing. Peter sat down. 'I'm not crossing,' he said when his brother tried to cajole him.

'But this means we're near home,' Gustav reasoned. 'It must be the same stream as ours.'

'I'm not crossing.'

Gustav's head swam as he stepped onto the bridge. The stream was in spate; twenty metres below, the black water roared. Something about the sound reminded him of his sister when excitement made her speech even more of a cascading torrent than usual. The wood creaked beneath his feet; the whole bridge bounced when he took a step. He crossed on his hands and knees but his brief surge of elation congealed when he saw the immobile heap of his brother still on the other side. He had to go back. This time he walked upright, deciding to get it over with quickly no matter the risk. A section of the handrail came off in his hand; both brothers heard it splintering on the rocks below. No matter what Gustav said, threatened or promised, Peter would not cross. 'You'll have to come,' Gustav said by way of last, resort. 'Or the witch will get you.'

A frightened eye peeped up through the red fringe of his younger brother's hair. 'You said witches weren't true.'

'Well, usually they aren't but — '

'You said Papa said they weren't true.'

'Look, I wasn't going to tell you this but I think maybe you *are* old enough to know. You see, Papa didn't think you were.' Gustav paused for a moment. A big bubble of snot bladdered from his little brother's nose. He felt terrible, but he had to do it. Later he could tell him that he was confused, and that it was just a story not the truth, but for now they *had* to get over the bridge before the wolves smelt them. Not to mention the elves, the goblins, the dwarfs, the pixies, the kobolds, the nixies or even the Nazis; so many different types of mischievous beings. 'There *is* one witch in our mountains.'

'Who is she?'

'Nobody knows her name, but she lives here.'

'Here?'

'This is her bridge. That's why some of the planks are missing. They get burnt by her feet.' The abject terror on his brother's face made Gustav back-pedal. The last thing he wanted was for Peter to become paralysed like a rabbit before a stoat. 'But we're safe on the other side, Peterli. You see, the water washes away her magic.'

'What happens then? Does she just become a normal old woman?'

'This one's young,' said Gustav, embellishing. 'She's not at all like your usual witch.'

'Doesn't she even have a black cat?'

'No, a tame nutcracker.'

'I'd like to meet her.'

Wasn't that just like a little brother? 'You wouldn't. Now come on.'

Peter took one step then stopped. 'But if there's a witch, there'll probably be a troll.'

'No there won't.'

'How do *you* know?'

'Because there's no such thing as trolls.'

'You're only saying that; five minutes ago you said there weren't any witches in our mountains.'

'You stay here then and I'll watch from the other side as the witch comes for you. She'll eat you most likely. Toes first, then nose, then the thing between your legs.'

At last he managed to drag the snivelling Peter across. At the far side he looked at the darkening patch on the front of his brother's shorts. He'd wet himself. Like a baby.

It wasn't long before beeches began to replace the firs. Both boys let out a cheer. They were near home. A woodpecker flew across their path. 'Good luck!' they said simultaneously, spitting on their hands and shaking. They reached the first landmark. It was a huge tree, the one that they called the Kaiser beech. Hundreds of years old and hollow as a hut, its great branches, themselves the size of most tree trunks, swept down to rest their knotty elbows on the ground. Papa had hung rope swings, and built a tree house. 'Papa, Papa!' the younger sibling cried and with a shout of glee set off at a run down the well-known path that led to their home.

Allowing Peter to beat him in the race, Gustav forgot all the doubts he'd had in the forest. He was going to see Papa again after his long trip to England! His papa was the best father in the world. The eaves of the woods appeared ahead. He could already see the thatched roof of their house when he remembered the book down his shirt. The enormity of what he'd done brought him to a halt. Before Papa had gone on his last field trip, he'd heard his parents discussing his old teacher. Mama had said that she *had* been sent to prison; Papa had laughed saying she'd probably left to get married. Up until now Gustav had believed Papa. Gustav listened to his brother's voice ringing through the valley. 'Papa! Papa! Papa!' But what if Papa was wrong and his teacher *had* been sent to prison? All *she'd* done was say the book was no good; what would the Nazis do when they found out that he'd actually ripped pages out? They would come to take him away, and when they did they'd see Lotte and they'd take her away. And it would all be his fault.

Gustav turned and ran back up into the darkness of the forest. He ran and ran until he reached the bridge. The roar of the water seemed even louder now, the bridge flimsier as he tested it with his foot. Would it bear his weight a fourth time?

2

The front door was open wide. Standing at it, Ernst listened to his daughter's happy babble playing through the afternoon stillness like the stream turning the mill wheel. Silently he entered the old house. Helga and the little girl were at the far window filling vases with the wild flowers heaped on the table. A butterfly had got inside and was fluttering over the blue blooms.

It was Lotte who saw him first. Scattering her bunch of gentians, she ran over and threw herself into his arms. 'Pa-pa-ba!' she laughed as he hurled her so high that her hair danced in the rafters.

'Yes, Papa's back, Lotte!'

'Ernst,' smiled Helga. 'Careful.'

Still holding his three-year-old daughter, the folklorist encircled his wife with his other arm, and drew them all together so that their noses touched. 'Three peas in a pod,' he laughed. Helga was still holding her flowers and they seemed to glow between them. Lotte blew on the gentians. Her breath was weak but one of the spreading petal tips quivered. 'Mistress of the Blue Lamp,' said Ernst, 'I am bound to serve you in everything. What would you have me do, O Princess?'

The little girl threw her head back and giggled. 'Loli-min-eh!'

'Yes, Lotte *is* a princess and Mama is the Queen. And this is what their faithful servant brings from a far-off land.' Reaching into his knapsack, Ernst brought out a brown-paper package tied with a blue ribbon.

Lotte gasped with pleasure at the ribbon. 'Wow-ah!'

'Yes! Blue just like your flowers.' Ernst leant over and whispered in his daughter's ear. 'The moon told me that you and Mama would be picking blue flowers.'

'Ah-oo, Pa-pa.' The child thanked him solemnly then took the present outside.

'She's taken it to the bench,' Helga said. 'That's her special place. We always open your letters there. She's missed you, Ernst; the boys too; we all have.'

Gently, Ernst placed a finger on his wife's brow. 'I'm back.'

Holding each other they could hear their daughter's happy prattle outside. 'How are the boys, Helga?'

'They ask me every day when you're coming back. How's Hans?'

'I've invited him to come tonight. He'll help me carry the trunk up from the car. But first this.' Ernst drew out another present from the knapsack. 'You didn't think I'd forget the Queen of the Blue Lamp, did you?'

'Oh, you didn't need to.' Ernst watched Helga giggle like a child as she opened the box he'd given her. When she found the hat inside, she gave a short sharp laugh. 'Where on earth did you get this from, Ernst?'

'Don't you like it?'

'It's beautiful. But how can we afford it?'

'It's the economic miracle, Helga. Now even peasants can afford to wear hats like a high-society girl!'

She turned the hat round in her hands, caressing its feather. 'But I can't wear this.'

'They're all the rage in Berlin; why not in our Keilburg? Here.' He placed the hat on his wife's head, flicking the feather with a graceful sleight of hand. 'Your panache.'

Helga blushed. 'Thank you,' she whispered.

Their kiss was broken by the cry of joy from the door. 'Mama-wee-wi-wown.'

'Queen Mama with her crown,' Ernst repeated.

The child tugged at her father's arm. 'Pa-pa-um-awine!'

Come outside! How Ernst had missed the swallow-like chatter of his little one. He followed her to the bench outside where the present lay unwrapped: a picture book. 'Oh Ernst, that's beautiful,' said Helga. 'Did you write it yourself?'

'And illustrated it too.' He winked at his daughter: 'With a little help from the moon.'

Taking his daughter on his knee, Ernst sat on Lotte's bench among the tubs of scarlet runner beans. There, stretched out before him, was their little valley. Lying hidden in the mountains like a secret, no matter what was happening elsewhere Keilburg was always the same. Even the mill wheel still turned though it had ground no flour for decades; and every year the meadow, quilted with the same flowers, echoed with cowbells tinkling in the distance. Summer had come in his absence. 'This story,' he said, picking up Lotte's book, 'is called *The Musicians of Keilburg.*'

Helga let the relief flood through her. How wonderful it felt! During the weeks of Ernst's absence her worries had been raging out of control. Each morning she would wake to Lotte's happy babble, but the moment of calm peace would then become terror as she imagined someone else listening. She tried to tell herself that no stranger was there, that the sound of a footstep on the landing was just the creaking of the house's old timbers, but her fears were like the spiders in the rafters: no matter how often she brushed the webs away they would immediately begin spinning again. The terror of prying ears listening to the little one's carefree gaggle of words grew in her breast like a cancer. And it wasn't just the speech impediment. Only this afternoon as they gathered flowers from the clearing in the forest, a sudden sunbeam had fallen on her daughter's face picking out the harelip so that the slight indenture on her mouth seemed to twist half her face inside itself. When the child had begun to sing for joy, her cleft palate had seemed like a hideous, gaping wound. *Why-Ma-ma-i?* the girl had asked. Helga had had to lie: *Mama's crying because she pricked her finger*. But now Ernst had returned, bringing with him his assurance, and the valley's sense of inviolable enchantment. Helga closed her eyes and listened to the story, laughing with her daughter at the antics of the donkey. As Ernst always said, what harm could come to them here? The present state of affairs couldn't last forever. Germany wouldn't let it; neither would the rest of the world. They were right to have come here. Lotte had three years before she had to go to school, three years before her affliction would become common knowledge. They could hide in Keilburg until then; by which time it would be 1939 and everything would be changed. Hitler just a bad memory. With her husband back, it seemed easier too to believe that the horrible stories one heard weren't true; to shrug aside the vile rumours that had managed to reach even Keilburg. After all, sitting in the sunshine, listening to a children's tale, who could give credence to such dark, twisted whispers? 'Non-ee,' Lotte cried, clapping her hands together as she pointed at the illustration of the donkey, 'Non-ee may oom mah-mah!'

'Yes,' Helga grinned. 'Donkey plays oom-pah-pah.'

'Non-ee lon-eeya.' Lotte held her hands up at her head like a pair of donkey ears.

'Donkey Longears,' nodded her mother.

A bee hummed drowsily in the runner-bean flowers behind the bench; already the first beans were forming. Helga stared across the valley. From here she could see the long length of the path from the road, the only access to Keilburg from the outside world. She closed her eyes gratefully. For a while at least she no longer needed to play sentinel. Tonight she knew she would sleep properly for the first time since Ernst had left.

When Ernst finished the story, Lotte acted it out, tramping the animals' long road, leaping out at robbers. Ernst took Helga's hand. 'She's grown, I'll have to put another notch on the measuring post. Her speech seems clearer too.'

'You think, Ernst?'

'Dr Wolff said the impediment might get better.'

'We do her speech exercises every day.'

With a final jump, the little girl collapsed in a heap. Her peals of laughter caused the real donkey grazing with the cows to lift its head and bray. Ernst leapt to his feet. 'Ah yes, our very own Frau Longears. She's reminding me that I have something else to show my Lotte.' Picking herself up, the child skipped over to the bench. *Look at her*, Helga thought, *as carefree as a foal*. 'Do you believe in magic?' her father asked. Lotte nodded. 'Good, then you can bring her to life.' Ernst stooped, and picking a seeding dandelion from beneath the bench, gave it to his daughter. In the bottom corner of each page he had sketched the donkey in a slightly different pose so that when you flicked through the book the animal seemed to come to life. Lotte blew on the dandelion. 'Frau Longears lives!' Ernst whispered, and the falling seeds appeared to be fanned by a living donkey whose hooves romped against a squeeze box as its eyes closed with pleasure and its ears flattened in the ecstasy of tune.

'Pa-pa-ma-i,' their daughter said, her eyes wide at the thumb-cinema.

'Papa *is* magic,' Helga echoed.

'Mama wee-wi-wown.'

Lifting her hand, Helga realised that she was still wearing the hat.

They were still laughing at the animated donkey when Helga spotted the figure on the path at the head of the valley. Her smile fell like a piece of dead wood. The dread that had thawed with Ernst's arrival gripped again. Seeing her mother's look, the little girl jumped from her father's knee and plunged into the house. The book tumbled to the ground behind her, closing like a lid on the musical donkey.

Lotte loved this game. They played it every day. She called it 'apples in the barrel'. Whenever Mama looked at her like that, the child had to hide. With the ease of a sparrow flying up into the thatching, she darted up the stairs to the top of the house; mounting the loft ladder, she pulled it up behind her just as Mama had instructed. Where should she hide? It was lovely lying under the hay but she liked the smell in the apple barrel even more. Today though she decided to creep into the secret mouth! The thought excited her so much that she remembered only just in time that she couldn't so much as clap once: she had to keep absolutely quiet. Opening the little door hidden in the loft wall, she stole into the cavity. How she loved the smell of the onions Mama had hung in here for her.

Listening with all her might she waited for mother stork to visit the nest just above her hiding place. When that happened the darkness was filled with the hungry chirrups of the young. But she had to be careful; when she heard mother stork's babies Lotte always wanted to call back to them, and the most important rule of 'apples in the barrel' was that she could not make a sound.

It wasn't only during 'apples in the barrel' that she had to keep quiet. *Lotte must never speak in front of strangers!* Those were the words Mama said to her every day, and every day Lotte would have to repeat them and then recite over and over again the names of the only people she was allowed to talk to: *Mama, Papa, Gustav, Peter, Uncle, Hans*. But who else was there in the world? Frau Longears; the cows; perhaps the storks circling overhead? Lotte did not enjoy the 'you can only talk to' game as much as 'apples in the barrel' even though she had put in her own name to make it sound better: *Mama, Papa, Gustav, Peter, Uncle, Lotte, Hans*. Of course she could speak to herself as well, just in her head. The funny thing was, *that* voice was not at all ugly like the one that sometimes made Mama cry.

Hidden in the loft, Lotte listened to the house whispering. It shared so many things with her. Each creak, rustle or scurry of a mouse was a secret being given away. Best of all, if she listened really carefully she'd hear her own heart stirring the darkness.

Mother stork still hadn't arrived when the call

came from downstairs. But Lotte's disappointment was tempered when she heard who it was: 'It's Uncle Dietrich!'

'Ung-ah!' Lotte laughed. Quickly descending the loft ladder and then the stairs, she burst outside. Uncle was still a long way off. Seizing one of the daisy chains she kept hanging on the door handle she ran down the long path to greet the newcomer. 'Ung-ah!'

Ernst and Helga watched their daughter. Falling down, she pulled herself back up and continued running.

The distant figure raised a stick and waved. Ernst waved back. When he glanced at his wife he was surprised by the look on her face. 'What's the matter, Helga, are you expecting bad news?' Disturbed by the little girl's shouts, a pair of storks rose from where they were drinking at the millpond edge and, circling the valley, landed on their clutter of sticks at the top of the house.

When Dietrich saw the little girl running towards him, he felt a catch in his throat. She looked so small against the back-drop of the valley with its mill wheel, towering thatched house and the steep tree-clad mountainsides. What times he had lived to see. To think that there were people who wanted to hurt this child. He practised a smile — it was imperative that the little one have no inkling of the purpose of his visit — and waved again. Only Ernst was waving back; Helga stood stationary as Lot's wife. The professor watched the storks landing on the apex of the old thatched house. The instincts of mothers and birds, he observed heavily, were eternal mysteries.

He slowed down in order to prepare himself to greet Lotte as nonchalantly as he could. How beautiful the house looked sitting between the millpond and the treeline; how calm; like a Tibetan temple. 'Ung-ah-hing!' Lotte gasped as she reached him. He bent low to allow the little girl to place one of her daisy chains on his head. 'Ung-a-hing,' she giggled, exposing the red gape of her palate like a nestling.

'Me, a king?' Laughing, Dietrich bowed. But as he did so anger surged through him. If only he could have that Adolf Hitler here with him now! He'd show him a thing or two. What kind of a monster could want to rid the world of children like Lotte? 'Lotte,' he whispered, embracing the child, 'I've brought you some sweets; the kind you like the best.' And with the daisy coronet on his brow, he let the child lead him on. 'You still haven't persuaded them to bring the autobahn a little closer then?' the professor called to Ernst as Lotte propelled him to the bench. 'Couldn't you at least widen your track a little so that a car can get up? Those two kilometres feel like five in this heat.'

Helga watched her uncle drink the water she brought for him. Her intuition had been sound: there was something the matter. Bringing out a small table, she placed on it a bottle of *Blutwurz*. 'And what have you got there, Lotte?' Dietrich asked as Lotte proudly held up her new book. 'How wonderful,' he said, flicking through it.

'Pa-pa-ma-i,' she urged, and blowing the

dandelion clock that Ernst plucked from beneath the bench she laughed again as the donkey was flicked into life.

'You'll stay the night, Uncle Dietrich,' said Helga.

'Of course he will,' Ernst said.

The professor tried to smile as he fingered his daisy coronet.

Lotte began to dance for joy. Despite his anxiety, Dietrich got up and danced with her for the length of his breath.

Blutwurz sparkling in their glasses, the men toasted each other. 'To your most recent trip,' the older man said. Although he was feeling light-headed, the professor drank. He even managed to wink at his niece. 'Helga, your husband's new research is brilliant; quite brilliant. If we don't find a way of stopping him soon he will have completely rewritten our subject.' Although her uncle smiled and talked volubly, Helga knew that he hadn't come out here to swap pleasantries. Her sense of foreboding deepened when she saw the way his hands repeatedly kneaded the head of his stick. 'Still birdwatching, Lotte?' Dietrich said, indicating the Zeiss binoculars hanging in the bean frame.

Lotte threw her head back and laughed. But Helga understood that her uncle had not given them these glasses to watch the storks. Through them you could spot a visitor ten minutes before he might reach the house. Uncle and niece caught each other's eye. *I would give everything not to have to tell her what I have come for*, the old man said to himself, *even my life itself.*

3

'You expect us to believe that?' Helga's voice rose angrily.

'Helga, don't get angry with the boy,' the professor soothed. 'Now tell us the truth, Peterli. They didn't close school early today, did they?'

Peter looked at the ground; he seemed to find inspiration there: 'There was a fire! We had to run for our lives. All apart from Thomas Hermann; he burnt to death.'

His mother threw her hands in the air. 'The boy's a liar!'

'Then a witch chased me through the forest. Only it wasn't a witch. It was a Jew!'

'Listen, Peter,' his father said gently. 'We have to find Gustav. He might be hurt. He was with you, wasn't he?' After a long pause the boy nodded.

★　★　★

Even before he reached the Kaiser beech Ernst could hear his older son weeping. He felt his knees buckle with relief. He had not mentioned to Helga his fears about the dilapidated bridge. How could he have gone off to England leaving such a danger? First thing tomorrow he and Hans would mend it. With his back resting against the tree, Ernst slid into a sitting position. Inside the broad hollow trunk he could hear Gustav trying to be silent. 'I wish I could find my eldest son Gusti,' Ernst declared. 'I've got a present for him.' He waited. The shouts of the others echoed in the trees as they searched the other side of the valley. 'Lotte's got her present already; Peter will get his tomorrow, even though he's been naughty. But what naughtiness lasts longer than the sunrise?' Ernst had to stifle a giggle. He could hear his son moving slightly. 'Such a nice present too; I'm sure he's going to love it.'

The abject little boy emerged from the depth of the Kaiser beech. Embracing him, Ernst could feel his son's heart beating like a sparrow held in the hand. 'Have they come, Papa?'

'Who?'

'I'll go. Tell them they don't need to take anyone else.'

'And who might *they* be?'

'I didn't mean to do it,' Gustav blurted. 'I didn't . . . ' His anguish too great for words, the boy buried himself deeper in his father's arms.

'You know something?' Ernst said brightly. 'When I was your age, I played truant too.'

'*You* did?'

'It's not the end of the world.'

The boy disengaged himself and took out an object from down his shirt. 'Papa, is *this* the end of the world?' The floodgates opened as his father took the torn *Hitler Youth Handbook*. 'And when they come for me . . . ' Gustav sobbed. 'They'll see Lotte and they'll take her . . . and Mama too for hiding her . . . and you . . . and even Uncle . . . Oh Papa, they'll take everyone . . . and when the storks come back to nest next year no one will be left in our Keilburg . . . '

163

Taking the little boy by the shoulders, Ernst looked him in the eye. 'Gustav, no one's going to take anyone away.'

'But — '

'I promise.'

The son looked back at his father. 'The Nazis.'

'Not even the Nazis. Gustav, I give you my word.' Gradually Ernst felt his boy's sobs subside. It was here, on a midsummer evening exactly like this one, that Ernst and Helga had lain together for the first time. In the following spring Gustav had been born, just as if he really had been brought by the storks. Ernst gazed up at the interlacing branches of the tree. Through its canopy he could see the long light of summer glimmering unflinchingly in the sky. 'Our tree,' the father breathed in the son's ear, 'will keep us all safe.'

Helga insisted that the boys be sent to bed without any supper. 'Who'd be young again?' Dietrich asked as his junior colleague joined him outside on the bench. The sun was sinking below the peak of the mountain; soon the smoke from their pipes rose fragrantly. 'After all, they only wanted to see their papa. And we know that he too was something of a rover at that age. How sweet the air is this evening. Ernst, come with your old boss for a turn round the millpond.'

Student and master walked down to the water. Frogs called from the lily pads; the fin of a fish stirred in the middle. Here at least, in this quiet corner of the world, Dietrich could find peace. But for how much longer? 'There's a pike a metre long in there,' Ernst said, stopping to take

164

his shoes off. 'He has his mayoral chair in the reeds. Can you see? His municipal sceptre is a reed mace.'

'Oh yes.' Without seeing, the professor looked over the water.

'He wears a chain of pond weed as his badge of honour. The frog, his alderman, naturally dislikes his habit of dictating at council meetings.'

'Funny that,' Dietrich said. 'Common character in Slavic tales, the pike; don't hear from him much in the Germanic versions.'

'Evidence of a more evolved culture.'

Pretending to laugh at the joke, the professor drew his arm through the younger man's, and moved him on. Usually there was nothing he liked more than to hear Ernst's imagination spin itself a line, but tonight his heart was full of other matters. Yet now that the moment had come, he felt an unwillingness to begin. 'When I first saw you, you were barefoot. And now here you are, a husband and father, and still without shoes!' He waved his stick at the house across the water. 'What a good job you and Hans made of that old ruin.'

'All done to the best specifications of Germanic-Nordic peasant design,' Ernst quipped.

'I can still remember the old miller. He died before your time, my boy. The wheel still turning too.'

'You know Hans. He's an expert on anything mechanical.'

'Yes, the Rosenbaums. The house had been empty for years. All three of the miller's sons were killed in the war. I used to think there was

165

nothing more tragic than a war.' The old man looked at his friend. Ernst was gazing over the water at the house, his feet gently treading the grass. 'I had a visitor today, Ernst. He left me a calling card.' Dietrich handed a piece of folded paper to his junior colleague.

Ernst unfolded it. 'A cheque. A generous cheque.'

'*Most* generous.' Again the professor looked at his companion, but Ernst continued to gaze over the pond.

'It's just what we've been waiting for,' Ernst replied. 'The department will be able to pay for a secretary full-time now, not to mention all the new books we can have. We could even hire an expert in folk curses; you've often said that you and I are hopelessly ignorant in that area.'

Dietrich did not return Ernst's smile. 'Yes. There's enough to repair the hole in the roof as well. In fact, we've never had so much money.'

'Your visitor must have been a fairy.'

'Do fairies come dressed in black uniforms?' A bat flitted from the eaves of the forest and hawked over the water.

'Fairies come in all shapes and sizes, Uncle.'

'More of a goblin, I think. Or a kobold. You see, I got the distinct impression that he wanted something in return for his gift. Ernst,' Dietrich tried to disguise the anxiety in his voice, 'do you recognise the signature?'

'I didn't look.'

'Well, look now. Oh, Ernst, what are we going to do? Our fairy was from the Office of Ancestral Inheritance.'

166

'Uncle, you shouldn't carry around a cheque for this sum. What if you lost it?'

'Look at the stamp on the back. Look!'

'I know, Uncle.'

'You know? I don't think you do.' The professor lowered his voice instinctively. 'Ernst, the Office of Ancestral Inheritance is run by Himmler. Look, you're a brilliant folk-lorist, but, forgive me, you're not a man of the world, you expect everyone to be as good as you. The Office of Ancestral Inheritance is nothing but a vehicle for propaganda of the vilest kidney.'

The reflections of the colleagues shimmered on the darkening water. Across the millpond Helga was closing the casements of the children's bedroom. The bean flowers by Lotte's bench flared in the dusk. Ernst's voice seemed an intrusion on the deepening silence. 'Do you remember how the roof leaked last winter, Uncle? We nearly lost half the volumes of the *Folklore Dictionary*, which are, as you know, irreplaceable. This cheque — '

'Ernst, the Office of Ancestral Inheritance is an SS organisation.'

'Hardly that. It's a funding organisation. That's all.'

'A funding organisation?'

'There's barely a folklore department in the country that isn't funded this way.'

'Are you serious?'

'Either by the Office itself or by Rosenberg's bureau.'

'Rosenberg.' The professor's face twisted.

'Rosenberg,' laughed Ernst. 'The great intellectual of the University of the Bierkeller! Him and Himmler, what a pair; can you really imagine them having anything serious to contribute to academia?'

'It's not *that* I'm worried about. It's this cheque — ' The old man broke off. The bat darted between them; a terrible truth dawned on him. 'You know about this already, don't you? This cheque; the *Office of Ancestral Inheritance.*'

'Uncle, it's a routine matter. This is just the way they do funding now. I don't like it any more than you.'

'What about our academic freedom?'

'It's not affected. The moment they tell us what to write, we'll tear up those cheques. Meanwhile let's use them, Uncle. Instead of letting them buy new weapons, we'll use their money to mend the roof. Don't you see? As well as benefiting us, using their money stops them from spending it on other things. Besides, they would only give it to another institution.'

Dietrich sighed. Things were much worse than he had thought. 'As long as I'm head of the department, I won't accept a thing from them.'

'Then you won't be the head of department, Uncle — there won't *be* a department. Oh, Dietrich, how do you think we've been getting funding all this time?'

'How long?' the professor managed to say. 'How long have we been funded by Himmler?'

'You think I could have bought the Magnetophone and the camera with the department budget? Do you think I could have gone as far as Switzerland on it, let alone England?' For the first time Ernst looked him in the eye. 'Uncle, there's nothing to worry about. Everybody's doing it. It means nothing. Just that we can continue our research. You want that, don't you?'

'Of course I do, but at what price?'

'Do you remember when I first came to you? There were candles in the department. You had to spend time doing inventories of ink and paper. The other faculties thought yours was . . . well, what did they call our department? The fairy-tale cottage. Now look at it. We've got the best facilities and three people working under us. Never forget those candles, Uncle. And do you know what? Today I gave Helga a hat!' Ernst's laughter ran out over the water and echoed under the trees. 'Fairy-tale cottage. I quite like that. But, Uncle, seriously, you know how well we're doing with our work. Making real, tangible progress. Stories; it's not just stories, is it? What we're doing is unlocking the soul of humanity itself. Story; it's the blood of our species. What separates us from animals. Understand the stories we tell, and the rest falls into place. It's examining humanity's common bond.'

'That's the very last thing the Nazis want to do.'

'I know, isn't it wonderful? They pay us to subvert them!'

'Ernst, have you forgotten one of your own English proverbs? *You need a long spoon to sup with the Devil.*'

'Look; Helga's waving. I'd better go and read

the boys their bedtime story. Just because they've been locked up in the keep doesn't mean their dad can't tell them a tale. I heard one in England that they'll love. Come up and give Lotte a kiss when I've finished.'

Walking back to the house Ernst did not see how stooped the older man was.

★ ★ ★

As he sat down heavily on the bench, Dietrich's stick clattered to the ground. Helga picked it up for him. Night was spreading slowly but inexorably from the trees. It was still warm although a cool chill was rising from the water. The gentle play of the wheel seemed to deepen the stillness. From the house came the murmur of Ernst's story. 'No harm done,' the professor said. 'With the boys, I mean.' He waited for the blood to stop drumming in his ears. What he had just discussed with Ernst was merely a prelude to his real business. He looked at his niece. It was the happiest he had seen her looking in a long while. Give her another minute, he told himself, one more minute before I destroy this calm perhaps forever. From the house the cuckoo clock called, then its regular tick seemed to settle into the very bones of the house. 'Helga,' he began at last, 'things are getting worse.'

'It'll blow over,' she replied.

'I don't know whether it will.' The professor swallowed back a reflux of bile. 'Helga, you know that family I told you about? The people from the valley after next; the ones with the mongol son? Well, they went to visit their son at the sanatorium.'

'How is he?'

'He . . . ' Dietrich took his niece's hand. 'They didn't see him.'

'What do you mean?'

'He wasn't there.'

'I don't understand.'

'They were told he'd been moved to another sanatorium.'

Helga's voice was hollow. 'Well then, did they go there?'

'They didn't find him there either.' The professor tried to clear his throat; he felt light-headed. 'In fact, nobody had even heard of him. When they were walking away, someone followed them. An old woman who lives by the sanatorium. She came up to them while they were waiting for their bus. She was terrified. At first they thought she was mad; an inmate herself. Helga, she told them that the patients who arrived there never left. She said that it wasn't a sanatorium but a laboratory.'

'What are you talking about?'

Dietrich paused. How could he tell his niece what he had found out? Especially after he had helped convince her time and time again that rumours were always worse than the truth. A cow bellowed from the meadow; the donkey brayed. 'Helga, the old woman knew that they weren't trying to cure their patients; she said that the sanatorium was in fact a place where patients were experimented on.'

Anger contorted his niece's face. 'Stupid old

171

woman. What a thing to say. Evil, cantankerous cow.'

'Helga — '

'To cause the parents pain like that. What sort of a person does that?'

'Helga, I've heard the same from other sources.'

Her voice was a low growl. 'Uncle, I'm surprised to hear you giving credence to such malicious gossip. You've always claimed to be a man of science.'

'Forgive me, Helga; God forgive me. All this time, deep down, I knew it was true. And now I can no longer lie to myself.'

'So you lie to me instead?'

Helga closed her eyes. It seemed only yesterday that she was holding her daughter for the first time. And now here was Uncle Dietrich telling her that she was going to lose her.

Right from the start Lotte had brought her mother pain. The birth had been difficult, far worse than either of the two boys, as though instead of a child her own insides were being drawn out. A doctor had to be sent for. Yet when Helga held Lotte for the first time, crumpled and still bloody, she had forgotten all the agony in an instant. So tiny; so perfect: a freshly minted miracle. Dr Wolff had placed in her arms not just one new baby but the creation of the whole world. She remembered too as though it were yesterday Dr Wolff ushering the midwife out peremptorily, and his face falling as he peered into the baby's mouth. Then came all those weeks and months in which the infant failed to thrive. With her cleft palate Lotte fed only with great difficulty so that day after day Helga watched the mite baffled by a breast which was so full of milk that it would leak at the merest cry of the infant, muffled even then. Instead of growing, Lotte seemed to shrink, as though she was slowly drifting away from them. At the time Helga suffered the recurring nightmare in which Lotte would be plucked from her useless nipples; running to the window Helga would see the Angel of Death flying up the valley with her daughter dangling like a stick the storks carry to their nests. Now it seemed this wasn't just a nightmare. The Angel of Death was flying above the world for real, and he was searching for Keilburg.

'Helga, Helga?' She opened her eyes. Uncle was leaning on his stick, staring intently at her. 'They're not going to go away. The Nazis. I was wrong to say they were. They're here to stay.'

She grasped his hand. 'You're getting all confused, Uncle,' she soothed. 'It's the strain. You've been working too hard. You know we've been talking for a while about you retiring. Leave the horror stories to the Grimms. Let Ernst take on the department. Come out here and live with us — '

'Helga!' His anguish was so savage that at a stroke the professor knew he had passed over the line into old age. 'My sweet, sweet Helga. We have to face facts. There are people like the ones you hear rumours about. People who will do things that we could never even guess at; people who would hurt children, the ill, the crippled.'

'No!' Helga's forced laughter was horrible. 'It's just Jews,' she begged. 'Jews and antisocials and halfwits . . . '

Dietrich felt his niece's hand twisting in his like a little animal caught in a trap. 'We can't wait any longer, Helga. We've talked about it before. And the time has come. Dr Wolff himself said it would have to be done when she was three or four.'

'But, Uncle, if we took her to the hospital someone would see. *They'd* find out.'

'I went to talk to Dr Wolff today. He's willing to come out to Keilburg and do the operation himself. It's a risk, of course, but what choice do we have? It's only a matter of time before someone sees her. There's talk of their running a telephone wire through the valley. The telephone today. A road tomorrow. Even in Keilburg you can't hide someone forever. If we don't act now, it may be too late. We must act tonight. I'll send Ernst to get Hans.'

4

His headlights scouring the firs, Hans went through the checklist: petrol tank full; oil changed; battery charged; brakes tested. 'We'll be there in half an hour, boss,' he said at last.

They did not speak again until the forest fell away and the lights of the town came into view below them. 'Hans,' Ernst began, 'this can't go

174

on forever, can it? The Nazis, they can't, can they?'

Hans exhaled deeply. They had never discussed politics before. 'A question in return, boss. Who's going to stop them?'

'But all their lies; surely they'll be found out?'

The driver shrugged as he joined a larger road and encountered the first other vehicle on their journey down from the mountain. In the flood of the passing car's lights, Hans glanced at Ernst. He had never seen that expression on his face before. 'Seems to me, boss, the easiest thing in the world is getting people to eat a lie they like the taste of.'

'And the hardest?'

'Getting them to cough it back up.'

'Do you know the way?'

'His surgery is on Kirschstrasse.'

'He lives above it.'

When Ernst pressed the bell he heard it clattering in the hall. There was no response. Laying his face against the cool of the building's stone, he rang again. The sound drilled through the empty house once more but brought no one down the steep stairs. Having turned the engine off, Hans joined him at the door. 'Try it again,' he urged, looking anxiously up and down the street. If they were stopped, the plan was simple: the little girl had broken her leg, she couldn't be moved, they needed the doctor to come out and set the bone. Although Ernst seemed calm, Hans could see the tension in his eyes as he rang again. Hans glanced up at the window on the floor above. The curtain fluttered. For an instant a face appeared like a ghost. 'He's seen us.'

Half a minute later, the door opened to reveal the bloodless face of the doctor. He followed them to the car. 'Has anyone seen you?' he said.

'No,' said Hans.

'You're certain?'

'I had a good look. It's past midnight.'

'You think they ever sleep?'

As they were leaving the town, a car came up behind them. Hans glanced into his mirror. The doctor dropped his head into his hands. 'Take the back road,' Ernst ordered. The tone in his voice made Hans obey implicitly. The other car did not follow.

Totally impassable in winter, even in summer the road was treacherous. Its tortuous zigzag, carved like a rune from the mountainside by centuries of donkeys and goats, was narrow and precipitous. Hans looked for the moon. It was pitch black. The car engine whined as it took another perilous ascent. 'Hang onto your hats.' The headlights picked out a deer bounding in front of them. Grass grew in the middle of the road; Hans felt the sweat falling off his forehead. 'How's the clock, Doctor?'

'I beg pardon, Herr Rosenbaum?'

'My grandfather's clock in your surgery.'

'Oh yes; of course; it's still as accurate as ever. Your grandfather was the greatest clockmaker to come out of the Black Forest. A Rosenbaum clock will still be working in a hundred years' time.'

'Well, at least that's one thing we can rely on.'

'They're on to me, you know,' the doctor said.

'It's just a matter of time. This isn't the first night-time call I've made. And then they're not very happy about the way I've been neglecting their paperwork. Christ almighty!' The doctor punched his hand. 'Things can't go on like this. You know they're actually paying us for it now.'

'For what?' Ernst asked levelly.

The doctor unzipped a side pocket on his medical bag. He brought out a piece of paper on which he shone the beam of his torch. 'Birth certificates. See that section? *Inherited birth defects*. We get bonuses for informing the appropriate authority. Fined if we don't.' At first Hans thought that the doctor was weeping. His shoulders shook as he wheezed like a broken accordion. Then he realised that his passenger was laughing. 'I was trained to *save* lives. Now they . . . ' The words, sticking in his throat, were expelled at last on a surge of bitter laughter. 'It's all of a piece with the way they're treating the Jews. Do you know that last week a Jew was openly beaten to death? I don't mean in a dark alley at night. It was during the day. And not punched once or twice either. It happened outside the church, a hundred people must have witnessed it . . . ' The doctor's laughter continued. 'One of my colleagues was even brought to treat the cuts on the assailants' knuckles. He treated the thugs as the Jew lay dying at his feet.'

'It can't go on forever,' Ernst said.

'Why not?'

Ernst lit three cigarettes. Although he normally didn't smoke, Hans reached out for one. At that moment his front wheel struck a large branch that had fallen from the trees encroaching on the road; he just managed to regain control in time. The car came to a halt on the sharp rise; the scree displaced by its screeching tyres plundered down through the trees. Giving a low whistle, Hans started the engine once more.

The doctor seemed to have regained his nerve. 'Fortunately I trained as a dentist,' he said. 'So I'm on familiar ground. Before becoming a family doctor, I performed this procedure a few times, but I must stress the dangers to you, Ernst. Even in the best-equipped hospitals things can go wrong.'

'Do we have a choice?'

'Without the operation her speech would give her away instantly. Although I have to tell you that even if the operation is a success there is still likely to be some speech impediment. But if Helga keeps up the speech exercises, and avoids trouble spots, it won't be insurmountable for her. I mean, she could go to school. And that would be impossible without the procedure. There will be some physical scarring but we can put that down to other causes. When I repaired Lotte's lip at three months, I explained the scar as a wasp sting; I left space in the records to write the fresh scars down as wasp stings in the mouth. Remember; it was that bad year for wasps? Not entirely plausible, perhaps, but the Nazis are not the brightest. Her nose might be slightly lopsided but I think her adult teeth will be all right. She's going to be little different from other little girls.'

'She nearly died,' Ernst said. 'When she was two months. She weighed so little. Do you remember, Dr Wolff?'

'Yes, I gave her up, Ernst.'

'It was a donkey that saved her.'

Years later as he lay dying on a lice-ridden bunk in Dachau, eaten by vermin, cholera and despair, Dr Wolff would remember these words. 'A donkey; really?'

'Have you ever seen a donkey foal, Dr Wolff?' The live tip of the cigarette cast a faint glow over Ernst's face. 'They're beautiful little animals. For weeks Lotte didn't stop crying, then one morning: silence. Helga was asleep. I took the little one outside and went for a walk. A walk? I didn't want Helga waking to find the baby dead at her breast. The donkey trotted after us, her foal too. A real procession. I didn't know where we were going, we just wandered, the four of us together, and Lotte about the size of a squeeze box in my hands; a similar shape too.'

'A squeeze box?'

'In the forest there's a large beech tree where we take picnics in summer. That was where I had gone without realising. I was sitting there holding Lotte, waiting for her to die I suppose, when the little foal started to suckle. That's what gave me the idea. A donkey teat isn't shaped like a human breast. Well, think of the foal's mouth. The nipple is like the chanter on English Border pipes. What I mean is: it fitted Lotte perfectly; cleft palate and all. And instead of watching her

179

die, I saw her feeding properly for the first time. The milk was just right for her stomach too.'

The doctor lit another cigarette. The flare of his lighter revealed a smile on the folklorist's face. The medical man exhaled. 'Ass's milk, a folk remedy; not without some basis in sound medical practice.'

'Cleopatra used to bathe in it, and it's what saved our Lotte. Ass's milk. Hans, do you remember the way she would drink? She drank and drank. To see her there at the teat like a donkey foal. And laughter came back to the house. Do you remember, Hans?'

'Boss, how could I forget?'

Ernst's smile did not fade. 'I would do anything to save my daughter's life, Wolff. Do you understand? *Anything*.'

But before the doctor could reply, the inside of the car was seared by a sudden bright light. A car had appeared on the road behind them. 'Gentlemen,' Hans said, 'we have company.'

5

'Peterli; are you asleep?' The only reply was Peter's deep, even breathing. Gustav had heard Papa leave but hadn't heard him return yet. Silently he slipped underneath his bed. Tonight more than ever he needed to know what was happening.

The knot came out easily from the floorboard. Gustav lay utterly motionless. It was all right; his brother was still sleeping. As he laid his cheek against the cool sweet-chestnut floorboard he breathed in the scent of beeswax. Carefully he lowered his eye to the hole.

Earlier in the evening his mother had scrubbed the table until the pine grain shone like the rings on a freshly felled stump. But now she sat motionless in the chair, Lotte asleep in her arms. Uncle hadn't moved from the window through which he was staring down the length of the valley; a daisy from the chain Lotte had given him remained behind his ear. The only activity in the whole room was the swing of the cuckoo clock pendulum and the water gently simmering in the pots on the range. Although it had not been bath night, Lotte had been bathed in the zinc tub. As she washed her, Mama had sung happy songs, but Gustav had seen her crying. The boys had been sent to bed early, their mother's unusual shortness of temper quelling any protest. *Keep them well away*, Gustav had heard her say to Papa.

Rolling silently out from underneath his bed, Gustav crept across the floor. He opened the casement and listened. All he could hear was an owl calling, and the water wheel clicking quietly like someone telling the rosary. What was keeping Papa? He had told Mama and Uncle that he would not be long fetching Dr Wolff. With no moon, the darkness was impenetrable; black as the swastika flapping on the school flagpole. The boy thought he could just make out the pond, a slight shimmer in the darkness as though a piece of the moonless sky had fallen into the little valley. The silhouettes of the trees

181

were not discernible but he could picture their watchfulness as they paused in their march up the mountain. *Be as quick as you can*, Mama had told Papa. *Make sure you're not followed*, Uncle Dietrich had urged. *The Nazis are everywhere these days*. But only the eye in the ceiling had seen the pistol Papa had put in his pocket.

The Nazis, the Nazis. That's all Gustav seemed to hear. Perhaps the Nazis really *were* nixies. Nixies who, having lain year after year in cold water consumed with jealousy and hatred for those who walked on the land, had decided to leave their pools and millponds and flood the whole world so that they could drown everybody in one fell swoop instead of having to wait for their victims to stray too near their banks.

'My name is Peter.' Gustav froze but it was just his brother talking in his sleep again. Stealthily the elder boy crept back under his bed. 'I live in Keilburg but I go to school in the next village. My friend is . . . '

★   ★   ★

When Gustav woke with a jolt he looked down through the hole to see Lotte lying on the table in a pool of blood as the doctor leant over her. So this was the operation his parents had been talking about earlier; Lotte's only chance of getting better and avoiding the Nazis. Heart beating sickeningly, the boy stared with a morbid fascination. Lying there, Lotte looked like a girl pulled to the bottom by a whole family of nixies.

On her face some kind of mask had been fixed, like a donkey's bridle. A sickly smell insinuated itself through the floorboards. Gustav blinked it away. He did not recognise the smell of chloroform. When, having rubbed his eyes, he looked back through the hole he saw that Peter was standing at the open door downstairs; he was watching the operation too.

Having been woken by the voices from downstairs, Peter had called out to Gustav; but his bed was empty. Halfway down the stairs he had heard his sister scream. Paralysed for a few moments he had listened to her whimpering.

Opening the door Peter could not believe what he saw. In the scalding brightness created by the burning of all the family lanterns and candles, Dr Wolff was killing his sister. First he poured poison on a cloth, holding it over her mouth until she had suffocated, then, to make sure, he began sawing her head off. And Mama, instead of fighting back, was holding her daughter as though to stop her struggling. Papa was weeping by the window. Woken by the bright lights and the chloroform, a butterfly fluttered agitatedly against the pane before falling senseless among the blue flowers.

Peter stared as the doctor leant over Lotte like a butcher; blood spurted from his sister in a thin arc like when you wee in nettles. With a silent cry of anguish, the little boy fled the house into the thick darkness.

Auvers-sur-Oise, May 1890

1

The rector quivered with excitement. The butterfly had come to rest just a few yards in front of him. He crept forward on his hands and knees as stealthily as a man weighing eighteen stone and sweating profusely may. The creature did not stir; the clergyman hardly dared breathe. Slowly positioning the net, he cocked his wrists and waited for the perfect moment to strike, motionless as an obese heron dressed in a black frock coat and shovel hat.

At last, with deadly speed, the net fell. Anguish fluted from the rector's pendulous lips. He had missed her. How beautiful she was! Long, dancing tail; wings: a scrap of Persian carpet, blue, red and yellow; and the dips and lifts of her flight as she fluttered away plotting the coordinates of a divine algebra. Yelping like a hound, the Rector set off after her. Despite the encumbrances of his specimen case, billowing net and tolerably female-sized mammaries, the clergyman moved with a surprising grace. It had been raining earlier that morning and as he waded through the tall grass, only a day or two from the scythe, it shimmered with drops as golden as a toad's eyes. Unaware of the titanic lepidopterist's pursuit, the butterfly landed daintily on a sprig of Queen Anne's lace. Surely now she would be his! But before he could cock his net again she was lifting effortlessly over a thick hawthorn hedge, like an embroidered handkerchief waving from the window of a first-class carriage.

The rector paused for a moment to take off his glasses, then lowered his head and pitched in. *O God*, he intoned against the barbs and thorns which ripped at him like the talons of some chimerical beast, *preserve thy humble servant, the bearer of thy ether and specimen case.* Flubbering like a washerwoman in spate, the Reverend Jonah Fairbanks shouldered himself through the nigh on impenetrable brake, bursting free with just a small cut above his left eye. But where was she? He looked around. This field had already been mown. It seemed utterly devoid of even the commonest species of Lepidoptera let alone the mysterious *Papilionidae* he had been stalking all morning. In the distance, the little train could be heard pulling in over the wheat plain from Paris.

The rector saw the butterfly at the same time that the Charolais bull saw him. Intent only on his quarry, currently tenanting a fresh cowpat, Jonah Fairbanks was raising his net when he heard the thunder of hooves behind him. 'Odds bodkins!' he murmured, sidestepping the ton of hurtling beef at the last possible moment like a globose matador. Smoothing down his side whiskers, the vicar returned to his butterfly. But already the steer had turned and was pawing the ground once more. The great hooves might crush the little beauty! Before he even had the chance to etherise her! With a blood-curdling yell, the rector raised his net and, brandishing it like an Agincourt standard, sallied forth to meet the charge head on. Confronted by this vision of enraged obesity, the Charolais stopped, its dewlap rippling. But the vicar's dander was up. 'Queensberry Rules!' he roared and, with a fist the size of a navvy's shovel, struck the bull flush on the nose. With a broken bellow the beast slunk off to his heifer harem leaving the field to the butterfly collector and his pearl of great price. She was off again. The strap of his specimen case creaking like a clipper in full rigging, the rector followed, convinced now that this was no common member of the *Papilionidae* family but an entirely new species. Dare he name it after his dear, dear wife? *Papilio campus fairbanki*. Chuckling, he began to sing:

'Queen, Queen Caroline
Dipped her head in turpentine.
Why did she look so fine?
Because she wore a crinoline.'

Still singing, he followed *Papilio campus fairbanki* into an osier bed, staggered through a quagmire where grass snakes whipped themselves from his step, and stumbling through a stand of umbelliferous flowers found himself teetering on the edge of a river. Only a frenzy of windmilling arms and muslin net prevented a ducking.

Beneath his feet, the Oise ran green and deep. Weeds swayed dreamily in the current; the rector waved as a kingfisher flashed by: a philosopher's stone cast by the teleological hand. But *Papilio campus fairbanki* was already halfway across the river. There was not a moment to lose. Putting down his specimen case and hanging the net on the branch of an obliging alder like an Israelite his harp, he began to undo his frock-coat buttons.

'I think you'll have to stop now, darling,' whispered the woman in the brightly coloured jolly boat concealed within the bell of a bankside willow.

'Can't,' came the stilted reply of the young man lying in the stern with her.

She, of middle years wearing a set of vivacious and highly fashionable skirts, and he, half her age and pinioned beneath her, were arranged as though in a clinch of resuscitation. 'But, darling, you will reveal us. We are no longer alone.'

The retort was a febrile groan. The boat rocked as the young man's limbs writhed spasmodically under the hoisted, voluminous froth of petticoats.

Jonah Fairbanks, however, had eyes only for the butterfly. She had come to rest on an eyot. The couple in the boat peered through the fringe of foliage, which stippled the light around them as though with a pointillist's brush. 'A veritable river walrus,' said the young man as the gallons of green water displaced by the clergyman's belly flop seethed over them.

'It's only the rector,' the lady replied. 'You

might as well proceed, Mr Dalrymple.'

'But I've already concluded, Mrs Oyster.'

'Oh.'

'Say, Mrs Oyster,' said Dalrymple, his tone once again the languid perfection of Harvard University after the brief contortion of passion, 'I suppose that fellow is entirely naked?'

'He's completely gaga, poor thing. He's one of Dr Gachet's patients.'

'Oh Lordy, Gachet; the mad medicine man. Still, decent of the chubby episcopal to keep his hat on.'

Hoicking up her skirts, Lucette Oyster stood, rising above her young lover like a masthead. Revealed like a snail in its trail, James Dalrymple took out his notebook. 'Scribbling already, Mr Dalrymple?' Lucette did not suppress her yawn. 'Well, boy I shall have to go. I have a prior engagement.'

'Ah yes, the painting party.'

'The painting party. To which you are *not* invited.'

Lucette Oyster sprang from the boat. What a lovely morning! Mayflies danced on the withers of the water; a cuckoo was calling. The scent of the river mixed intoxicatingly with the bottle of ether she curiously uncorked from the Rector's specimen case. 'Mr Fairbanks,' she called, shuddering slightly as the warm semen dribbled down her thigh like a wand of freshly laid toad spawn, 'do come out and get attired. I'm relying on you to be my chaperone.'

The clergyman did not seem to hear her. Having forgotten his lepidopteron quest, he was revelling in the special gift that water reserves for the adipose. Sporting in the Oise effortlessly as any butterfly, pirouetting like a Degas dancer, Jonah Fairbanks frolicked in the sense of weightlessness:

> *'I have a bonnet, trimmed with blue*
> *Why don't you wear it? So I do.*
> *When do you wear it? When I can,*
> *When I go out with my young man.'*

'Yessir, the old satyr is absolutely two Colts shy of a gunfight,' remarked James Dalrymple, then, scribbling another sentence in his note-book, he stepped rather awkwardly onto dry land. The boat shot treacherously from him and scrambling free he left an immaculate if undignified imprint of his size 8 left leather bootee in the mud. 'So, Mrs Oyster, what's the admired Gachet prescribing for Padre Pump-head; foxgloves? Fellow I know says Gachet always prescribes foxgloves.'

'I believe the doctor's methods are the most modern available, Mr Dalrymple.'

'And how did the rector come to be toddling along Bedlam Avenue?'

'It's rather romantic, darling; he's never been able to accept the death of his wife. Or something like that.'

'But I thought the old sport was married.'

'As does he. That's why he sees Dr Gachet three times a week.' For a moment more the pair watched the rector, half-man, half-seal, creaming through the Oise, then Lucette Oyster lifted two fingers to her mouth and emitted a whistle that might have pierced to the far end of Billingsgate fish market.

Bobbing in the river, the rector expelled an arc of water. Seeming to see the two on the bank for the first time, he lifted his hat. 'Mrs Oyster, is that you? Good morning. I trust you are hale and hearty?'

'Indeed I am. But, you naughty man, our engagement commenced five minutes since.'

'Engagement, madam?'

'The painting party, Rector. When I met you yesterday you agreed to escort me thither.'

'Did I indeed? I thought there must be something I'd forgotten. I'm always forgetting, you know.' Hauling himself onto the bank, Jonah Fairbanks wistfully watched his newly acquired svelteness drain away; once again he was a towering, ungainly caterpillar with little hope of chrysalisation.

'*Forgotten?* My dear Rector, it's only the social event of the week. Dr Gachet gave me my invitation personally. An art jamboree hosted by a compatriot of Mr Dalrymple's; a certain young artist by the name of . . . What do they call your friend, Mr Dalrymple?'

'I don't call him my friend for a start,' twanged the young man without looking up from the notebook into which he was scribbling again. 'But I believe you're referring to Chip Coakley.'

'Forgive Mr Dalrymple's rudeness,' Mrs Oyster said expansively. 'He's a writer.'

'I'm nothing of the sort.'

'*Will* be a writer one day,' Mrs Oyster

explained. 'I'm collecting him. But, dear Mr Fairbanks, your face is all cut. Have you been sticking yourself with entomological pins again?'

'A hedge,' the clergyman replied vaguely. 'A bull.' He looked at the fully-clothed couple before him and then glanced down at his penis. It hung below his belly bowl like a withered dolmen floating free of its earthwork. 'But, Mrs Oyster,' he said with profound bafflement. 'I appear to be . . . as Adam.'

Lucette Oyster laughed until she nearly choked then sobered abruptly. Tenderly she began to dress him. 'First the apple and then the pear,' she coaxed, holding out the tent of the clergyman's drawers for him to step into. 'How can you have forgotten about the painting party? Now the cherries,' she sang, doing the same thing with his trousers. '*I've* thought of little else all week. It will create quite a stir in our little republic of art. Our mutual friend Dr Gachet shall be present; as will that Hollander artist everyone seems to be talking about. Who is he again, Mr Dalrymple?'

Dalrymple looked up. 'Vincent Van Gogh's coming to Chip Coakley's painting party?'

'And the gooseberries,' said Mrs Oyster, buttoning the vicar's fly. 'Don't feign interest, boy. Rector, during our brief acquaintance, Mr Dalrymple, latterly of Harvard, has asseverated the demise of the visual arts at least a score of times.'

'Picture art is finished,' Dalrymple said with lethargic conviction. 'The modern era has no use for hieroglyphics.'

'Isn't he like something from a Zola novel?' Lucette beamed.

'But Van Gogh, he's something different,' Dalrymple continued. 'Did you read that piece about him in *Le Mercure de France*? Makes him out to be some kind of tortured genius.'

But neither Mrs Oyster nor the Reverend Fairbanks was listening. Arm in arm, they were already walking down the path through the willows, singing in tandem:

> *'On a hill there is a lady*
> *Who she is I do not know*
> *All she wants is gold and silver*
> *And a fine young man, you know . . . '*

Shrugging off a shiver of despair, the young man dipped his hands in the river to flush away the distracting aroma of coitus, and opened his notebook again: *Auvers-sur-Oise*, he wrote. *A veritable Arcadia of thatched cottages, villas and madness. And whither hasten the bedlamites? To a painting party hosted by Mr Chip Coakley, stolid, talentless son of a railroad king. Painting party? Mad Hatter's tea party rather. Whom of the mental misfits shall attend? Mrs Lucette Oyster, soiled Venus of the London rookeries; the Reverend Fairbanks, an Icarus brought down by the folly of his own obesity; Gachet, also known as Dr Foxglove; and of course, guest of honour, the coming man and chief goofball Vincent Van Gogh, devourer of Utopias, stinking Pan.*

On the plain above the village, the train could

be heard bringing her day-trippers from Paris. James Dalrymple wrote for a little longer then threw down his notebook in disgust.

2

There were supposed to have been sunflowers. He had specifically asked the gardener to place pots of sunflowers under the laburnum. Although Mr Chip Coakley was from California, he prided himself on his French. *Sacré bleu!* he had even begun reading Zola in the raw original. And he had distinctly told the gardener — in French — that he wanted a whole mass of sunflowers for his painting party.

Admittedly everything else in the garden was passing perfect. The pink roses were fragrant and the lilacs nodded in the breeze coming from the river. In the lane the chestnut candles still burnt brightly. Chip had arranged the easels in an inviting fan, a full set of marten brushes poised on each, along with an oyster-shaped palette. On the trestle table, dressed with a clean white cloth, a line of steam sketched itself from the coffee-pot spout. As well as telling him that the Dutch artist loved sunflowers, attached an almost religious symbolism to them, Dr Gachet had intimated to Chip that the painter was addicted to coffee. Well, perhaps there were no sunflowers but he would find enough caffeine here to keep him happy; and anything else he might need too. The rolls were warm in their basket, and on the adjoining table, also looking good enough to eat, the tubes of paint. In short, everything was as perfect as any still life. Under the doctor's guidance, as well as providing the most expensive oils, Chip had bought in great quantities of the pigment favoured by the up-and-coming artist. Even the canvases had already been mounted in varying sizes. The only thing required now was for the Dutchman to arrive, and the sun to shine. The young man looked up at the sky doubtfully. Were the rain clouds drifting away over the wheat fields to Paris, or *coming* from that direction? Back home in California, a fellow could trust the weather; here the sun and the rain might play chequers with each other for days. Chip shivered slightly in his thin, short-jacketed summer suit. Well, he'd be warmer once he had his smock on. The smocks were his *pièce de résistance*, hanging from the golden boughs of the laburnum like pods of art. Gachet had also said that the Dutchman had a sense of humour. Once again Chip Coakley felt a frisson at the coming encounter. It was on account of Van Gogh that the young Californian had picked on Auvers-sur-Oise in the first place. Freshly arrived in Le Havre, he had chanced to read the article about the painter in *Le Mercure de France* and, although Chip had never heard of him before, it was clear his was the rising star. The last words spoken to Chip by his father on the New York quay echoed in his mind now. *Remember, son, the successful hunter always marks the lead buffalo.*

Picking up the green bench he placed it under

the blooming laburnum. Dr Gachet had said the artist had a passion for reading; well, here was the perfect place should he require a novel between bouts of creativity. Chip sat on it now and reflected. With its thatched cottages and villas, its green river and multicoloured pleasure boats, its plain of young wheat rising above the village and stretching into the distance, this Auvers-sur-Oise really was a million dollars. A garden of Eden. His only grouses were the numbers of other Americans here and the weather. Nothing but rain since he arrived. *Her-umph!* Chip Coakley's sneeze startled a black cat from the ranunculi bed. Picking up a stone, he hurled it at the bolting animal. Why did the gardener persist in allowing the filthy beast in the garden? Hadn't Chip repeatedly pointed out the defecations in the flower beds, the mangled song-thrush corpses? Adjusting the position of the easels one last time, Chip consulted his fob watch. His painting party had officially begun.

For the third time that morning the young Californian walked carefully through the irises down to the knothole in the garden fence. The lane was still empty; no sign of the guest of honour. What kind of a man was he? Was genius instantly recognisable? Chip pictured a great, tortured giant whose blond hair flamed as brightly as the artist's own suns so vividly described in *Le Mercure de France*; a kind of Odin of the paintbrush. Up on the plain the Paris train was pulling into the village, but still no inkling of the artist. Hearing the squeak of the wheelbarrow among the shrubs, Chip hurried over. He intercepted the old man at the laburnum. 'Excuse me, monsieur,' he said using the French of which he was so proud. 'But I am puzzling; where is it that one is able to find the sunflowers?'

The gardener, his old face a cracked walnut, looked at the pots in his wheelbarrow. 'Sunflowers,' he announced in English.

'Sunflowers? But no; you is wrong; you is making mistake,' Chip persevered in French. 'I am able to see the sunflowers back home. What is it that these are in your barrow of wheels? Sunflowers? But no!'

Turning to the little boy who was with him, the old man said something in French that Chip could not quite pick up. The little boy handed over one of the pots for examination. 'Sunflowers,' reiterated the gardener.

Chip pointed at the fibrous, green, flowerless stalks and shook his head. 'Sunflowers? Big yellow faces that follows the sun.'

'*Is* sunflowers,' the gardener insisted.

Chip looked again at the plant. Something in the neighbourhood of a bean sprout, perhaps even a turnip green, but definitely *not* a sunflower. He had given the old guy ten francs extra for the party too. More spondulicks, the young man wagered, than he'd see most months. The plan had been to welcome the Dutch artist with an extravagance of sunflowers; he wouldn't be stirred by this mess of weeds. With a Gallic shrug, the gardener and his grandson began unloading the offending pots.

Helplessly, Chip watched the pair empty the

196

barrow. His father would know what to do here. *Labourers in the vineyard are worth their dollar, but only if they tread their mess of grapes. If not, off you go, Joe.* But Chip was not a self-made millionaire, he was an artist, and this old man was a true son of the soil. Just look at his fingers, misshapen and fibrous as old roots. He should be painting him, *not* wrangling like this. He could do the boy and the old man together as though they too were the products of a garden: the old woody bush, the young sapling taken as a cutting. The young Californian held a coin out to the boy. 'Here, you like *bonbons?*' But the boy bolted from him, just like the cat. The gardener grunted with laughter, then wheeled away the empty barrow. *Her-umph!* Chip's sneeze rang out through the garden. This crummy Northern European weather; no wonder everyone had permanent head colds. The cat seemed to laugh at him as it stretched in a brief sunbeam on the green bench. Chip's stone missed by a whisker.

Yes, mused the young Californian, consulting his timepiece again, money *was* certainly a danger to the artist, and he could never allow himself to become one of those young men who seemed everywhere in Auvers, those fellow countrymen like James Dalrymple whose independent means outweighed their talents, but there again who could deny the uses of cash? For instance, how swell it was to be able to rent this villa and host a painting party where so many great artists had been over the years: Daubigny, Cézanne, Pissarro. Sitting back on the bench, Chip looked at the famous white house with its green shutters. It seemed to float in the verdure of the garden like a boat. He clapped his hands in triumph. *That* would be his subject for the day. The white house as a boat bobbing in a green water whose waves were now geranium blue, now rose pink, now laburnum gold. Perhaps he could already have begun by the time Van Gogh arrived; perhaps he could have something to impress him with. That would be the ideal introduction. Dr Gachet had told him that within a year the Dutchman would be recognised by the whole world as a hero of art. *The lead buffalo!*

Chip Coakley had already selected his canvas when something flew over the fence from the lane and plunged into the laburnum above his head. An instant later, a second object followed it. Somebody was hurling missiles and he guessed he knew who! Sprinting over to the fence, Chip reached the knothole just in time to see a figure slinking away down the lane. Yes, it was *him* all right. That shambling, stooped fellow was the simpleton who'd been hanging around all morning. Why, about an hour ago he'd come right into the garden, fingering the paints and everything; he'd even begun to pour himself a coffee. Red hair on a grotesquely blunt head, smelling to high heaven and mumbling all sorts of double Dutch to himself, Chip had had to dry off the trail of saliva he'd left on the tube of titanium white. He'd sent him packing in no uncertain terms but as he'd done so in the corner of his eye he had seen the gardener and his grandson smirking. They seemed to think that the trespasser was harmless. Perhaps he was the local village idiot. But now he didn't seem so harmless. What if Vincent Van Gogh had been there and a missile had struck him, or even worse one of those canvases so brilliantly described by *Le Mercure de France?*

'Excuse me?'

Straightening up from the knothole, Chip saw that the first of his guests had arrived. The surge of excitement dissipated instantly. It wasn't the artist. That smear of pink among the greenery revealed a lady; and a young one judging by her stature. Chip tutted with annoyance. The matter of the other guests had been left in Gachet's hands but surely on such an important day he wasn't going to be inflicted with kids barely out of the schoolhouse?

'Is this the painting party?' enquired the figure, still obscured by herbage.

'Yes,' he returned rather testily.

'I seem to be early.'

'Welcome, welcome . . . ' Chip declared, his good, down-home breeding winning through as he waded back through the irises.

'Miss Fairbanks.'

'Welcome, Miss Fairbanks.' Chip was just wondering about whether the gardener's daughter, also on a ten-franc retainer for the day, would be up to making some lemonade for his juvenile guest, when he saw the new arrival properly for the first time.

She was youthful certainly and unequivocally dressed in pink, but the figure revealed so tantalisingly by her gingham belonged to no child. She was a young woman in the first full flush of herself; nineteen, perhaps twenty. Unaccountably, the young Californian felt his mouth run dry. 'I'm Mr Coakley,' he heard himself say.

'I thought my father would have arrived by now.' The young woman looked about the garden in some confusion. 'Perhaps I'd better come back later.' Her hair, worn free-flowing rather than in that constricting, inhuman bun of fashion, was raven black; her nose slightly turned up at the end. As she began to retreat the tips of her dainty brown boots showed exuberantly like the noses of a pair of puppies.

'There's no need,' Chip said. 'To withdraw, I mean; the arrival of the other guests is imminent.'

As the two young people gazed at one another, Chip, to his mortification, felt his cheeks blushing. 'You're fond of sunflowers?' she asked, gesturing at the pots with her parasol handle.

'Yes,' he replied.

'They're lovely, aren't they?'

'Yes.'

'And these will be a veritable feast for the eyes when they flower later in the summer.'

'Why yes, they will.'

At that moment a stick flew over the fence. It was the loon in the lane again! 'Are you all right, Miss Fairbanks?' the host gasped.

'Perfectly,' she replied.

'Excuse me one moment,' he declared dramatically. 'I guess I have a public nuisance to quash.'

It was some relief to be running back down through the irises. For the past minute all he had been able to do was stand and stare at that girl. What had she been saying about sunflowers? Chip could only hope that his mouth had not opened as it did when he was a child waiting for marshmallows to melt. Another stick crashed into the laburnum, setting the smocks swinging. The young Californian's resolve stiffened. He was going to formally identify the miscreant, village idiot or not, then get the gardener to summon a gendarme. But instead of a view of the offender scuttling away between the thatched cottages on the lane like a crab with a broken back, Chip Coakley found an eye waiting for him in the knothole. He reeled back in shock. As he sprawled on the ground, a chewed face and bony torso reared above the fence. It was the loopy malefactor: gaunt and bearded as a starving goat, no teeth, one eye partly congealed and the lobe of an ear missing as though he was a street dog. For a while the madman held himself in position, his gingery head peering over the fence like a mangled, masticated piece of the sun, then issuing a weird gurgle he dropped from sight. Still lying on the ground, Chip heard him arguing with himself down the lane. My God, but what an apparition. If Auvers was an Eden then here was its serpent. It reminded the young Californian of the Indian braves he'd seen on a visit to the reservation with his father. The very dregs of humanity. Thank the stars that Vincent Van Gogh hadn't had to see such offal.

The arrival of the next guest announced itself

with the click of the wicket gate. Chip hurried back through the irises. Surely *this* couldn't be Vincent Van Gogh, this slight, frail figure in a blue coat leading a large dog on a leash and cackling to himself. No; it wasn't a dog. It was a goat! 'You must be Dr Gachet,' Miss Fairbanks was already greeting him.

'Me, Dr Gachet?' the elderly man replied in a heavily accented English which was further mangled by the mask he suddenly thrust before his face: a grotesque, barely human visage of bulbous eyes with a thick protruding tongue. 'Mademoiselle is mistaken. My name is Serge Dechamps. Late of the 14th arrondissement. Permit me to introduce myself. I am a criminal of passion; a murderer.' Beneath his death mask the doctor's head shook with laughter. 'I killed the man I found in bed with my mistress. The penalties of living in a bourgeois society. If she had been my wife, they would have spared me the guillotine.'

The girl looked at him without seeming to register either surprise or unease. 'I'm Georgiana Fairbanks.' With a flourish the doctor bowed. He took off the mask to reveal a face the colour of an overheated brick. The two ginger wings of his hair were folded over his skull like the feathers of a melancholy Cupid.

'Ah! So *you* are the daughter of my friend the rector.' Taking her hand, the little man kissed it then stared lengthily into the young woman's eyes. 'I have heard *much* about you. Forgive the death mask, mademoiselle; I hoped for a droll effect.'

202

The wicket gate pealed again. *This* wasn't Van Gogh either but perhaps the fattest individual Chip had ever clapped eyes on. There certainly wasn't a smock that would fit him. The man appeared to be some kind of minister, and was carrying a large net and leather bag. With a twinge of irritation Chip recognised the rather gaudily dressed woman with him as one of Dalrymple's dubious acquaintance. When was the Dutchman coming? Genius was whimsical; perhaps he would see all these people and flit away without alighting, like a shy forest bird veering from the smoke of the slums. Welcoming the new arrivals perfunctorily, the young Californian hurried back to the house with the coffee pot. Yet again his instructions had been ignored. They were supposed to ensure a supply of *hot* coffee. The goat was cringing in the shrubbery, licking its balls; having made a beeline for the interesting smells within the folds of the lady's skirts, it had received a sharp kick. At the door to the white house, Chip found himself turning to look through the greenery at Georgiana Fairbanks. Just as well that he'd decided not to allow himself to fall in love before making his mark. Artists had no time to form romantic attachments. Especially not on the day they were marking the lead buffalo.

Carrying the hot coffee jug Chip Coakley found himself intercepted. 'We meet at last,' the newly arrived woman said with a throaty significance.

'Are we acquainted?' Chip asked, quailing somewhat under her searching gaze.

'I know your work. It means everything to me. It fills my heart. Just here.' Chip felt his hand enfolded in the deep front of the woman's garish bodice. 'My name is Lucette Oyster,' she breathed. 'An amateur artist but a professional connoisseur. And your work, Mr Van Gogh — '

'Forgive me, madam; I am Chip Coakley.'

'You're not the Dutchman?'

'Alas, no. I'm still waiting for him.' Allowing him to pull away, for a moment the woman seemed overcome with disappointment before appearing to rally precipitously and tugging him towards her again. Chip felt his hand sinking ever deeper towards her heart; how deep down could that organ be? His anatomical knowledge was sparse but he felt certain it couldn't be *there*.

'I feel *sure* that you must be an artist too,' she whispered conspiratorially.

'Well, I am.'

'And a great one too, of that there is no doubt. Let me see your eyes. Look at me; look at me. Yes; I can see it in your eyes.'

'Please, madam, choose your smock,' floundered Chip, then to hide his confusion he used the phrase he'd been saving up for the Dutchman. 'They're fruiting on the laburnum.' The minx-like look that Lucette Oyster cocked at him revolted the young Californian. There was something insatiable about her. Reptilian. Was she some kind of artists' model, or even a courtesan? The young man accompanied her to the laburnum tree, then peeled off from her, skirting the ranunculi. Chip had been repeatedly warned about such figures by the family pastor back in the States. Her association with Dalrymple was in itself sufficient reason for wariness. Oh yes, Chip knew the kind of establishments his peer frequented during his trips to Paris. It was quite possible that this woman was a streetwalker! What on earth had Dr Gachet invited her for? Mind you, Gachet seemed little better himself. A doctor, my hat. Rather he seemed some kind of cheap carnival huckster. And still Vincent Van Gogh had not arrived. 'Watch out for that one,' a voice murmured. Dalrymple was leering at the wicket gate.

The two rivals regarded each other. 'I'm surprised to see you at such a gathering, Mr Dalrymple,' said Chip coldly. 'Times out of mind I have heard you talk about the necessity for painting to be expunged from the human repertoire.'

'How flattering of you to commit to heart the least of my sayings.'

'In addition to which I don't recall an invitation being extended to you.'

'You're a dark dobbin, old sport.' Blowing out smoke from his cheroot, Dalrymple pointed to where Georgiana and the doctor had already set up their easels. 'Hold a painting party: good way of meeting the pretty pink filly.'

'I assure you, it's nothing of the sort.'

'So why blush like a bride?' James Dalrymple sniggered maddeningly. He was wearing a large striped apron and a billycock hat. 'As you see, I have come to the fancy-dress party as a butcher.'

'It's *not* a fancy-dress party.'

Dalrymple poked the billow of Chip's smock. 'Then why are you attired in masquerade?'

'I'm not.'

'Why certainly you are. A perfect rendering of the son of a railroad magnate play-acting as a hobby-artist. And my dear Casey Jones, you handle the role admirably. With *plum aplomb* as your friends out west might say.'

'As ever, sir, your meaning is evasive.' For some time now Chip had regretted travelling to Europe in company with his fellow Harvard alumnus.

'Not here yet, is he?'

'Who?'

'Gachet's pet lion. The star of *Le Mercure de France*. Vincent Van Gogh.'

'Not yet.'

'Say, what's he like, Chip?'

Without replying, Chip joined the rest of the guests and taking his easel pitched it at some distance from the girl in pink. Although he had tried to avoid it, he found himself painting beside the Lucette Oyster woman. *Her-umph!* Another sneeze racked through him.

'I wish you'd be careful on your excursions, Papa,' Georgiana was saying as she tenderly touched the wound on her father's head.

'Where's your mother?' the rector replied, a little pettishly. 'It's not like her to be late.'

'She'll be here later,' Georgiana lied gently. At his easel Chip could not help but notice how her glossy black hair crackled as she pulled on her smock.

The painting party had begun at last; but the guest of honour was missing. Sitting on the green bench James Dalrymple observed all, scribbling in his notebook as the others sketched or painted. Voices of the boating parties rose from the river on the chilly wind. The sun kept threatening to come out from behind steel-grey clouds. Lucette was just about to move her easel even nearer to Chip when she smelt something unspeakable on the air as though one of Gachet's animals had shat right behind her. She swung round in disgust. The stench was rising from the man standing directly behind her. His stink struck her a low blow like an Indian club in the crotch. She'd seen him before about Auvers; some kind of dropsical indigent. From her woeful childhood in Clerkenwell Mrs Lucette Oyster recognised that rank odour of piss and shit: the unmistakable cocktail of despairing poverty. In the days before artistic modelling rescued her from walking the gaslit streets of Piccadilly, she'd also had ample opportunity to recognise the grip of syphilis. Her face, so dovelike a moment ago when praising the lines of young Mr Coakley's drawing, became the hooded glare of a hawk. But before she could send the cripple-cock packing, Dr Gachet spotted him. 'Vincent!' he gushed. 'I was beginning to worry that you weren't coming.'

Hearing the name, Chip turned too. 'Mr Van Gogh, what an honour. I — ' He broke off, his hand only half extended. It was the loon; the eye in the knothole; the stick thrower; the goat head; the paint fondler; the dum-dum for whom he was going to summon a constable.

Vincent Van Gogh stared at the members of the party for a few moments then, without a word, shambled over to the easels and dragged one to the other side of the laburnum: a starving scavenger with a slab of carrion. The fine marten brushes, the oyster-shell palette pattered to the ground. Above on the plain, the half-hourly train could be heard pulling into the station.

'*And so,*' James Dalrymple wrote, '*tearing himself from the cave where he had been hidden for epochs, the modern primitive man arrives in polite circles. Homo artisticus.*'

'That's Vincent Van Gosh?' Lucette cried incredulously, her native cockney accent resurfacing in her agitation.

'*Oui, madam,*' Gachet replied drily. 'But try and pronounce his name correctly; throttling it like that is liable to make him, how you say, tetchy.'

Lucette peered in naked revulsion at the seedy hobo, who was snatching up the tubes of paint like a thief stripping lead from a Bloomsbury roof. It wasn't his short blue jacket that caused her such offence, threadbare and streaked with paint as it may be; nor the battered straw hat more proper to a gardener — after all, this *was* the *demi-monde* of art. His boots too, a labourer's cast-offs, were not what made his presence so irredeemable. Even his ugliness was not his irredeemable feature, although with that great, blunt, chewed ginger head he looked like a testicle with mange. What Lucette Oyster could not forgive was the little monkey of death

208

perching on his back. As a girl she had encountered it too often and from too close a distance ever to mistake the leer on a dying man's rounded shoulder.

'Work, work, work,' implored Dr Gachet.

'*A sailor went to sea, sea, sea,*' the Reverend Jonah Fairbanks sang to himself as he daubed gaily.

Unfortunately Chip Coakley could not find a similar fluency. Through the corner of one eye he was gazing at the vision of Miss Fairbanks in pink gingham; through the other, without a corresponding admiration, he gaped at the Dutch artist. Having snatched up the tubes of paint, Van Gogh was peering at them famishedly. A worm of saliva slid from the corner of his mouth. He spread his fingers wide and squeezed out a dollop from each tube then stared in amazement as though he had just dipped his hands into a rainbow. Zinc white, emerald green, orange lead, ultramarine, canary yellow; malachite green, crimson lake, chrome, cobalt, carmine. The tendons on his wrist corded; he began to chuckle; his tongue flickered at the greasy dollops of tincture. His beard and chin now shining with saliva, he craned his neck forward. Nose sniffing loudly, Vincent Van Gogh closed his eyes and, opening his mouth, leant forward like a communicant . . .

'Time to work now, Vincent,' said Dr Gachet gently catching his elbow just in time to prevent the artist from tasting the colour. 'Remember, we must always work.'

For a few moments Chip thought that the

Dutchman was going to strike the doctor, but instead he threw his head back, and, roaring with laughter, wiped his hands on his trousers. 'I am taking a risk,' the doctor confided to the host. 'He does not thrive on occasions such as these. Yet his fame is growing so that in a few months, maybe a year, who knows, he will not be able to avoid them.'

'Is Mr Van Gogh ill?' Chip asked.

For the second time that morning the young Californian was subjected to the Gallic shrug. 'He is an artist, monsieur.'

'Are the colours to his liking? I got in the ones you specified. And the brushes are — '

'Return to your painting, monsieur, and try not to stare. Please, everyone, do not stare, you will only unsettle him.'

'Unsettle *him*?' Lucette Oyster shuddered.

Behind his easel, eyes hooded as a lizard's, the Dutchman's gaze travelled slowly round the garden. He peered at the white house as though half recognising it. At last, with a salacious grin, he took out the lid of an old cigar box from within his jacket, and put out his colours, the tubes farting their evacuations. Mumbling to himself in a garbled mixture of Dutch, French and English, the artist began to apply the paint in thick, sweeping sketches. Loaded now with green, now with yellow, now with white, the brush quickly conjured up the scene before him in bold strokes. His wrist hefting like a bricklayer's, he built the foliage, the house, the damp spring day. Nose dotted with orange from when he had sniffed the paints, eyes narrowed to slits, the artist worked in a frenzy. Only the rector, singing to himself as he coloured in his childlike picture of a butterfly, did not watch the stinking whirlwind that had blown into Daubigny's garden.

'*Who is this monstrous angel?*' James Dalrymple wrote. '*Christ, not risen from the dead but exhumed, creating new worlds with the wrist of a hopelessly dedicated onanist. Take care those who would follow him. His brush is a serpent bearing the warning colours of venom. This is a postlapsarian world.*' Then feeling a sudden wave of nausea at his own pose of world-weariness, as well as a cramp in his arm — he really ought to follow Dickens's lead and learn shorthand — James Dalrymple put down his notebook, and simply watched the artist at work. How wonderful his picture was, he thought, but poor son of a bitch, he's not long for this mortal morass.

Georgiana blew a strand of hair from her eyes and painted over her composition. Having watched the Dutchman conjure the spring garden in a few hefty strokes, her simple, rather delicate picture of dainty lawn, laburnum tree and green bench seemed wholly inadequate. Copying the artist's technique this time she dispensed with preliminary sketches, drawing her picture with the paint itself.

Gachet grinned complacently behind his easel. Vincent seemed happily at work; that was his friend's only hope: uncomplicated and unfettered work. Wasn't it everyone's only hope in such a cruel, flawed world? Work, as well as digitalis purpurea of course: essence of foxglove. Well, the artist had passed the first test of his coming fame. He had not yet come to blows with anyone, nor suffered a seizure.

All at once the garden was filled with light; the countless colours deepened. The sun had emerged from behind the clouds. The voices of the boating parties also rose as though in response. The rector's belly began to growl. Looking up from his own canvas, which wasn't progressing as well as he'd like, Chip began to wonder if the gardener's daughter had forgotten lunch. Seeing the little boy at the wicket gate, he was about to send him to the kitchen with a message when Vincent Van Gogh shot out so quickly from behind his easel that the wooden support toppled to the ground, throwing his canvas face down. The rufous Dutchman sprinted violently to the gate and snatched up the boy.

It was clearly a game they had played before. Hoisting him over his shoulder, the painter whirled the child round. The gardener's grandson screamed with delight. 'Encore, encore!' the boy begged when the ride ended.

'Encore,' Van Gogh complied and spun him even more dizzyingly. The boy's laughter filled Daubigny's garden, his hair a whorl of golden brushstrokes set now against the blue of the sky, now the yellow of the laburnum tree, and now the white of the house with its green shutters.

'Encore, encore!'

'Encore.'

'That's enough for now,' the old gardener

declared in French, smiling from the wicket gate. 'Can't you see that Mad Red is tired?'

Releasing the child, Vincent Van Gogh fell to his hands and knees and fought for his breath, his great blunt head lolling like a seeded sunflower. The child climbed on his back and began kicking him with his heels. 'Donkey!' the artist yelled, then with a loud bray rode the child through the ranunculi bed. The child shrieked with joy.

As she lifted the fallen canvas back onto its easel, Georgiana Fairbanks gasped at the beauty of the painting. It was the garden, but how you would see it in a dream.

3

Only when the tureen came back for the second time did Chip declare it warm enough. He looked anxiously at his guest of honour; he didn't seem to have much of an appetite. There were seven of them lunching round the trestle table but the rector alone drank his soup with gusto. The Dutchman, having kneaded his bread into little pills, chewed laboriously on his single tooth, gums working like a cow at the cud. Dr Gachet also left his bowl untouched. 'But you were not painting, monsieur,' Gachet said to James Dalrymple as the conversation languished once more. 'I see you with your notebook; you are a devotee of literature?'

'Well,' Dalrymple shrugged, 'I guess.'

'No doubt you are enamoured of our French

writers. Honoré de Balzac perhaps?'

'He's all right for insomniacs, I suppose.'

'You prefer Zola then, monsieur?' the doctor asked, nettled.

'Lord, no; he's a dreadful idiot.' Dalrymple gave a little yawn. 'You French are good at crêpes and canapés, but your literature's a tad gastropodous.'

Coughing away his irritation, Dr Gachet turned to the Dutchman, who was continuing laboriously to masticate his bread pills. 'Make the case for the defence, Vincent. Next he'll be desecrating Maupassant, the Goncourt brothers and Daudet.' Van Gogh mumbled unintelligibly to himself. 'Vincent went to Arles because of Alphonse Daudet's description of that matchless creature, the Arlesienne,' the doctor explained to the company. 'The most beautiful women in the world are from Arles, are they not, Vincent?' Waving the comment away, the Dutch painter spat out his sot of bread and lit his pipe. 'Vincent is saying nothing,' Dr Gachet continued. 'But I challenge anyone sitting here to remain unmoved by his picture of the Arlesienne. Indeed, I issue an open invitation to come to my villa and view this portrait: true beauty on a canvas.' As all eyes gazed on Vincent van Gogh, the painter's pipe gurgled like a snail dropped in salt water.

'I should love to see it,' Chip put in.

'And I should love to see *your* work,' Mrs Oyster said sotto voce to the young Californian. 'I am sure *you* are going to achieve great things. I suggest that you and I form a little alliance. Tomorrow we shall go painting in the young corn above the village. I know just the spot: a perfect portion of paradise.'

'Dr Gachet,' said the rector, looking regretfully at the empty tureen, 'may I have a word? In camera, so to speak.'

'*Now*, monsieur?'

'It *is* rather urgent.' Rising from the table, Dr Gachet took the clergyman by his elbow and drew him out of earshot to the green bench. 'I'm afraid she's late, Dr Gachet.'

'Who's late, Reverend Fairbanks?'

'My wife. Serve the next course; don't wait for her. She would be mortified to cause the party any inconvenience.'

'That is all?'

'I was also wondering whether . . . ' The obese vicar broke off delicately. 'When I was at your house the other day browsing through your curios . . . such a fine collection of bibelots — death masks, the pickled finger, the skull, the antiques.' The doctor bowed. 'Well, I was wondering whether you happen to have any chronometers among your cornucopia of oddities.'

'I have a number.'

'One set to the hour in the Galapagos Islands?'

'The where?'

A ravenous hunger flared on the rector's apple-sized cheeks. 'The Galapagos Islands, it's a matter of the greatest moment.'

'Alas, no, monsieur.'

'How about Babylon?'

The doctor considered the rector with professional fascination. Behind those spherical

215

glasses the vicar's eyes seemed to be frying like eggs in a pan. Gachet had been wondering when Jonah Fairbanks would return to his *idé fixe*: his belief that by finding a new species of butterfly he would rebut Charles Darwin's theory of mutability. 'This chronometer, it is important, Rector?'

'Let me say only this, Doctor: it is of sufficient significance to prove the existence of God once and for all; and thereby confirm Charles Darwin's true message.'

'Ah yes, Charles Darwin; I understand you knew him.'

'It was to me he dictated his last will and testament,' the rector whispered. 'And it was likewise from me that he extracted the promise that I would never rest until I had fulfilled his life's work. His true work, mind you; not that cyclopean farrago of natural selection to which so many seem to subscribe. You see, he entrusted me with the task of showing that his work actually *proves* the existence of God.' Looking around furtively, he gestured Gachet closer. The doctor obeyed, fascinated by the sheer bulk of the clergyman's paunch — there was barely room for his thin shanks on the green bench. Zola had divided the world between the fat and the thin, but here was something new: the gargantuan. 'And today I was within a trice of bringing that undertaking to fruition.'

'With your butterflies, Monsieur?'

The rector emitted a curious giggle. 'Tee-hee. Yes, as you say, with my butterflies. Butter. Flies. What a ridiculous sobriquet; how demeaning a diminutive.' Jonah Fairbanks darkened. 'Give a thing a silly name and then you won't have to admit that it is the hinge on which the whole of existence relies. But you and I know very well that butterflies are angels in disguise. Not figuratively. They bear the message. They — ' He broke off and smiled sadly. 'How I wish he could have lived to understand how butterflies provide his missing link. He would have loved that, you know.'

'Who, Rector?'

'Charles, of course. It was the only thing we argued about. Tiff would be a better word. You see, he was convinced that pigeons were the divine birds. Little did he know that it would prove to be the pretty genus Lepidoptera.' The clergyman gave a little sigh of forbearance; his eyes misted. 'He was pretty himself. Do I surprise you, Dr Gachet? We've all grown used to that rather beetle-browed egghead promulgated by the celebrated daguerreotype; but as a young man he was lovely. His smile, Dr Gachet, his smile was like a butterfly.' Jonah Fairbanks remained locked in a fond memory for a while longer then, clapping Gachet on the back, chanted:

> 'Fatty and Skinny went up in a balloon,
> Fatty went pliff and blew Skinny doon.'

Watching the clergyman return to the table, Gachet wondered if he had made any progress with this interesting patient of his. If anything, the rector's condition seemed to have grown more acute since his arrival in Auvers. Yes, he meditated, there are many rooms in the mansions of melancholy.

Smoothing his little goatee beard, chin resting on his hand, Gachet considered the others gathered for lunch. Utterly alienated from the company, Vincent had begun sketching on the tablecloth. Had the doctor been right to bring him to this thrusting young American's *salon au jardin*? He hadn't said a word. Yet he *had* produced a fine picture. Tilting round on the bench, the doctor could see it now on the easel. Incredibly, it seemed almost finished: all the freshness and riot of spring distilled on a canvas. Although an atheist, having watched Vincent Van Gogh at work Dr Gachet was disposed to believe that the Bible was right in one respect: creativity was rapid; if there was a God it would have only taken Him six days to make the world. *Le Mercure de France* was also correct. Vincent Van Gogh was a towering figure. Not the finished article yet but what would he be in a year, five years? If they were given to him. Unlikely. Rarely had Gachet seen a man more worn away. His melancholy was raging out of control like the Japanese rhododendron, which, having been introduced to European parkland as an orna-mental shrub, was now strangling the life out of the native flora. Well, well, work and digitalis purpurea, but was it too late? Yet, after all, madness was the artist's stock-in-trade; what else was artistic vision but the strange second sight of a brain fever? Finally a fire consumes itself.

The doctor rose stiffly, and, wandering back to

the table, looked at his protégé's sketch on the cloth. He was drawing the party at lunch: a kind of last supper without saints. At that moment he was scratching out the figure of Mrs Oyster. Lucette Oyster, yet another interesting refugee from modern living. Gachet was loath to call them patients. Hers was an odd case. From what he could gather, Lucette Oyster seemed to have a number of distinct personae, any of which she could embrace on any given day with complete conviction. Today she was clearly the former streetwalker who had risen from the cockney rookeries to be the model for many minor English Pre-Raphaelites, but only last week she had told him of her childhood as the daughter of a duke, and when she had first come to see him she had shared a decidedly harrowing tale of how, as a governess in Cornwall, she had been forced to flee the amorous attentions of a local tin magnate. She played each role entirely convincingly, but like a novelist of limited invention, her characters shared one constant symptom. Nymphomania was too pallid a word for it. Gachet was in favour of free love, it was one of the things for which he had taken to the communard barricades, yet Lucette Oyster's appetites were of a prodigality he could not even begin to imagine. What sadnesses and sorrow did she seek to sink in the well of her lusts? Shaking away the sudden weight of despondency — the sad suffering of his patients always made him think of his dead wife — he sat down. His eye passed down the table to Georgiana. She was the most fascinating case of all. If her father was to be believed — *severe caveat* — then until coming to France a few weeks before, she had spent her life in complete isolation. Immured in a moated rectory hidden deep in the countryside of northern England, she had grown from babyhood thinking that the human race consisted only of the rector himself, a female retainer and the occasional passing farm labourer. Yet she bore no signs of this deprivation. Drawing most of what she knew of the world from the pages of fiction, she seemed to be blossoming rapidly in her newly acquired freedom. Look at the way she was conversing with the young Americans now. Hers was a beauty that appealed to the doctor; and not only because of her exquisite retroussé nose. There was something of the gypsy about her. Before lunch he had taken her as his subject, trying to capture her on canvas as a kind of modern sylph of spring, but she would also have been the perfect model for a barefoot harvester painted by someone like Millet or Jules Breton. She had painted quickly so that a light glow of perspiration had sheened her skin like dew on fruit. Her brushstrokes had been executed with all the power and majesty of a gleaner asserting an ancient right. The doctor studied her now. The freckles on her face were stippled as though glimpsed through a stand of ripe wheat; her eyes were dark as a corncockle seed. His own wife had been beautiful too once, a laughing girl just like this one, but in the end she had weighed no more than a small stook of cut corn in his arms. Yes; his own wife. His thoughts were never far from her. She remained real to him although her body was long since food for the worms. Georgiana on the other hand was very much alive as she talked with the young men. Well, that was how it should be. The young turn to the young for love; and the old die, and before you die, you remember. Dr Gachet felt his own melancholia settle around his shoulders like a peasant her yoke. Work and digitalis purpurea.

In his absence the conversation had languished. The next course arrived, a dish of moules mariniére from which his poor digestion banished him. Vincent, ominously quiet, was still sketching on the tablecloth. 'So, Monsieur Dalrymple,' Gachet began, 'I understand you believe that art is dead. Perhaps you yourself are the only writer worth reading. No doubt any day now Hatchards are selling your magnum opus.'

'Lord, no,' Dalrymple drawled as he scribbled in his notebook, 'being published is the worst thing that can happen to a writer.' Vincent looked up and appeared to nod vehemently before spitting at his sketch and shading in the lines. James Dalrymple yawned theatrically. 'Dr Gachet, you're asking the wrong person about such matters. Miss Fairbanks is the real expert on literature.'

'*Vraiment?*' Gachet turned to the young woman; again he wondered whether her life really had been as her father described: the imprisoned existence of a kind of Lady of Shalott. He feared for her during the inevitable, perhaps imminent climax of her father's cerebral neuralgia. 'You enjoy literature, mademoiselle?'

'Oh yes,' Georgiana replied with an emphasis

that made the cat curled in the tree open half an eye.

'Her particular favourite is Thomas Hardy, is it not, Miss Fairbanks?' Dalrymple put in.

'Assuredly; but not exclusively,' asseverated the young woman.

'And what do you think of art, mademoiselle?'

Miss Fairbanks shook her head. 'I don't know much about art, Dr Gachet.'

'Yet your picture is very good — I took the liberty of glancing over your shoulder as you worked. You have painted before?'

'Only dead lapwings and gollies and things.'

'What is this *lapwings* and *gollies*?'

'Gollies are what Jessie calls nestlings. She's our servant. They often fall from the hedge. I have also painted our own garden and Sir John Franklin, but he was dead too. Sir John Franklin, our dog.'

'And who is your favourite artist?'

The girl flushed slightly as though unused to such lengthy intercourse. 'Well, I like the stained-glass windows in our little church at home. But I don't know the name of the artist. He lived in a tent for two months; I never saw his face. But he wore fustian trousers.'

'Indeed. But your favourite artist, mademoiselle?'

'I suppose . . . Edward Springrove.'

'Edward Springrove? I have not heard of him. An English artist?'

'Edward Springrove?' repeated Dalrymple, putting down his pen. 'Do you mean the Edward Springrove from Thomas Hardy's *Desperate Remedies*?'

'You too like Mr Hardy, Mr Dalrymple?' Georgiana asked.

Gachet laughed. 'How droll! How Anglo-Saxon! But I am asking which *real* artist you admire.'

'But he *is* real,' Georgiana replied.

'Georgie,' the rector's voice suddenly boomed out, 'pass me your mother's bowl; she must still be visiting with the cottagers; and you know how much she'd hate to see it go to waste.'

Georgiana passed her father the untouched dish of moules marinière. The rector tilted his head back and with a smack of the lips, poured the contents into his mouth, separating the glutinous gobs of sea fruit from their shells with a shockingly fibrous tongue.

It was as the beef course arrived that Chip realised the painting he had been wrestling with all morning was no good. Oh, it was all right in its way, his white house boating through the garden, but it was as nothing beside the piece he now knew he had to begin. Georgiana Fairbanks was his real subject. All morning he'd been fighting against it. But why — didn't every artist require a muse? The way she was sitting now would be an ideal pose; eyes smouldering even as she listened politely to the nonsense drivelling from Dalrymple's mouth. On the visit to the Indian reservation, among the drunken, listless native braves sleeping their liquor off in the tepee, there had been a squaw. She had stared back at Chip with such blackly intense eyes that even though he'd paid his admission fee he looked away. Georgiana's gaze burnt with the

223

same jet flame. Glancing at her now he deeply regretted the smocks; she would look much better unadorned in her pink gingham dress; in fact she would look much better completely unadorned. With a furious blush Chip Coakley realised that the picture of Georgiana Fairbanks in his mind was a version of Manet's *Le Déjeuner sur l'herbe* in which one of the lady picnickers is utterly naked. A nude; the very thing he had promised Pastor Cash never to paint. *Her-umph!* Much to his mortification, the young man sprayed his phlegm over the table, the loud noise finally flushing the cat from the branches of its tree.

'Mr Coakley, I see you are suffering,' Dr Gachet said. 'I have a linctus for such a malady. I prescribe — '

'Don't tell me,' smirked James Dalrymple quietly.

' — digitalis purpurea. The homeopathic remedy for 90 per cent of our modern ills. The essence of a plant you will know by the name of the — '

'Foxglove,' the young writer mouthed the word at the same time as the doctor spoke it.

'As for your other malady, there is no other cure save for the universal cure of all such ailments: the passing of time.'

'My friend and esteemed colleague is the sufferer of *two* illnesses, Dr Gachet?' Dalrymple enquired brightly.

'You too, monsieur.' The doctor took Georgiana's hand. '*Ma chérie*, if only my wife was here. Together you would form the perfect juxtaposition of complementary colours.' With a sorrowful little moue, Gachet lifted up Chip Coakley's and then James Dalrymple's hands and placed them on the young woman's. 'Yes,' the doctor declared, 'some call love an illness, but I believe it is the cure.' For an instant, their hands joined, the young people held a single gaze. Then Georgiana looked quickly away. In all her long years of musing about young men, she had never dreamt they would blush so tenderly. Did they, she wondered, also have rounded, glutinous buttocks?

'Stone the bloody crows!' Mrs Oyster screeched.

The doctor leant forward to investigate the small crablike insect crawling over the pristine tablecloth. '*Pediculus humanus*,' the rector intoned, crushing the creature between finger and thumbnail. 'A louse.' Getting up, Mrs Oyster moved her chair further from the Dutchman.

After long consideration of the steak on his plate, Vincent picked it up with his fingers. Placing it in his mouth, he worried the slab of beef like a dog with a rabbit. Eventually managing to break a piece off, he chewed, the dentures he had just affixed champing loud as a cab horse. But it was no good, his stomach could take nothing so solid. With a violent retch, he spat it out. Having studied the partially masticated meat lying on the table before him, the artist stood up solemnly and then began to address the company. The ill-fitting dentures made his words unintelligible as his hands painted ever more extravagant meanings on the air. Growing increasingly earnest, his voice was little more than a whistling, spitting sibilance.

'Perhaps if you took them out,' Gachet urged gently. With growing agitation the Dutchman continued to hiss at the people round the table.

All at once James Dalrymple clapped his hands in delight. 'Thank you, I will, Mr Van Gogh.' Laughing loudly, the young Ivy Leaguer took out a cheroot and having lit it held his Lucifer match over the artist's pipe. Van Gogh nodded and puffed his pipe into life. The hissing of his words was matched now by the gurgle of nicotine juice and saliva in the bowl of the pipe. 'He was speaking Japanese,' Dalrymple explained. 'Inviting us all to smoke. *Anatanominase!* Those were his words. *Anatanominase!* It means 'please smoke' in Japanese. Not only that but I believe he's expressing his literary preferences vis-à-vis our earlier debate. The quotation is from Pierre Loti's novel *Madame Chrysanthème*, is it not, Mr Van Gogh?'

'Just call me Vincent,' the Dutchman said in English. Taking out his dentures, his face fell like a corpse but his words became instantly clearer. 'It's giving me a headache having to listen to you jawing my name like that. What is it with you people? Anyone would think Dutch was a language spoken on the moon.' The artist jabbed the stem of his pipe at the writer. 'Tell me, lad, do you really think art is dead?'

'I think your picture is splendid, Vincent,' Dalrymple replied. 'I can honestly say that I have never seen spring so wonderfully portrayed.'

'Forget about me. Did you or didn't you say that art was dead?'

'I did,' Dalrymple conceded uncertainly. 'But — '

'No buts. Why?' Under this quick-fire interrogation Mr Dalrymple experienced a new sensation: he found himself speechless. Red bonehead bristling like a badger, Van Gogh shot out from behind the table. 'I'm-fucking-asking-you-why-you-fucking-said-art-was-fucking-dead?'

'Vincent,' interposed Gachet. Although the Dutchman had been relatively quiet since coming to Auvers, Gauguin had warned the doctor about his violent persona, his propensity to carry a knife. Of course Gauguin was a braggart and a self-aggrandiser, but there was no disputing the fact that Vincent Van Gogh had cut off his own ear.

'What is it now?' Vincent barked at the doctor.

'Mr Dalrymple meant no harm.'

'Let him speak for himself.' The artist placed his pipe on the cloth where it continued to hiss. His face inches from James Dalrymple's, he lifted a fist. But just as he seemed about to punch him, the artist broke into a broad grin and shook the American's hand. 'Of course it's not as good as it was, that's for certain; I mean, none of us are Millet or Delacroix or even Josef Israels, but I think there's still some life left in us yet.' He turned to Chip. 'What do *you* think?'

Chip floundered. Watching Georgiana through the corner of his eye, he hadn't really been listening. But still, *this* could be his opportunity. 'I want to be an artist like you, Mr Van Gogh.'

'Just call me Vincent. Vin-cent. That's easy

enough, isn't it?' To Gachet's relief his protégé was still smiling. 'So you want to be an artist? Let's look at your hooves then.'

'My hooves?'

'Hooves, hooves, hands!'

As the Dutchman grasped Chip's hands in his own, the young Californian tried to hide his disgust. Gunk encrusted the long fingernails; filth engrained his palm; warts ringed his knuckles, their cratered tops multicoloured with paint. 'You'll have to toughen these up before you pass muster with St Luke.'

Chip smiled wanly, wondering how he could extricate his hands before they became infected. 'Monsieur,' Gachet explained, 'Vincent is referring to the medieval guild of artists. Their patron was St Luke; their emblem an ox.'

'And to be an artist you have to bloody work like one too.' Dropping Chip's hand at last, the Dutchman struck the table. A bowl of caramelised blancmange danced. 'On, on, on!' he cried. 'And how do they reward us? By muzzling us as we work. Feel my fucking ribs. This nag is ready for the knackers.' He exhaled; softened. 'So you want to be an artist, son?'

'I'm committed to it,' Chip replied more unflinchingly than he actually felt.

'Pass me one of your scratches then. Your drawings, your drawings.' Van Gogh snatched up the sketch pad in which Chip had been doodling before lunch. Looking at three or four pages he grinned. 'Well, at least you can draw. Give it another ten years and you might get somewhere.'

Chip smiled uneasily. 'I was hoping to begin

selling a little sooner.'

'Selling? That's not hard, but really painting or drawing something worthwhile, that's different. Any whore can sell sex, but what price love?' Vincent tossed the sketchbook to Georgiana with a giggle. 'I wondered why he kept on looking at you.' The sketchbook landed with one of the sketches visible; it was of a young woman with thick dark hair and turned-up nose. The Dutchman cackled like a fishwife. 'Don't blush, lad. You'll have to grow a thick skin as well as hooves if you want to be an artist. Paint her by all means, but if I were you I'd watch her work. I agree with the doctor. She's got something. She's better than you. Better than me too, if she gives herself to it.'

'Come now, Vincent,' Gachet expostulated. 'No false modesty. Only a short while ago your work was praised in *Le Mercure de France*.'

'Yessir, I have a copy here,' said Chip bringing out the magazine and placing it on the table. This was exactly the moment he'd been waiting for.

The Dutchman twitched. 'Come now, gentlemen, none of that. He wasn't writing about me.'

'But he was, sir.' Chip opened the copy and handed it to Gachet.

'*Vincent Van Gogh*,' Dr Gachet translated from the passages highlighted by Chip, '*a fellow countryman of the great Dutch masters and indeed their worthy descendant . . . a thousand details thrust at us his heartfelt and childlike sincerity, his passion for nature and truth. Vincent Van Gogh is not only a great painter but*

229

a dreamer, a fanatical believer, a devourer of beautiful Utopias living on ideas and dreams. He is an intense and fantastic man of colours, grinder of golds and precious stones — '

The painter's voice was ominously quiet: 'I've written to tell the bastard to keep his mouth shut in future. He's writing about how *I should* be, not what I am.'

'But, monsieur, your time is coming.'

'I don't care about me; my pictures are — ' He shook his head. 'Maybe those coming after will be able to take it further. This girl here; who knows.'

'But, Vincent,' Gachet said, 'people are beginning to talk about *you.*' Like a cab horse beset by flies, the artist shook his head and shoulders. 'And the buyers will soon follow.'

'I'd sure like to buy one of your pieces, Vincent,' Chip said.

'How much?' Van Gogh demanded, rounding on him.

'Ten thousand francs,' the young Californian blurted.

'Are you joking?'

'No, Mr Van Gogh.'

'Call me Vincent.'

'I'm not joking, Vincent.'

'You've got ten grand to spend just like that?'

'My father, he . . . ' Chip trailed off.

Dr Gachet braced himself. Was Vincent's violent side about to assert itself with catastrophic results? But the anger in the Dutchman's bloodshot eyes was a brief flare. 'If someone really had that kind of money to spend on art,' he reasoned,

'I'd say: my friend, you seem to be sincerely moved by this picture; good; but bear in mind it was produced not only by me but my colleagues; so give me a thousand of those francs and then go and have a look at their work too; come back again later, in a week's time perhaps, a month, and then you might see something else to catch your fancy. For instance, today,' he gestured at his painting on the easel, 'I have tried to show this garden as a blind man might see it getting his sight back for the first time; how spring might feel after a hundred years of winter.' Vincent Van Gogh faltered. 'Ten thousand francs? We don't even get a single sou.'

'But I'm willing to buy that picture now, Vincent.'

The Dutchman waved him away. 'It's too much. You want to be an artist? My advice: don't. You'll have to die first.'

'But only last month someone bought a Millet for half a million.'

'What?'

The doctor half rose. Now it really was going to begin. The young American boy might as well have waved a red rag at the local Charolais bull. 'And now, Vincent,' he interposed hastily, 'back to work.'

'What did you say?' The Dutchman asked softly, ignoring Gachet.

'Why,' said Chip, 'the Barbizon artist Millet, not so very long ago he went for half a million Francs.'

'He did, did he?'

'Sure! Even my papa was impressed by that.'

231

'Well, half a million; good for Old Father Millet,' the painter murmured. 'Half a million you say?' The Californian nodded uncertainly. Something was going wrong. He thought he was offering the painter a favour; but there was a glint in his eye that presaged . . . 'Half a million? Yes, well, now he's safely dead, I suppose the butchers will get their cut of him. Funny thing is, when he actually *needed* the money nobody would touch his work with a Drenthe bargepole. Did you know that, Yankee boy? That's how it is with dealers. To the money-makers, you're nothing until you're dead. Oyez, oyez, who will give me half a million for the corpse of Jean François Millet? You have to kill an artist before he can feed himself. I mean, that's how it is. An artist has to be a carcass before a dealer tries to sell his work. That's true, isn't it, Doctor?' The painter was dangerously still. 'The galleries are dealers in dead men; aren't they, Doctor?'

'Sometimes, Vincent, sometimes.'

Vincent Van Gogh's voice rose in irritation. 'Not sometimes. *Always*. I mean, why not go the whole hog and just be a grave robber?'

'Vincent is upset by the art establishment's lack of initiative,' the doctor said.

'Let me speak for myself! Art establishment! That's the right word for them. Oh, they put on their airs and graces, their high and mighty ways, these gentlemen dealers, but what are they but a gang of bloody body snatchers? Fucking toerags. Scrofulous bastards. Not only do they muzzle the ox as it treads out their corn but once the poor beast's caved in, they flog the hide, the eyelashes, the bollocks, every little fucking titbit.'

'Please, Vincent, do not upset yourself.'

The Dutchman rounded on Gachet. '*You're* the one that's upsetting people. Have you hung those paintings yet? You haven't, have you?' He turned to the others. 'He's got some fantastic paintings, one by Guillaumin, and he doesn't bother hanging them; he just leaves them leaning against any old wall.' The artist's skull seemed to be splitting his skin. 'Pah! You're the same as the rest of them.'

'Monsieur, take heart, the time is coming when your work will hang in the finest galleries of Europe. Monsieur Aurier in his article in *Le Mercure de France* said — '

'Shut up with that shit!' the painter screamed and snatching up the magazine tore out the pages of the article. Cursing in a mixture of English, Dutch and French, he screwed the pages into balls and hurled them at Dr Gachet. 'You dealer in dead men. You fucking necrophiliac cunt!'

In the ensuing silence, the first few gobs of rain pattered on the crisp white tablecloth. Dark clouds drifting from the wheat plain drew themselves over Auvers-sur-Oise like great winding sheets. 'My darling,' the rector greeted his spectral spouse. 'You're here at last.'

London, July 2008

1

She did not notice the rain; she did not notice the traffic ploughing through the puddles; she didn't even notice the other pedestrians jostling her from the pavement. Concentrating only on one thing — the blond head twenty yards ahead — Zohreh had followed Piers all the way from the bank. It wasn't easy. She had to maintain a certain distance in case he happened to look over his shoulder, yet if she allowed him to get too far away she would lose him. In London, a person can be lost in a second. Ambling down London Wall, he had threaded a circuitous route through Little Britain before wandering along Newgate onto High Holborn. She had nearly lost him at the intersection of Farringdon Road when he had crossed after the green man disappeared. Zohreh had plunged out after him into a hail of car horns. At Chancery Lane tube station, he had glanced back and she had willed him to see her, imagining in that single, long instant a pavement reconciliation, an anguished declaration of his love, an ecstatic proposal. But he had simply turned back and continued. When they reached Bloomsbury the rain intensified, hissing on the hundred roofs of the British Museum, and bouncing off the striped awning of the Forum Cafe. Piers quickened his stride, a copy of *London Lite* rapidly growing sodden over his head. Zohreh's thick black hair was crushed flat against her skull; at the kerbside the parked cars huddled like whales. *Surely* he felt something for her too; how else could he have made love to her those four unforgettable times since the awful day after Amsterdam? The last time he had even asked how she was; not just for the sake of speaking but as though he were genuinely interested; as if there was so much more he would say if only he could. Yes; she had gone over it a hundred times, a thousand: he must care for her. Otherwise.

Gav was already inside the Cafe in the Gardens when Piers arrived. He was reading an email on his BlackBerry while talking into his phone. Piers sat down and ordered an espresso from the Eastern European waitress. 'I'm not even going to pretend I'm pleased to see you,' Gav said when his call was finished.

'How's Emily?'

'She's fine.'

'Aren't you going to ask about Mimi?'

'I would if I thought you cared about her.'

'Ah.' Piers cleared his throat. He hadn't seen Gav for weeks; not since the day he came back from Amsterdam. 'Shouldn't you be out somewhere saving the world?' Gav lifted up a forefinger as he read the email just coming through on his BlackBerry. 'That's a breach of etiquette,' Piers continued, 'reading mail when you're with someone. Seriously, they're compiling a book about it; a kind of new Debrett's. A guide to acceptable behaviour. Don't you want a latte?' Gavin shook his head without looking up from the small screen. 'Another contravention of the new Debrett's. Inviting someone for a coffee and then not having one yourself.'

'Piers, I haven't come here to piss about.'

'Put the crackberry down, Gav; didn't you know excessive BlackBerrying is bad for the health?'

'Look, I told you to give up the sixth-former.'

'Well, I have. I told you.'

'Yeah, you tell me a lot of things.'

'For fuck's sake, Gav, you've got to — '

Gav's phone rang. He took the call outside under the cafe awning. Through the plate-glass windows Russell Square Gardens loomed desolately. One or two people were hurrying through the rain; a lone figure sat hunched on a bench under a dripping plane tree. 'It must be a fake bake,' Piers bantered when Gav came back. 'More *stand as you tan* than Torremolinos. Your radioactive glow.'

'Delete the crap, Piers.'

'You *did* have that nose job, didn't you? Come clean, Gav.'

'For fuck's sake, can't you take anything seriously?'

'Language. Auntie Beeb will have to wash your mouth out with soap and water. Here I am being insulted and I thought I'd just got soaked to the skin so that I could meet my oldest friend for a coffee.'

'Friend? You're a cunt of the highest water.'

'Whom am I to defend myself?'

'What?'

'It's the example in the *New Shorter Oxford Dictionary*. You know, to help lost souls and BBC Special Correspondents decide between their *whos* and their *whoms*. Actually the entry reads: *Whom am I to defend Daphne Du Maurier?* By shorter they mean 3,578 pages. How's that for dumbing up?'

'Now I see it, you've never taken anything seriously in your life.' Gav stared at Piers in disgust. 'You're a child. You can't be a normal responsible adult. You're to be pitied. Anyway, you've got a chance to do a good act. That St Trinian's girl you've been fucking — '

'I told you, that fling thing is long over.'

'Right, until the next one starts tomorrow. Anyway, I don't care. What I care about is Sally.'

'Do you indeed?'

Gav's face reddened. 'Any more from you, Lupine, and so help me God I'll punch your lights out.' *Lupine?* Piers hadn't heard that nickname since school. He drained his small cup. At this mention of his old sobriquet, the haunting, distant intimacies of childhood seemed to cluster around Piers for an instant, as though the voices of the other customers were those of a classroom of boys moments before a master comes in to take prep. 'You've driven me to this,' Gav continued. 'Well, actually you've driven yourself so I have no sympathy.' The BBC Special Correspondent shook his head in disbelief. 'Sally Twentyman, everybody fancied

237

her, but it was you who smarmed his way in. And you've brought her nothing but grief. I mean, you've obviously never given a toss about her.'

'That's bollocks. I — '

'Let me have her, Piers.'

'What?'

'You heard. Oh Christ, wake up and smell the coffee. Sally and I have been in love with each other for years. We've only denied ourselves because of you. Talk about misplaced bloody loyalty. Otherwise she would have left you for me ages ago.'

Piers's voice was small. 'And your own wife?'

'We're getting divorced; been on the cards for ages. She's fucking our Polish skivvy. Yes; Katya, our plumber-nanny. I thought you'd like that. For Christ's sake, you're actually laughing.'

'And what else am I supposed to do, Simian?' Piers replied, in his turn using Gav's nickname from school.

Gav shrugged it away. 'Whatever. So now there's nothing to stop Sally and me. As for Mimi, well, I think we can safely say that she'd prefer living with someone who actually respects her mother, don't you? She and Emily are already like sisters. Don't go all pathetic on me, Guest, it's not as if you love Sally.' The BlackBerry began to ring.

Out in the gardens Zohreh was shivering; the wet had seeped through to her skin. She recognised the man with Piers from the television. Yes, she'd be the first to admit that to begin with it had been Piers's success that had

238

attracted her: his famous friends, television appearances and reputation. But it had grown into something far more. A tide of misery broke over her. How had she become the sort of person in such a situation? At every turning of their relationship she had behaved in a way that once she could never have imagined of herself. Relationship? There wasn't one. Yet if he cared nothing for her then why did he keep sleeping with her? The agony of his tenderness took her breath away. It couldn't be that he didn't feel the same way as her; it was because of his family. He was denying his feelings because of them. Zohreh peered into the cafe. The BBC newsman had stood up.

'So that's it,' Gav said. 'That's what I wanted to sort out. All you need to do for Sally's happiness is to tell her the truth about yourself.'

'How long has this — how long have you and Sally felt this way about each other?'

'Oh, since about two minutes after your wedding.'

'And it's *me* that's despicable?'

'Whatever. Anyway. I'm giving you twenty-four hours to tell her. Then I'll do it myself.'

'All this time, and you were supposed to be my best friend.'

'Fuck it, Guest, you have no right to deliver the emeritus lecture on fidelity. You've got until tomorrow. Then I'll tell her for certain. It's time she started living for herself.'

'When I came here I was going to do you a favour. There's a story about to break. I thought I'd let you know about it.'

'Story?' Gav's eye glittered coldly.

'Scoop of the month; maybe the year.'

'Art?'

'Yeah, but bigger than that.'

'What, like a lost Michelangelo?'

'Different map, same atlas.'

'High profile?'

'Oh, I'd say you'd definitely get a *Panorama* out of it.'

Gav's phone began to ring. 'What is it, Piers? Come on, don't you think you owe me?'

'*Owe* you?'

'Yeah.' Gav stared in distraction at the phone until the tone stopped. 'You've *got* to tell me now; you made me miss a call.'

'You've been whoring among the media tarts too long, Gav.'

'Whereas in the art world, you're all pukka chaps.' Gav's sneer bunched his features into the simian snout which had earned him his nickname back at school. 'Art world? You're a fucking salesman, Guest. A second-hand salesman. Why not go the whole hog and change your name to Swiss Tony and open up a car lot in Romford?'

Zohreh was nearly knocked down by the door when the BBC Special Correspondent thrust himself out of the Cafe in the Gardens. 'Sorry, I missed your call,' she heard him say into his phone as he strode out into the soggy Bloomsbury afternoon. She paused before going to Piers's table; it wasn't too late to turn away; but the memory of that last time under the table in the stateroom convinced her. She had to do

240

this for him as much as for herself.

Piers looked up from the BlackBerry, at whose blank screen he had been staring, to find Zohreh standing there. 'What are you doing here?' he stammered. She did not reply. 'How did you know I was here?' All at once, it hit him. How stupid he'd been! All those seemingly chance meetings, her uncanny habit of joining him in the gym or the coffee queue, her knack of sharing his lift. And now this. She must have followed him. This wasn't just infatuation. He should have left well alone when they had come back from Amsterdam. For the sake of a couple of hurried fucks, he'd . . . well, it was clear now just what he'd done. How could he have missed the signs? The rain and tears had washed away the usual patina of the young woman's make-up. Standing before him she seemed as raw and unadorned as an unfledged blackbird fallen from the nest. Before he could even begin to take in what Gav had said, he needed to get rid of Zohreh. Permanently. It was time for plan B. Piers had only ever used it once before. With a loud groan he buried his head in his hands.

'Piers! Are you all right?' Zohreh cried. His reply was a broken sob. 'What is it?'

'I can't tell you,' Piers whimpered.

''Course you can.'

'Not this.'

'What is it?'

'No, no, no, no.'

'You can tell me *anything*, Piers.' The art adviser looked up, face contorted with anguish, gulping air like a drowning man. Leaning over the table, Zohreh embraced him with such force that the sugar bowl spun giddily. 'I love you,' she said. 'I'm here for you.'

'Zohreh, it's my daughter.'

'What is it?'

Piers's bellow of anguish drew looks from the nearby tables. He'd already checked there was no one he knew. 'Mimi's not well. She's . . . sick. My lovely daughter's sick. No, no, no.' *No life! Why should a dog, a horse, a rat have life, and thou no breath at all?* the words he had delivered as King Lear to Sally's Cordelia at university popping into his mind. Seeming to gasp convulsively, Piers borrowed the clawing heart clutch he had used during that production. 'They say there's a chance she's not going to make it. Oh Zo, when I see her lying there, I feel . . . I feel . . . ' Something wet splashed onto his nose. It was a tear. Using it to his advantage he ostentatiously wiped it away. 'It's going to be months, maybe years; and even if she pulls through we'll have to give her constant care. Oh shit, shit, shit.' The last plaintive shit pealed on the air. With a moan he plunged his head into his hands. Risking a furtive glance through the webbing of his fingers, he tried to gauge her reaction. She appeared to be stunned. 'I keep on picturing her lying there so small and helpless; as though she's been run over by a train. Zohreh, I'm so, so sorry but this is going to have to be goodbye. I can't see you any more.'

Pulling himself to his feet, Piers caught his reflection in the plate-glass window. Grief creased the face interposed on the sodden

Russell Square Gardens. The last time he had seen his reflection like that was when he was ten years old, the night he had found out about his father's death. The art adviser stumbled outside. The rain was a relief; he ran through it, head tilted back, eyes still wild from the play-acting: a very Lear of Bloomsbury.

2

The tube shot through the yellow clay of London. '*I should be back tomorrow,*' Piers tapped into his BlackBerry. '*Day after that the latest. Couldn't get out of it I'm afraid. Mikey bloody Durrant's clients again! Been thinking. Let's have a holiday. Couple of weeks somewhere. Tuscany? Maybe go and stay with your mum and dad in Cumbria? Just the three of us.*' After some consideration, Piers deleted '*I have only ever loved you*'. As the train throbbed on — Leicester Square, Piccadilly Circus, Green Park — Piers pictured Sally reading this message sitting at the computer in their bedroom with the summer rain coursing down the window. Were these the only words he could send her at a time like this? Yet there was no point in meeting trouble halfway. Having recovered somewhat from the shock, he'd decided that he didn't believe Gav — wishful thinking on his part. Simian had always had a tendency to view reality through his own desires. The real danger lay in whether he would tell Sally about Zohreh. As for Zohreh, well . . . Gloucester Road, Earls Court,

West Kensington, the litany of his life. Piers allowed himself to be more forthcoming in his email to Mimi: '*I want you to know just how much I love you and your mother. You keep me going in the loony bin they call modern art! By the way, Mikey Durrant is thinking about selling helium-filled pterodactyls at his installation!! Each one £10,000!!!!!!*' Piers erased most of the exclamation marks. On *miscellany.com* he had once read that exclamation-mark saturation is often subconsciously interpreted by the receiver as insincerity. The tube roared through the suburbs: Turnham Green, Acton Town. South Ealing. Schooldays came to Piers's mind again. Boys chanting behind a line of desks: *this is the night mail crossing the border.*

★   ★   ★

At Heathrow, Piers stood beneath the twirling destinations board. He had come here instinctively. All he wanted was to be on the move; disappear while everything blew over. Things usually did. As Amsterdam flipped over on the roulette board, he recalled Maria Hertz. 'So you've got something to show me?' he said when he had got through to her.

'Piers, I knew you'd get back to us,' Maria replied.

'Well, I can't resist the smell of frying fish. Do you want to meet at the Van Gogh Museum again?'

'No, it's not in the Netherlands. Where are you?'

'Heathrow.'

'Remain there. I'll arrange everything. I'll email you the various bookings. Flights, hotels. And Piers? Get excited, get very excited.'

Sitting in the club-class lounge, Piers tried to distract himself by calling Mikey Durrant. The artist's voicemail sounded like a group of foraging cavemen attacking a woolly mammoth. 'Fuck off,' Mikey's message declared duosyllabically. Piers left an insincerely expletive message then scrolled through his mail. Maria Hertz was sending him to Switzerland. Not that he really cared where he was going. As for Sally, no news was good news. 'Espresso,' he replied to the oriental barista who had hovered until Piers looked up. It was as he was waiting for his coffee that Piers found himself thinking of his father once again. He got up. 'I'll have it later,' he said to the baffled barista.

He hastened down the retail malls but the thoughts of his father pursued him. In the Perfumerie Gallery, the air thrumming with chemical static, he saw the purple willowherb growing rampantly on the railway cutting. Piers let the colour fill his mind; like an artist he concentrated on its texture, imagining it spreading over a canvas. Usually this was enough; a way of stopping his thoughts deepening, heading them off before they could lead him to the place he had spent his life avoiding. But as he quickened into the chocolate store, mindlessly staring at the giant Toblerones, he found himself thinking of that 7.12 train to London Victoria, the one that had killed his

245

father. The body had been identified by the medical bag and clothing, and his dental records.

★ ★ ★

Landing in Basle, Piers picked up the car that Maria Hertz had booked for him. His itinerary had been preprogrammed into the satnav. It took him north. As he crossed the border into Germany, after lying dormant for weeks the tooth he had snagged that day on Zohreh's nipple ring began to twinge again. With a swig of bottled water he washed down some aspirins. He'd never been to the Black Forest before; he had a brief, splendid view of the Rhine then for the rest of his journey the trees seemed to crowd in on him, as though shuffling right to the edge of the road, the odd branch shouldering the windscreen. At last he reached the city of his destination. Pulling the car over, he checked his emails. Nothing from Sally. The half-sob of relief escaping his lips surprised him. Two psychological factors were at work here, he figured. Firstly, Sally was the sort of person who would contact him the moment someone accused him of anything; secondly, if Gav *was* going to tell her he would have done it straight away. Among his regular art-world emails was one from Zohreh. He scanned the long, heart-felt message, then, finding the all-important information — she'd taken the bait — he deleted it. One less problem to deal with. Having got up Gav's address Piers typed a message offering reconciliation, hinting at the stress Gav was under, and that words spoken in haste between friends can be forgotten. With a flush of gambler's optimism, Piers clicked on *send*. If it turned out that what Gav had said *was* true then nothing Piers could do would make it worse anyway. It wasn't long before he found the little art gallery. He was expected. 'I will drive you there,' said his contact, a woman who seemed to own the gallery. 'The roads in that part of the mountain are not for the faint-hearted.'

'Mountain?'

'Yes, that is where I am to take you.' Her sing-song German-English made Piers think of the war films he had watched as a boy in which the stupidity of the Nazis jostled with their greed. He had to force himself not to smile. 'As the English say, we must go to the back of beyond.'

The smooth Audi climbed and plunged its way round the sharp hairpin bends. Once again the trees seemed endless, beeches then pines and finally impenetrable firs: a fairy-tale landscape. He closed his eyes. He hadn't eaten since breakfast at home with Sally, but felt no hunger. 'This is an area very famous for cuckoo clocks,' the woman told him.

'I thought that was Switzerland.'

Her lips tightened. 'A common mistake. Cuckoo clocks are very much of the Schwarzwald. Of course these days the old craftsmen are fewer. Where we are going is near to the birthplace of our greatest local clockmaker. But surely you have heard of Rosenbaum's cuckoo clocks?'

'Oh yes, of course,' Piers lied. The plush

upholstery of the Audi cushioned him from the worst of the bumps as the car slowed to less than walking pace. When he looked out of the window he saw a sheer drop falling away from the side of the road. 'You weren't joking.'

'What do you mean?'

'It's not for the faint-hearted.'

'Before the war a Gestapo car plunged down from this bend, killing both occupants.'

'Gosh.'

'Gosh? Yes; gosh. It was the dead of night; they were following a doctor — so the tale goes.'

Whether it was the aspirin he'd taken reacting with the flight drinks or his rising hope that the double shock sustained in the Cafe in the Gardens was nothing but a storm in an espresso cup, Piers felt almost euphoric. 'The Gestapo? Nasty.'

'He was a great hero. They say he treated many people against the wishes of the Nazis. Of course they caught up with him eventually.'

Through the air conditioning the scent of resin was entering the car. On the road a chamois bounded out in front of them. Settling back, Piers wondered where he was being taken. He'd hardly given it a second thought. It was a wild goose chase of course. Yet what if it *was* a Van Gogh? Crazy and impossible as it sounded what if he was being whisked into these mountains and trees to be shown a masterpiece by Vincent Van Gogh? After all, Maria Hertz was no fool. He smiled cynically. It was more likely that Mikey Durrant would one day be considered an old master.

He had lost track of how long they'd been driving when the woman pulled the car onto the side of the road. 'From here we must walk.' The slamming of the Audi doors echoed through the ranks of trees lifting from the path. 'Even in the Schwarzwald there are not many places like Keilburg left. Not even Hitler could get an autobahn up here.' Some unseen animal bolted in the undergrowth. The woman walked very quickly. Piers tried to hide his growing breathlessness. 'If you want I can telephone the vendor. He offered to come for you with a quad bike.'

'Not at all, I like the walk. I'm just a bit tired. Such beautiful scenery. It's like following in the footsteps of the Brothers Grimm.'

A bird plunged into the firs. 'A nutcracker, Herr Guest; now you can say we really *are* in the heart of the Schwarzwald.'

'Do you make nutcracker clocks as well?'

His guide did not return his smile. 'No, they lack the pleasing vocal of the cuckoo.'

They were still in the trees when the whine of a power tool rang out. 'Like a wolf,' Piers said. 'You know, in *Little Red Riding Hood*.'

'You are fond of children's stories?'

'I used to read them to my daughter. She loved *The Musicians of Bremen*. The one with a donkey. Do you have wolves here?'

'They are coming back; ask the vendor what he thinks of them.'

'Who is he?'

'An artisan; forgive me, a real Schwarzwald peasant; he knows nothing about fine art.'

'So where did he get the picture from?'

'I understand he was cleaning out an old loft.'

They crossed a stream, mountain cold and crystal clear, and passed through a particularly thick belt of ancient firs. Even though it was the height of summer the air here still felt damp; tiers of brightly coloured toadstools studded the steep slope like the sweets on the walls of a candy house. It was late afternoon but already night was pooling in the forest.

When they reached the top of a little hill, Piers checked his BlackBerry again. Now there was a message from Sally. He felt his eyes twitch as he quickly scrolled it down. It was an answer to his earlier message: *Yes, let's. Holiday just what we all need.* His breath still jerky from the ascent, Piers exhaled. If he could get out of this scrape he would never risk losing Sally and Mimi again. Piers typed: *Remember how we always used to talk about opening a gallery in Cumbria? What think you?*

'Welcome to Keilburg,' the woman said. The art adviser looked up to see a little valley spreading below his feet. At the far side there was a pond and a huge chalet-type building whose thatched roof formed a steep apex. 'Perhaps the finest example of a traditional *Schwarzwaldhaus* in our part of the Black Forest,' his guide explained. 'There are not many like this now with the thatching and balconies. It is an old mill house. Of course, to see it in its full glory you would have to return. The vendor has erected scaffolding; he is renovating it.'

'What's he called?'

'Herr Mann. I apologise for bringing you out here, but it was a stipulation. Some mountain people can be a little strange.'

'My wife's from Cumbria,' Piers said. 'Near the Lake District.'

'Then you will know.'

Piers only saw the little girl watching them from behind a giant fir when she broke cover. Barefoot, she sprinted down the path into the valley before them. They followed. On the pond, the lily pads were out in white bloom. Overhead a pair of storks slowly circled. When the little girl reached the house, the power tool stopped. The sudden silence was immense. From the scaffolding a man was waving. 'That must be Herr Mann,' the woman said.

Piers watched the slight, almost childlike figure clambering gracefully down the tiers of scaffolding. When Herr Mann reached them he was grinning. The dust clung to his eyebrows and ginger hair. Piers shook his hand; the grip was surprisingly light. 'I'm sorry,' Piers said after the builder had talked to him for about a minute. 'I don't understand a word.' He turned to the woman. 'I speak a little German but — '

The gallery owner laughed. 'This is Alemannic. It is the local dialect. He has welcomed you and told you that his daughter has gone to tell her we are here.'

'Tell who?' Piers asked.

The gallery owner and Herr Mann talked for a while. The woman nodded. 'Now I see. He is not the vendor.'

'Who is?'

251

'His aunt. This is her house. She is called Lotte Mann. Should there be any transaction you will require her signature.'

As they waited, Piers checked his emails. Mimi had sent a picture of the new phone she wanted, and lots of kisses. Piers counted them. There were twenty. But before he could send his reply, the signal had gone dead.

'Ah yes,' said the guide. 'Hitler could not get his autobahns to Keilburg, and we can't get our mobile phones.'

3

Although the child barely made a sound climbing the stairs, Lotte heard her coming as surely as if the little girl was calling out to her. Nothing could stir in the old wooden house without her hearing, and when the middle rung of the loft ladder creaked, she turned, ready to greet the little one with a smile. The child grinned back: how was it that Omi always heard her coming? The little girl gestured with a finger, telling Lotte what she already knew. The strangers had arrived.

The storks had been the first to alert the old woman. The pair had risen abruptly from the marshy ground close to where the path leaves the road. Only strangers on the track could have made them circle the valley like that; if they'd caught a frog or a newt the birds would have brought it straight to their nest. Sitting on the bench in front of the house, her nephew's power drill wailing, Lotte had then seen the little girl running. A minute later, the strangers had come into view and with them the moment for which she had been waiting for decades. Finally the time had come to say goodbye.

The girl buried herself in the old woman's arms. There'd always been a special bond between them. They'd named the child after Helga, Lotte's mother. But *this* Helga Mann would never have the heart ripped out of her. *I tried to creep up on you*, Little Helga giggled with a barely discernible lift of her thumb.

I heard you, Lotte replied with a silent finger.

You hear everything, Omi.

The house tells me. Lotte looked at the child. Who could have thought something so beautiful would grow on such scorched earth? She was a flower blooming on a grave. Today, more than ever, Little Helga's resemblance to Lotte's lost father was striking. Not just to look at; she too went around Keilburg barefooted. Well, that was fitting. Reaching up, the child touched the mark on the old woman's lip, the wasp sting; Lotte reached down and did the same to the little girl's mark. It was their most intimate way of saying *I love you*. Even before Little Helga had been born Lotte knew the child would share her mark.

Strange voices began to whisper in the loft rafters. The outsiders had entered the house. Lotte breathed in deeply; the little girl did the same; both savouring the aroma of apples, nuts and the other produce stored there. But something was different today. The child looked around. The trunk was open! Padlock and chain, over which her fingers had speculated endlessly, lay spilt on the floor. For as long as she could remember, Little Helga had wondered what Omi stored inside the trunk she kept so carefully locked in the old house's loft. Omi — Little Helga called her that although of course she wasn't her real granny but her great-aunt. *Hasenscharten-Omi*: Granny Harelip. Seeing the direction of the child's gaze, Lotte nodded. *Yes, her eyes murmured, today I have opened the trunk.*

The smell of naphtha greeted Lotte as it always did as she leant over the trunk; through the years the scent had become so deeply linked to Papa in her heart that now she had to remind herself it had nothing to do with him; it was just a side effect of memory. For the last time, she reached inside her father's chest to bring out the photograph. Lotte's Mama, the first Helga Mann, had always believed she had destroyed all the pictures of her husband, but one had escaped her, and here it lay on the palm of the old woman's hand: torn and brittle through long years of handling, faded and curled like a leaf from an old October. The sight of it filled Lotte's heart with countless memories: Papa racing her round the millpond on the donkey's back; Papa swinging her high on the Kaiser beech; Papa sitting her on his knee and reading her his endless stories. Stories. Always stories. How good it was to remember these times, to peer through this little window and look at the lost world. But she must not even keep this photograph; *everything* had to go. The second object she took from the chest was *The Musicians of Keilburg*. She flicked through the book Papa had written for her. At the bottom of the page Frau Longears came brilliantly to life. Although she had seen it so many times, Lotte gasped at the magic of the thumb-cinema.

The old woman paused. Behind her, she could hear Little Helga's curiosity: a pursing of the lips, a hand playing with the skirt of her dress, her foot lightly tapping. Should she show her what was in the chest; reveal what had been hidden for so long before it was gone for good? Yet what could she tell her about it; how could she say what she really wanted to express? *This is my Papa, he was a man not a monster.* Even in the wide vocabulary of her hands and face, a language the child had picked up effortlessly, there were not the words to express the inexpressible. Still, the little girl might like the book. No need for her to know the tragedy behind the antics of Frau Longears. The story of a musical donkey stands on its own.

Beckoned, Little Helga came forward uncertainly. Omi was holding out a book. There was a donkey on the cover. *It's yours*, a lift of the old woman's finger told her. The same finger opened the book and quickly flicked through the pages. The donkey came to life! The child's sudden laughter rang through the loft. Lotte watched the mark on the little girl's lip dance. There *was* progress in the world after all. Little Helga's affliction had been totally healed; she could talk with only the merest hint of the cleaving. *Her* life would not be that of a mute. Lotte kissed the top of her head. After all these years Frau Longears was playing to the laughter of a child again. The old woman breathed in the scent of her great-niece's hair, her brother Gustav's granddaughter: fresh and lovely as a fir sapling — oh, may she grow healthy and strong! Here, where she had spent so many hours playing 'apples and pears' when she was a child this age, here where she knew every smell, was a new scent: the scent of the future. She was right to say goodbye to the dead. Life *was* going on untainted in this little girl. The last of the dandelion spores fell from the pages of *The Musicians of Keilburg* and fanned out over the loft. Let them go. Let everything go. Taking out the hat with the long feathered plume, Lotte placed it on the child's head.

Both barefoot, the child followed Omi down the loft ladder and then the stairs.

Taking her by the hand the old woman went to the kitchen to prepare drinks for the strangers. Little Helga gazed at her in amazement: *Hasenscharten-Omi* never met strangers. Lotte's nephew too was so surprised to see his aunt come into the room bearing a tray of drinks that he stopped in mid-sentence. He'd been explaining to the Englishman, through the woman from the gallery, how hard it was to renovate old properties like this; where, for instance, could you find seasoned sweet chestnut to replace the floorboards without paying an arm and a leg? Having set the tray down, Lotte's hand flurried expressively. Although Herr Mann didn't speak his aunt's silent language as well as his daughter, he knew what she was telling him. He gestured for the guests to sit down at the table.

'No thank you,' Piers said as a glass of red liquid was offered him. Blank faces met his refusal. 'I've been taking aspirin.' He looked at the gallery owner. 'I'm on medication.'

'It's a local tradition,' she replied. 'I think you're expected to drink.'

Herr Mann downed his *Blutwurz* in one; Piers copied him. It burnt his throat, but wasn't unpleasant. He did not complain when the old woman refilled his glass. From somewhere deep within the house the mechanism of a cuckoo clock began to whirr, followed by the cuckoo calls. Through the window Piers could see the lake; it was about the size of a Cumbrian tarn. He thought of the message he had sent Sally. Why *not* leave the rat race; why not go to Cumbria or somewhere like it and open a gallery? He looked at the little girl hiding behind the old woman, holding her apron string and wearing a hat with a plume. Under her arm was tucked a little book. As the alcohol suffused its pleasant glow through him, Piers smiled at the child. Perhaps this business with Gav and Zohreh had been timely, giving him the jolt he needed.

As she mounted the stairs once more Lotte already felt lighter. But it wasn't just a matter for her alone. She must consult her brothers. From the threshold of her bedroom, she gazed at the three beds. One was her own in which she had slept every night since leaving her cradle, apart from those weeks at the end of the war when

Mama had taken them across Germany. The other beds belonged to her brothers, Peterli and Gusti. Peter's presence was the faintest. He had left Keilburg while still a boy. Lotte felt Gusti much more keenly. Not only had he remained at Keilburg until qualifying as a doctor, he had come back to it again at the end of his life when the cancer was already too widespread to operate: brother and sister sharing their bedroom once more. Gustav's colleagues had given him weeks to live; he had managed five months, largely pain-free until the last days. Some recompense for their lives. Good, kind Gustav, tireless doctor and gentle husband and father; what a pity he had died before his granddaughter, Little Helga, had been born. Still, at least he had known life, unlike their brother Peter.

Peter. Peterli. Even his name had grown strange. She could barely picture him sleeping here. What sounds did he make in the night; what did he look like? No photographs of their lost brother remained, although twice since the war Lotte had dreamt of him. Once when the Berlin Wall was being put up, and then again when it came clattering down; on each occasion she had woken with such a vivid sense of him that he might still be lying in that unoccupied bed. It was apt that those were the two occasions of his visiting, for his body lay somewhere beneath the stone and concrete of Berlin. And with him lay her voice: the very last words Lotte had spoken had been to Peter.

Gusti, Peterli, she whispered with a finger, edging into the room. *I am saying goodbye to*

Papa today. Lotte was concentrating on the past so strongly that this time she did not hear the child until she saw her running across the floor. She gasped with the wonder of the shock. The little girl was like a sunbeam flowing through a door opened for the first time in years. *Look at me, Omi*, little Helga's fingers cried, *look at me!*

It was Little Helga's favourite room in the house. There were three beds just like in the story of Goldilocks and the three bears; and just like Goldilocks she loved to try each one in turn, jumping from one to the other. Omi never told her off. Little Helga loved coming out to Keilburg with her father. It was a place of fun and light. Here there was a different set of rules. Not just about jumping on beds. Because of this Little Helga was not surprised when Omi crept under one of the beds and beckoned her to follow.

As they slid underneath, Omi took her by the hand and guided her fingers to a hole in the floorboard, a little eye of light. *Look,* she whispered with the gentlest of touches to the child's brow. Little Helga found herself peering down onto the living room. How funny to see it from up here! The strangers were sitting round the pine table with her father. 'Yes; it was all by accident,' Little Helga's father was saying, his hands smoothing the polished grain of the wood. 'I've been going on about the state of the house for years then at last, out of the blue, Auntie gives me the go-ahead. Anyway, there I am in the loft banging away when I hear something hollow. Hello, I say to myself, this isn't an outside wall.

And sure enough it was just a partition.' Little Helga looked at the strange man. Why did he keep on touching one of his teeth; lifting the lip like Omi's donkey? 'This house is hundreds of years old,' her father continued. 'Should get a good price when the time comes. The miller kept his flour up in the loft, away from the rats. So the floorboards are as strong as gold blocks. Seasoned chestnut again. It could easily be another bedroom. I don't know what the old miller was keeping in his cubbyhole. Maybe it was for his moneybags when the tax inspector rode round. You know what those peasants are like for hoarding. Anyway, I took the partition out and there was this old trunk. And in it, the picture. The trunk itself is magnificent; I'm going to keep my tools in it. You know, it's probably a hundred years old. The picture looks like a load of rubbish to me; a dog's dinner; but you never know; you hear the oddest stories of such things being worth money.'

When Little Helga looked up from the knothole, she realised Omi was no longer under the bed with her. The girl watched the man from England drink another glass of *Blutwurz* then she came out from under the bed. Omi was standing at the window beside the vase of gentians that they had gathered together. The flowers were bluer than the sky. Was that the sound of Omi weeping, or the storks calling hungrily in their nest? The old woman sat at her dressing table; the girl came over and picked up the old pearl-backed hairbrush. The skeins of Omi's hair had long since faded to grey but as

Little Helga unpinned them they fell over her shoulders in a brief flash of red. It was at this moment, in the stillness of the old house, that the child began to fathom one of life's greatest mysteries: Omi had once had hair like hers. Now only the rust remained but this old, kind, playful woman, her *Hasenscharten-Omi*, had once been a little girl too! Helga's father said that Omi didn't speak because of what had happened to her as a girl; in those days they hadn't been able to heal the lip and mouth so well. Stiff bristles crackling lightly, the child pulled the brush through the tangles. Soft but supple, the old strands reminded her of the spiderwebs she had loved to feel breaking against her face in the loft before her father had ripped out the cavity. Why did Omi let him do that when they had played there together so many times? It made things in the loft seem different somehow; as though a secret had been told, or a spell broken. Then there was the way the old woman had greeted the strangers, normally she disappeared into the loft quick as a sparrow whenever anyone came down the long path. She was being quieter than usual too; Omi's fingers usually played ceaselessly, joking and laughing. Raising herself on tiptoes Helga glanced over the old woman's shoulder. No wonder *Hasenscharten-Omi's* hands were so mute. They were holding a photograph. Having brushed through a stubborn tangle, the child looked again. The photograph was gone. Later, she would often puzzle over the picture of the Nazi Omi had held the day she died.

4

When Piers's foot slipped on the ladder, he
wondered whether three glasses of the local
gut-rot had been such a good idea after all. His
chin jammed against the lip of the loft, and a
sharp pain lanced the cocoon of aspirin and
alcohol. From the kitchen downstairs, he could
hear the voices of Herr Mann and the gallery
owner talking. At the foot of the ladder, in the
shadows, the little girl stood watching him. The
old woman was waiting in the loft above. As he
boosted himself into the attic her hands seemed
to swoop at him like a bird. He followed her
beckoning gesture, ducking beneath the rafters.
What the hell was he doing here? The moment
he was finished he'd go home. They could be in
Cumbria this time tomorrow. The old woman
showed him a large trunk, and still without
speaking made it clear he was to reach within.
Deeper than a coffin, its wooden slats were black
with age. He reached inside. There was only one
thing within: a long thin object rolled like a rug.
The first touch of the cold, slightly clammy
material told him what it was. When he'd
brought out the canvas Piers turned to the old
woman. Nodding, she kindled a lantern and held
it out for him. He knelt and unrolled the picture
across the globe of lit floor with some
impatience. Why couldn't Maria have simply
sent him a photo? Even in the half-light, Piers
could instantly see the composition: a garden in
spring. He could also instantly see the relation it
bore to the gardens of Vincent Van Gogh's

Auvers period. The same white house, lush garden, golden laburnum tree, green gate, black cat; even the roofs of the church and town hall peered over the garden as they did in the masterpieces like neighbours not on speaking terms. If only forgers could show more imagination. Searching for the telltale signs of fakery he felt a sudden surge of adrenaline. There weren't any.

Blinking against the sudden swimming of his vision, the art adviser took the lantern and travelled it the length of the canvas. What had he been expecting? Certainly nothing like this. Most forgeries give themselves away instantly: a mumbled blunder, a garish shout, an entirely wrong accent. This one was as silent as the old woman watching him so intently from the shadows. Stooping even lower so that his nose could feel the sheen of the old paint, Piers gazed. He still couldn't spot the note of inauthenticity. Surely it couldn't be genuine after all; surely he couldn't be looking at the handiwork of one of the world's greatest painters? No; of course he couldn't. At that moment the attic was filled with a weird whispering. Piers looked up to see the old woman laughing to herself. The art adviser tried to keep his voice as calm as possible. 'Can I look at this downstairs, in the light?' Clumsily he mimed his meaning. Pointing up at the sound of the storks on the roof, she laughed silently. *Dementia*, Piers thought, his mind quickly turning over any legal implications in the event of a transaction.

When the foreigner had descended the ladder,

Lotte went back over to the trunk. The child had the book — that was right and proper — and the hat too; and the Englishman had the picture — whatever money it realised her nephew was free to keep, he could also have the chest itself, for those tools of his. As for the letters and photographs, tonight, alone again, she would burn them. She brought the letters out now. Two were still unopened: the ones addressed to Peter and their mother; well, they would remain forever unread. For a moment she was filled with the desire to open them, but it passed. Why bother the dead? Gustav had only opened his on his deathbed. And then he had wept. Lifting the lid of the trunk in order to close it forever, Lotte paused. As she stood there in the familiar half-darkness, she recalled the day she had brought the chest back from the university. It was after the death of Uncle Dietrich, who had been assembling Papa's archive. She had found it in a cellar with the rest of the documentation. From all the many pieces stored in that dank hole, she chose only the personal things, placing in the trunk letters, photographs, souvenirs from his travels, *The Musicians of Keilburg* and some of his other stories. It was when she had got the chest back home that she discovered its secret cavity, and the two things concealed there, one so ugly, the other supremely beautiful: the black uniform and the painting of the beautiful garden, whose colours had brightened the world at its darkest time. Lotte shuddered at the memory of the first time she had seen the picture. It had been right at the end of the war when instead of fleeing like the rest of Germany, they were heading towards the invading Red Army.

Having closed the lid of the chest and locked it, Lotte Mann lifted her thumb and forefinger delicately to her mouth and blew as though telling the hours of a dandelion clock.

★　★　★

Downstairs, Piers had washed his hands meticulously, and was placing the canvas on the scrubbed pine table. 'Can you tell them to put the lights on?' he asked the woman from the gallery, disguising the excitement in his voice. 'Every lamp, light, torch, everything they've got in the house.'

'You like what you see?'

'I don't know.'

With great care he unrolled the canvas over the tabletop. Closing his eyes he waited for the swirling sensation to pass. He definitely shouldn't have drunk so much alcohol on top of the medication. His judgement had to be watertight. He was tired too after that business with Gav and Zohreh; he'd been on the go for hours. Yet when Herr Mann brought over a lamp and switched it on, the art adviser's weariness fell away. In the fuller light the foliage seemed even more verdant. Piers was looking at an explosion of spring; a garden of Eden for Northern Europe, where spring ends winter not by burning it with the heat of the sun but by healing it with lengthening light and soft sunshine. Where was the error that revealed this as a clever fake? It *must* be somewhere. His pulse drumming, Piers searched the garden for the flaw but his fingers were tingling as though he was handling a holy relic. Beneath the burning bush of a laburnum an artist stood at his easel. Blunt-headed, rufous-bearded, he was hunched over his easel like a blacksmith at his anvil. It could only be Vincent himself! *Where the fuck was the bloody forger's thumbprint?* Heart beating in his ears, Piers lifted up the picture delicately and looked at the back. He turned it over once more then burst into laughter.

'It is funny?' the gallery owner asked.

'Well, I'm almost entirely certain that this is a Georgiana Fairbanks. She often signed the back of her pieces.' Piers looked at the canvas more calmly. It was clearly from early in her career. But why was it so similar to Van Gogh's Auvers oeuvre; and why should the figure of the artist at the easel be so similar to the Dutchman: blue jacket, boots, straw hat? Fairbanks was never one for such coded references.

'When Maria Hertz said you were coming personally, I must say I was a little surprised,' the gallery owner said. 'The market for Georgiana Fairbanks may be bigger in Britain and America than here, but even that is not large. Yet you clearly love her work. Now I understand why you insisted on coming here personally. I can see you have the genuine collector's passion.'

'Yes,' said Piers vacantly. 'Would you excuse me for a moment?'

As Piers stepped outside, the late-afternoon

sun struck his eyes. Some bean plants were growing in a wooden trough behind the bench; Sally grew them like that. The water of the millpond glimmered. How perfect a place for a little gallery this would be. There was still no signal. He strode up the hill that rose behind the house. The BlackBerry beeped in response. He couldn't wait any longer; the need to speak to Sally had become a physical urge. But he reached only her voicemail. He told her about the Georgiana Fairbanks. 'And by the way,' he concluded, 'I'm serious about the gallery. I think we should do it now.'

He was still standing there looking over the lake when his phone rang back. 'Sally, I — '

'Did you like it then?' a voice asked. It took Piers a few seconds to recognise it.

'Is it some sort of joke, Maria?'

'I've booked you into the hotel airport for tonight. There's something else I want to show you.'

'I'm going home.'

'The Georgiana Fairbanks is yours, Piers. A tiddler for your net. But you wouldn't believe the size of fish I'm frying here. And it just happens to be a Dutch fish. It's time for you to see the real thing, Piers.'

5

Maria Hertz was sitting under the row of tropical fish tanks in the foyer of the airport hotel when Piers walked in. 'Maria, I meant what I said;

you've got ten minutes.'

'I'm not going to need that long.'

As he followed her down the carpeted corridor he nursed his jaw. He had taken more painkillers but the jolt in the loft rim had set his tooth throbbing like a marching band. At the gift shop, a thickset man dressed in black left the postcard stand he was revolving and came after them. He wore an earpiece. 'Brought your own personal bodyguard along, Maria?'

'The insurance people provided the security team.'

Inside the conference room, the man with the earpiece checked under the table and around the light fittings, he studied the waste-paper bin and the blinds. Two security guards brought in a large metal case. 'Have I walked onto a film set?' Piers asked.

'You know, I think Hollywood *would* like this story.' The security team withdrew and Maria Hertz punched a code into the lock of the case. 'Maria Hertz,' she said into the voice activator. There was a click.

'Welcome to Fort Knox,' said Piers. 'You've got eight minutes left.'

Maria brought out a transparent container. 'Item one. Newly discovered letter by Vincent Van Gogh, dated late July 1890, Auvers-sur-Oise. You've seen this already, Piers. Let me just say that further tests have now made us as confident as we can be that it *is* indeed the artist's last letter. Now look at this.' She brought out a second box; just as flat but larger. Piers found himself considering a rough sketch of people gathered round a lunch table; one of the figures was recognisably Dr Gachet, another seemed to bear more than a passing resemblance to Georgiana Fairbanks. 'Item two, drawing on linen, probably a tablecloth. By Vincent Van Gogh. The sketch is referred to in the letter above. Item three.' Her eyes inscrutable behind dark glasses, Maria Hertz brought out a third, much larger flat box. 'Untitled canvas by Vincent Van Gogh, dated between May and July 1890. Also referred to in the letter.'

It was a garden scene, the same one that Piers had seen earlier in the day. The same place, anyway, but everything else was different: the brushstrokes, the combinations of colours, the dizzying fluidity. Whereas Georgiana Fairbanks had captured a garden in spring, this piece had captured spring in a garden. Piers was looking at nature itself caught in the very act of creation. Neither of them spoke for a full five minutes. 'You've got authentication?' Piers heard himself mumble at last.

'Exhaustive. To start with generalities. Note the unusual canvas size: twice as long as it is wide. The very dimensions Vincent Van Gogh utilised in Auvers-sur-Oise. Note also the weave. Most importantly perhaps, observe the reverse of the canvas. Do you see those marks? Identical to those on other Van Gogh canvases, made of course by his home-made stretcher.'

'Van Gogh's fingerprints.'

'You are familiar with the quotation? Well, yes, his idiosyncratic canvas stretchers certainly leave unique physical indentations.' Maria turned the

269

picture over so that once again Piers was confronted by the blinding green beauty. 'Other generalities. You will note the lack of cracks, the so-called craquelure, which are the hallmark of so many forgeries; a physical blemish resulting from the habit of copyists stacking their work while still wet in the manner of Van Gogh. There is no layering either; by his time in Auvers Van Gogh had reached the stage of being able to apply his paint all in one go. Notice also the — ' Maria Hertz broke off. 'But since you are so pressed for time let's cut to the chase. The specifics.' She brought out a bound document from a briefcase. 'These are the findings of our exhaustive scientific report.' He recognised the name of the laboratory. Its credentials were impeccable; each member of the group of chemists and physicists was a recognised expert in their field; Piers had used them when making his own film about the artist. 'In sum,' Maria continued, 'the report concludes that this canvas fulfils all the strict chemical and physical criteria of belonging in the oeuvre of Vincent Van Gogh's last period. It's long and exhaustive, and you are more than welcome to study it fully, but now perhaps I shall just flag the salient points. Maybe we should sit down.' Piers made no move to sit, but continued to stare at the canvas. 'I turn to page 45,' said Maria Hertz leafing through the report. 'Can you see the heading: 'Results of the SEM-EDX Process'? SEM-EDX stands for scanning electron microscope; it's the latest development of the microfluorescence procedure.'

Piers's voice was a whisper. 'I know what SEM-EDX is.'

'Naturally; an examination of the paints under the highest possible magnification. Allow me to read their conclusion on page 278: '*The results of our SEM-EDX process proves that the characteristics and proportions of the ingredients of the grounds of the paints used in this canvas are identical to those on Vincent Van Gogh's Auvers palette. Both the spectral and texture SIMS analysis prove beyond question that this is a work created from the exact make of paints favoured by Van Gogh in the last weeks of his life.*' Put into simple words, the paint on the canvas in question was squeezed from the same kind of tube as all the authenticated Van Gogh pieces from the Auvers-sur-Oise period. Figure 20 on page 28 is a diagram proving the diagnostic identity of the common binding oil medium. Figure 25 on page 40 shows the common organic compound geranium blue, that most democratic of blues, cheap but vivid. Incidentally, it's unlikely that a forger painting before recent scientific developments, say up until the past two or three years, would know to use geranium blue; and as I'm sure you're aware all serious forgeries of Van Gogh's work date back to the early years of the century. I'm referring to such people as Otto Wacker or the Schufenegers. We can deal with all of these matters in greater detail, but now let me just also indicate page 61, figure 26, which shows the results of chemical analysis; it states that the organic red we know Vincent Van Gogh used is used also on this canvas. Page 87, figure 27 depicts the aluminium emulsion lake mixed with lead, a potentially deadly cocktail much used by the Dutchman and also on our painting — '

'Wait, wait.' Piers sat down.

'I know,' Maria Hertz said. 'It's a shock. We've all dreamt of this moment. It's like a Catholic getting to meet the Virgin Mary at last.' She poured him a cup of water from the cooler. Piers drained it at a gulp; she poured him another. 'You follow so far?' He nodded. 'Now, this is even more interesting. Through advanced micro imaging we have been able to chart the deterioration of chrome-yellow pigments in all authenticated Van Gogh pictures of Auvers and match them against this one. What did we find out? Figure 28 on page 134 shows that our piece has aged at the same rate: it was painted at the same time Van Gogh was creating his Auvers pieces!' She looked at Piers. 'You feel the thunderbolt?'

Dazed, Piers thumbed through the report; its stark diagrams and figures seemed like the shapes of a contemporary artwork. The words lost their meaning: . . . *paint grounds . . . coarsely chopped and poorly sorted lead white in linseed oil . . . mixed with finely divided gypsum . . . some of the smallest particles found have been identified as earth pigment, clay . . .* '

'You can examine all the evidence as fully as you wish; the basic point of the report is that beyond all doubt this piece was painted with the colours that Vincent Van Gogh used.'

Fighting against the sense of awe building up

in him, Piers shook his head. 'Maria, let's be charitable; even the best laboratories can make mistakes. Especially when large amounts of money are involved.'

Maria Hertz produced another great dossier. 'This is the work of a second independent laboratory.' Once again Piers recognised the name on the bound document. 'This report is even longer than the first. It comes to exactly three hundred pages. Its findings are identical, although it also throws up a few interesting vignettes of its own. For example, look at page 198.' Leaning over, Maria flipped through the computer-printed sheets and Piers found himself looking at what seemed to be a monster. 'This is a magnification of the bacteria that the laboratory found on the canvas. Very painful; apparently it's from a fully blown abscess on the gum. As you know, he didn't have many teeth by then. Maybe what we're looking at is the death throes of Vincent Van Gogh's last tooth. For your interest, there's the string of his DNA on page 220.'

'You could have stumbled on something there,' said Piers. 'A new theory for his suicide. He couldn't bear the pain so he shot himself.'

'So, you're recovering your humour after the shock? Good. Actually, some of what has been found might cast a new light on his death. But the question for now is this: Is *Spring Garden in Auvers* a genuine Vincent Van Gogh? To quote one of your top British authors, if it looks like a duck and quacks like a duck then we must be prepared for the fact that it is indeed a pretty bird of the aquatic kind.'

Piers drank down another beaker of water. The chill lanced his gum. 'And now you come to the difficult part.'

'The provenance? Of course. Well, let's deal with that now. The history of the artwork as a separate entity from its creator Vincent Van Gogh.'

'*Possible* creator.'

Maria touched a key on her laptop. 'I've been working on this for two years now. You mentioned a Hollywood film? Believe me, that's *nothing* on this.'

'You're giving me a PowerPoint presentation?'

'I agree, rather prosaic, isn't it?' An image of the painting appeared on the screen set against the wall. Superimposed on the projection of the garden were the words: *The incredible life of a secret masterpiece: the provenance of Vincent Van Gogh's Spring Garden in Auvers.*

Piers got up. 'Maria,' he said, 'I think you can save yourself the trouble of going through all this.'

'I may?'

'By answering this simple question. Did this painting come from the same source as the Georgiana Fairbanks I've just seen?'

'Originally, but that in itself is a long story.'

'I see.' Piers strode to the door.

'Where are you going?'

'Your ten minutes are up.'

Maria lifted her shades in amazement. 'You're walking out on an undiscovered masterpiece by Vincent van Gogh?'

'You said that you'd been working on this for two years? Well, Maria, I'm sorry to be the one to have to tell you this, but you've been wasting your time.'

'Excuse me?'

'You might as well have been pissing in the wind.'

'Pissing in the wind; what is this, more British irony?'

'Irony? No, nothing could be less ironical. Thank God I never cashed that cheque. You can get all the scientific proof in the world, Gregor Mendel, Albert Einstein, Stephen bloody Hawking, and they'd mean nothing. You see, there's a huge tear in this canvas about the size of a jackboot. What's going on, Maria?'

'What's going on is the remarkable discovery of a new addition to the Vincent Van Gogh oeuvre.'

'Cut the crap. You've just sent me on a day trip to a loft in an old German house. Now a loft in an old German house is about as reputable a place for a work of art as Eva Braun's boudoir. Old master plus old German loft equals 99 per cent chance of swastika. You know that as well as I do. So I repeat: what's going on?'

'And I repeat: what's going on is — '

'What the fuck are you trying to get me mixed up in here?' Piers voice rattled in the room.

'The renowned Guest charm is flagging somewhat, Piers.'

'That tends to happen when someone's trying to get you to be part of an illegal piece of Nazi theft.'

Maria touched her laptop. 'Look at the screen. You may recognise the home page of the Loot List, the internationally respected body that monitors works of art stolen during the Second World War. Let's enter the relevant information.' Piers stared blankly at the screen as Maria rattled the detail of the picture into the laptop. 'No match.' Maria scrolled slowly through the list of missing pieces of Impressionist and Post-Impressionist art. 'As you see, there is no mention of this piece as missing or lost. We've searched thoroughly. There is no record anywhere of previous ownership of the artwork provisionally titled *Spring Garden in Auvers*. Nothing approximating to it; nothing — '

'I'm really beginning to wonder about you, Maria. Either you're stupid or you're . . . Even if you can put the morality to one side for a moment, there's another factor here: you'll never find a buyer. It takes years to prove the validity of even squeaky-clean artworks. With something like this any potential buyer is likely to be involved in a court case that will make Jarndyce and Jarndyce look like a bubble of brevity. As far as the market's concerned it won't even exist. Look, why do you think everyone's so keen to push modern art: because it's so good? You really think that sharks in fucking formaldehyde or menstruating knickers represent any great insights into the human spirit? We push modern art because there's no chance of it being soiled by Hitler and Himmler. Everyone knows that most of it's a pile of complete crap but it's the only safe way of making money out of paintings.

If you deal in anything pre-war the lawyers will pick your bones. Modern art has one virtue: it's a stable currency.'

'Mikey Durrant too?'

'What the hell has Mikey Durrant got to do with this?'

'Is Mikey Durrant also a pile of complete crap? In your programmes you compare Mikey Durrant to Rembrandt.'

Piers snorted in frustration. 'Mikey Durrant is a complete muppet. Actually, he's worse than that. He's the head muppet. In fact, he's the arch-druid of all muppets. The fucking Reichs-führer of muppets.'

'Your opinion of the rest of contemporary art is that low?'

'I wouldn't wipe my arse with most of the stuff I sell.'

'A strange thing for one of the most important dealers in contemporary American, British and German art to be saying.'

'Neither would I piss on it if the whole lot was on fire. In fact, I'll tell you this. If the collective contents of the next Frieze art fair went up in smoke, the world would be a significantly better place.'

'What about the artists?'

'Flies congregate on shit. Capital won't go near the real stuff in case of the Nazis.'

'But your books, television programmes — you've championed contemporary art for years.'

Piers shook his head wearily. 'Whatever. All I'm saying is that you'll never find a buyer for this.'

'You think not?'

'I think most fucking certainly not.'

'I already have. And all we need is your signature. Piers, forget about the provenance. You can forget about the science too if you want. Just give me your eye. Do you think this is an original from Vincent Van Gogh's Auvers-sur-Oise period?'

'You realise I'm going to have to inform the authorities, don't you?'

Maria looked levelly at Piers for a moment. 'Perhaps I forgot to mention that for your signature we will set up an offshore account to the tune of four million euros. Today. Now.'

'My God, you're not joking, are you?'

'The buyer requires only the opinion of two connoisseurs. Myself and you.'

'Well, I've done plenty of things I've been ashamed of but this is new.'

'Ashamed of what? You're not being asked to do anything illegal; all we want is your opinion.'

'Maria, if I take those four million euros, then how am I different from the Nazis? We're treating art like a commodity.'

'Isn't that what we've been doing all our lives? By the way there's no sign of the Georgiana Fairbanks piece on the Loot List either. What a tasteful peace offering that will be for your wife.'

'And what the hell's that supposed to mean?'

'How many Fairbanks pieces have you got now? Four in London; and is it just the two in your Tuscany house? Where will you keep this new one? But this isn't just about four million and an early Fairbanks. Aren't you curious to know what Georgiana Fairbanks was doing in Auvers-sur-Oise with Vincent van Gogh? If you choose to be involved herc then I will be able to make you privy to the art story of the century. Not only will it significantly swell Georgiana Fairbanks's market but also your own international kudos. You wouldn't believe what we've found out about her. Did you know her husband was a writer? Wait until you read his characterisations not only of his wife but of Dr Gachet and Van Gogh. We have photos too. You've seen one. It's quite an archive. There's never been such an insight into *fin-de-siècle* Auvers. You realise what this means, don't you? It's the kind of biographical narrative that will very probably catapult Georgiana Fairbanks into the stars. And you with her.'

Piers sat down heavily. 'I want to know how you've found out I have four Georgiana Fairbanks pictures hanging in my house.'

'And why I know you need to make peace with your wife?' The ghost of a smile hovered round Maria's lips. 'Grow up, Piers, when there's this amount of money involved people are very cautious; they like to know exactly who they're dealing with. And the money we're talking about here makes Mikey Durrant's value look like that of a pygmy. Now, Piers, be sensible. I didn't think you'd react like this. You don't need to think about anything else, just the painting. So tell me, does it look to you like the work of Vincent Van Gogh?'

Piers found himself gazing at the picture. All the hallmarks of Van Gogh were there: the brushstrokes, the vision, the titanic struggle between artist and subject, the sense of freshness as though the piece had just been finished moments before and any moment he might step back to touch up a detail. He nodded. 'As far as I can tell at this early stage.'

'I knew too, the moment I first saw it. But there's no hurry. I've booked this room for a week. I want you to be certain. All my resources are at your disposal.'

'Why me, Maria?'

'You're a world-renowned expert.'

'No; I'm not; not really.'

'You have a reputation. My buyer has enjoyed watching your programmes. And let's just say: you're the flexible type.'

'I don't think I like that piece of character analysis.' He shook his head and then said, as though to himself, 'I might be a bastard but I'm not worthless.'

'An interesting distinction. Look, Piers, why are you making this so hard?'

'Why? Probably because I don't want to be party to trafficking Nazi loot. I think it's time I went to the authorities.'

Maria exhaled in frustration. 'You leave me no choice. I've tried to hint but . . . ' She handed him a document. 'Does this look familiar?'

The art adviser's voice broke. 'How did you get hold of this?'

'I've told you, the money involved makes the buyer extra careful.'

'You bitch.' Piers stared at the page. It was a list of the biggest deals he'd been involved in over the past few years with all the figures including his own inflated percentages.

'The pot calling the kettle black is the English saying, I believe. Do your clients know how much of a rake-off you've been taking, Piers? Do your buyers? To coin another of your English phrases, you've been taking bungs up both nostrils and the arse; so I don't think now is quite the time for moralising.' She took out another document. 'I'm not at all sure that some of these transactions aren't illegal. In fact, I think some of your activities are getting perilously close to insider trading.' She handed him the second sheet. 'Now *that* is a crime in the Netherlands. You could be extradited for that. Artificially raising prices. Naughty, naughty.'

'How did you get hold of this?'

'You think that with all the money here a little computer hacking was so hard? Don't be alarmed; these measures were taken only as a precaution.'

'I could fucking screw you for this. Tampering with emails; *that's* a criminal offence.'

'We've left no trace. You think the people I work for employ schoolchildren? Incidentally, you might like to know that we're not the only ones who have been snooping in your email account. Someone at this address has been using your password and number.' She handed over a piece of card on which was written: zohreh@aol871.com. Piers stared at the card. 'You're not handling your mistress very well, are you?'

'My God, you're like the Gestapo.'

'If we've been a little overzealous, please forgive us.'

'*We*? Who is this mystery buyer, Maria?'

'You don't need to know.' If it hadn't been for the sudden twinge of his tooth the art adviser would have laughed outright. 'Piers, you know very well buyer anonymity is perfectly standard practice. We still don't know for certain who bought the portrait of Dr Gachet. Anyway, as for the vendee of *Spring Garden in Auvers*, I genuinely can't tell you; I don't know myself.'

'Come off it.'

'My contact is a Chinese woman.'

'Chinese.' Piers now did allow himself a bitter laugh. 'This just gets better and better. Step one: you're asking me to authenticate a piece of dodgy loot from the Holocaust. Step two: and oh, by the way, it's going to China.'

'I suppose that's just where the money happens to be.'

'China is a black hole.' Piers pointed at the canvas. 'If this *is* an undiscovered masterpiece by Vincent Van Gogh and it goes to China then it could very easily never be seen again.'

'Well, since you bring it up, Piers, that brings us to another matter. In this case, as well as his or her own anonymity, the buyer wants the shroud of silence to extend over the work of art as well. No one's ever to know about it, Piers. When you sign, you accept the condition of silence. You must never mention it to anybody, never refer to it. In fact, for all intents and purposes, you must forget it ever existed.'

There was a pause during which, in vain, Piers

tried to evaluate the exact depth of the shithole he found himself in. 'So what are you getting out of it, Maria? No, don't tell me. It's the letter, isn't it? They've given you the letter. Van Gogh's last letter. That's your cut of the corpse.'

'Piers, there are more masterpieces in private vaults than in all the world's galleries put together. What harm will one more do? Besides, it'll come to light eventually. They always do, eventually.'

'And for now, it's as though it never existed in the first place.'

'Which technically it didn't. Look at it this way, Piers, without the investment the buyer has made it *wouldn't* exist. You know how sceptical the market is about Van Gogh. No major Van Gogh piece has been sold for ten years. The market doesn't believe in Vincent Van Gogh any more.'

'You make him sound like a religion.'

'And isn't he? Realistically speaking, it's the buyer's money as much as the master's brush that has created this masterpiece.'

'Jesus, this isn't a philosophy course for undergraduates: when you walk out of a room do its contents cease to exist? It's an actual work of art, one whose reality you have been at great pains to successfully prove.'

'A process only made possible by money from the buyer.'

'OK, so you've managed to pull my tongue out, Maria, but how can you possibly hope to keep something like this dark?'

'By letting as few eyes as possible see it; that's

why I had to be so sure of you before I showed it to you. For which I profusely apologise.'

'You're not doing a very good job then.'

'What do you mean?'

'Well, the trainload of scientific experts for a start.'

'The labs were simply given a large number of different paint samples to compare; the context was utterly divorced. None of them know it's by Van Gogh. As for the wording of their reports I simply replaced their rather cold reference system with the words *Van Gogh* and *Auvers*. Here's some irony for you since you're so fond of it: how many people does it take to make a masterpiece? In this case, you, me and a billionaire.'

'And presumably the artist too?' The tooth throbbed. 'Let me just make sure I understand you here, Maria. Firstly, the Nazi connection doesn't bother you; and secondly, neither does the fact that you're committing this picture to the black hole of some secret vault?'

'I was asked to rescue an artwork from oblivion; resurrect it, if you like. What then happens to it does not concern me.'

'That doesn't make it sound any better.'

'There have always been patrons of the arts.'

'The people you're talking about aren't patrons; they're hoarders.'

'You think there's a difference?'

'I see. Thirdly, but by no means least; have I got this completely wrong, or are you in fact blackmailing me?'

'For which I apologise.'

'Apology not accepted.'

'It may have been heavy-handed but would you really call four million euros blackmail? As for keeping it quiet, I just happen to accept that in the real world someone who is willing to spend in excess of one billion pounds sterling in salvaging a work of art is entitled to a little silence.'

'One billion?'

'I believe that's the insurer's figure. And now, four million euros for your signature.'

'A signature? Wasn't that how people were sent to the concentration camps?'

'We're going in circles.'

'I'm sorry, but I just can't seem to forget the little fact that what we're dealing with here is a piece of poisonous booty from the Holocaust.'

'Firstly, it's no one's property; secondly, the man who appropriated these paintings was never posthumously indicted for the more serious war crimes.'

'So he *was* a Nazi? I knew it. Pity there isn't such a thing as a moral SEM-EDX process. I wonder what that would show up on the surface of this painting. Who is he?'

'Nobody of any consequence.'

'Ah. Not the best answer given the situation.'

'You met his daughter today.'

'The nutty old woman?'

'He was called Ernst Mann. Something of a small cog. A folklorist, if you can believe it. Mossad turned every stone but his only specific crime was as a propagandist. They couldn't even pin the theft of the painting on him.'

285

'Mossad? Hold on a minute. You're saying that the Israeli government is involved in all of this?'

'I'm not saying anything, and neither are you. Listen, Piers, do you really think I'd have anything to do with a piece of Nazi loot?'

'I don't know, Maria, would you?'

'If it's bothering you that much let me assure you that the vendor of this piece has got nothing to do with that family in the Black Forest.'

'So who the fuck is it then?'

'I'm afraid I can't tell you that.'

'That's a new one on me; vendor anonymity too.'

'Let's just say that the vendor has every ethical right to make the sale. Now, Piers, I give you my word: there's nothing to stop you signing.'

Piers got up and paced around the room. Unbidden, the sums came into his mind. With the money Maria had mentioned and all the accruing growth in Georgiana Fairbanks works, in tandem with the London house (what other exclusive address had such a large garden?), the gallery in Cumbria would be more than viable. They wouldn't even have to sell the property in Tuscany. It was in his grasp; a new life, far from all of his mistakes. Just one signature and he would no longer have to kowtow to people like Mikey Durrant; or have an office in a fucking bank. It was his one-way ticket from the Republic of Muppetry. And no one would ever know.

'Piers, if you'll just watch the presentation all this will be explained.' Maria touched a key on her laptop. On the screen loomed the face of

Vincent Van Gogh; it was the self-portrait with bandaged ear and pipe; his eyes seemed to bore into Piers. Smoke fluttered from the pipe and formed the words: *The Secret Journey of a Masterpiece: The Provenance of* Spring Garden in Auvers *by Vincent Van Gogh.* Words and portrait were replaced by the picture of the garden, whose colours now seemed even more wonderful. Slowly the painting faded. For a while Piers thought that the screen or the presentation equipment was damaged in some way because all he could see was a grey snowstorm of interference; then the figure of an old woman emerged. She was swaying back and forth in a rocking chair. Piers realised that he was watching some primitive film footage. The definition sharpened. The old woman's nose and chin were pointed; a cat sat on her shoulders; a ball of wool on her lap. How a child might imagine a witch. Her hands were knitting. After a while the old woman suddenly got up and, walking across an ancient kitchen, administered a few blows to some children who were sitting nearby. The camera froze on a man watching from the shadows. 'Ernst Mann,' Maria's recorded voice intoned. 'Birthplace unknown. Celebrated throughout Europe for his folkloric work, including the seminal text *The Donkey's Song: Why Humans Tale.*' On the screen, the image of the man melted and was replaced by the same figure in a black uniform. 'The squalid tragedy of Ernst Mann, and other folklorists, is a lesser known footnote of the Holocaust . . . '

6

Piers woke abruptly. He reached out for Sally but the space beside him was empty. Gaping into the unfamiliar orange darkness for a few disorientated moments Piers thought he was back in his school dormitory; no, he was lying in the narrow bed at his parents' home. Even as the table, television and chair of the airport hotel room established themselves he felt as though he only needed to get out of bed to find the desk and bookshelves of his childhood waiting for him. Any moment, it seemed, he would hear his father's footsteps as he crossed the landing to the bathroom, followed by a satisfied grunting as the jerky jet peppered the porcelain.

Piers fumbled for his watch. Could he only have been asleep for an hour? He snapped the light on and opened up his BlackBerry. There was the picture of Sally and Mimi they had sent last night: they were both smiling. Despite his tooth, which was in danger of becoming something he could no longer avoid, Piers smiled. Gav wasn't going to tell Sally after all. He took some more aspirin and turned off the light. But the jaundiced darkness was filled with the insomnia of corporate hospitality. A male voice droning from one of the adjoining rooms; the wailing of the plumbing as one small-hours shower followed another — what was everyone so keen to wash away? — the Sisyphean click of the lift shouldering its way back up the many floors; the footsteps that built softly out on the corridor, and, breaking at his door in a soft spindrift of voices, ebbed away. It was perhaps during the tenth wave of feet that Piers realised once again he was listening out for his father's footsteps on the landing. Piers had been at school when his father died. He did not go to the funeral but came home for the next holiday to find that even his father's dogs were gone.

Abandoning all hope of sleep, Piers turned on the television, and, flicking channels, found himself looking at Gav's face. What wouldn't his friend give for the story he was sitting on? As far as the internal market of the media went, an undiscovered Van Gogh masterpiece and the Nazis beat the crap out of yet more pictures of starving African children. With the sound of the television turned down, he took out his BlackBerry. Browsing through miscellany.com he read that if Pamela Anderson had one wish it would be for the world's fur coats to come back to life and attack the people wearing them. He moved onto the famous-last-words section. His father's own last words, at least to Piers, had been: '*You'll see; everything's going to be just tickety-boo.*' Piers recalled how one evening he had been called out of prep to the telephone. His father had never rung him at school like this before. It was the night before his accident. 'I'll take you to the Test match in the summer,' he had said after a strange rambling conversation. 'We're playing India. *You'll see; everything's going to be just tickety-boo.*' His father's dogs had been border terriers.

Getting out of bed, the art adviser made himself a coffee and opened the hospitality cookies; but his tooth growled warningly at the first bite. Listlessly he browsed through the drawers of the chest: a Gideon Bible, a remote control, trouser press, and a tangle of pubic hairs. Did he really have the resolve to see this matter through? After all, walking out on Maria Hertz during her presentation might have been the easiest part. He was almost certain that the criminal charges were just a bluff; still, it might mean having to keep out of Holland for a while. As for the *bungs*, well, wasn't all that just expected and accepted? If it became known he might lose one or two clients but that would be it. Maria's veiled threats about Zohreh were toothless too: that business was irrevocably finished now. There was no proof. He knew Sally would never believe the word of a stranger against his. Piers was prepared to weather any storm. True, he'd be losing a hell of a lot by walking away from this thing, but wasn't truth and integrity important too? No matter how tempting, no matter how Maria dressed it all up, the painting was tainted. Piers padded into the bathroom. Before going to bed he'd got some salt sent up from the hotel kitchens and now, mixing it into a saline wash, he sluiced his mouth. Lifting his head back to swirl and then spit he caught his reflection in the mirror. He glanced away instinctively but there was no getting away from what he had seen. It was the face that had flared in the plate glass of the Cafe in the Gardens when he was dumping Zohreh, that he'd seen in the mirror of the plane toilet; the face of his own father. Something in the brow, in the deepening set of the eyes, in the emerging fretwork: this was how he remembered his father looking. People thought he was a Peter Pan figure, a Dorian Gray, but as he grew older Piers consistently avoided mirrors; he did not like being taken by surprise by his dead father like this. But tonight he found himself being inexorably dragged back to consider the reflection. There it was, stark in the unforgiving truth of the high-wattage lighting. Was this how his father had looked as he stood on the narrow bridge above the train track that ran through a cutting banked with willowherb?

Footsteps were just walking down the corridor as Piers came out of the bedroom. He waited for them to build and then break, echoing slightly on the melancholy acoustic of the passageway, but they stopped at his door. Someone was trying the handle. The art adviser listened for a few moments then called: 'Who is it?' When there was no answer, he thrust the door open. Zohreh stood in the corridor.

7

Piers drained the last from the bottle of Veuve Clicquot but the tooth continued to throb. In the bathroom Zohreh was filling the hot tub. He began to laugh. He laughed until his whole body shook. They'd fucked on the floor — the shadow where Zohreh's arse had taken the weight still lay in the carpet; the table was skewed from her kicking heels. She had wound herself round him like ivy. Of all things, just before arching in his final spasm Piers had found himself thinking of Mikey Durrant's *Highway of Progress* installation. Did monogamy exist among Stone Age people, or were their male-female relations more like those shared between herd animals: one male annexing as many women as he could into his harem? Her scent had engulfed him and he had been as helpless to fight against it as a rutting stag. 'I knew it,' Zohreh had whispered, cradling his head. 'Knew you loved me; knew we had to be together.' After the sex he had lain there without moving as she talked about the future. They could live in Amsterdam; make a fresh start; some things just had to be. Then the bombshell. 'Piers, we're going to have a baby.' The hot tap continued to keen in the bathroom; abruptly Piers stopped laughing.

'Hello, Piers,' his father had said when he picked up the phone that night. 'It's Daddy here.' *Daddy*. The first and last time he ever used that word. To get to the telephone Piers had had to walk through the school, deserted and eerie at the prep hour. Had it been the *grey lady* or the *headless butler* who was supposed to roam that long, long corridor? He had been terrified but did not run; in those days he obeyed every rule.

The hot tap reached a crescendo in the bathroom. Piers could hear Zohreh luxuriating in the water.

★ ★ ★

Piers had dressed and was ready to slip away when he saw that something had been pushed underneath the room door. A small square envelope with his name on. He looked out into the corridor but it was deserted. Inside the envelope was a DVD. He put it in the player, and saw instantly that it was film footage taken earlier that day when he had been with Maria Hertz. The definition was uncomfortably high.

'*Mikey Durrant is a complete muppet. Actually, he's worse than that. He's the head muppet. In fact, he's the arch-druid of all muppets. The fucking Reichsführer of muppets.*'

'*Your opinion of the rest of contemporary art is that low?*'

'*I wouldn't wipe my arse with most of the stuff I sell.*'

As Piers watched himself destroying his own career, he thought: how old I'm getting; one day I will be as old as my father. The footage broke off; another scene appeared. It took a while for him to realise that it was a toilet cubicle. The picture fragmented; when it reassembled, Piers and Zohreh were screwing. The screen filled with Piers's face. It was the toilet from their flight to Amsterdam. So. That Viking soccer fan had been doing more than evacuating his bowels.

The light of dawn was almost showing at the window when Piers opened it. Far below, a security guard roamed between parked cars. Piers was trapped. Even if Zohreh wasn't really pregnant, what did it matter? Whoever had filmed him would not scruple to send Sally a copy. How he had let it happen didn't matter; it had happened, just as on the morning after ringing his son, Piers's father had climbed onto a railway bridge and fallen in the path of the 7.12 London train.

Piers felt a jet-fuel tainted breeze reach him from the runway. A busload of Filipina domestics debouched at the hotel entrance. Vincent Van Gogh had also committed suicide. It had taken two days for the bullet to kill him, during which time he had smoked and chatted amiably with his brother. There was no time to chat amiably as you jumped from a railway bridge and had your body parts broadcast over the willowherb. The first plane of the day swept up from the runway, the heat from its engines a mirage on the greying air. Piers leant against the windowsill feeling its pressure against his body just as his father must have felt the parapet of the railway bridge pushing against his diaphragm. Earlier on miscellany.com he had read that 29 per cent of British men are unable to look their father in the eye; and that males are so vulnerable after orgasm that their reaction time to potential danger is impaired by up to 215 per cent. *How often did this prove fatal in our hunter-gatherer days?* queried some Silicon Valley philosopher. Why had he just fucked Zohreh? Was suicide always the act of insanity, or was it that of cold, unadorned, selfish sanity? It was too late now of course but how he would have loved to have given Sally a good life. He had always thought of moving from London, to Cumbria or somewhere with real soil for the roots. Instead, he had become this stereotype: a philandering businessman run to earth; one of countless ants caught under a child's stomping foot. Was this how his father had felt as he stood on the bridge? What else is despair but life without illusions? But there are different kinds of despair. Miscellany.com said that the despair of shame was the most frequent motive for suicide. Untenable grief ran only second, fear of pain third, and fourth, ironically, fear of death. It didn't say whether toothache was a factor but the way his gum was beginning to hurt now, Piers wouldn't be surprised if it ranked somewhere. He looked about the room. Zohreh was singing softly in the bath. He wondered whether anyone had ever killed themselves in this room before. He leant out of the window. From here it would all be over in a matter of seconds: the fall, the impact, the snooker cue of the spine potting the skull. Then three hours later a Filipina chambermaid would be tidying up, getting ready for the next guest, perhaps even screwing up the suicide note without realising. *Why did he do it?* her co-workers might ask her during their break. *I don't know.* No one knew why his father had taken his own life; he had left no note.

In the bath Zohreh raised her leg and eased in a little more hot water with her toe. Her skin shone with the bath oils, the large pores opening hungrily in the steam. How lovely it was to lie here in the warmth with Piers's child knitting in her womb. She'd known all along that he loved her; and now at last he'd proved it. In years to come she would tell their child about the lengths to which she'd had to go to make Daddy follow his heart. 'Are you all right, Piers?' she called.

'Yes,' he replied.

Rising from the bath Zohreh watched the soapy water cascade from her; there was no sign of the baby in her flat stomach but any day now she would begin to show. Poor Piers, it had been a shock to him too; but in the end it would be what saved him if — God forbid — Mimi died. Nature had its own balance. Drowsy with happiness, Zohreh draped herself in the luxuriant bathrobe.

When she came out of the bathroom, the room was empty. The window was wide open. Zohreh strode across the room to shut it. No doubt Piers had gone downstairs to personally arrange room service. She lay on the bed and, pressing her face into the sheets, breathed her lover in. Just after they had made love and were lying on the carpet still locked as one, she'd looked at his hand. With its lovely long tapering fingers it was the hand of an artist. His ring and index finger were the same size. In one of the baby books she'd bought, it said that this was a sign of creativity; their baby too was going to be creative, just like Piers.

8

Squinting in the sudden bright white light, the art adviser threw up a shielding arm. Gently but irresistibly it was pressed back down. He grinned in blessed relief; at last the pain had gone. Two cold blue eyes evaluated him from above a paper mask. 'Perhaps you shouldn't floss so zealously,' the English dentist at the airport said. 'You've managed to saw right through the gum; the whole thing is badly infected. How long is it until your flight?'

Concentrating on a single white square of the wall Piers tried to distance himself from the shining dental implement invading his mouth. Over the years this dislike of dentists had grown into something like a phobia. He'd far rather have a prostate probe any day. But he hadn't been able to put it off any longer; walking into the airport he had thought he was going to puke with the pain. Even just ten minutes ago as he sat in the waiting room it had been as though a rat was gnawing his gum. So great was the agony that he had hardly even noticed the needle sliding into his mouth. Not entirely successfully fighting off an urge to giggle he wondered what Mikey Durrant would have to say on the subject: *Teeth are everything; they fucking say it all. It's how them archaeologists date their digs, and the forensic teams find out who was murdered. In the wild nothing dies of old age; their fucking teeth wear away and they slowly starve. I'm telling you, Posh Spice, at the installation we'll have teeth and dental records strewn over the rotting carcasses. Forget space travel and books; it's false teeth that are humanity's greatest achievement.*

His mouth still beatifically numb, Piers left the dentist and walked down the terminal concourse. The last call for some missing passenger

297

on the flight to Kiev rang out. Piers had never been to the Ukraine before. He'd reached the Kiev gate when he stopped himself. The time for running was over.

At the duty-free shops he filled two carrier bags with chocolate. Wandering through the retail area and then through the food village, he found himself instinctively reaching for his BlackBerry. He stared at the screen for a number of seconds, then, dropping it onto the hard floor, ground it underfoot. On the flight home to London, the pain slowly reasserted itself. Sitting on the toilet he shat out the first wave of the antibiotical diarrhoea. Without really realising what he was doing, he began to sketch on the back of a gold-card brochure. The drawing was of Sally and Mimi playing on the slide in the back garden. He had no other plan than to come home and tell Sally everything. He would miss nothing out; it would be the whole truth.

The Heathrow tube rattled him back into London. Emerging from the Underground, Piers broke into a run, only stopping when he saw the tree of heaven. He had never noticed it looking so beautiful before. According to the elderly couple from whom he and Sally had bought the house, it had germinated during the refuse-collecting strikes of 1976; a small but tenacious sprig growing between the unemptied bins and mounting piles of trash. More than anything, it had been the tree of heaven that had sold the house to Sally. Slowly Piers approached until he could hear the bees in its canopy. Everything else he had ever done in his life was as nothing beside what the next half an hour or so held. Would Mimi be at home?

The sound of his key in the lock — once so familiar as to go unnoticed — seemed to detonate in the hallway. The French windows were open. Sally's voice was coming through them from the garden. Just about to go to her, Piers realised she was not alone. Someone was with her in the garden; they were laughing together; a man. Raising a glass to his lips, the man presented a profile. Piers instantly recognised Gav. He was leaning towards Sally and removing something from her hair, a ladybird or a fluff of dandelion seeds: a gesture of proprietorial intimacy. Exhaling softly, Piers put a hand against the pane of glass. Although the day was warm, the glass was cool to his touch. He withdrew without being seen and, gently closing the front door behind him, passed back under the tree of heaven down the avenue of four-by-fours.

The tube was packed. Piers just managed to squeeze in through the doors. Blindly changing trains a number of times, going with the flow of passengers, he finally alighted at Russell Square. He pushed through the passengers waiting for the lift. How could people exist like this; how far had we come on Mikey Durrant's highway of progress? A hot wind leapt down the tunnels, throwing grit in his eye. At the Cafe in the Gardens he ordered an espresso but left before it came. After spending twenty pence to squat in the toilet Tardis at the gate, he lingered in the gardens for a while. At the fountain, the down-and-out was feeding the pigeons. *Do not feed the pigeons*, a sign on the tree said, by order of the *Friends of Russell Square Gardens*. Filled with what felt like a sudden inspiration Piers rushed into Bloomsbury to buy a sketch pad. Armed with both chocolates and pad he walked down Judd Street. Pausing outside the North Sea Fisheries for a moment he scanned the price list. Was it for Mimi's sixth or seventh birthday party that he and Sally had ordered fish and chips from here? He passed a pub, the jovial laughter of the Friday-lunchtime crowd strafing him through the open door. Did his mother still believe that he thought his father's death was an accident? *Was* it an accident? After all, he didn't know for sure.

The taxi took him through the thick traffic to Victoria; he travelled south on the train, unable to get a seat. Colourless even on a summer's afternoon, the sallow strands of housing stretched endlessly: Battersea, Clapham, Wandsworth, Tooting. On the sides of the cutting the willowherb was raging purple. The first time Piers had been aware of the existence of willowherb was in the holidays after his father's death. The library in the next town kept back copies of the local newspaper. It was in these pages that he had found the headline: RESPECTED LOCAL SURGEON MYSTERY DEATH PROBE. Below it was the black-and-white picture of a railway cutting with its willowherb; but he didn't realise that willowherb was purple until he had gone himself to that 'railway bridge on a bridleway popular with dog walkers'. Standing on the narrow bridge at the scene of the incident — the local newspaper recorded the coroner's open verdict — Piers had stared at the blaze of purple, and the tracks whose parallel lines seemed to stretch away forever. On the night he had been called to the phone at school he had been writing about parallel lines for his maths prep. *Parallel lines will never ever meet*, the master had told his class, *not if they run forever and ever world without end amen*. Five more weeks had passed at school and then he came home for the summer holidays to a house where very little seemed to have changed. He missed the dogs chiefly; not that he had ever liked them. Working late in London during the week and also staying there many weekends, his father had never been much of a presence. On his first afternoon home, Piers had sat in the snug having tea with his mother, the only concession to his bereavement the extra Jammie Dodgers on a plate.

The southbound train rattled on; at last there was room for him to sit now. Wimbledon, New Malden, Surbiton, Woking. The first sustained flashes of green through the window. Fields, cows, trees, children playing. What had those travelling on the 7.12 train that day nearly thirty years ago seen through *their* windows? They wouldn't have seen the body falling from the bridge onto the line, although the ones in the front carriage might have witnessed a gentle red rain dowsing their window. At 7.12 maybe they were all half asleep anyway. His was the next station. Was the journey really so short? Yet an hour and a half had gone by. At school, prep had lasted an hour and a half, and that had felt like an eternity. Through the window he registered an elbow of river and the slight rise in the landscape where an oak wood grew. Behind there somewhere was the house that the well-known local surgeon had left early one morning on his way to rendezvous with a fatal accident. In the local library, as well as the newspapers, the young Piers had looked those words up in a large dictionary. But just like the parallel lines, it seemed that their meanings were destined never to meet. Fatal: *decreed by fate, destiny, that which must happen*; Accident: *chance, an event without apparent cause.* The train took a long curve then straightened into a deep cutting. The sides of the cutting rose steeply, purple with rampant willowherb. When the train passed under the bridge, the whole carriage bucked with the impact, like a forehead striking a wall.

Piers caught a taxi at the little station. As he was driven through the Sussex countryside he looked for something he might remember from his childhood, but even here everything had changed. Car dealerships on the pastures where cattle had grazed; country lanes throbbing with traffic. The village green remained, but where there had been donkeys now stood twenty new houses; chastened into a straight channel, even the meandering little river had been disguised as a dyke. 'You said the Old Parsonage?' the Asian taxi driver asked.

'Yes.'

'Is that near them new houses, up that

Parsonage View estate?'

'I suppose it must be.' Piers looked past the driver's prayer-dangle. He barely recognised what had once been home. 'Just drop me outside the pub. I'll walk from here.'

Piers avoided homecomings. His mother had always been welcome in London, and through the genuine hospitality of Sally she stayed with them every Christmas. Sally pressed her to come more often but there was a diffidence that nothing could pierce. Since leaving home for university Piers had returned no more than five times. The last occasion had been four years before. Or was it longer? With its eighteenth-century colonnades and flat roof, the Old Parsonage remained standing in its three acres like a location for a Jane Austen film, but the twenty-first century was encroaching all around in the new houses huddled right up to its glebe edge. Although he had repeatedly told her not to, his mother still kept the key under the door mat. Piers let himself in quietly; she would be having her afternoon nap. Strange how sure he was of that fact.

The usual faint scent of lavender water was just as it had been on his last visits, but underneath it lay the unmistakable odour of decay: that unforgiving barometer of mortality that no scent or unguent can mask. Seventy-five now, she insisted on still doing everything for herself. She had never even employed a cleaner. *I left all that behind in South Africa*, she had said to him when he brought it up again last year. Piers walked through the snug where he and his mother used to have tea in the holidays and crossed the hall to his father's study. He had not been in here for nearly thirty years and when he opened the door he half expected the two Border terriers to come rushing out. The room was unchanged. The few books on his father's shelves were medical volumes; the pictures on the wall prints of Joseph Wright of Derby. Piers gazed at one: a claustrophobic bubble of light in a dark experimental laboratory in which faces intently watched a pigeon dying in a vacuum. Behind the solid desk, Piers tried to sit the constantly tired man in tweeds that his memory held. A slight Scottish burr; a furrowed brow; something of a Dr Finlay.

Piers found his mother sleeping soundly. She had always been a heavy sleeper; and never so much as during the long summer after her husband's fatal accident. Standing in the doorway of her bedroom, he waited for her to stir. She usually woke for what would have been afternoon tea. Her supine form was surrounded by the emblems of her day-to-day life like a primitive corpse set among its burial goods. At her elbows were copies of *Good Housekeeping, Country Living*, the *Radio Times*; on the pillow by her head the television remote control; on the bedside table her formidable selection of medications, and a bowl of lavender potpourri; at her right hand the novel she had been reading as she fell asleep. Was she dreaming? Her face was as wrinkled as Miss Havisham's. This was how she would look when she came to die. He stood there, the carrier bags full of chocolates still cording his wrists. He had not known about his father until she sat him down in the snug a few days after he had returned home. Yet how could he judge *her* long silence? Neither Sally nor Mimi knew that in all probability his father had taken his own life. A fatal accident, as linguistically contradictory as it may be, sits more easily in the history of a family.

'Is that you?' A crumpled voice came from the pillows.

'Yes,' he replied from the doorway but felt the need to add: 'It's me, Piers.'

'Piers.' She seemed to savour the word as though it had an unexpected flavour. Who else might it have been? he wondered.

'Are Sally and Mimi with you?'

'No, I've come alone.'

'We'll have tea in the snug. Just give me two ticks to get dressed.'

'All right, Mother.'

He lingered at the threshold, peering through the crack in the door as she hauled herself upright. Dishevelled, hair a frayed grey rope, her mouth gaping. Piers turned away.

The snug with its wide hearth, comfortable settee and sprawling armchairs was the only territory mother and son had shared; cool in the summer, in the winter the large fireplace crackled with logs. Faded hunting scenes decorated the wall, mute witnesses to a hundred of Piers's childish hobbies and fads. A thousand games of solitary chess and Top Trumps. He had drawn here too, keeping his sketch pads under the hefty settee seats. Why he should have felt the need for secrecy, Piers could no longer remember. It was here too that his mother finally broached the matter of the fatal accident: *Darling, put down the sketch pad for a moment and listen. Your father has suffered a terrible misfortune . . .*

'I've opened the windows in your room to air it,' she said now as she wheeled in the same tea trolley she had that day. Its load was identical too: little ham sandwiches, a bowl of crisps, and a plateful of Jammie Dodgers; he might be nine years old again. 'You are staying the night, aren't you, darling?' He didn't know whether she wanted him to or not. 'When did you get here?'

'Oh, just before you woke up.'

'How did you get in?'

'The key. There's no need to go to all this trouble, Mum.'

'It's no trouble, Piers. Should I light a fire in here? It seems cold but I've always thought it was a shame to light a fire in summer. Like those people who put Christmas decorations up in October.' When Piers bit into a biscuit he found it was soft. 'Are you all right, darling?'

'It's my tooth.'

'I see. I had a nice chat with Mimi on the phone yesterday.'

'Really?'

'That girl has more sense in a little finger than you have in the whole of your body. She said you were in Switzerland.'

'Germany. The Black Forest.'

'Lovely country. Cuckoo clocks. You look tired, Piers. Haven't you been sleeping?'

'You know what these hotels are like.'

'So you let yourself in, you say?'

'You shouldn't keep the key there, Mum. We've talked about it a thousand times.'

'Don't exaggerate, darling. Anyway, it's just as well, otherwise how would you have got in? Why are you looking so thin when Sally's such a fine cook?'

The conversation languished for a moment. 'I see they've built on the field,' he said.

'I objected of course. It's madness. That's a flood plain. But they just build anywhere these days. You used to play on it as a little boy; do you remember?' He nodded warily, references to the past were rare. 'Sometimes I wish you'd been brought up under the sun.'

'You mean with apartheid and Kaffirs?'

His mother smiled slightly. This was part of their long-running banter. 'We weren't all like that. Anyway, it's changed. I was very happy when they let Mandela out. But this new one, he's in cahoots with Robert Mugabe. Shameful. Have you given up shaving, Piers, or are you growing a beard? If so let it be a proper hirsute affair; I can't stand these little scraggly fungi you see these days.'

'I'll be a real Voortrekker.'

'Don't be facetious, Piers.'

'Mum,' Piers said, 'I'm in trouble.'

'Now my grandfather had a true beard. Mother's father. He *was* a Voortrekker. *His* grandfather had come up to Transvaal to get away from the British. He'd turn in his grave if he knew that his granddaughter would end up marrying one. *Rooineks* he used to call them. He fought in the Boer War. Piers, just tell me this and nothing more. Has it got anything to do with Sally?'

'Yes.'

'Then I don't want to know.' He watched her bite into a dry sandwich. A smear of crumbs adhered to the light down of her moustache. 'I can't say I'm surprised. Whatever you've done to that girl you'll just have to undo.' A crumb fell from her top lip and her face tightened. 'My grandfather would have thrashed you with a sjambok. Have another sandwich; you're looking thin.'

'Mum.'

'Oh Piers, she's such a good girl, and you've run her ragged. By the way, did I tell you, I got the piano tuned.' As a boy, if she wasn't sleeping then his mother would be at the piano. Playing her sonatas she was as oblivious to him as when she slept. Climbing the trees in the orchard, he would peer through the blossom and watch her in the music room. 'Where have you parked your car, darling?'

'I came by train. Got a taxi at the station.'

'And you let yourself in. Now aren't you glad I used the key rock?'

'But you don't; you keep it under the mat. If anyone saw it — '

'Darling, Sussex hasn't quite yet become Johannesburg.'

'Can I ask you something?'

'I've told you. I don't want the details.'

'Not about Sally. It's about — '

'So you had to get a taxi? I'm forever writing to the council about bus services. But it's the same as their jerry-building. When you're old, you cease to exist.'

'You're not old, Mum.'

'Oh flimflam, boy. Now after tea I want you to run through a few papers of mine. The finances are a bit rucked up.' She pointed at a huge pile by the letter basket.

'You know, Mum, you should open some of the letters they send.'

'I don't want to encourage junk mail, the planet's ailing as it is.'

Ailing: one of his father's words. Piers caught an unfamiliar disturbance in the room. 'A jet,' his mother said. 'They come over all the time these days. We're under one of the new flight paths. Sometimes I wonder if it's you, away on one of your jaunts.' Mother and son caught each other's eye. 'You're very like him, you know. Your father.'

'What was he like, Mum?'

'How nice for you to have dropped in without warning, darling.' Piers reached for another Jammie Dodger. It was just as soft as the first. Delicately he bit as far from his wounded gum as possible. 'You see,' his mother continued, 'he was artistic too. Of course, when we first met that was already long behind him. Something happened in the war, I suppose. That's how it was for his generation.' Piers held his breath; it was the first time she had ever talked like this. 'Tell me, Piers, what's your excuse?'

'Excuse?'

'For stopping drawing? You used to be ever

309

such a good drawer. Did something happen to you? Times you've sat in that very chair sketching away. Do you remember that exhibition of yours I went to? It was in an old warehouse. Dirty, damp place.'

Piers remembered the incongruity of his mother at the exhibition he had organised for himself and a few other artists. In her twinset and pearls, white gloves and handbag, she had stood all evening by a Calor gas heater talking to Mikey Durrant. 'Now, *Durrant*. Is that a Cape Huguenot name?' In terms of sales it had been a disaster. Mikey Durrant had sold one piece; somebody else another. Piers hadn't sold anything of his own but when he organised the next exhibition, he found other artists approaching him for a share of the space. By the third show, he had given up trying to sell his art and was selling spots in his warehouse exhibitions. They had become the toast of the art world. He arranged them in Berlin, Paris, New York, Tokyo. All at once he had found himself as the spokesman for the Young British Artists. Television had followed. When New Labour won their electoral landslide in 1997, he was one of the luminaries invited to 10 Downing Street.

'Wherever you went, you had a sketch pad,' his mother said, breaking the silence. 'I've still got them, you know. I'll never forget the picture you drew when we were up in London for the day. Do you remember, Piers?'

'Mum, that's a thousand years ago.'

'You were such a lovely little boy. We'd been to

the British Museum to see the mummies. You sat in Russell Square Gardens and drew a tramp. He was feeding the pigeons. It was a fine day in spring. You were only so high.' She lifted the flat of her hand; the veins were twisted like blue tree roots. 'Oh, the plane trees were beautiful that day. So green. They reminded me of the withaak trees in the bushveld.'

'Mum, why did Dad — '

His mother got up, using a little pivoting motion to make the most of her momentum — another new sign of her ageing. When she had gone, Piers reached for his BlackBerry. Then he remembered he'd disposed of it. As his mother struggled back through the door with a heavy box he got up from his chair. He wanted to embrace her; instead he took the box. 'You shouldn't carry heavy loads like this.'

'Ah.'

'You'll strain yourself. What's in here anyway?'

'I kept all of them,' she said. 'When you were a little boy you used to give them to me.' For a moment the veiny hand hovered around her son's head. 'Little gifts from my little one.'

Spoors of mildew rose as Piers opened the box and lifted out a sketch pad. 'The damp's got to them, I'm afraid. In South Africa it was always the white ants.' Piers leafed through the sketch pad. Page after page of boyish doodling: footballers, cricketers, the orchard, his father's dogs. It was only occasionally that Piers caught his mother's South Africa intonation but it seemed more pronounced than ever before when she said: 'Look at these, hey. They're all so good. So lifelike. I used to wonder whether it was because you were an only child; you had to conjure up your own company. But of course, your father drew too.'

Piers brought out another pad; more of the same; then leafed through the others. Although it was summer, the paper was cool to Piers's touch. The edges were curled with damp. 'Where was that?' he asked, showing her a picture of a stretch of water fringed by pines.

'Scotland, darling; we went there on holiday. There's the cat on the farm where we stayed. You loved it so much you cried when we had to go.'

'I don't remember.'

One of the pads had been used for watercolours. They looked at it together. Halfway through there was a portrait of a woman in her forties. It was his mother sleeping. 'You little tyke,' she laughed. 'I remember telling you not to do that. You always were a stubborn little fellow in your own quiet way.' Piers turned to the next page. Their eyes collided; the pad slipped to the ground. It was a railway line stretching through a cutting of purple willowherb. 'Well, Piers darling,' she said softly, 'I think I'd better be getting your bed ready.'

'I'm not staying, Mum.'

'I thought you were.'

'No, I've got to get back.'

'To Sally?'

'I don't know.'

'But you've only just got here.'

Piers turned to her. If he didn't speak now he

never would. The coroner's report had said that due to lack of any note or explanatory circumstances the verdict could not be suicide but had to remain open. 'Mum?'

'Yes?'

'Are you all right?'

'Don't fuss, darling.'

'I got you this.' Piers's voice rose as he lifted up the dutyfree bags. 'Chocolate.'

'Piers, go back to her and make right whatever it is you've done before it's too late. Some mistakes last a lifetime.'

★ ★ ★

From a stump in the dead orchard a blackbird watched Piers passing back down the drive with the box under his arm. He walked through the village. After the pub the pavement gave out and he walked along the side of the road, the passing traffic rippling his hair. In the adjacent field a tractor was spraying a cloud of pesticides. Leaving the road, he skirted a cornfield. The crop barely reached his thigh; hadn't it stood so much higher when he came this way as a boy? From behind barbed wire a herd of bullocks followed him, torn between curiosity and fear. Climbing the stile left foot first, Piers followed the path through a thicket of brambles and blackthorn, the barbs forming an arching roof above. He heard the train before he came to the cutting, its sudden rattle showing how close the track was.

The bridge had been built originally for cows

and horsemen; there was no room for a car. Placing the box on the parapet, Piers looked down. Unlike the rest of his native place, everything was as he remembered: the lines of the track, the bridge, the cutting; all lying before him like an exercise in geometry. Here and there on the sides of the cutting the tall purple flowers had already seeded, and each breeze lifted clots of the down and sent it drifting over the tracks.

Piers looked through the rest of the sketch pads. Impossible to think that he'd ever drawn them. On miscellany.com he'd read how the human body follows distinct cycles, the atoms completely changing themselves every seven years. If this was true then physically he wasn't even the same person who had welcomed Mimi into the world. The Piers who had fallen in love with Sally was ancient history. As for the boy who had stood here sketching the place of his father's fatal accident, he was a veritable Australopithecus. And if this was true of the body, what of the heart, the soul? Some of the pads had flicker drawings on the corner of their pages. Someone slipping on a banana skin, a batsman hitting a rotten tomato. One, however, had not been drawn to raise a smile. Piers flicked it into life. It showed a man jumping from a bridge into the path of an oncoming train. In keeping with the slapstick nature of the other flickers, the different body parts were thrown hilariously free. Arms, legs, hands, feet, a head.

Even as he felt the bottom of the box Piers

knew that the last sketch pad was different. Heavier, older, even more eaten by time; bringing it to the light of day he saw that its stiff black cover was warped. Without taking in the subject of the first sketch, he realised that it had been drawn by a different hand. Focusing, Piers found himself looking at a line drawing of a dead body. No, it wasn't quite dead; although the body was emaciated the artist had tried to convey some sense of life in the eyes. Piers flipped through the pad. On each page was starvation in a different pose: ribs covered only with skin, bones protruding, large shaven heads with wide staring eyes. The eyes drew Piers in as he leafed through; huge but sightless they seemed to have been burnt out by what they'd seen. Piers blenched as he looked at a drawing of corpses piled five-deep. The next page showed a long line of barbed wire; behind it British soldiers stood guarding a mass grave. A single word had been written beside his father's initials: *Belsen*. Down in the cutting, the London train sounded its horn. Closing the pad he put it on the parapet of the bridge.

Piers had known that his father had been in Europe at the end of the war as a medical student. He had always thought that he'd been with the regular army. Now it seemed that he had been at Belsen. As he looked at the drawings, he made the calculations. Twenty-one years old and a medical student at Belsen.

The bridge began to vibrate. A train was coming. Louder, louder, then there it was exploding underneath him. Shaken free, his father's sketch pad fell. The train continued along the cutting; a loose sheet from the gutted pad spiralled gently onto the track ballast. Piers peered down at it as the willowherb shivered.

Auvers-sur-Oise, June 1890

1

The Paris train, *La Petite Vitesse*, chugged over the wheat plain. The corn was still green, stained here and there with the first scarlet poppies; the hay meadows were in full bloom. A wonderful pastoral fragrance drifted through the open window of the carriage. James Dalrymple shifted uncomfortably in his seat. Was it just his imagination or did the sad savour of last evening's whore linger about his person? He smelt under the cuticles of his fingers. As the baby with the couple sitting opposite him started crying again, he shuddered at the memory of the night before in Paris. He hadn't really wanted to visit that depressing little Left Bank hovel, with its malodour of fried onions and sour perfume clinging to the rickety stairs, and the dirt visible even in the gaslight. Sighing, the Ivy Leaguer looked through the window of the rattling carriage. There was the river running through the valley; there the wheat fields. Just to look seemed to heal some kind of wound hidden within him. In a moment the village itself would come into view. Auvers with its thatched roofs and winding little streets; its steep steps and sudden views; its villas, artists and crackpots. He had laughed when Georgiana had called it a garden of Eden, yet now at the sight of it, to his surprise, James Dalrymple felt a surge of something peculiarly like innocence. He looked at the crying baby but this time to smile. 'You're visiting our Auvers?' he asked the father of the infant that had grizzled the entire length of the journey.

'Yes,' the man replied. 'I'm sorry if Baby is bothering you.'

Dalrymple raised a finger in forgiveness. The young father was ginger-haired and rather blunt-headed; the American felt he had seen him somewhere before. Then he realised that he bore an uncanny resemblance to Gachet's Dutchman. Strange how nature threw up these meaningless similarities. Why, he'd once had a whore who was the spitting image of his mother. What could a well-dressed man of the world like this one, with his pretty, boyish wife and a bouncing baby, have to do with Vincent van Gogh? 'A day trip, monsieur?' Although both were foreigners, they conversed in French.

'Yes, we're going to see my brother. He's — '

The baby started to choke, and both parents fluttered round in alarm.

Dalrymple looked out of the window again. Was he really growing attached to the place? How different it was from Paris with its claustrophobic attics and frowzy little ten-franc tarts who were already squatting over their bowls of permanganate as one lay freshly slain on Venus's rusty-springed battlefield. As the baby wailed, a goose at the back of the coach started flapping wildly. Good to know that there were still genuine peasants on the Oise. If only he hadn't drunk that champagne and cognac last night. Dalrymple's head throbbed as the chateau hove into view, and he caught sight of Auvers lying shrewdly beneath the lofty confrontation of its church and town hall.

La Petite Vitesse began to pull in at the station. 'Auvers-sur-Oise!' The cry swept down the platform as the doors opened and the passengers disembarked. It was the usual Auvers fodder: weekend artists, commuters, summer visitors and a solitary peasant with a hooded goose under his arm. Dalrymple recognised the peasant as the man who worked in the gardens of a number of villas, including the one in which he stayed with the insufferable Chip Coakley, and was just about to nod to him when he saw Mrs Oyster. Discreetly he turned away and blended with the crowd. Then there she was: Miss Georgiana Fairbanks. So she'd been in Paris too. She was hurrying down the platform. Without quite knowing why, James Dalrymple donned the larrikin hat he was affecting that morning and hastened after her.

'Are you all right, darling?' the ginger-haired father asked his wife who had been jostled by the American's haste.

'Yes, but Baby is restless,' she replied, the infant wriggling in her arms. Her husband began to cough. She watched him anxiously. 'Are *you* all right?' she asked.

'Just the steam, Jo,' he explained in between his paroxysms. 'From the engine.'

Helplessly his wife watched him bend double. He was still coughing when a man bearing the kind of similarity to him that an old chewed mangold bears a newly grown turnip swept down the platform with a shout of joy. 'Vincent!' the husband managed to cry.

'Theo!' The man ran down the platform; he was dressed in a short blue jacket streaked with paint, battered straw hat and derelict boots. 'Jo too; dear sister! And little Vincent!'

Jo tried to smile as she watched her brother-in-law scoop up the baby from her arms. The painter's long fingernails were encrusted with dirt but he held the infant so gently that the child stopped grizzling and cooed happily at the great ugly face of his beaming uncle. One look told her that Theo's brother had deteriorated since she had last seen him. When he had stayed with them in Paris, Jo had been obliged to open the window the moment he left the room; now she doubted she could share an enclosed space with him without being overcome. Yet there was no denying the depth of his emotion. 'It's Uncle Vincent,' she said to the baby. 'Dear Uncle Vincent.'

'Vincent,' the painter whispered to his namesake. He looked at his brother, awestruck. 'Theo; it's little Vincent.'

Equally moved, Theo squeezed his elder sibling's elbow. 'Your nephew, old chap.'

'Careful.' Jo stepped forward protectively when Vincent hoisted the baby high.

'He's still just a tiny little one,' Theo said.

'And he's rather particular about the way he is

held, dear brother-in-law.'

As the crowd of disembarking travellers parted around him, Vincent Van Gogh squatted down and took his nephew on his knee. 'This is for you,' he whispered, bringing out an old nest.

'How lovely,' said Theo, taking in the look from his wife. 'I'll look after that, shall I, Vincent? Baby's still small.'

'No, it's all right,' said Vincent. 'I've brought him the softest one. It's a long-tailed-titmouse nest. Look. Feel it. Moss, wool, goat hair from Dr Gachet's pen. It's the most beautiful nest there is.' Breaking a piece off as though from a loaf, he tickled the child's face. Grinning, the baby tugged at the artist's scabrous beard. Vincent Van Gogh the senior burst into laughter.

'He's taken to you,' Theo beamed.

'May I carry him?'

'Of course, dear brother-in-law,' said Jo, trying to make herself sound happy about the arrangement. 'Perhaps if we moved away from the edge of the platform first.'

As the train pulled away, Vincent held the baby out. 'Bye-bye, puffer train!' The infant cooed happily. After another look from his wife, Theo guided his brother down the platform.

'How are you feeling, old chap?' Theo said as they walked into Auvers.

'Better. The symptoms have nearly all gone. But *you'll* never be cured of that cough until you leave Paris. I heard you on the platform. Have you thought any more about what I wrote in my letter?'

'Which bit?' Theo replied cautiously.

'Which bit? You know! How children are healthier for being brought up in the open air.' He hoisted the baby high above his head. 'He doesn't like being a fourth-floor apartment baby, do you, little fellow? He might fall. After all, he doesn't have wings. Do you, little Cupid?' Vincent let the baby drop. Jo and Theo gasped. Caught inches from the ground, the baby grinned. 'By the way,' the artist mumbled, 'many thanks for the paints. I'll show you some of the pictures. You can take what you want.'

They ambled up into the village. After days of rain the river was full, the greenery of the chestnut trees intense. 'Quite some place,' admired Theo.

'I'll take Baby, if you like,' said Jo. 'He can get heavy.'

'I could carry him for a thousand miles!'

'Careful, old chap, his head's still not very steady. But where are you taking us, Vincent?'

'Come on, I want to show little Vincent something. It's a Noah's ark of sorts. And I know he won't have seen many animals in Paris. Oh, Theo, how can you stay in that shithole when you can breathe air like this?' Stopping abruptly, Vincent closed his eyes and inhaled deeply. 'And you, little Vincent,' he laughed. 'Breathe in deeply. This is fresh air. Not like that Parisian muck you're used to.' He looked sharply at his brother. 'You *must* be able to see that a village like this is the only place to bring up a child. Agree here and now that you'll leave Paris and come here.'

'Ah!' Theo laughed.

'For the sake of the new addition!'

'Do you want me to take Baby now, dear brother-in-law?'

'Not until I've introduced him to some friends of mine. Look at the roofs of the thatched cottages. See that one there with the flowers and the birch tree growing on it? How little Vincent would love to live beneath that roof, Theo.'

'Rather damp I should say, old chap.'

'Well, a villa then. Look at those earthenware pantiles. What marvellous effects. Don't you love the way the houses seem to grow out of their gardens here, as if they're a bed of flowers or a tree? I think if you lived here you wouldn't be able to resist any more. You'd become an artist too. And you, little fellow, you'd soon be running around. I bet you've never even touched a flower. You want Daddy to be an artist, don't you? The Van Gogh brothers, and junior partner! What do you think about that, Jo?'

'Are you sure you don't want me to take Baby, dear brother-in-law?'

Vincent kissed the top of his nephew's head and breathed in deeply. There was nothing like the scent of a baby. If only he could capture that on canvas then he really would have done something. His mind raced. To paint the portrait of a baby boy as the child's father might picture him if he was a miner trapped in a flooding shaft, or a sailor on a sinking ship, or a prisoner in the condemned cell; to capture the image of a baby girl that stays in a mother's heart through all the years even when the child herself becomes a parent. But *that* was not for him. Only a father or a mother could do that. Real life was passing him by like a man watching a train from the platform.

'Are you all right, Vincent?' Vincent felt his brother's gentle touch on his arm. 'I'm fine,' he said, 'fine. Come on, little one. There are some very important people I want you to meet.'

Theo walked on with his brother. He hoped the visit was going to be a success. From what Monsieur Penyon at the asylum in Saint-Rémy had said the fits might reappear at any time. Coughing behind his hand, Theo felt a bead of sweat falling from his brow. He himself was far from well. In fact he was becoming feverish once more; and the pain in his bladder was growing. He'd have to try and urinate again soon. At the station in Paris only a few, scalding drops had dribbled out, and sitting on the train each jolt of the tracks had seemed to pierce his insides. The important thing was to hide his condition. Jo needed all of her strength for Baby, and Vincent was not to be worried, especially now that he had turned the corner. Those canvases that he had painted after Millet in the asylum at Saint-Rémy were staggering; not copies but translations into another tongue! That was how his brother had described them, but how flimsy was the bridge carrying him over the chasm of his temperament. Please God that it hold up a little longer. For underneath it at long last his tide was turning. Not only had he recently made his first sale — at the same time as the little one's birth! — but there were the exhibitions, and finally a favourable notice in the press. After all he *was* going to prove everyone wrong.

Walking past the town hall, Theo watched his brother holding up the baby as though for a better look. He sighed; he knew how much Vincent yearned for family life. Theo too had his own dreams; if only he really could throw everything up and move to Auvers. But he had his wife and little Vincent to support, not to mention his brother. No; Theo's future lay at Goupil's art dealership. He felt his forehead moisten at the thought. Although he had worked there for years and created a vast amount of business, Vincent was right, his bosses treated him like a boy on his first day. Just yesterday they had questioned him about his frequent trips to the toilet. It had been so terribly humiliating.

At first Jo was worried that they were trespassing. Having opened a gate off the street, Vincent ran up some steep steps into a terrace garden. She looked at Theo. 'Who lives here?' Theo called after his brother. 'Friend of yours, old fellow?' But the artist was already scampering out of sight.

'What happens if he drops Baby?' cried Jo.

The young mother would not forget what she saw as she rushed round the side of the large house. For at least two beats of her heart she was convinced that her brother-in-law was feeding Baby to a huge, bristling goat. Then the two namesakes exploded with laughter. 'I'm introducing him to Henrietta,' Vincent announced. 'Dr Gachet's favourite mistress.' Still laughing, the painter swooped his nephew over to where a peacock stood spreading his fan. 'Did you see that, Theo?' he asked. 'A peacock! If only one could capture that effect.'

'Why not, Vincent?' Theo returned. 'After what you've been achieving lately. Dr Gachet is fanatical about your portraits. *The Arlesienne*; and the ones you've done of him.'

'And now allow me to introduce you to Monsieur Cocorrico,' Vincent announced, as the cockerel who had been watching the human trespassers with increasing irritation strode over. His tail was long and green; his comb an argumentative red. When the baby reached out to pull it, the cockerel pecked his finger before crowing loudly.

Jo watched in horror as little Vincent reddened. He might easily lose an eye. She knew how important her brother-in-law was, shared Theo's view that he was little short of a genius, but sometimes Jo could not help feeling that it would be better all round if he was just a little more ordinary. 'Please,' she said. 'Mind Baby.'

'Cocorrico!' the cockerel crowed.

'Cocorrico!' Vincent laughed.

'Cocorrico!'

Baby began to scream. 'Be careful of his eye!' Jo cried.

'The cock crows: cocorrico!' hooted Vincent.

2

'Won't be a minute,' Theo called weakly from behind the tree. The paltry patter of the few

326

drops dribbling from his bladder barely darkened the green moss of the tree bole, yet the pain was scalding, as though he was passing boiling water. When he'd first contracted this condition he'd gone practically a whole week without urinating. Surely there was no worse pain. In the parsonage at Zundert where he and Vincent had grown up there had been a fruit tree that grew thorns in a drought rather than cherries. Theo thought of that tree now as he waited for more urine to barb forth. Auvers-sur-Oise was so beautiful, yet how hard it was to appreciate beauty when your piss was like fish hooks.

'It's so lovely here,' Jo was saying to Vincent as they waited for Theo. It was a little unnerving the way her brother-in-law watched her feeding Baby so intently. 'Do you think you'll stay long in Auvers?'

'Well,' the artist replied without taking his eyes from her breast, 'that depends on Theo.'

'Theo?'

'When he moves here I'll have to stay too.'

'Theo's moving here?'

'Jo, you're *all* moving to the country!'

'Is it certain?'

'Well, tomorrow I'm going to look for a place for you all. Dr Gachet might put you up for a bit. How about that, little Vincent?'

Knowing not to contradict him, Jo looked down at the feeding infant. At least little Vincent was feeding properly. Some days it was a real struggle. At the beginning he'd been such a bad feeder that they'd often feared for him.

'That's good, your breasts are still nice and

full,' the painter remarked. 'Is there plenty of milk in them?'

'I think so,' said Jo, blushing.

'Well, they'll get even bigger once you get here. Swell up like Midi melons! Perhaps we should all move into one of those thatched cottages. A gardener I know has the snuggest little place you could picture. Somewhere you imagine you might open the door and find Millet sitting talking with a peasant.' Jo looked around. Why was Theo taking so long? 'That's one thing about the country for sure,' the painter continued, 'you get a fuller tit. Are you drinking enough — both of you, I mean? Dr Gachet says young parents should be drinking at least two litres of beer a day.'

'There you are, darling,' Jo said quickly when her husband finally emerged.

They walked along the river watching the day-trippers on their brightly coloured jolly boats. 'Pure Maupassant,' Theo said. Vincent took them past the chateau. 'No end of subjects, old boy,' Theo remarked. 'We saw the poppies in the fields from the train. There were cornflowers as well. The sun's shining today too. Did you get that rainstorm the other day? We had it bad in Paris. You should have heard the streets hissing.'

'I tried to paint it. I've always loved storms. By the way, Jo and I have decided everything.'

'What's that, old fellow?'

'About your moving here of course.'

'Ah,' said Theo. 'Tell me, Vincent, apart from Dr Gachet, what are the people like round here?'

'What do you mean?'

'Are you getting to know anyone?'

'There are a few other artists. A lot of Americans. But you know I'm no good at that, Theo. When they see me they just think I'm something else that's escaped from Gachet's menagerie.'

When they came back to Auvers through a newly mown meadow Jo was amazed to see that little Vincent was asleep in his uncle's arms. 'Look, Theo,' she whispered.

'He's taken a shine to you, old fellow,' Theo remarked, and in the corner of her husband's eye Jo could see a tear, but the moment was short-lived. Theo's sudden coughing fit woke the infant.

Vincent tried to soothe the child but he was growing querulous. Grizzling, he cried for his mother. 'I'd better take him,' Jo said. 'He needs winding and cleaning too by the smell of it. Why don't you take Theo to see your paintings?'

'Well, Jo, if it's all right, I'd like to watch you clean his shit away.'

'Watch me?'

'Yes. Paint it too. It would be a kind of alternative Virgin and Child.' Vincent held his face straight for a few more moments then roared with laughter. 'Just joking!'

'Go on, Theo,' said Jo. 'Vincent's eager to show you his work. I'll wait here with little Vincent under this chestnut tree. You know how Baby Bobbin is, he won't settle now until I've sorted him. And you've got things to attend to.'

'Well, if you're sure.'

Undressing Baby, Jo watched the two brothers

hurrying up the narrow lane, boys again in their enthusiasm. For a while after their wedding it had angered her the way the older one seemed to sponge on the younger, like a cuckoo in the nest. It still worried her. How much longer could they keep on supporting him like this? What if they had another little one? And what if Theo's illness took a turn for the worse? Yes; she knew he wasn't well despite how valiantly he attempted to conceal it. Yet seeing them together like this, like two pilgrims on a journey between thatched roofs, she realised how close they were. Besides, she always found it easier to feel sorry for brother-in-law when he wasn't actually with her. All the same, he was right about the country. It was lovely and cool under the shade of this chestnut tree. From somewhere the lowing of cattle reached her. When she had cleaned Baby, she lay with her face beside his and gently sang a Dutch lullaby. Grinning, little Vincent Van Gogh kicked his naked legs.

⋆ ⋆ ⋆

'I'll definitely paint this,' Vincent said, pointing at the church as the brothers paused outside the imposing building. 'Doesn't it remind you of Father's old church?' The congregation were just coming out of midday Mass. They cast haughty glances at the Dutchman. 'By the way, Theo, are you still having trouble pissing?' Theo nodded. 'The same thing happened to me that time in The Hague when I had the clap. It was misery.' Vincent nodded at the church. 'I'll paint it on a stormy day; give it a sky like when the veil of the temple was rent in twain.'

Noticing the looks from the worthy parishioners, Theo guided Vincent gently down the steep steps away from God's house. 'Come on, old chap, it's time for you to show me your work. I've thought of little else for days.' In their descent both brothers made use of the handrail. Yes, Theo thought to himself, the years have not been kind to the Van Gogh brothers.

Vincent took him down a narrow lane between thatched cottages and past a row of villas into the main square. 'This is it,' Vincent announced, pointing at a dreary-looking building with peeling stucco, a wide awning and lopsided roof. 'The cafe where I'm staying. They charge three francs. Did I tell you the doctor tried to get me to stay at a place where they charge six? Still, three francs is too much. That's what really fucks me off, boy. The way they treat artists. After all, they wouldn't charge a peasant that much. When will the world realise that an artist is not a gentleman of leisure on a rest cure but an artisan as much as any shoemaker or jobbing weaver.' An old man with a hooded goose under his arm was the only customer sitting at the tables outside the cafe.

'Afternoon, Monsieur Leblaine,' Vincent greeted the gardener. 'This is my brother, Theo.' The goose hissed uncertainly.

'Fine bird, monsieur,' said Theo in his affable way. 'I saw you on the train. Remarkably docile fowl — most of the time.'

'No different from people,' the gardener

replied. 'If they can't see, they don't fret.'

'Where's your grandson today?' Vincent asked.

'He's helping his grandmother at Dr Gachet's. There's a lunch there for you later.'

Vincent turned to his brother. 'I forgot to tell you, Dr Gachet's giving us lunch.'

'Pulling out all the stops,' cackled Monsieur Leblaine. 'It's a high day and holiday in our house when the doctor invites your brother for a meal. Dishes of all shapes and sizes, and neither of them eating so much as a mouse. We eat well those days, I tell you.'

Hearing the voices and laughter, a face parted the lace cloths which hung like curtains at the dingy cafe window. There was a scurry of little feet and a toddler came rushing out from the dark interior to greet Vincent. 'And this is a shipmate of mine,' Vincent grinned, saluting the child. 'The son of the cafe owner.'

'You know, Vincent,' Theo said, 'every day I pray that you too become a father.'

Vincent went into the cafe and led the way up some stairs, but when he came to his door instead of opening it he rested his forehead against it. 'Of course, what I'm about to show you is nothing beside what you're doing. Falling in love, having a child; that's the real business of life. I'd swap everything for that.'

'It'll come one day.'

'No, it's too late. There comes a time when the barren apple tree must be cut down. You know, just before, at the station, I was thinking of the woman I left behind in The Hague. Her little one was like a son to me — '

'Vincent,' Theo interjected, 'I forgot to tell you. Guillaumin has given me a canvas to swap with you. And he specifically instructed me to tell you that he knew he was the net gainer by such a transaction.'

'Oh, that's good.'

'I thought you'd be pleased. And Gauguin is saying the most wonderful things about you.'

'Gauguin, really?'

'Aurier too; he's talking of doing another piece in *Le Mercure de France*.'

'Theo, I don't want any more attention from the press. Tell them to write about the real artists.'

'But you *are* a real artist, Vincent. Come on, show me your work, there's a good fellow. You're answerable to your little nephew now too, you know.'

'He likes me, doesn't he?'

'He's taken a real shine to you. Everything you paint is for him too now.'

'Yes, it is, isn't it?'

Vincent pushed open his door. Theo heaved a sigh of relief. The last thing he wanted was to get his brother brooding on his childlessness. It always led back to The Hague where he had lived with that whore and her brood — as if they really would have been like his own children. Theo shuddered at the recollection. He was convinced that it was Vincent announcing his intention of marrying that woman and taking on her children that had dealt the fatal blow to their father. He had never recovered. A minister of God with a trollop as a daughter-in-law!

'Welcome to my salon,' Vincent declared.

Through a skylight in the sloping ceiling a blue eye of Auvers sky scrutinised a bed, a chair and countless paintings. 'My God,' whispered Theo solemnly.

'You see, I haven't been taking your money for nothing.'

'Please, Vincent, don't ever refer to it again. You deserve every penny I send.'

The painter gestured at the canvases which were stacked against every available inch of wall. 'You know how it is; each one's yours as much as mine.'

'The chestnuts,' said Theo, bending over a group of canvases. 'They're exquisite.'

'They were still in bloom when I got here, but really I should have come a couple of weeks earlier. Still. What more can I do? I work every hour as it is. Bed at nine and up at five. It's easier to get through the days that way. Look, I've put some Japanese figures walking under the chestnuts.'

'Yes, I see. A memory of Arles, Vincent? And the thatched cottages too.'

'I've tried to show them growing there as naturally as the moss and lichen on their roofs.'

'And these portraits of Dr Gachet. Oh Vincent, I think these must be the best thing you've done.'

'Do you think Gauguin would like them?'

'I'm sure he would, old fellow.'

'He's completely mad, you know, Theo. Easily as mad as me. Gachet, I mean. He misses his wife to the point of insanity.'

334

'You're not mad, Vincent.'

'Well, whatever word you want to use. Bricks that the builder rejected. I've tried to show that in his expression. It's a very modern face. A new kind of broken-heartedness for a new age.'

'You've really got something here, Vincent.'

'You think?'

Theo exhaled softly. In fifteen years of professional connoisseurship he'd seen nothing to compare with what was in this humble little room. 'Old fellow, you've done something that's never been done before.'

'You see, what modern art needs is someone to do for the portrait what Monet has done for the landscape. Of course, it won't be me.'

'I think it already is. But why the foxgloves, Vincent?'

'The doctor's a great believer in anything like that. Natural medicine, he calls it. Maybe you should have him treat you. By the way, if you need to piss, there's a cabinet downstairs. If anyone asks you who you are, you don't need to answer. If they charge me three francs a day then my visitor's got the right to piss in their hole.'

Theo knelt by the canvases as though in prayer. 'Yes, you've really got something here.'

'Take what you want.' Vincent strode over and plucked up a canvas, one that Theo hadn't seen yet. 'Here, have this one.'

It was a garden scene. On it a laburnum tree burnt with a bright yellow flame; flower beds roared with colour; a black cat ran across a lawn; a green bench stood invitingly. 'Remarkable,' murmured Theo. 'Absolutely remarkable.'

'Yes,' said Vincent, turning his head this way and that like a jay as he studied it. 'After all, it might be the least bad thing I've done.'

'I've never seen anything so beautiful.'

'At first I wasn't sure but it's growing on me. I tried to make it look peaceful. The opposite of Gethsemane. I did it in a morning, in Daubigny's garden, but I've been retouching it.'

'You've caught something of eternity, Vincent.'

'It's yours. Take it home with you today.'

'It's still wet; I don't want to spoil it.'

'Take it, then I won't be able to interfere with it any more. Here. Hang it on your wall at home, it'll remind you of what a real country garden has to offer. Think of it as a prescription: *for a complete physical overhaul move to the country.* Yes, and then when you come, bring it back. Now, Theo, you'll have to move quickly if you're going to get here while it's still summer.'

The younger brother sighed. 'How can I just drop everything and come here, Vincent?'

'How can you *not?* That cough of yours isn't getting any better. I wasn't going to say this but you look terrible. Pale as a lily. There's Jo and the little one to think of too. Theo, I'm glad you like this painting but the real thing's even better.'

'What will I do here?'

'Come now, we've been over this a thousand times.'

'Have we?'

Vincent chuckled. 'You're the man of business but it's me having to deal with the practicalities.' The painter's enthusiasm raged like a fire. 'I've worked it all out. Set up something here in

336

Auvers. With your own contacts and Gachet's you'll easily be able to get enough Impressionists to sell.'

'Vincent — '

'Not a combination. More a cooperative. Anyway, a concern dealing with living artists *for* living artists. Forget the trade of dead men. You've seen yourself how busy Auvers is. How many people got off that train? It's quite an artistic hub. There's even a girl painting here. She's English. What an ideal base for you to set up on your own. Why put up with being a lackey for Goupil when you can stand on your own two feet? Ah, Theo, once you're here I really think you'll realise that it's painting you want to do more than selling. What's the matter, what's that look for? You know I've never seen you as being the same as those cunts at Goupil's. You're an artist not a merchant. You're the same as that old gardener outside. In that temple of Mammon in Paris, you're no happier than he would be. Monsieur Leblaine has to feel the earth between his fingers, and you need it too, flowing to you through a brush and canvas, like water reaching a tree through its roots.' Telling himself not to react, Theo continued to look at his brother's canvas of a spring garden. Remarkable the way someone so turbulent could produce such an oasis of peace. 'Don't go silent on me, Theo.'

'But, Vincent, what can I say?'

'Just say you're coming.'

Theo sighed. It was the same thing over and over. Once his older brother got an idea into his head, he hammered away at it like one of the woodpeckers they'd watched in the parsonage garden as children. Sometimes his brother seemed to be like a woodpecker with a broken beak. 'And what about little Vincent and Jo?'

'Well, why do you think I keep going on about it? A move here would be for them. Escape your drudgery. Why break your back pulling someone else's cart? By the way, you'll have to frame it simply, I think, for the best effect. What's the matter, don't you like it?'

'The picture? Of course I do.'

'Then what the fuck is it? That look you've just given me, Theo, I swear it's pure Dad. Don't tell me you're turning into a minister of religion on me.'

'There was no look, Vincent. I'm just thinking how beautiful your garden painting is.'

'Yes, well, here it is. Take it.'

'I don't want to spoil it. The train gets so crowded and with the baby and everything it could easily get damaged.'

'Don't be a prick like those fucking ever so grand bastards you work for. Why don't you just come out with it and say you don't like the canvas.'

'But I love it.'

'Then move to Auvers!'

'Those aren't the same things.'

'Fine, so you don't want the picture. You'll just chuck it under a bed anyway, like you do with the rest.'

'Every single space in the apartment is taken up by your canvases, Vincent. There's no room left. And with little one — '

'Well, here's one less to clutter it all up then.'

Snatching the painting of the springtime garden, Vincent stepped up on the chair, and, thrusting open the skylight to its widest extent, flung out the canvas.

3

'Well I never,' Monsieur Leblaine said to himself when a picture fell from one of the upstairs rooms in the cafe, and landed practically at his feet. 'Strange rain we're having.' Bouncing off the awning, the picture had landed face up. The old gardener smiled. 'I've seen a thousand artists working in Auvers,' he said later on many occasions, 'but there were only two paintings I ever liked. And one of them was done by the maddest of them all. But say what you like about him, he must have been a gardener himself to have painted something like that. It's the kind of thing a gardener dreams of. A place where everything comes just right, and there's no late frosts.'

With a twinge in his back, and the hooded goose still under his arm, Monsieur Leblaine bent down and picked up the canvas. There was no one about. Removing the stretchers and rolling it up, he placed it inside his jacket. From Mad Red's room in the cafe came a raking cough. The hooded goose murmured once as the old gardener hurried off to his thatched cottage in the narrow lane.

Eastern Germany, February 1945

1

Don't look up. Helga told herself, *don't look up.* As she passed under the tree, a dangling foot struck her forehead. Burying Lotte's face deeper in her breast she hurried her on. The girl stumbled. There were five bodies hanging from the beech bough. At the beginning of the journey, Helga had made detours round the improvised gallows that were springing up all around Germany, now it was all she could do to keep one foot in front of the other. And if *she* was tired how did her children feel? For the thousandth time Helga asked herself what she was doing dragging them halfway across Germany when everyone else was fleeing headlong in the other direction. There, ten steps ahead as usual, walked Gustav, the great clouds of his breath drifting over the ice-bound earth. But where was Peter? He was always lagging behind, wandering off, disappearing for hours on end. Soon it would be dark, but Helga lacked even the strength to call her youngest son's name. For three days now she'd eaten nothing, giving all the food to the children. Another step; another; another. *Don't look up, never look up.*

Standing below the beech-tree gallows, Peter looked up at the bodies. They were frozen solid. One of the corpses was swinging on its creaking rope. Agony contorted the dead face, a long tongue protruded from the wide open mouth as though he had swallowed the rope that had hanged him. Peter reached up and touched one of the bare feet. The toes were black; the nails cracked. The boy shook his head with disdain. This is what they deserved; they were cowards. Nailed against the trunk was a sign saying: *These men talked of defeat, they are not worthy of their Führer and must die the death of shame.* Peter plunged a hand into his pocket. Even through his mittens he could feel the exact shape of his Pistole 08. No talk of defeat for him; when his turn came he would be ready to use it. Years in the Hitler Youth had prepared him. Hitler had secret wonder-weapons; everybody knew that. Any day now he would unleash them; it was the duty of each German to keep the Russkis back until that moment. Feeling a stinging sensation on his numb face, Peter realised that it had begun snowing again. He gazed up at the million flakes; against the black silhouette of the tree with its twisted branches and rigid corpses, they seemed to shimmer with a soft translucence. Yes, he was more than ready: at the age of fourteen Peter yearned to die for the Fatherland. On the road the worm of refugees continued to wriggle west. Rage noosed his throat. They all deserved the same treatment as the cowards hanging above him. His father wasn't a coward. *He* was staying in the east to face the enemy. Perhaps they could die side by side; perhaps Peter could find Papa and fight beside him. It was what he dreamt of every day. Seizing hold of the frozen foot, he thrust the corpse into motion. All five bodies began to swing, ropes groaning, five dark shadows swaying over the pure white snow.

★ ★ ★

Gustav waited patiently until his mother caught up then spoke the words that had been burning him for days. 'You're never going to find him,' he said. 'Papa. He could be anywhere. How do you know he isn't one of those; how do you know that that one right there isn't him?' Helga followed her son's pointing finger to the endless column of refugees, a defeated, anonymous mass wound round in as many coats, rags and sacks as they could find against the bitter cold. 'Or one of those, Mama.' Helga peered through the snow to the hanged men her son was pointing at. 'We've got to turn back,' Gustav pleaded.

How could Helga answer him? Whatever she said he would not understand. Perhaps she didn't even understand it herself. She squinted; was that Peter standing beneath the gallows beech? 'Go and find your brother, Gustav. It's going to be dark soon.'

'All right. You and Lotte get some firewood. I saw some trees over there.'

★ ★ ★

342

Although he had only been still for a minute, Peter was already beginning to feel the cold. Icicles hung from the trousers of the hanged. They reminded him of the lightning bolts on the Waffen SS insignia that Papa would be wearing when he found him; that he himself would soon put on. Despite the bitter cold, he felt a warmth within.

Gustav was halfway to the hanging tree when he heard the plane. On the road the line of refugees parted, people diving for whatever cover they could find. *Just like the Red Sea*, he thought to himself for a moment, then he too began to sprint, throwing himself headlong under the beech just as the Soviet fighter roared above. Cringing beneath the roots of the old tree, Gustav blocked his ears to the bullets. Yesterday he had been hiding like this with a group of refugees, and a little girl had been neatly decapitated; her head had lain on a snowdrift, her eyes questioning the survivors.

The din of the Soviet fighter faded as it strafed its way down the long road to Berlin, but nobody moved from their hiding place. Often a plane would come back. Among the moans of the wounded, Gustav could hear a strange, musical tinkling. He looked up. Sprayed by bullets and mud, the corpses were swinging so that their icicles chimed together. The icicles had a green tinge: the piss that had frozen even as it left the dying bodies. The hanged often piss as they die. The past few weeks had enormously increased Gustav's knowledge of death. It seemed there were as many ways of dying as of living. He

343

looked for his brother. A cart was burning nearby. Gustav could make out a small figure standing alone in the middle of the road. It was holding something that glinted in the flames of the cart. He realised that it was his brother just as he heard the plane returning. The din of bullets and propeller shook the frozen world but Peter did not move. Gustav looked on in disbelief. His brother was standing in the middle of the road brandishing a Pistole 08 at the approaching Soviet fighter. The plane seemed to fill the sky; the pilot was clearly visible. And there was Peter and his pistol like a boy facing a dragon with a catapult. 'Peter!' he screamed. 'Peterli!' But his brother did not reply.

At first Peter thought that he'd been hit. The moment he'd longed for had come at last: he was dying for the Führer and Fatherland. Then he realised that it was his brother who had knocked him down. The receding shape of the plane was shimmying its wings in recognition of the challenge. 'What are you doing?' Peter screamed.

'It'll come back again.'

'I've still got two bullets left.'

'You've got to take cover.'

'Leave me alone.'

'Don't be an idiot, Peterli.'

'You're a coward like the rest of them!'

Gustav snatched the pistol; Peter caught him by the wrist. In the thickly falling snow, they grappled in silence. Cumbersome in their many layers and thick mittens they lay locked on the ground grunting face to face, half concealed by their own steaming breath. With tears of rage

344

Peter found himself being overpowered. For about three or four seconds Gustav held the gun at his brother's forehead. How easy it would be for him to pull the trigger. As easy as it had once been to dangle spit over his face. For a few seconds he felt consumed with a desire to fire, then with a cry he threw the weapon from him and covered Peter with his own body so that when the plane came back, the pilot, who had been looking forward to dealing with the cocky Kraut, saw only a bump of frozen earth already whitening with the snow.

Climbing back onto his feet, breath steaming from him like a geyser, Gustav thought that he was dreaming. A smell of roasting meat basted the air. Both brothers looked at each other, hunger brokering its instant, although untrustworthy, truce. How long was it since they'd tasted meat? Slipping on the ice, Gustav stumbled over to where the odour was coming from. An ox which had been pulling the burning cart was beginning to roast in the flames. For a moment the brothers stared open-mouthed. 'Quick,' Gustav commanded. 'Help me.' Taking out a piece of metal that he had salvaged from a smouldering vehicle a few days before, the older brother began sawing at the haunch of beef as the younger pulled. Although the metal was razor-sharp, the sweat soon stood on their foreheads. The dead animal peered at the falling snow through its glassy, unseeing eye.

'What the hell are you doing?' A small figure had materialised from the snow. 'That beast's mine, you bastards.' Gustav shrugged off the man and continued hacking. But he came back. 'Get off, you thief!'

Having retrieved the gun, Peter pointed it at the figure. Eyes only just visible in the swathe of sacking over his head, the owner of the cow stared in disbelief. 'Jesus Christ, put that toy away, you crazy kid.'

'You fucking deserter. I'll blow you into the middle of next week.'

Attracted by the smell of meat, people were appearing from the snow. Watching as one brother aimed the gun at the owner of the cart while the other hacked at the carcass, the crowd held for a moment then surged forward. Ripping hands descended on the beast. Tearing their haunch clear, Gustav pulled himself free of the melee. But as he did so he felt the prize being tugged away. He swiped with the sharp piece of metal. A dull scream was followed by a stream of scarlet blood onto the snow. Swaying like a drunkard, the owner of the dead beast held up a thumbless hand.

With the meat secured under his clothes, Gustav ran to the beech tree. 'Come over here,' he ordered his brother. 'Brace yourself against the trunk.'

'What are you doing, Gusti?'

'Stand still.'

'Why?'

'Just do as I say!'

Peter flinched under the weight as his brother hauled himself roughly onto his shoulders.

'The tree?' said Peter. 'I'll go up. I'm better at climbing.' But as usual Gustav wasn't listening to him. His heel clipped Peter's ear. The younger brother bridled. He'd done that on purpose.

Careful not to fall — best not think what would happen to them all if he sprained or broke an ankle — Gustav squirmed his way across the long bough on which the corpses dangled. They'd already been stripped, but two of them still wore their shirts. From these he could make a little screen; not much but enough to form a rudimentary roof or keep the drifting snow off as they slept. The garments were frozen onto the corpses. If he ripped them, they would be useless. As he peeled the clothes off, strips of the skin came away too. Jostling his way down the bough to the second corpse, Gustav looked down. At the sight of his brother huddled below, a memory pricked him like an icicle: the day they had truanted from school. Conquering his own terrible, lurching fear, Gustav had had to return for Peter over the rickety bridge. To get him to cross he'd pretended there was a witch watching them from the trees. They had been on their way to Papa then too. As Gustav carefully teased the shirt from the dead man's back he found himself wishing that it was his father hanging here. Dangling from the branch, he let himself drop. For the first time since leaving the Black Forest just after Christmas, he was thankful for the deep snow that broke his fall.

2

Helga tightened her grip on Lotte's hand. Gusti might be all right, Peterli too, but Lotte was only eleven years old; if they got separated even for just one night she wouldn't survive until the morning. As if this journey wasn't hard enough without it being the coldest winter she could remember.

When they reached the wood and found some ash poles under the snow Helga felt her strength rally. Long, dry, light: the perfect firewood! Carrying as many poles as they could between themselves, mother and daughter scrambled back to the road. The boys were just coming. Although they were exhausted, Gustav insisted they camp back from the road among the trees. Peter argued against it, and for a moment Gustav thought that he would have to fight him again. In recent days, Peter had been getting worse, contesting everything that Gustav suggested. It was only reluctantly that the younger brother gave ground. When Gustav brought the meat out, his mother began weeping. As she lit the fire, he constructed a small shelter among the ash saplings with the shirts of the dead men. The haunch of cow had already frozen. Mama stuck it between two ash-pole skewers. Mesmerised, they sat in a ring round the fire, watching the juices slowly bubbling into a tin set to catch them. As though sharing a communion cup, Mama passed round the billycan of blood-yellow glutinous fat. 'Don't take all of it,' Gustav ordered Peter. 'And eat slowly, otherwise you'll get the shits again.'

The meat was almost ready when the three men came, fleshless faces protruding from shapeless rags. Without a word they grabbed the food. Ripping at it with their bare teeth, their incisors glinting, they stripped it from the bone. When Peter tried to stop them he was knocked to the ground. 'Please,' Helga begged. 'We are starving.' The men continued to gnaw ravenously. 'Leave us some.' Still, they didn't seem to notice her. 'I'll pay,' she screamed, hanging on them. 'Leave us some and I'll pay.' One of the men cocked half an eye at her, and pulling off a morsel tossed it to her. Helga gave it to Lotte. She gripped the second man by the arm. 'I'll pay.' He grunted; and gave her a piece, which she passed to Peter. 'I'll pay,' she said to the third man. He too pulled some of the fibrous steak free, a larger chunk than the others. It went to Gustav.

'Where did you get the wood?' one of the men demanded when they had finished the meat. Helga pointed into the darkness. 'Show me,' he said.

She had barely walked beyond earshot of the fire when the man grabbed her. In the dark whiteout she could hardly see him, her senses filling instead with the beard chafing her face, and the smell of meat juices coating the chin that butted her nose. 'Don't rip them,' she said, as he began pawing at her clothes.

'Jesus,' the man whispered as the cold gripped his penis.

A searing pain gashed its way into her body. He had thrust her against a young tree and seemed to be probing her insides with a knife. *Don't look*, she told herself and forced herself instead to look at . . . food. It was never far from her thoughts anyway. Just a simple apple to begin with, freshly picked from the little orchard at Keilburg; then some warm, fragrant bread and a round of goat's cheese. In her mind, a table quickly laid itself, bearing all the delicacies of the Black Forest: *Schäufele*, a feast meal served with sauerkraut and potato salad; speck, the thinnest slices of smoked bacon dowsed in mustard, plum flan . . .

As the tree shivered with the impact of the stranger's climax, showering its rime over her, she found that her mouth was watering. As he withdrew, her belly rumbled.

The second rapist came just moments later. Skull gurgling with lust, he threw himself onto her. They tumbled to the ground. He bit and chewed at her neck, soaking her with saliva. Helga did not resist. The amount of meat she had been able to get for her children was about the same as a penis. At least she'd got something; other women were not so lucky. *Don't look up*, she told herself as she lay under the rapist like wood beneath the axe. Once again to distract herself, she pictured the table at home, placing more and more items on it; and among all the many mouth-watering dishes, a Black Forest gateau. The finest she had ever made: cherries that burst with flavour in the mouth, cream whose richness made the eater close their eyes in appreciation, and dark cake that melted in the throat like dusk in the forest. The first time she met Ernst she had made him a gateau. *I'm bringing home a student this evening,* Uncle had said nonchalantly. *He doesn't seem to have any family; he might appreciate a decent meal.* With a mewling grunt the second rapist ejaculated, but even after he had withdrawn, leaving the woman lying motionless in the snow, she continued to masticate over her memories. Had that table with its Black Forest gateau and young girl falling in love for the first time really ever existed?

She waited but the third man did not appear. It was so warm lying there in the snow like an ash pole. Then a terrible thought, even worse than the rape itself, penetrated her. Lotte. Ripping herself up out of the snow, falling repeatedly, as Helga ran back to the fire she pictured the third man fucking her daughter. When she reached the fire she saw that the two satiated men were already slumbering, noisy as pigs. They had gathered more wood, and the flames were leaping high. The third sat staring into the dancing tongues of fire. Lotte too was sleeping, huddled with Gusti. Looking up into the mute, snowy night, Helga fell to her knees and thanked God. Without rising she went over to the third man. 'Please, I'll pay you now,' she whispered. He handed her a piece of meat and for the first time since Gustav was born Helga thought only of herself. Weakened by her memory of lavish food, she snatched the meat and began to bolt it down. A tearing pain ran

351

through her thighs. Some of the semen had frozen and the movement had torn off the skin. Heavily hooded, the man's features were hidden. The growing firelight hinted at a scarred and pockmarked face. From within the hood, grey eyes watched her eating, like a wolf peeping through the undergrowth. 'Let me pay you now,' she repeated. 'I won't be able to do it later.'

As he leant forward and raised her to her feet, she saw that his lips were black; his left ear was missing. 'We parted company on the eastern front,' he said, touching the missing ear. 'Frostbite. Funny thing is, I can still hear the shells. You don't need to stare at me like that. I'm not going to hurt you. Those two are not travelling companions of my choice.'

'Where are you from?' Helga heard herself ask. It was not fear that made her stare but his shockingly gentle voice.

'Somewhere I'll never see again,' he replied.

The same intonation; the same vowels; it might be Ernst talking. She sat down by him. 'This place; is it far away?'

'Ah, now you're asking. All right then. The Baltic. You want my address too? Well, you're welcome to it. I come from north of Königsberg; the home town of Immanuel Kant. I'm a citizen of the dead dunes.' And so, unlooked for and in the most woeful of circumstances, one of the mysteries of Helga's life solved itself. Ernst was from the Baltic. 'Why do you ask?'

'I just knew someone who spoke the same way.'

'They say we speak with a grain of sand in the throat.'

Helga drew on her last well of strength. 'Please, let me pay you now.'

'I've committed enough sins without adding that one to the list.'

'Thank you,' she whispered, and then found to her surprise that she had grown too weak to weep.

In the ensuing silence they found themselves smiling at each other. Tentatively, his lupine eyes searched her face. 'Forgive me for asking, but I'm a little puzzled myself. Here I find you in the eastern enclave of our glorious Reich and yet your accent has nothing of the Prussian in it.'

Helga paused before saying: 'We're from the Black Forest.'

'I'm not convinced that this is a good time for holidaymaking.' She did not reply. Again the searching, iron-grey eyes. 'If you want, you can come with me. All of you. We'll leave these two dogs behind. I'd shoot them if I had a gun.'

'We're not going in your direction.'

'One of the ports is still open. I know the way.'

'We're not going to the sea.'

'Believe me, it's the only way out. If you keep going west the Russkis will catch up with you. They're in Poland already.'

'We're not going west.'

'So now we're dealing in riddles. You're not going north; you're not going west; you're not going east. True, if God had given us wings we might fly over the Red Army. Look, I'm not prying, God knows we all have our own business to attend to, but I assure you the only hope is north. I've just been fighting in the east. Ivan's going to wipe Germany off the face of the earth. Not that you can entirely blame him. Our own visiting manners were not exactly impeccable.'

'My husband's there.' Helga's voice did not seem to be her own. 'He's an officer in the SS.'

The man shrugged. 'Well, from now on I wouldn't let on to that little fact if I were you. Where abouts was he from, your Baltic friend?'

'I don't know. He never said.'

Bathing in the unaccustomed warmth, the children continued to slumber soundly. Helga closed her eyes. Her body was numb; her mind too. The voice of the stranger had brought to the fore everything she had lost. After that first supper, they had gone for a walk. Simple as a child, Ernst had taken her hand. 'Will you do me a favour?' she heard herself murmur to the stranger. 'Would you tell me about your home?'

'What do you want to know?'

'Oh, what's it like?'

He had not been talking for long when the stranger felt the woman's body next to his own. Imperceptibly, they had been drawing closer. He lifted an arm and found her underneath it. In the past few years he'd seen enough to realise that Germany was damned, but this woman would have been enough evidence on her own. 'The dunes go on forever,' he told her. 'They have a life of their own. They blow from one place to another so that the coast is never the same two years running. In winter the whole sea freezes, just about the time the geese arrive. Chain after chain of geese. When I was a boy — '

At that moment, wandering in his boyhood memories, the soldier's brain registered a thundering flash and then nothing more. Woken by the gunshot and seeing the Pistole 08 in the firelight, the stranger's chance companions lurched away into the snowy night. 'Scum,' Peter screamed brandishing his pistol. 'Deserters. Traitors.' He stared at his mother in the arms of the coward he had just shot and then he too disappeared into the night.

'Peterli!' screamed Helga as she struggled out of the dead man's embrace.

Not listening to the voices calling after him, Peter kept running. At last he had struck a blow for the Führer! At the Hitler Youth meetings they had said it was every German's duty to exterminate vermin. Well, that was what he'd done. He'd eradicated an enemy of the Fatherland; Papa would have shot him too. Finally the time had come; Peter had made up his mind; he wouldn't stay to be told what to do by that coward Gustav for a moment longer. It shouldn't be too hard to locate the nearest Waffen SS unit then he'd lie about his age if he needed to. Other members of his Hitler Youth group had been doing the same for months. It was only Gustav who had stopped him. Gusti! Ever since Papa had left home, Peter's brother had done his best to hinder him in his work for the Führer. Who was it that told the authorities that he was only fourteen when he had joined up last autumn, coming all the way to Freiburg to take him home? Who was it that refused to fly the swastika at Keilburg? Who was it that had dared to defend that Jew doctor? Stopping abruptly, Peter let out a howl of wrath into the great snowy night. Although Gustav had always lied, saying the doctor was trying to help her, with his own eyes Peter had seen him trying to kill their sister. It was the Jew who had maimed her, cut out her voice. Another wail of anguish escaped Peter's lips. There could only be one reason for Gustav's behaviour: he himself was a Jew. Ever since Peter had realised this fact, he had fought against it. He could do so no longer. Gustav was not his brother; his parents must have adopted him; he was a filthy Hebrew bent on destroying Germany and the world. Pain gripped Peter's guts. The meat he had eaten lay heavily on his stomach; the shits would begin any moment.

Enraged by his weakness, he lingered, leaning against a tree, the snowflakes lancing his upturned face. Even though he was going to join Papa it was hard to say goodbye to Mama and Lotte. 'Leibstandarte Adolf Hitler,' Peter whispered to himself, reciting the litany of the SS divisions to give himself courage. 'Das Reich, Totenkopf, Viking, Hitlerjugend . . . '

The sudden touch on his shoulder made the boy spin round. It took him a few moments before he realised that the figure standing there, at whom he was pointing his gun, was his sister. Then for the first time since she was three years old, Lotte spoke to another human being: 'Pe-er.'

'Lotte?' He tried to push her gently away but she caught his arm.

'Pe-er.' Her voice was like a baby's; like the ugly, stuttering gasp the stranger had made when he shot him. 'Pe-er — ont-go.'

For a moment he seemed about to speak, then he pulled himself free from her and crashed into the night. Papa had done it; and now he was doing the same. A man had to renounce *everything* for the Fatherland.

As Lotte watched the snow obliterate her brother she rubbed her hands together but they would not come warm. It was a new sign for her to teach Papa when they found him. Hands rubbing and rubbing but staying cold: how she felt when they were apart. When she came back to the fire, Gusti was stripping the dead man of his clothes. He did not even ask her if she'd found Peter.

As his sister and mother slept, Gustav threw the last of the ash poles on the fire. Wood never lasted as long as you needed it to. All the same, when was the last time he had felt this warm? The tent he had improvised round them kept off the snow, its panels bellying in the wind. The dead man's sheepskin waistcoat had been a godsend. Gustav looked at his mother; she had cried and screamed when he stopped her from going back out into the night to search for Peter. Through a tear in the tent, Gustav could see the corpse lying there but all he could do was flip him over so that his buttocks and not his penis faced them. In these weeks travelling across the country, the young man had seen more ways of dying and being dead than he could ever have guessed were possible. Once Uncle Dietrich had told him about the Finnish Eskimos, who had a hundred different words for snow; his own language would now have to develop the same lexicon for death. How would Peter die? In their deep, even breathing Mama and Lotte seemed to be one living creature. He watched them for a while, envying their temporary oblivion. Papa was somewhere out there in the horror beyond their frail womb of warmth. Peter too. Gustav wasn't quite sure when he had begun to hate his brother. The acrimony between Cain and Abel doesn't grow in a day. Yet he could pinpoint the exact moment he had started to despise his father. It had been in the autumn of 1941.

The three of them had been collecting sweet chestnuts as a special treat for Papa's return from a field trip in the Ukraine. The crop was fruitful that year and Gustav had raced back to the house for another basket. Running past the pond, he saw Papa's trunk by Lotte's bench. He was back already! As Gustav crossed the threshold of the house, the boy had heard something he had never heard before. Mama was shouting. Silently he went inside, mounted the stairs and, creeping into his bedroom, slid under the bed. Years later as he lay dying on that very same bed, Gustav Mann would recall in searing detail what he saw through the knothole. The black tunic and hat, the flashes of the swastika: his father wearing an SS uniform. Even the words of his parents' conversation were punched onto his heart as though recorded by a stenographer.

'Take that thing off,' his mother had snarled.

His father's voice had been as gentle and calm as it always was so that for a while Gustav couldn't quite grasp what they were talking about. 'And for how much longer do you think we can keep her a secret, Helga?'

'For as long as we need to.'

'She should have been at school two years ago.'

'Dr Wolff will make us another birth certificate. He'll change her birthdate.'

'And what will we do next year, and the year after?'

'Dr Wolff — '

'Helga, Dr Wolff was arrested today.'

'Ernst.' Gustav's mother's voice had been a strange hissing. 'That uniform. Burn it.'

'Another six months, a year. Yes, maybe if we're lucky we might be able to protect her that long.'

'And by then the war will be over!'

'You're right, Helga, the war will be over by then because Hitler will have won it. He's running through the Soviet Union like a knife through a gateau. I've been in the Ukraine — ' At this his father had broken off with a sigh that Gustav had never heard him make before. 'I've seen such things, Helga. Such things.' Again the sigh, so unlike Papa, almost a sob, a donkey-like bray. 'Hitler's not going to stop until he's killed everyone who isn't with him. And who's going to stop him? Russia's on the point of collapse.'

'The British — '

'The British themselves are living on borrowed time.'

'The Americans.'

'What do they care? One after the other the capitals of Europe have fallen to him and they never lifted a finger. Why change now?'

'I'm telling you to get that black crow out of our house.'

'Helga, this is our only hope.'

'Are you out of your mind, Ernst? It's that uniform that wants to kill her.'

'But don't you realise? It's our cloak of invisibility.'

Once and once only would Gustav hear his mother swear: 'This isn't one of your fucking fairy tales now!'

'Nevertheless,' Papa had replied, his tone still even, 'it's the only thing that can save her. I've joined them, Helga.' And this was the moment. At a single stroke all the boy's idolatry for his father had been recast in hate. Papa had given himself to the Nazis; weakness can be forgiven by a son, betrayal never. Tears stinging his eyes, Gustav had come out from under his bed, run back down the stairs and fled the house.

'Helga, you must believe me,' Ernst had begged that day in Keilburg — without eavesdroppers now. 'I've thought long about it. Done nothing else but think about it. There's no other way of protecting her. This uniform bestows a special dispensation on those who wear it. I've seen it myself. Helga, I happen to know that some of those who wear it are even married to Jewesses.'

'What are you talking about?'

360

'Even some right at the very top. If you keep loyal and keep quiet then nobody probes.'

'I won't hide our daughter in that pillar of smoke.'

'Then where *will* you hide her?' Now it was Ernst's turn for his voice to rise. 'Are you going to keep her in the store loft for the rest of her life? Are you going to turn her into a stork? Helga, if you'd seen what I saw in those birch forests out east — '

'I will trust my prayers rather than that abomination.'

'And you're the one accusing me of weaving straw into gold?'

If Gustav had remained at the knothole he would have seen something else that he would never forget. But the slap Helga gave her husband rang out unwitnessed through the empty house. 'Who are you?' Helga had murmured. 'You blew into these mountains like an autumn leaf and now, still with no explanation, you want to turn the world black. Let me ask you this. If nothing else, are you not worried about your soul?'

'For my daughter, I'm willing to risk it.'

'For your daughter, or your career?'

Helga woke. And for an instant, she thought she was back in Keilburg stirring in Ernst's arms one morning before the shadow of the uniform had fallen over their little valley. Day was breaking, grey as the lice in the folds of her clothes. She rose. Somewhere in this godforsaken world her second son was wandering lost.

361

3

'Heads down; get your fucking heads down!' The whine of the shell became an explosion that seemed to flip the dugout high into the sky like a pancake. A halo of fire flared over the foxhole. Lethal lumps of frozen mud and metal crumped through the air. It was only when Ernst Mann felt the lice stirring in the cuffs of his tunic that he realised he wasn't dead.

He spat the soil and grit from his mouth. He was unlucky; it hadn't been a direct hit. The boy who had been wounded yesterday continued to moan from somewhere under the wreckage. 'I must have *Panzerschrecks*,' a hoarse voice demanded from inside the dugout. 'Will you listen to me? I must have some goddamned *Panzerschrecks*.' Ernst looked at the layer of dirt and detritus covering him. Leave it; maybe the next shell would bury him properly. All around him coughs hacked from the rubble. In the dugout, the officer continued to rasp into the radio, requesting anti-tank personnel that no longer existed.

'I wish I had a *Panzerschreck*,' one of the men stirring in the foxhole said. 'The first thing I'd do is stick it up his arse.'

When the clouds of smoke had lifted a little, Ernst thought he must be dreaming. Standing there on the edge of the crater was a donkey. *Am I losing my mind*, he thought, *or am I dead already?*

'I must have anti-tank personnel,' the officer continued. 'I've received intelligence of heavy tank units coming this way. They've just started shelling us.'

'Intelligence?' the man beside Ernst mocked. 'Ivan's so near I can smell him. What a stink! He's just pulled his pants down and had a shit. That's your intelligence!'

'This fucking thing's frozen again,' another soldier said, brandishing his weapon in disgust.

'Piss on it then, that's the only way.' Ernst's neighbour smirked. A thin jet of yellow urine arced against the frozen grey. 'You've brought us luck,' he said to Ernst. 'I thought we were meat for the maggots just then.' From somewhere amid the nest of living limbs and severed body parts, a hissing sound started.

'Looks like your luck's run out,' another hidden voice said.

Ernst's lungs were racked with smoke. 'What is it?'

'Something about to explode. I'd fucking run if I hadn't lost half my leg already.' The man began desperately to crawl his way out of the hole he'd spent yesterday digging for himself. Like a rat with a broken back he scrabbled over the earth. Ernst closed his eyes. At last he was going to die. But instead of the explosion he was waiting for, he heard a detonation of laughter. 'Of all the fucking things!' his neighbour declared. Feeling a sudden searing pain at his side, Ernst grabbed at it instinctively. With a yelp, he recoiled. His fingers had been singed. A piece of shrapnel was wedged in his hip. So, this was his fate. He'd seen it in others. A slow death of blood poisoning and lockjaw. But the one with

363

the injured leg was no longer trying to escape; he was lying back laughing. 'I thought I'd seen everything,' he cackled. 'Hey, everybody, you've got to see this. This is something to tell the grandkids.' Like wraiths materialising from the drifting smoke, a pack of gaunt, wizened faces emerged from their hiding places in the rubble and crawled across the foxhole towards Ernst. They all began to titter. Ernst looked up. The donkey had gone. The pain in his hip was excruciating. With a dull scream he tried to rip the molten shard of metal from his flesh. The others wailed with laughter. The piece of red hot shrapnel had not entered his body but pierced his water bottle. The hissing was the water coming to the boil. 'Soup, we must have soup,' said the man with the mangled leg.

Some bouillon cubes were crumbled into the perforated canister and stirred by the giggling Waffen SS veteran with the nozzle of his gun. Suddenly solemn, the men passed the watery potage round. But the shell that landed without warning on the lip of the crater dispelled any hope. Ernst saw what looked like a mouth opening to spew fire, as though one of the dragons of English legend had hopped onto the battlefield. Half of the soup drinkers were killed instantly, the others left writhing on the frozen ground like maggots.

For a long time the folklorist did not open his eyes, but at last he was forced to admit to himself that once again he had somehow survived. Among the mangled limbs surrounding him was a donkey's hoof. Shells shook the ground. He picked up the hoof; it had been filleted at the fetlock.

'Goddamnit!' the officer roared brokenly. 'Get me those *Panzerschrecks* or are we supposed just to suck Ivan's cock when he arrives?'

In the east, a rumble began; it growled like approaching thunder. Ernst crawled to the top of the dugout. For an instant the dense cloud of battle smoke parted to reveal a thick phalanx of T-34s. He felt his throat tighten. Behind the tanks came the Red Army itself, only three hundred metres away.

The squad of anti-tank personnel with their *Panzerschrecks* arrived just in time. 'What's the matter with you?' one of them asked Ernst as he primed his bazooka. 'Never seen a stovepipe before?' He laid an affectionate hand on his anti-tank weapon. 'Ivan's on the menu.'

'How long can we hold them?' Ernst asked.

'Today,' the man replied. 'We're the only squad in the whole sector.' All around them more troops were arriving. 'Are you the only one of your unit left?'

'Tank shell.'

'Want to be a hero? Go and get a lollipop from that man over there.' The soldier made the sign of the cross. 'And make your final confession.'

Less than a minute later Ernst was crawling over the frozen terrain. The instructions were simple. He'd been given a hollow-charge grenade and told to find a hole. He was to hide there until he heard a tank overhead. Having stuck the magnetic grenade on the tank's underside, he would have nine seconds to get away.

The frozen ground was already trembling under the weight of the rolling hardware as the folklorist threw himself into his hole. He hacked at the dirt with his entrenchment tool until his fingers bled. Was it deep enough? Too late to change hiding places. One last look showed him the line of tanks advancing, and behind them the Ivans, near enough now for him to see their contrast to the grey, frostbitten Germans. Dressed for the weather, the Red Army was warm, mobile, and lethal. Behind them Ernst could sense the whole weight of retribution: the creeping shelf of an ice age that was going to cover Germany, perhaps the entire world, for many years, maybe even the thousand that Hitler talked about.

How much longer would it take? Not for the first time since joining the Waffen SS Ernst questioned his motives. Why was he killing himself like this? After all, what had he done that was so bad? There was, of course, the Ukraine, but what had he actually done there that made his own death so necessary? He clung to the sides of his hole. The whole earth around him seemed to be rumbling as though the world's fairy tales had emptied their pages of giants and scattered them over Berlin.

The first wave of T-34s passed wide of him. The *Panzerschrecks* seemed to ignite the world; for a long time he just lay there gazing at their brilliance as though struck dumb by a wonder of nature. Then all at once his rathole was plunged into darkness. Before he had chance to move, the tank had gone and once again the sky was filled with smoke and the aurora borealis of battle. Human screams mixed with the rattling of the vehicle. The T-34 had dropped its caterpillar track into another soldier's hiding place and was crushing the cowering inmate. A saying from Helga's native mountains came to Ernst's mind: *The hare dies screaming, the fir giant falls with only a sigh.* How would he himself die? The final question of his life.

When the second tank came he was ready. He fumbled off the safety cap as instructed. Nine seconds now separated him from oblivion. He placed the device onto the belly of the beast but it didn't stick. The tank had been coated with some kind of non-magnetic paint. Head pounding in the thundering darkness, he tried again, thrusting in desperation, but the magnet would not fix. Was this going to be the way it ended? How would it feel, the obliteration of every thought, every nerve ending, every single atom of his being? Would it be a screaming agony, or nothing more than the prick of a spindle? The next moment there was a barely audible clump. The magnetic explosive had found purchase on the tank's metal underbelly. Only just clear of Ernst's hole, thick smoke suddenly billowed from the tank followed by a roar as the T-34 blew up.

4

When Ernst opened his eyes, his body seemed to be hovering above the ground; a face he did not recognise was looming over him. The face was speaking but Ernst could hear only a buzzing. He looked about and was puzzled to see a row of bunks lining a sandbag wall. This certainly didn't correspond to the underworld of any myth he had ever read about. Although it was difficult, he lifted his head to get a better view. What he saw was reminiscent of no Valhalla; in fact, it seemed to be the barracks that he had left this morning. Neither was there a boatman to ferry him over the river of death, just this stranger chatting to him as he smoked a cigarette. The stranger was wearing the same uniform as the folklorist although his was a higher rank. His face was pocked with small, livid, burn marks. Was this a special room for the Nazi dead? 'Did you use a grenade?' The man's Austrian voice finally reached Ernst through the ringing in his ears as though on the crackle of a short-wave radio. Ernst nodded, recalling the T-34. 'Congratulations, you're a hero. You're entitled to a decoration. By the way, we're withdrawing.' The lights flickered then died. A ragged claw of daylight groped through a tear in the roof. 'They've taken the generator,' the Austrian said. 'It's a general retreat. Although naturally we don't call it that.' Along the corridor, which Ernst could see through another hole torn in the sandbag wall, members of the divisional staff jostled, bearing sheets of paper and obsolete maps. 'We've lost the war for sure; don't you think, my friend?'

'I try not to think.'

'Please, I'm not trying to trap you — you're a

hero for pity's sake — I'm merely expressing what we both know. It's finished. There's no secret weapon, only halfwits harbour such thoughts. But my manners, please accept tobacco.' As the Austrian took out his cigarettes, Ernst noticed that the case was covered with human skin. Having accepted a light he leant over the edge of the bunk and retched. Squinting to avoid the smoke scouring his eyes, the other man cleaned him, tenderly wiping away the bile and vomit. 'It makes a pleasant change to meet another educated fellow in this inferno. I hear you were a professor? I was nothing grand like you; just a village teacher.' The Austrian took out a wallet. Opening it, he held out a photograph to Ernst. It showed two girls.

'What are their names?' Ernst asked mechanically.

'Gretchen is ten and her sister Katharina thirteen.'

'Lovely girls.'

'Yes. Do you have children?'

Ernst opened his mouth. His ears popped but the buzzing did not clear. 'I never married.' If he *had* died, the folklorist reflected, then certainly his interrogation might begin like this.

'Ah. What was your subject?'

'Folk tales.'

'Well, we find ourselves in a gruesome enough tale now, don't we?' The Austrian tittered; a plane flew over the bunker; one of the clerical staff screamed. Daintily the higher ranked officer of the Waffen SS flicked away a fleck of cigarette ash from Ernst's blood-soaked collar. 'Were you in the east?' There was the slightest of pauses. 'I mean, on special manoeuvres?'

The buzzing between Ernst's ears blurred the Austrian's words so that he seemed to be speaking through a cleft lip. The folklorist nodded. 'In the Ukraine.'

'So you know what it was like. When I was there, I often took out the picture of my girls just to remind myself what I was doing it all for. I mean, what normal human being could do what we had to do without the purest of motives? My God, do you remember it? All that blood day after day. The children were the worst. No matter what you did one of them always survived. Some little hand poking up through the bodies like a bean sprout.' Again the titter. Ernst felt rather than heard the explosion that rocked the headquarters. One of the bags in the roof above began to weep sand. The grazing caress of it on his face brought back the way Lotte would draw her eyelashes down his cheek to tell him she loved him. 'If you were there, you must have seen it too. Those fucking little hands. The children shook even the strongest faith. But it's all over now. A bad dream. Our part is played. One day they'll honour men like you and me. Pogroms? Anyone can hate. What's the point in breaking a few heads? What we've done is to cut the cancer out once and for all. The blood on our hands comes from scalpels. That is why we must *never* be ashamed. We've done what everyone knew had to be done but no one else would do. The Yanks understand that, that's why they let us do it. And just think, I might have spent the rest of

370

my life failing to teach the sons of Tyrol shepherds how to count goats.' The Austrian dug into a pocket and brought out a metal flask. He took a deep draught then handed it to Ernst. The schnapps burnt the folklorist's throat. With the air of an after-dinner raconteur, the schoolteacher leant closer to the folklorist. 'You like stories — I'll tell you one. Every year a pair of swallows nested in the rafters of our little schoolhouse in the Tyrol. Charming. I used to leave the window open and the parents would swoop in to feed their young, darting over the heads of my charges. And every year without fail the nestlings would fall from the nest; with only one ever fledging. Not so charming. For a long time this baffled me. Perhaps the nest was shoddy? I provided the birds with a fresh supply of wet mud so that their nest was as fine a cup of wattle and daub as you could hope, but next spring the same thing happened. Was it one of my pupils coming in at night? As a schoolmaster you quickly come to understand the unreasoning cruelty of some children. I beat the naughtiest; I even beat the law-abiding. No one confessed. I found out only by accident what was happening. Getting to school earlier than usual one day, I saw the single youngster emerge from the nest. This giant fledgling was no swallow but a cuckoo. Aha! Each year a cuckoo had laid its egg here, and each year its chick, growing fat and acquisitive, pushed out its foster-brothers and -sisters!' Overhead, Ernst could feel the vibrations of the Soviet fighter planes raking the sector. The Austrian took out a fresh cigarette.

371

'Moses of course is our cuckoo. Generations of parasitism; the eternal leech. *The Jew is our misfortune*. I hung those words up as a banner in our schoolroom. How true they are. Just like cuckoos, the Jews have always pushed us from the nest. Mind you, I've never been a primitive Jew-hater, I readily acknowledge their accomplishments, their financial abilities, cultural achievements, their musicians. And so forth.' He waved his cigarette with expansive tolerance. 'After all, the song of a cuckoo in spring is delightful. But for the other birds it is also the sound of death, parasitism and persecution. For swallows to live, the cuckoos must be killed. It's a law of nature.' The Austrian reached out and laid a hand tenderly on Ernst's cheek. 'I did it for my family. You are more noble; you did it for others, for the world. Is altruism a quality one comes across often in folk tales?'

A long face appeared round the corner of the wall of sandbags. 'Obersturmbannfuhrer, we're launching the counter-attack.'

'One moment, soldier.' The Obersturmbann-fuhrer scrabbled under the bunks and pulled out a tight tube of rags. Tossing aside the outer casing, he unrolled them. Ernst got up. In the brown dusk of the bunker, he found himself looking at two paintings. Each one showed the same thing: a garden in spring. 'I picked them up in a village on the River Oise somewhere, at the beginning of the war,' the Austrian explained. 'The woman I got them from had some story about her husband's grandfather being the gardener for some famous artist. Lies, naturally.

Which artist can afford a gardener? I paid for them of course. I always taught the children the virtues of honesty. Even though in this case she scarcely deserved it. The pictures were being used to stop the draught in a broken window. Can you believe that? The French pretend to be so cultured yet they are little more than pigs.' Ernst gazed at the spring scenes: a riot of flowers, yellow tree, black cat and green bench. One of the pictures showed an artist at his easel. Wearing a battered straw hat and clapped-out boots, the painter was shown from behind, hunched over his work like an exhausted blacksmith at his anvil. He was so thin that his spinal column could almost be made out, marking the sloping back like a track winding up a long, insurmountable hill.

'They're beautiful,' Ernst whispered.

'Obersturmbannfuhrer,' urged the young man from round the corner.

'In a minute,' the Austrian replied. He rolled the paintings up and handed them to Ernst. 'I was saving them for myself but with today's order I know that I'm going to die.' He tittered. 'It's my honour to cover the withdrawal. Besides, I've just found out that this photograph of them is all I have left.' The Austrian produced the photograph from his wallet again. 'My wife and daughters were killed in an air raid.'

'I'm sorry.'

'Well, well, well . . . ' The Obersturmbannfuhrer waved as though swatting a fly. 'The dead are dead; what we've done is for the living. You know about the network of course?' Ernst shook his head. The Obersturmbannfuhrer swore softly. 'Damn, they should have told you. Who were you working under in the Ukraine? Look, the network is an organisation for setting up active party members with new homes and identities after the war. No one will want to be in Germany once Stalin has finally mastered us. Christ, he doesn't scruple at sending millions of his own people to their death in Siberia. I mean, that's what we've saved the world from, but is there any gratitude? We call it Noah's Ark; the network. They'll be able to arrange a new life for you. Argentina, Brazil, South Africa. Your choice. Only perhaps not Palestine.'

'But I'm part of your unit, Obersturmbannfü-hrer. I'm going to die too.'

'No you won't. Soldier!' The long-faced young man appeared. 'I'm ordering this man — what's your name again?'

'Ernst Mann.'

'I'm ordering Ernst Mann to go with the general withdrawal. You are to accompany him. Do you understand? See that he gets away safely. Now just give us one more minute.' The sounds of battle were growing louder. A new urgency seemed to seize the Austrian. 'You don't think I'm helping you solely through the goodness of my heart, do you? Someone has to tell the true story of what we were doing in the east; someone has to explain the Ukraine; someone has to tell how we gave our souls for the future of the human race. Your job was to deal in stories, wasn't it? Well, here's a true one. Make sure you tell it well: how we sacrificed ourselves for those who were to come.' The Obersturmbannführer wrote on a scrap of paper then held it out to Ernst. 'This is the name and address of your contact. Commit them to memory. Got it?' The folklorist nodded. 'Repeat them to me then.' As he did so the Austrian ground out the stub of his cigarette on Ernst's cheek. The folklorist fell to his knees with a shriek. 'I'm sorry,' the Obersturmbannführer said. 'That's my little aide-memoire.' He touched the burn marks on his own face. 'We must make sure you survive. You see, you're our only hope. Without you we'll never be understood. For fuck's sake do they think we *liked* it in the Ukraine?' The throbbing of Ernst's cheek seemed to echo with the ringing in his head. The Austrian knelt down and took one of Ernst's hands. 'We had to go back, you know. To burn the bodies. The next summer we had to dig them back up and burn them. Soldier! Soldier!' The young soldier reappeared just as the Obersturmbannfuhrer, still kneeling by Ernst, gave a final snigger and, pressing a pistol against his own temple, pulled the trigger. Ernst felt the fine spray of the Austrian's brains lacerate his burning cheek. He looked up at the soldier.

'Did you see a donkey. Or was I imagining it?'

'There are no vehicles,' the soldier replied, 'to pull the field kitchens. Horses, cows, donkeys, we used anything we could. But they've all been eaten.'

5

They never did find Peter. By the time they reached Berlin it seemed even colder; if that endless pile of smoking rubble and destruction could really be the capital city. The war was so near now that it could be heard as a continual drone like storm winds rising through the tall firs above Keilburg — The next morning there would always be one or two of the giants uprooted. They had been in Berlin for two days when Helga, leaving Lotte and Gustav in a shelled house, disappeared for an hour or so. When she came back she said nothing but that night as mother and daughter slept together, Lotte could smell Papa. Touching Mama with her eyelashes, Lotte invited her to talk, but she did not reply. And never once in the years to come would she so much as mention it. But Mama had not come back from the meeting empty-handed; Lotte knew that. 'Here,' Helga had said as they bedded down, handing Lotte some of the rags that she herself had been wearing during their journey.

'Won't you be cold without them?' Lotte had asked with her hands.

Waiting until she could feel her mother's breathing slow to its deepest reach, Lotte began to investigate. Carefully probing the layers of her sleeping Mama's clothing, her fingers encountered a fabric that they did not recognise: an unevenly smooth texture, cool even in the warm membrane of their shared sleep. Mama was wearing something new. Whatever it was, it had come from Papa. Lotte was about to look more closely when the sleeper stirred. In the morning the girl asked outright about Mama's new clothes; Helga did not reply, and when Lotte reached through her mother's outer layers, she flared. Never having seen her like this before, Lotte realised that for the first time there was a secret between them that would never be shared willingly.

★ ★ ★

In Berlin they had come so near the front line that Gustav had been able to differentiate between the small-arms fire of the Red Army and the defending Germans, but now, fleeing west, the war seemed to recede quickly like a spent tide. All around was the flotsam of the flight: bodies, broken carts, burnt-out vehicles, discarded weapons; but in the fighting itself there was an eerie lull. For one whole, unforgettable day they rode in a cart; blessed hours of rest and peace, slowly moving under a sky untroubled by planes, along a wayside suddenly innocent of corpses. It was only at night when the horizon flickered with a troubled red that the raging conflict reasserted itself. The next morning Gustav asked an old man about the fires to the northeast. He replied that it was the Red Army being driven back. When Gustav told him about the Soviets being in Berlin the old man threw stones at him. And this wasn't the only person who still believed the propaganda: the Ivans had been turned back by the Führer's secret weapon.

If you mentioned Berlin, people always got angry, even the ones who were also in flight. Finally someone else told Gustav that the burning they could see at night was Dresden. The British were erasing it.

★　★　★

At last, after patiently biding her time, Lotte found out what it was that Mama had brought back from her meeting with Papa. Having fallen in with another family who had shared their food with them, they were resting at midday under a sun that for the first time gave real warmth. Mama was sleeping in the new grass, having loosened her clothes. Lotte could see the rags she had brought from Berlin. But this was no dull piece of sacking; colours shone brightly from it like a tapestry. Then Lotte realised that it was a painting! A springtime garden with blossoming trees, a cat, flowers, a green bench. So intently was she looking at the picture that Lotte was taken by surprise when her mother woke and reached blearily for her clothes. For the rest of the journey home, as Lotte forced her body onwards, her mind wandered constantly through that painted garden. How different it was from the ravaged countryside through which they were passing. Here spring spilt itself reluctantly, bringing no hope, only a greater depth of destruction. In the painting the sunshine conjured flowers and blossom, here it melted the snow to reveal corpses. Closing her eyes, the girl would imagine herself sitting on that green bench, warm and sleek as the cat. And at night she dreamt that Papa would come into the garden and play with her as he always used to. For the rest of Lotte's life, the painting of the garden would be like a dream of everything she had lost.

★ ★ ★

Helga had her own dreams too on that journey home. The old nightmare came back, the Death Angel now carrying not only Lotte but Peter too. Once when the Angel turned round to look at her, Helga saw her own face whiskered and wizened.

★ ★ ★

Gustav suffered no nightmares; what he saw in the day was enough. As they slowly moved south-west, he made himself a promise. If life ever returned to anything like normal, he would become a doctor. He decided this on the evening that he encountered the twelve skeletons. Having separated from Mama and Lotte to forage he had met a group on the road shuffling slowly as sleepwalkers. Gustav had learnt many tricks of survival on their desperate trek through a disintegrating Germany, some of which would be a secret shame for the rest of his life, but what he saw as he drew level with the straggling group made him do something he had not done for months. Instead of looking to snatch and steal, he had given away what little bread he had.

Perhaps it was the horror of the emaciated bodies — how could people so fleshless still be alive? — or the blank whiteness of the eyes. Dividing the hunk of bread and a cabbage which had taken him all morning to procure, he distributed it among them. The next morning back on the road with Mama and Lotte, they had passed the same group lying on the roadside, every single one dead. Some of them were still holding the small pieces of bread he had given them, as though they were diamonds. A woman spat at the bodies as she walked by: 'Jews,' she said. 'Are you happy now, Jews? Are you happy with what you've done?'

6

Ernst sprinted across the rubble. Any moment he expected to feel the kick of a bullet, the fist of a shell, but nothing knocked him from his feet and he reached the far side. Hurling himself under a pile of debris, he waited to get his breath back. How long had he been in Berlin, days or weeks? The end was very near. Ivan was everywhere, crawling through the city like the rats. Well, for as long as he had left he would fulfil the promise he had made to Helga during their final meeting. Finding a knot of corpses, once again Ernst began the search. They were freshly dead; five of them; thirteen, fourteen years old; the same age as Peter but not Peter; it was never Peter. It seemed that he found every dead boy in the world except his own son.

As he moved through the ruined city searching, Ernst's mind kept returning to the meeting with Helga. He had been so surprised that he hadn't known what to say. Even now he wasn't entirely certain that it had really been her. Exhumed from a shallow grave of sleep, he had opened his eyes to find her standing above him. Neither had been able to speak. It was only as she turned to go that she found her voice: 'Peter's gone.' She explained what had happened. 'I'll find him,' Ernst had replied.

Ernst's head thudded dully with the sounds of firing that came from all around. The ringing from the tank remained between his ears as though he had swallowed a wasp. This search for their son was all he had left; and like a carrion scavenger he had to scour the battlefield. There had been so much he had wanted to tell Helga. At least she had taken the paintings, stuffing them into her clothes. With those she would be able to buy a new life for herself and Gustav and Lotte. Hans would assist her. Ernst had even written out the contact and address for her.

Through their daughter, Helga and Ernst had both grown used to communicating in silence, but the folklorist had been unable to read the last look he ever saw on his wife's face. Instinctively, he had gone to embrace her only to find his machine gun coming between them. With the paintings, she had also taken his final letters. One for Hans and the old professor, one for Helga, and one each for the children — even Peter, because in all the multitude of its horrors war sometimes permitted a single miracle. But

how could any written words express what he'd
been unable to tell Helga? How could he explain
that he had never meant any of this to happen,
that there was nothing he could have done
differently to change things, that the moment
never came when he could have jumped from the
juggernaut? That he would do it all again to keep
Lotte safe.

Calling on his last reserves of strength, Ernst
got up and ran. Maybe his son would be round
the next corner.

Before he was halfway across the street, he
knew that at last he'd been hit. It felt like little
more than a slamming punch in the belly; one
sharp, winding pain. His momentum took him as
far as the door of a building, half of which was
still standing: a miracle in its own right. He
crawled inside and was amazed to find himself
not in one of the ruined caverns to which Berlin
had been reduced, but a grove of Ukrainian
birch trees. No longer machine guns but a bird
singing on a branch. Some of the leaves were
already yellow. Although spring was stirring even
in the grey debris of Berlin, these woods were
touched with autumn. Ernst was just musing on
how such a place could have missed the
destruction wreaked on the rest of the city when
he saw Gustav and Peter. They were playing in
the trees; little boys again! He called out to them
but as he did so they changed from children into
men with the blunt, Asiatic features of one of
Stalin's Far Eastern brigades. Both wore now not
the traditional Black Forest garb that they had
often worn in childhood but the uniform of the

Red Army. There was a deafening blast. When the smoke had cleared, the boys had gone; in their place was a little child, just a toddler. What could she be doing here? Lotte! She was picking blue gentians. Seeing him she toddled over and giggling threw herself into his arms. The giggling became a piercing scream. Lotte's chubby little arms were all gashed. Ernst looked down at his hands. He had grown claws. Springing from behind him, Helga snatched Lotte and fled through the birches. Ernst yelled after them until his veins throbbed. 'They can't hear you,' somebody said calmly from behind him. 'There's no point shouting.'

'You're here too, Hans?' said Ernst. 'But how did you get here?'

'On Sleipner,' his old friend replied. 'You know, Wotan's steed.'

'Ah, Sleipner. He must be very fast.'

'No one knows better than you that he has eight legs.'

'But where is he?'

'Can't you see him tethered?'

Ernst gazed through the doorway onto the street. 'I can only see a Soviet tank.' He could hear his friend shrug. 'You'll help Helga and the children, won't you, Hans?'

'What?'

'There's no time to lose. Follow them. They've got the pictures. The network. I've explained it all in the letter.'

'I can't understand what you're saying, Ernst.'

'You can go with them too if you want. To South Africa . . . '

'You're talking gibberish, Ernst. Why can't you speak Alemannic like the rest of us? Who are you anyway; where did you come from? Why are you growing those big teeth?'

'Teeth?'

But Hans had gone.

Ernst had lain there for what felt like a very long time when he heard a rustling in the leaf litter, a pattering as though of small paws. Someone had crawled out of the woods and now lay beside him. It was the old professor. 'Well,' the old man said, 'you want to know whether we'll forgive you?'

'Uncle,' Hans whispered, 'what have I done that is so bad?'

'You need me to tell you?'

'At least tell me why I've grown such big teeth.'

'All the better for . . . But you ask me what you've done. Ernst, once and for all you've proved the value of our subject. You have shown conclusively that the fairy-tale view of the world is in fact the correct one.'

'Witches; giants; malicious sprites?'

'Exactly. Naked avarice, reasonless murder, envy, irrational hatred, the full ridiculousness and cruelty of greed.'

'I've proved this?'

'And the old truth of the folk tale. Wolves *are* interchangeable with people. But that's not all. You've taken away our only consolation. After all of this, who will ever be able to believe in a happy ending again? Now that's something that can't be forgiven.'

When the rats found that there was no longer even a hand to knock them away, they grew bolder. Perching on Ernst Mann's face they gnawed at his features: eyes first, then lips. His heart was still beating when they began on his testicles.

Some men of the Red Army, having secured the sector, decided to spend the night in the partially standing building. They barely noticed the chewed corpse in the uniform that had destroyed half the world. Throughout the night, rats the size of small dogs kept returning to gorge on the carcass. Enraged, one of the soldiers shot blindly at the mass of vermin. His bullet splashed a small fresco of guts on the wall; a second rat took the rest of the dark hours to die, a grey grimace on its narrow, whiskered little muzzle.

Auvers-sur-Oise, July 1890

1

Since six o'clock that morning the world had been turned upside down — at least in Auvers and her surrounding fields. Emerging from the black photographic cape, James Dalrymple took a few moments to orientate himself to the sky and the swelling wheat plain standing once again in their true relation to each other. It was a feeling akin to that which he had experienced on the rather rough passage over the Atlantic; as though the world had slipped from its moorings. Surely there were cameras that didn't invert their image in the viewfinder like this? And lighter ones too: each time Van Gogh moved his easel to a new subject, the young Harvard man had to tote the thing after him, tripod and all across his shoulders. Since 5 a.m. he'd been stalking the environs of Auvers like a coalman with his sack. Not forgetting the photographic plates; they weren't light. He had five in all. He'd already used four; and was just about to expose the last, once he'd made sure of the composition.

Dalrymple looked down to where Van Gogh was working. With the naked eye the scene looked perfect. The wide sweep of wheat billowing under a blue sky, and the single figure of the artist toiling away. A few minutes before, the sky had been entirely black but the wind had borne the clouds away revealing an azure that rang like a bell. Not that the camera would capture the splendour of the rain-washed sky; nor the red poppies dancing in the crop; nor even the Dutchman's fevered toil as he filled yet another canvas. Still, the end product would be wonderfully atmospheric if those photographs Dalrymple had seen in the Paris studio were anything to go by. No doubt the scene would be further enhanced if he could capture his subject from a greater proximity or even from the front, but after what had happened when he'd tried to do so earlier, he decided to maintain a safe distance. Perhaps he ought to try and get a *little* closer; at this angle and range the amateur photographer had the sneaking suspicion that the figure of the artist would show on the developed plate as little more than one of the crows gathering round him; yet perhaps there was something poignant about seeing an artist from such a perspective: lost, drowning almost in his subject. A cockroach stranded on its back, a sea defence inundated, a frog about to be eaten by a crow. *So help me*, Dalrymple said to himself, *I'm turning into a goddamn sentimentalist*.

Dalrymple hadn't set out specifically to document the Dutch artist like this. Woken by his recently contracted disease at the ungodly dawn hour and finding further sleep elusive, he had decided to rise and indulge his new hobby. The book of instructions had recommended first

387

light as being a particularly felicitous medium for photography. Sallying forth he had encountered Vincent Van Gogh quite by chance. The artist had been standing motionless in front of the church as though transfixed by something only he could hear. Dalrymple had frequently witnessed Van Gogh in this trance-like attitude, and it had always struck him. Before he even knew what he was doing he had set up his tripod, inserted the plate and climbed under the black cape. The cape! Dalrymple liked the cape; it made him feel like some villain from a penny dreadful. At first he had also liked the way the camera made the world leap on its head, but the novelty of that had quickly worn off. He didn't hold much hope for that first photograph, the painter having moved before the stipulated period of time had passed for the perfect exposure. Still, he might get one of those ghost effects that had looked so striking in the window of the photographic studio. The second exposure had been more successful. With the peasants taking breakfast and the commuters in their villas still dreaming on their lace pillows, the young East Coaster had followed the Dutchman through a deserted Auvers-sur-Oise usually so busy. Peace lay like deep water over the thatched roofs and red tiles. Dalrymple had tried to talk to the painter, but Van Gogh had refused to look at him or even recognise his presence. The perfect situation! The instructions had likened the role of the photographer to being a bodiless eye; the observing genius loci. They had just got clear of the village when Van Gogh had stopped abruptly

388

to peer into some undergrowth. This time the artist had remained stationary long enough for the duc process to be concluded. The third photograph too seemed to have been satisfactorily accomplished albeit with unpleasant consequences. Having gone out onto the fields above Auvers, Van Gogh had pitched his easel at a vantage point that commanded a line of haystacks and was mixing his colours when he spotted the trespasser on his privacy. Like a bull perceiving an intruder, the Dutchman had stared intently for a while then, putting his head down, charged. Dalrymple, fiddling with some mechanism under the cape, saw what was happening only at the very last moment: Vincent Van Gogh bearing down on him wrathfully. Seen upside down through the lens, the painter seemed to dart at him from below like a seal twisting after a salmon. The photographer had fallen heavily on his coccyx. The exposure, however, seemed unaffected. The fourth plate had been taken only a short time ago with Van Gogh in the same place as he was now, down among the wheat, but the amateur photographer worried that the picture might have been ruined by the flock of crows that was continually lifting and falling in the corn. Of course, such a plate might too have its own atmosphere. Well, now for the fifth and last exposure.

Taking one last look with his naked eye at the artist waistdeep in the wheat, James Dalrymple withdrew back under the cape. Once again everything turned higgledy-piggledy: the sky became the ground, the ground rose up to take its place, and all the colours drained from the cheeks of the world so that the wonderful poppies sobered to a solemn Calvinistic sepia. Inverted, Van Gogh's distant toiling figure bore an even greater resemblance to a crow, his easel the trap a farmer sets for the flying vermin. The Dutchman's ragged voice rang out once more; he was shouting at the birds again. They rose in a tattered cacophony. The sound cut through Dalrymple; he didn't like things that fluttered or crept or crawled. The corvine flock had gone to feed on the abundant frogs and mice exposed on the nearby strips where the wheat had already been cut. Dalrymple shivered. Earlier when he'd been following Van Gogh over a newly stubbled field, a rat had run over his foot. He'd shrieked like a girl.

As he lined up the shot, a splash of white emulsion landed on the camera lens. Fearing the brush of the irate Dutch artist, Dalrymple emerged hurriedly from the cape. But Van Gogh was still at work. It was bird guano on the lens. One of the crows had pooped on his camera. By the time the Harvard man had cleared it off, he felt a sharp drop of rain.

Dalrymple only just made it under the tree in time. The wheat seethed. Van Gogh, however, remained working. Dalrymple watched him, the image of a captain at the bridge of his sinking ship coming to mind; then one of the lame Hephaestus toiling at his anvil. *So help me*, the Ivy Leaguer said to himself, *I really am going soft*.

The rain had become a deluge and the Dutchman ran for the tree too; all elbows and knees, head thrown back, mouth open wide. 'Simply shocking weather,' Dalrymple greeted him, but still Van Gogh made no sign of hearing him. Staring out at the rain, the artist narrowed and widened his eyes ceaselessly. Dalrymple fought the impulse to take out a handkerchief and cover his nose against the stench rising from the other's wet clothes.

'Not easy,' Van Gogh said at last, speaking French.

'No,' agreed Dalrymple, grateful he'd hidden the camera round the other side of the trunk.

'Can *you* do it?'

'Probably not; no,' Dalrymple decided to say.

There was another pause as the heavy drops speared into the thick canopy of the tree above them. 'Yesterday I tried. With the crows flying through it like black seagulls. I love the crows. But to paint? They're bastards. Almost as hard as the rain.' Another lengthy silence. 'I was on a height,' continued Van Gogh, as though talking to someone else. 'Auvers below. The houses nestling in the hollow had the look of Noah's ark. The crows were flying towards them. Black doves.' Abruptly he turned to Dalrymple and as though seeing him for the first time spoke in English: 'Isn't there a story about the crows being the last to get on the ark?'

'I don't know it.'

'Yes; I heard it once, they were too busy looking for carrion when Noah shouted everyone on board. So God punished them by making them the ugliest, most despised birds in the world.'

'Are you all right, Mr Van Gogh?'

'For sugar's sake, call me Vincent. Listening to you foreigners mangling a good Dutch name is enough to make Rembrandt turn in his grave. Anyway, what are you doing up here?'

'I'm . . . taking pictures.'

'You've become an artist? I thought you were a writer or something.'

'Well, the lure of the visual age, I guess.' The Harvard man looked nervously to where the beak of his camera protruded from behind the trunk.

'It's you, isn't it? You're the bastard who's been following me all morning with the camera.'

'Yes,' said Dalrymple, unable to think of any other answer. He had read of natives on South Sea islands dying through having their photograph taken. Fearing their spirits had been taken, they wasted away. He hadn't expected to find such primitivism in the heart of the most cultured nation on earth. Ought he to run?

'You're lucky I don't shove it up your arse.'

Emboldened by the Dutchman's smile, the amateur photographer said: 'Don't you care for the medium of photography?'

The painter snorted derisively. 'Do you?'

'Well, yes.'

'You mean to say you don't like Zola?'

'On the contrary.'

'Zola said that art was nature seen through a

temperament. Where does that leave a photo-graph? Nature seen through a machine. What good is that to us?'

Dalrymple cleared his throat. Odd bird though he was, the Dutchman was susceptible to a bit of aesthetic bantering, as long as you allowed him to finish up the winner. 'I can't agree there,' he yawned, resurrecting his old role of the *flâneur*.

'Oho!'

'That's why I've given up the pen. Art is dead; literature too. What modern man needs is the truth, not stories. Railway timetables, yes; butcher bills, yes; details of court proceedings, by all means; literature, no. And why paint something when you can photograph it as it actually is?'

'If I thought you really believed that I'd throw you into the Oise. Look over there. What can you see?'

'A wheat field.'

'What else?'

'Some hills.'

'What colour are the hills?'

'I don't know; green?'

'How will you show green hills on that contraption?' Van Gogh pointed round the tree trunk.

'There's talk of someone developing colour photography.'

'That will be even worse. You see, those hills aren't green. They're blue.'

'They don't look very blue to me.'

'That's because photography's made you colour-blind. What colour is the corn?'

'Yellow surely.'

'No, today I think it's violet.'

'Well, if you're going to say anything can be any colour — '

'Not just *any* colour. Not just *any*. Anyway, if you come anywhere near me with that little machine of yours, I won't be answerable for my actions.' Turning his back on the American, Vincent set up his easel. Although the rain was drumming in the leaves overhead, underneath was totally dry. From beyond the protection of the chestnut tree came the stirring smell of dampening earth. Dalrymple looked at the canvas. Twice as long as it was wide, the bottom half had already been filled in — a large sweep of corn. Above it, a dark sky was assembling. 'I hope it pisses down,' said Van Gogh. 'I want one of those black skies. A real storm. There was a lovely one yesterday; and the gardener told me we'd have another one by the end of today. The crows are cunts. If only I could get them in the air, but they keep on settling to feed. They seem to be getting used to me. They come so close I could wring their necks. Do you like my picture?'

'Yes,' Dalrymple said simply.

'You know those posters advertising health resorts? They've got them in England. On the side of omnibuses; at railway stations. *Come to Ramsgate*, one said. *Get in the swim at Scarborough!* I liked that Scarborough one, it showed a real Rubens woman in a bathing costume. But I never got to Scarborough. Well, my canvas is supposed to be like an advertisement for Auvers. I'm hoping that when my brother sees it he'll move here. The silly bastard's thinking about going to America. You know they're raising their child on the fourth floor in Paris? And Jo's tits have dried up. Luckily there's an ass that does the rounds; they've kept the mite alive with milk from it. But a child will never be healthy in a city.' Van Gogh turned round so abruptly that Dalrymple thought somebody else had joined them. He was amazed when he saw only the wheat slowly flattening in the rain. And still Van Gogh stared as though someone was calling him from the rain just beyond the chestnut canopy. Suddenly, with a gurgling whimper, the artist threw himself at the base of the tree. For a long time he cowered there, clawing, grovelling at the ground as though to bury himself under the tree roots. It was the image of him that Dalrymple would never forget. No room for sentimentality now: a kind of Caliban tortured by spirits, a mange-ridden mole unable to dig a way back into the ground. The fit or whatever it was ended with the artist giggling. '*Get into the wheat at Auvers*,' he laughed.

'*Come to corn country*,' Dalrymple hazarded.

Laughing, the painter took out his pipe. As he sprawled among the tree roots — like a hedgehog king on his throne, Dalrymple could not help but think — the smoke rose thick and rank from the gurgling bowl. '*Auvers, where the discerning crow goes.*'

'*Auvers — where the world is your oise-ter!*'

After a great paroxysm of laughter, Van Gogh fell silent. Backing away until he stood directly in the rain, he stared at the tree roots for a good five minutes. 'By God,' he declared, coming back under shelter, 'that's worth something.' And taking down his wheat field and crows, he placed a fresh piece of canvas on the easel. If Dalrymple had thought that the painter worked quickly in the garden that day, now he could barely see the Dutchman's hands. On the canvas a gold background darkened to an earth tone, out of which writhed whorls of green and twisted shapes of milky blue. The artist was painting the tree roots; but not as any camera might see them. Giggling to himself Van Gogh seemed to have forgotten the other man's presence. '*Come to Auvers for healthy roots. Healthful and deep: Auvers soil*,' he cackled. The whole thing was done in less than half an hour at which, beyond the canopy of the chestnut, the sun had come back out. Van Gogh stumbled into the sunlight like an ejected drunkard. Dalrymple gazed at the picture. At first he had thought that the painter's tree roots were like veins on the back of a hand but now they seemed more like bones: femurs, tibia, the pelvis. Was it a tree or a human body? Up to now, he had liked Van Gogh's work, admired it; for the first time it truly touched him. The artist came back and considered the painting. 'Yes,' he nodded. 'Roots like that are good for many a storm.'

Humming a Provençal brothel song, which Dalrymple recognised, the Dutchman gathered his brushes and all the other accoutrements of his trade and hitched his easel on his back. Dalrymple watched him wade through the wheat on whose ears the raindrops glinted in the sun: a penniless pedlar walking through a world of diamonds. Dalrymple shook his head and then smiled. His sentimental side was burgeoning just like the wheat all around; and he knew why: Georgiana Fairbanks. The young man took out his fob watch. Was that the time? He'd have to hurry if he wasn't going to be late for her. Humming the Provençal air he hoisted tripod and camera cruciform over his shoulders and hurried through the wheat in the opposite direction to the painter. *His* path lay to a certain rented villa in Auvers.

At the chateau, contrary to his usual habits, he burst into a jog; by the time he reached the river his whole body was covered in a film of perspiration. Yet he felt an amazing swell of well-being. After all, Auvers-sur-Oise *was* the Garden of Eden. *I really am going mushy*, he laughed to himself. Then, with sheer joy, he laughed out loud. Soon he would be seeing her! And for the first time in his life he began to sing spontaneously:

> '*All I want in creation*
> *Is a pretty little wife*
> *And a big plantation . . .* '

'Ah,' declared an English voice sharply from the undergrowth, 'so you're here at last.' For a moment James Dalrymple thought about simply carrying on — he should have been at the villa ten minutes ago — but the voice grew imperious; after all, he *was* her father. 'I've been waiting for you,' said the rector, stepping out onto the path.

'Why, Reverend Fairbanks, how are you this morning?'

'Another dismal failure, I'm afraid.' The muslin butterfly net hung limply over the clergyman's shoulder. His clothes looked the worse for wear; mud splattered his globosity from toe to black shovel hat; he had clearly been out on one of his all-night hunts. 'But what a good idea, boy; to bring your daguerreo-typer in order to capture the moment. Alas, I have no image for you to secure. And yet, I have a plan.' Tittering, the rector burst into song:

> *'Gathering up the shells by the seashore,*
> *Gathering up the shells from the shore,*
> *Those were the happiest days of all, Moll,*
> *Gathering up the shells from the shore.'*

'Are you going home, sir?' Dalrymple asked, although he had been banking on the rector being absent from his rented villa at this hour, as had become his habit over the past weeks.

'Home?' The word seemed to cause the clergyman to brood bitterly. 'There can be no home for postlapsarian man.'

'Well, I shall be going then, Rector.'

'But, my young friend, we're not giving up; here, hold this.' The vicar thrust his net into Dalrymple's midriff then stalked back into the undergrowth. 'Shan't be a tick.' A few moments elapsed and then the clergyman began to groan from the bushes.

'Are you all right, sir?' The groaning

398

intensified. 'Are you pained, Reverend Fairbanks?' The Harvard man peered into the undergrowth. He could just make out the shape of Georgiana's father squatting like a buffalo cow giving birth on the prairie. A rolling white eye showed through the foliage.

There was one final 'Gruugh!' and then a shout of triumph. A foul stench insinuated itself into the Ivy League man's nostrils. Once again the vicar began to sing:

'A friend of Darwin came to me
A million years ago, said he,
You had a tail and no great toe.
I answered him: that may be so
But I've got one now, and I'll kick you up
the arsehole
Grrr out!'

Chuckling, Jonah Fairbanks emerged from the brake. The reek intensified. On the cushion of his capacious white drawers the clergyman was carrying a large sceptre of ordure. 'Tee-hee! This is how we'll catch him. Moths can't resist the old night soil. We'll smear it on a tree and hey presto, there he'll be in the morning. The meaning of everything!'

How strange it is, Dalrymple thought to himself, *that the most beautiful woman in Christendom should emerge from the loins of this man.*

By the time Dalrymple had been able to extricate himself he saw that he was to be punished for his tardiness. Coming through the gate of the Fairbanks villa he perceived Chip Coakley sitting proprietorially on one of the metal garden chairs. The two rivals nodded coolly. 'Miss Fairbanks is not yet risen,' Chip informed the latecomer. Sitting down at the same table, Dalrymple looked up at the young lady's window towards which his rival's gaze was also fixed. 'I don't know why you bother,' said Chip witheringly. 'You're only wasting your time.'

'Same to you, old sport.'

2

At that very moment Georgiana was gazing down at the gazers. *They're both here*, she whispered, and then felt herself flush. With a clever assemblage of her father's mirrors and lenses, she had erected a periscope whereby she could watch unobserved the two gentlemen. They sat for her like this every morning. Having read most of the classics of literature, she knew that it was obligatory to keep young men waiting. And really, that was the extent of her knowledge on the subject.

With uncertain but pulsating emotions bubbling inside her, she ran through the empty villa. How different life was here from everything she had known before. Nothing ever happened in the rectory; there were no events except for the fat carp stirring in the moat during heavy, endless mornings, and the frogs emerging at night. And now here she was leading the kind of life she had read about so fervently in the pages of Thomas Hardy. But out of the two suitors below, which was Farmer Boldwood and which Gabriel Oak to her Bathsheba Everdene? For she was tolerably certain that neither of them was the dashing although ultimately useless Sergeant Troy. Yes, how strange and marvellous life was here. The landscape far richer than anything Elizabeth Gaskell could summon, the characters rich beyond even Dickens' or George Eliot's invention, and the plot, well, that was so urgent she sometimes felt as though she might explode. For the first time in her life she found that her blood flowed with a far greater intensity than any ink from the tip of a writer's pen.

Having run through the empty house, her hair and night clothes flapping like the wings of the barn owls she had used to watch through interminable Cumbrian dusks, she came to a halt in her father's room. Still breathless, she opened the wardrobe. Here was one thing that *hadn't* changed from home: three clerical suits hung there just as they did in the rectory wardrobe; three clerical suits and her mother's dresses. Georgiana pressed her face into the folds of a crinoline but it was no good, they always only ever smelt of her father. Of her mother she retained not a single memory, although sometimes she thought she recalled the ghost of a face, pain-wan and anxious, peering in at her through the bars of a crib. Her father had brought something else to France that had once belonged to his wife: the cheval looking glass. Standing before it now, Georgiana peered at her reflection. She shivered with pleasure as the lace garment whispered to the floor. The breeze coming through the open window was a pleasant caress. The reflection showed that the freckles on her face were lightly echoed on her shoulders, back and buttocks. Georgiana gazed in wonder. What a great mystery the body was! Why did people like her father bother themselves over such distant enigmas when a view of themselves in a looking glass could furnish enough food for a thousand years of thought? For instance, there was the matter of the male mammary. It was a question that had exercised her, ever since she had watched her own grow in this cheval mirror. Did men also have breasts? Her father certainly did, but the old carter back at home didn't seem to. It was one of the first matters that Auvers had answered for her. Right at the beginning of their stay she had been on her way to Mr Coakley's painting party when she passed a group of mowers. Lolling in a hayrick they were stripped to the waist. Already stimulated to excess by the freedom — it was her first time wandering alone in the great world — she had seen to her amazement that although they had little pink teat tips there was no fleshy swelling around them. Yet this was just the beginning of the mysteries that France seemed willing to reveal. Did they have buttocks similarly as rounded as her own? Tilting herself, she looked over her shoulder at her reflection. Just last week when Mr Coakley had been most obligingly stretching to get her a cherry from the tree, she had not been able to avoid seeing how his short summer jacket rode up the small of his back to reveal a shape that while definitely indicating the same hemispheres as her own, strongly suggested something toned on altogether more muscular lines. Her eyes had been curiously drawn to the taut orbs, and every day since then she had not complained when the young man offered to pick her more fruit. What would it be like, she wondered, to see Mr Coakley similarly déshabillé in her mother's cheval mirror? A blush seemed to radiate from her own buttocks up to her cheeks. If the young male posterior was differently designed, then what might they have round the front? Striking a Lucifer, the girl lit one of the cigarettes that Mrs Oyster had given her, and considered the matter. She was certain they *were* fashioned differently; how else could she explain seeing the same party of mowers later relieving themselves from a standing position? She had tried that herself with incommodious results. A number of times while painting in Mr Coakley's proximity she had noticed a distinct movement in that part of his anatomy. Mr Dalrymple too demonstrated a similar propensity. Just yesterday when he had emerged from the black cape behind his camera having taken her portrait, she had seen the same stirring amidships as though a field mouse was domiciled there.

Blowing out smoke meditatively — how had she ever done without the pleasure Mrs Oyster had introduced her to? — Georgiana stared at herself. Of course, the body alone was just the beginning of the mystery. It was the way it seemed to call and be called by other bodies.

Back in her own bedroom she looked through the periscope. The boys were still there; it was time to go down. As she dressed she looked at her paintings. She'd done ten self-portraits in a week, and each one already possessed the candid, revelatory flavour that would become her hallmark: the freshness of vision that comes after a childhood confined within a moated grange.

When Georgiana emerged at last from the villa Chip Coakley had to stifle a whimper. She was wearing a flaming-red dress that expressed her figure at its most poetic. James Dalrymple gazed at the sight. It was a zephyr dress much popular with paddle-boat whores; nicknamed *old cling to 'em*. If the Harvard man wasn't mistaken Mrs Oyster had lent it to her — a dubious if liberating influence. Yet all such carping thoughts disappeared as he watched her come towards the metal table and chairs where he and Coakley stood. In the scarlet dress her natural grace gave her the look of a young poppy bending in the breeze. 'It's a truth universally acknowledged — ' he put in quickly before his rival could speak.

' — that a single man in possession of a good fortune . . . ' she replied with a laugh. 'Too easy, Mr Dalrymple: *Pride and Prejudice*. If you're going to beat me, you'll have to choose a more obscure author than Miss Austen.'

'I took the liberty,' Dalrymple said, taking a package hurriedly from his pocket and moving quickly to present it to the young lady. He watched her open it up with a childlike enthusiasm that no amount of sophisticated

Louisiana steamboat scarlet could conceal. In the periphery of his vision he observed Coakley's helplessness. If he could only keep the conversation on literature he would always have the whip hand. He was certain that that Californian dolt had barely read anything other than *Last of the Mohicans*. 'It's the latest Zola novel, Miss Fairbanks. *La Bête Humaine*. I would render that roughly as *The Beast in Man*. Perhaps you will allow me to translate it for you.'

'Oh, would you? I loved those stories of Maupassant you read me last week.'

Dalrymple recalled the dappled hours spent sitting with her in the rose arbour as he translated the stories. It had been even better when after an hour or so Chip Coakley had gone off in disgust. 'It's my greatest pleasure,' he said simply, but when she handed it back to him a memory of the night before intruded. The copy of the novel had been in his jacket pocket during his visit to the brothel; one of the whores had picked it up and joked: 'For me, monsieur?'

Sensing his rival's momentary confusion, Chip Coakley played *his* trump card. 'I thought we could paint the wheat today, Miss Fairbanks. I have your easel all ready. And your oils.' Chip lifted the easel with a physical ease calculated to undercut the other man. 'They're harvesting; if we don't move soon it will be gone. Nor is the weather to be trusted either, I fear.' Waiting for the girl to decide between book and brush, the former friends eyed one another without affection. 'Perhaps you'd care for some cherries, Miss Fairbanks?' Chip volunteered, sensing the outcome hanging in the balance.

Scampering to the tree, the rivals bumped into each other; with satisfaction Chip Coakley felt his shoulder barge send Dalrymple reeling. If it came to a fisticuffs, the sponging Bostonian was no match for the frontiersman. 'Thank you,' said Georgiana, slightly flushing as they each held out their offering of fruit.

Despite the scene's biblical flavour — Chip could imagine the Coakley family pastor's unquiet witness — the shape of the mouth puckering for cherries seemed to rob him of all will. Ever since the day of the painting party, he had been lost: try as he might he could think only of Georgiana Fairbanks. Last night, tossing between his sheets, the feverish memory of the day's fruit-feeding ritual had caused him to abuse himself, leaving his body pallid but unexhausted. This morning when he had seen his features in the mirror, as a desultory prelude to another half-hearted and no doubt unfinished self-portrait, he had been shocked to see the dark rings beneath his eyes.

'Pray, let us sally forth then,' Georgiana pronounced, licking the juice from her lips. 'As Mr Coakley so rightly divines, they've already begun to cut the corn. But, Mr Dalrymple,' she added, seeing his face fall, 'bring your *Beast in Man* and translate it for us as we work.'

The three of them set off through Auvers, passing between thatched cottages and under expansive chestnut trees. 'Let's hurry, Miss Fairbanks!' Chip suddenly urged, seeing how the tripod and camera incommoded his rival.

406

'They're cutting the wheat, and it's sure to rain soon.'

Georgiana and Chip ran through the village and up into the cornfields. At Harvard he had been something of a sprinter yet despite her relative lack of stature and restricting dress he could barely keep up with the young woman. With her dark hair flying she seemed like some fleet animal with a long tail. Reaching a rise, the young woman stopped to gaze hungrily at the spread of land. So long used to a view of the world circumscribed by tall rectory walls, in which the panorama even from the very leads of the roof yielded nothing more than the tall hedgerows of the neighbouring fields repeating themselves like the casings of a Russian doll, the unbridled horizons of Auvers-sur-Oise never failed to take away the young woman's breath. She shuddered slightly at the grand spaciousness with a pleasure not entirely dissimilar to the sensations she received from contemplation of herself in the cheval mirror. The body of the world was beautiful and mysterious too! The gently undulating terrain spread out before her vast as a sea; and the sky, with its black clouds billowing in the blue, also seemed an ocean: troubled perhaps, but deep, and full of wondrous fish. A hunger to capture it all on canvas swept through the young woman. Impatience flared in her cheeks as Mr Coakley appeared to fumble with the erection of her easel. 'Allow me,' she said. Setting out her colours, she stared at them for a while in the way she had watched Vincent Van Gogh do. Then she began. She had already assembled the anatomy of her landscape when she saw the figure in the midst of it. 'Who's that down there?' she asked.

Fearing Dalrymple had found them, Chip followed the direction of her gesture to the tiny black figure standing deep in the crop. 'Oh, nobody.'

'Are you sure? It looks a bit like Vincent.'

'It's just the crowstarver,' he replied, the fanatic Dutchman being, after Dalrymple, perhaps the last person on earth with whom Chip Coakley would want to share the girl. In fact, the one thing he would change about Georgiana was her propensity to hero-worship the painter. And no, that *wasn't* putting the matter too strongly. 'Look, at those crows, Miss Fairbanks; what a flock.'

'Oh yes,' she said absently, dreary murders of crows drifting overhead being one of the things that her life in Cumbria *had* produced in abundance.

By the time Dalrymple found the couple he had vowed to give up cigars. Surely he shouldn't be this breathless after such a short run? Perhaps it was the treatment he was receiving for his medical condition. He'd heard a few disquieting rumours about mercury; Dr Gachet had prescribed foxgloves. Well, henceforth he would abstain from both cigars *and* whores. Setting up his tripod, he gazed through the viewfinder at the young woman. Somehow now it seemed fitting that the world should be turned upside down.

'Hoy, Dalrymple,' Chip called with as much disdain as he dared show in front of Georgiana.

'You can't set up there; can't you see you're blocking our view?' For the hundredth time, Chip felt the temptation to blurt out his adversary's secret. That flowery way he goes on when all along his Uncle Sam is falling off ... *He visits tarts!* That's where his East Coast primrose path has gotten him. *He goes to Paris and picks up prostitutes!* Chip returned wearily to his own canvas. The brush felt distastefully incongruous in his hand, like the bone of a bird's wing. It was all he could do even to pretend that he was actually interested in painting. Art meant only one thing now: being able to be near Georgiana.

Georgiana paused for a moment in her work. The view was so rich that she felt like shouting. The wheat flecked with poppies and cornflowers, the reaping machines boating across the horizon, the brooding sky above, and from time to time the train chugging across. The world itself was the most amazing work of art. 'Are you sure that's the crowstarver down there?' she asked.

'That? It's Vincent,' Dalrymple said from behind his cape.

' 'Course it isn't,' Coakley asseverated acidly.

'I believe you'll find it is, old sport.' As Dalrymple came out from behind the camera, the full glory of Georgiana Fairbanks nearly knocked him from his feet. Perhaps Van Gogh had a point about photography. Rendering such a complexion in monochrome was like translating Baudelaire into a language of technical instruction. Still, it had *some* uses. It was the perfect medium through which to gaze unobserved at Georgiana Fairbanks. 'Shall I begin *The Beast in Man?*'

'What's he doing down there?' Georgiana asked.

'Vincent? He seems to be getting annoyed by the crows,' Dalrymple said. He looked at Georgiana's canvas. The influence of Van Gogh was glaring but still there was something of her own passion too. Standing behind his rival he studied *his* picture. 'Now, Mr Coakley,' he said almost pronouncing the *k* as a *t* in a way he knew annoyed his fellow countryman, 'your canvas seems to be plodding the trail a little slowly today, old sport.'

'Don't you old sport me.'

At that moment a shot rang out; down below them the crows lifted in a ragged, complaining murder. 'Small calibre,' Chip declared. 'Pistol, I would say.'

A cloud of smoke rose from where the artist had been a few moments before. Like a sea closing over the head of a drowning man, the wheat shimmered but showed no human presence. 'It's Van Gogh,' Dalrymple said. 'I think he's shot himself!'

3

From where he lay sprawled in the corn, it looked even worse. The dark clouds, supposed to be a symbol of the brimming energies of nature, were overpowering. His heightening of the gold

410

of the wheat had served only to make the sky seem even more threatening. This wasn't a storm to invigorate but a deluge; Noah's flood. Theo would take one look at it and steer well clear of Auvers. As for the paths he had put into the composition to relieve the sense of claustrophobia; well, they seemed to peter out like roads that led nowhere. Then there were the crows. No matter how he tried he just couldn't get their effect as they drifted overhead. As he scratched the ulcer on his leg, the defects of his canvas were all too painfully manifest. Having been brought up in the country, Theo knew as well as he did that too great a storm at this time of year was the farmer's worst fear: it would ruin the whole harvest. If you tried going for an invigorating walk in this storm it would blow you off the edge of the world. Having tried to paint Theo and his family a tempting invitation, he had produced a great big *fuck-off*.

Vincent lay back; the old gargoyle was perched on his chest again. To have worked so hard and so long, endured so much, and still be unable to capture the simplest of things. But he felt calm enough about it all; in fact strangely tranquil. He touched the gun in his pocket. All morning it had pressed against his trousers like a persistent erection.

A spider was spinning its web between two ears of corn. *Don't bother*, he whispered. *Can't you hear the reaping machines?* But the spider wasn't listening. Labouring ceaselessly, the little creature pulled itself back and forth like the weaver's shuttle the artist had once watched in the Dutch countryside. In Arles there was a dance named after a spider. A tarantella, it was supposed to mimic the behaviour of those bitten by the tarantula spider. Victims were said to dance uncontrollably for twenty-four hours, during which time the male was blessed with a permanent erection. The painter took out his own penis. Perhaps he should get bitten by a tarantula. He began to masturbate, desultorily at first but with growing conviction as he pictured Jo feeding the baby, her snow-white paps frothing like a tankard of English milk stout. How tender she had seemed, a single blue vein showing like a brook beneath ice. Grunting like a cab horse, the artist flailed his rather sore penis up the hill of his flaking foreskin. With increasing momentum, other more tawdrily erotic memories knocked the Madonna and child from his thoughts, flooding his mind as he continued to jerk with a collage of all the whores of Paris, Antwerp, Arles, The Hague. Vincent felt himself soften.

As the palliative of his lust wore off, the painter noticed the sharp stinging of his penis and the stench rising from the mange around his testicles. In the distance he could hear the whistle of *La Petite Vitesse*. He tried to wank himself solid again but it was no good, his body had dried up; there were no juices left. The only thing he could ejaculate now was the paint from his tubes. Lighting his pipe, Vincent puffed it into life, his one last tooth resting against the nipple of the stem. On the ear of corn, the spider was still spinning. Far above both man and spider, the clouds were gathering again.

Pulling up his trousers, the Dutchman stood up. There was the voicc again. It had been calling off and on all morning but now it was much nearer. *Piss off*, he mumbled.

Coming back to the north from the asylum in Provence, Vincent Van Gogh had hoped to be free from these interruptions; and so it had seemed at first. He had heeded Dr Gachet's advice and put them from his mind, thinking only of his work, but during the past few days it had all begun again. Clearly he wasn't meant to have peace of mind. Even a cow chewing the cud in the pasture has its stinging gadflies. Determined not to heed the voice, he gazed instead at the spider's little web. Such a work of unfathomable art. What did the intricate weaving of these silken strands mean? Yet what comfort did beauty like this bring? Here she was toiling like any poor artist and for what end? Soon her web would disappear under the teeth of the reaper. He too was like the spider, spinning his paint between the ears of July wheat. 'I'm not listening!' Van Gogh suddenly growled through clenched teeth. At all costs he must not turn and look to see who it was calling his name. Yesterday he had done so and found his father standing there, and last week pushing through the thicket by the river he had discovered the Dutch weavers waiting for him. Apparition or not, at least they'd stood there long enough for him to paint them. How right Gachet was when he said an artist's delusions can be useful. Vincent had given the weaver a high-peaked cap, and his wife a white

413

Brabant bonnet. But it was highly dangerous to trust these delusions. When he had done so in the south they had led to the asylum. And yet earlier today, what he had taken to be another delusion mocking his artistic travails with a camera, had in fact been one of the young Americans, a harmless enough fellow. One thing was clear, however, this voice speaking to him now was not out to do him a good turn, and he knew that if he looked round he would lose the rest of the day, maybe even his whole mind. 'I'm not listening,' he insisted.

Vincent Van Gogh watched the reaping machines at work. Their arms lifted and fell like the sails of a windmill; their rhythmic clack, clattering over the wheat fields, recalled the turn of the miller's wheel. Yet more reminders of the Netherlands. 'You're not there,' Van Gogh cried to the Dutch-inflected treble besieging him.

'Why have you abandoned me?' the child returned.

'I didn't; you're not there.'

'I came again just for you. Only this time I wasn't born in a stable.' The Dutchman placed his hands over his ears but he couldn't keep out the piercing words. 'I came into the world in a prostitute's rookery in The Hague. And you, Herod, what did you do? You slaughtered the innocents.'

'How could I have taken you with me?' Van Gogh begged.

'How could you have left me?' demanded the urchin Christ.

When Van Gogh gave in and finally looked his

accuser in the eye, he saw again the only child ever to have called him Daddy, even if it had been a mistake. 'Sorry,' he whispered to the whore's son.

Before the painter's very eyes, the boy's face grew old and wizened until he was a piece of shrivelled carrion being fought over by the crows. With a cry the artist reached for his gun and fired.

4

The crows were frothing overhead as Georgiana raced through the wheat. Her instincts told her that something terrible had happened, like in *Far from the Madding Crowd* when Farmer Boldwood shoots his rival Sergeant Troy only to hang for it later. Yet, as she kept on having to remind herself, this wasn't a book; it was real life. You couldn't just skip over the pages you didn't like or simply choose another novel from the shelf.

When she arrived at the Dutchman's abandoned easel, breathless with exertion, he suddenly jumped up from the corn. 'I've got it!' he cried raucously. 'The crows!' As the birds flapped overhead, the artist's wrist strummed a black tremolo of brush against the canvas. 'I used the gun to get them up. Look!' There was another shot.

Many years later, when Vincent Van Gogh was celebrated above all other artists, Georgiana Fairbanks would often wonder if she had imagined it all. Did she really spend that day, those weeks with him in Auvers? Had they actually worked side by side in Daubigny's garden? Had she met him so often by the river or in the fields above the village? Could she really have witnessed him making one of his finest pictures, the wheat field with crows, a piece that would touch millions with its strange paradox of despair and hope? In her own work she would try to capture him in many of the figures she painted, disguised of course as a tree, a horse, an ear of corn. Why did she never tell anyone about their acquaintance? Was it the intimacy of her memories, the contrast between this pulverised victim and the hero he became so quickly after his death? Was it because some things, especially in a secular age, must remain sacred? But these thoughts were in the future; for now she simply marvelled at the way he had captured crows flying above a wheat field.

'I'm sorry,' he said quietly, his head hanging like a child, 'I can't work with people watching me.'

'Vincent,' Georgiana said simply, 'I want your advice on how to become an artist.'

'That's easy. Don't.'

'But I think I have to.'

'In that case learn how to dance, fall in love. Now will you fuck off, please?'

'Come on, Miss Fairbanks,' Chip said, bristling at another example of Mad Red's uncouthery.

But Georgiana would not move. 'You've got them perfectly; the crows.'

'You think so?'

'Yes. And the sky. The fields too.'

'The heavens are going to open any minute,' Chip insisted. 'There may well be lightning.'

'By the way, are you from Scarborough?' the artist asked abruptly. Georgiana shook her head. 'You are English though.' She nodded. His toothless smile reminded the young woman of a benevolent Mrs Gamp from *David Copperfield*. 'I nearly went to Scarborough, but they didn't want me. So you like my picture? Do you hail from Ramsgate?'

'No.'

'Now my road *did* take me there. Would you like to see some of my other work?'

Then, as Mr Chip Coakley had surmised, the heavens opened.

It was a strange procession that walked back to Auvers through the driving rain. The leader of the band seemed to be a scarecrow that had just risen from its wooden cross in the corn, and beside him a young girl dressed like a Mississippi Delta whore; this vanguard was supported by two young porters dressed in the latest fashions, one carrying a large tripod and camera, the other, two easels and painting boxes; between them they bore the young woman's canvas protected from the rain by a black photographic cape. So, modern literature has it all wrong, Dalrymple mused; earlier savants such as Chaucer knew it: on the whole love makes one ridiculous. Over his shoulder he looked at the scene they had just left. For a moment he experienced again that peculiar *mal de mer* that he had felt when coming out from under the photographic hood. Then he understood. Nothing would ever seem in kilter again until he had won this woman's love. There and then he decided to stop at nothing in marrying the amazing Miss Georgiana Fairbanks.

'Do *you* have more milk in the country?' the painter was asking the object of Dalrymple's affections.

'More milk?'

'For your baby.'

'Oh! But I'm not married.'

'Not being married doesn't stop women having babies.'

'Doesn't it?' said the girl with widening eyes.

'I was thinking about what you said, about advice. There's an English word. It's how you become an artist. You have to be beset by the world.'

'Beset?'

'No, that's not it. Besotted. That's it. To become an artist you have to be besotted by the world.'

The procession wound its way through the lanes of Auvers, and came to a halt at the door of a thatched hovel. *Oh, Lordy*, Chip Coakley said to himself as he followed the others across the darkened entrance, *where on earth is that hobo taking us to now?* The stink unbalanced the Californian. It was something like the smell in the tepee he had gone into on his trip to the native reservation. In the festering gloom, shapes seemed to be regarding him with listless intensity. His foot sank into something softly

418

unpleasant. A light was kindled and what he saw made him shout out. The Devil, in multitudinous form, was staring at him from the shadows. The pastor had been right after all. Only when Dalrymple lit another lantern did Chip Coakley see that Beelzebub was in fact a stall full of goats. The revelation did little to cheer him up: he was sodden and miserable. What on earth was a young woman of her breeding and beauty doing in this hobo hotel? The lantern, a rudimentary affair of tallow and goat horn, smeared its sallow light over a madman's art gallery. Like a great orange orang-utan, the Dutch artist was climbing into the rafters where more of his canvases hung just beyond the endeavour of the goats. One by one Van Gogh held them for Georgiana to see. The thatching above dripped monotonously.

Just as his father did in that tepee, Chip took out a large cigar and blew the fragrant smoke big. But still the stench was poisonous. *Why do the Indians smell so bad?* he had asked as a boy. *Ain't you never smelt a dying buck?* his father had replied. Chip felt a sneeze gathering. Since coming to Auvers he'd had one cold after another. It was time to get back to the Golden State. Still, the trip to Europe had been most useful. As well as finding a wife, he had also found his true vocation. That art was not for him he'd known for several weeks now but it was only a little while ago that he had seen how he *would* make his mark on the world. To be precise, the revelation was as yet still only an hour old. The reaping machines had been the source of his epiphany. As Georgiana had painted, he had watched the harvesters eat their way through the crop faster than an infestation of tater bugs. Hitherto he'd thought of agriculture in terms of scythes and mowers; in short, Jean François Millet and the Barbizon school of artists. Now he saw that the new machinery offered a dizzying potential. When purchasing the land for his trans-American railroad his father had bought a mile or so on either side of the track in case of expansion. These endless acres of prairie, entirely ownerless save for the drunken redskins, had been dirt cheap, and had long lain useless, but now Chip had visions of planting them all up; with a team of those reaping machines he could harvest ten, twenty, a hundred, a thousand miles of wheat! It only depended on how many machines he could get. Those old stories hadn't been so far wrong after all; there *was* a way of spinning wheat into gold. Funny how entirely he'd got the preposterous business of art out of his system, like a snake sloughing its skin. Leave art to people like this lowlands skunk and the feeble East Coaster! His father was the railroad baron; *he* would be the wheat king — and Georgiana his queen. Chip looked over at her. Having been soaked in the rain, the red dress clung to her contours, swelling almost to breaking point as she reached for a canvas. Her black hair hung in passionate waves. Despite the goaty smell, Chip felt himself bursting. How swell he'd treat her! He'd buy her the best of everything; luxuries she'd never dreamt of. Naturally there were a few things he would have to be stern over to begin with. Certainly the art would have to stop; he saw that clearly now; in time she might be allowed watercolours but only when the more pernicious aspects of the instinct had purged itself from her. Chip shook his head. Holy-moly! Just to think, a few short months ago, weeks, he'd arrived full of his own artistic ambition. Well, the Dutchman had taught him everything he needed to know about art. If this poor broke-back sulking in a goat shanty was what art had to offer then he'd pass. He'd seen enough destitution among the redskins to last him a lifetime. His was the calling of the millionaire; and he would have a wife to suit.

'Yes,' Georgiana was saying as she looked at the canvas of thatched roofs that Vincent Van Gogh had just handed her, '*that*'s what they feel like.'

Chip looked over. To him it seemed a daub for which an eight-year-old ought not to be praised. The impasto was risibly thick, as though the canvas had lain below one of the swallows' nests that studded the rafters.

'Amazing. Your thatched roof seems part of the undergrowth,' James Dalrymple said. 'I wish I could live under it.'

'Perfect for the galloping consumption,' Chip put in.

'What I tried to show,' returned Van Gogh, his fists pushing against his head in the pale pool of tallow light, 'is that there's no difference between landscapes and portraits. *Everything*'s a portrait. Do you know what I mean; well, do you?'

'I want to,' said Georgiana.

'Look, this might explain. I've been thinking of a triptych. Three canvases together.' Chuntering to himself, the artist went through his canvases and selected a picture of two women walking across a field. 'This is the central panel,' he announced. 'Now if we place this one beside it.' He brought out a painting of thatched cottages. 'For the other side,' he said, lifting up a wheat field with cornflowers, 'we have this. And there you have it; everything that needs to be said; Christ between the two thieves.'

'What do you mean?' asked Georgiana.

He laughed so loudly that the goats began to bleat. 'It's transubstantiation. Here are the two women walking in the cornfield; they've sowed this crop and they'll eat it too in the form of bread; once eaten this bread becomes their flesh. And next year they'll sow it again. So that's why the second panel is a wheat field. Where does the wheat end and the body begin? We are wheat and wheat is us. But the Catholics got it wrong, it's not a miracle; transubstantiation is the norm. Bread always becomes flesh.'

'What about the third panel?' said Dalrymple, fascination waxing on his wan face. 'The thatched roofs.'

'Simple enough. In Auvers they thatch their roofs out of wheaten straw; what's left after the threshing of the ears. Another link in the chain. The trinity.'

'What a load of baloney!' Chip Coakley scoffed from behind his cigar.

Calmly the Dutchman dismantled the triptych 'Now, you'll have to go; I must work.' Georgiana was at the entrance to the hovel when the Dutchman said: 'You're not paying six francs, are you; at your inn?'

'No,' she replied.

'That's good, because the cunts would charge you that if you let them.'

When the others had left, Van Gogh stood there a long time looking at all his pictures. These were what he had given his health and sanity for. Just like the corn, his ear too had been threshed but the bread produced was meagre. The lanterns went out one after the other. The small eyes of the tallow wick continued to peer into the gloom. When he and Theo had been boys they would lie awake for hours chatting with just a rushlight. The pricks of light died. A strange feeling of being near the end of his journey came over the exiled Dutchman. He still had some bullets left in his revolver. 'No,' he replied to the Christ child of The Hague lying in the straw, 'I won't do that; you're not real.'

5

It was still raining as they left the goat hovel. Throwing her head back and opening her mouth wide, Georgiana ran. Dumbly, the two men followed her. 'Fuck off!' she cried exuberantly.

Chip bridled as he gave chase. So, she was picking up that Dutchman's foul language too; not that she could possibly understand what such words meant. Just as well they were unlikely to encounter anyone in Auvers from the sphere into which he would take her once they were married. Dalrymple was following her too, laughing to himself in a share of her access of spirits. *Please help me*, he begged his infrequently invoked deity, *I love this girl more and more*. But the young, syphilitic Ivy Leaguer was the first to tire, unable to keep up even when he'd cast aside his photographic equipment. The plates were consequently ruined, save the single one in his pocket: the Dutch artist among the crows in the wheat field.

With Dalrymple out of the race, Chip caught up with Georgiana among the corn. The reaping machines stood idle; their drivers had returned to the village until the weather cleared. Although Chip had planned a suitably masterful coup — less a proposal of marriage than a statement of fact — when his quarry turned to face him, words deserted him. Instead of being commander of the situation he felt himself being drawn to her like a train on points. She waited until he was within kissing distance then slapped him. 'You bully.'

'I love you!' he declared impetuously.

'Sir, you love none but your own self!' she returned, quoting from one of the thousand books she had read.

'Why, that's plum nonsense talk and you know it too, Georgiana Fairbanks!' he replied, in extremity reverting to the manner of speech with which he had grown up.

Georgiana considered an apt reply from the countless literary quotations she had for every conceivable situation, but nothing seemed to cover this. It was real life again; thrilling, vexatious, wonderful. In the goat pen she had decided that she hated Chip but now . . . Certainly he was handsome; more Anthony Trollope handsome than Brontë handsome, but still handsome; yet his personality, she feared, for all his talk of art, partook of the hobbledehoy. 'You bully!' she repeated.

'I ain't no book-reader, and I ain't so horse clever as Dalrymple, but I love you.'

'Oh piss off.' The second slap was just as satisfying. But as Chip bore the brunt of the blow, his sodden shirt ripped exposing a chest hereditarily toned. The young woman's eyes narrowed. As she had seen among the reapers, there *was* the semblance of a breast but it was muscled. What followed was to become the abiding mystery of Chip Coakley's life. In the future, though he became rich beyond belief, no pleasure he could ever buy came near to the moment when the wild British girl stepped towards him and placed a kneading palm on each of his buttocks before moving searchingly to the front of his trousers.

London Art Fair, 2009

No matter how hard Piers gazed at it, the exhibit before him remained a kettle. It had a nozzle, a cord and a switch. It *was* in fact a kettle. 'Challenging, isn't it?' the gallerist said, coming over. 'All year she's been working in electrical goods. Have you seen her washing machine?'

'No,' Piers replied.

'The kettle's £10,000. But there's a remote control over there for £5,000.'

'Does that come with or without batteries?'

The gallerist looked suspiciously at Piers. 'The iron's already gone; and that had a reserve of £7,500. Are you buying for yourself?' Piers took off his dark glasses. 'Fucking hell! Is that you, Piers?'

'Yes,' said Piers.

'Where have you been? Where's the white suit? No one's seen you for months. By the way, did you know the BBC are here? I saw Alan Yentob before. Hey, I've got to tell you, the Mikey Durrant thing is really kicking this year! People are going mad over it.'

'I don't work with Mikey Durrant any more.'

'Oh.'

Another customer came browsing through the electrical goods and the gallerist pounced.

Piers wandered for a while up the crowded hill and down the glinting dale of the greatest contemporary art show in the world. All the voices of contemporary art were represented: a pink Cadillac car rotating slowly on a turntable, ladders with untrustworthy rungs, a cage full of restless helium balloons.

Every now and again cutting through all the voices and competing attractions he heard the roar of what had been Mikey Durrant's ringtone: the yells of Stone Age men attacking an elk or beating back a sabretooth tiger. After the hunting cries had died down came a brief din of what sounded like a pack of rats. Smiling, he was musing to himself when he practically walked into another art lover. 'Piers!'

'Maria.'

Maria Hertz and Piers Guest looked at each other in silence. Their triple air kiss was executed woodenly, each scanning the throng of people furtively. 'Congratulations on the book,' Piers said. 'You're making waves. Van Gogh's last letter; a real insight.'

'And I hear the gallery in Cumbria is up and running?'

'Yes, we've got a stall here.'

'I've seen it. Seems you too are about to make some waves of your own. I picked this up at your stall.' Maria brought out a book entitled *The Sleeping Beauty Awakes: A Life and Critical Study of Georgiana Fairbanks*. 'Phaidon are publishing, eh? Quite an honour.'

'Actually, we're launching at the show today.'

'Have you seen Alan Yentob? He's over at your pitch right now.'

'He's making a programme about it.'

'About Georgiana?'

'About what we're doing in Cumbria. Actually, I've just signed with Channel 4 about Georgiana; I'm doing a three-parter for them. Her extraordinary life and works; that kind of thing.'

'You know, I've heard her prices have shot up. Who could have guessed her connection with Van Gogh? I hear on the grapevine that a certain important museum in Amsterdam may soon consider running a dual exhibition of Van Gogh and Fairbanks.'

'A certain important museum of which I hear you are soon to be made the *supremo*. Or should that be *suprema*? I was never much cop at the Esperanto side of things.'

'Glad to see you haven't lost your sense of humour.'

'No matter how hard I try.'

'I see you're exhibiting some of your own work too.'

'As I say, the sense of humour is the last of the organs to fail.'

'Talking of humour, I liked this; although it was rather melancholy as well as funny.' She brought out another book: *The Painting Party* by James Dalrymple. 'When we gave you all Georgiana's papers, I didn't realise that her husband's bits and pieces would form such a compelling whole.'

'Well, there was a little editing to do. By my wife mainly.'

'How hauntingly he evokes Auvers. And what funny characters he describes. I loved the mad rector — and of course Mrs Oyster. We've got plans to exhibit the tablecloth sketch in the museum.'

The shouts of bloodthirsty hunters rang through the large exhibition centre, followed by a cacophony of squeaking rodents. 'Those rats of your former associate are rather amusing.'

'Sounds like they've just turned on their Pied Piper.'

'I hear Alan Yentob nearly fainted when he realised one of them was still alive.'

As he came down the aisle leading to their own gallery space, Piers could see the television cameras and Sally in the bright-bake of the lights. How right he'd been to make the move. He pictured the rectory with its moat and pilastered chimneys; the walled garden in which Georgiana Fairbanks grew from child to young woman. It hadn't even cost him the whole four million to buy and renovate. Yes; it had all turned out rather well.

Piers waited until the TV crew were taking a break before slipping into the gallery. 'How's it going, Sally?'

'I wish you'd stop sloping off, Piers.'

'Yours is the pretty face they want.'

'We've sold one of your pieces.'

'This place really is going to the dogs then.'

'Daddy, you'll never guess,' Mimi cried, clapping her hands together. 'Mikey Durrant's challenged you to a corpse-eating competition. He has, hasn't he, Alan?'

Alan Yentob nodded sagely. 'Could we film it, do you think, Piers?'

'You're going to have to dress up as a rat too, Daddy.'

'So everything's going well,' Piers said to Sally.

'Actually,' Sally dropped her voice, 'The gallery assistant's a bit of a disaster. I can't believe you chose this one when the others had much better CVs. She couldn't even work out a 10 per cent discount on £10,000. Why on earth didn't you give the job to Giles?'

'Oh,' said Piers, 'I just thought she had the, I don't know, right interpersonal skills. She's got a degree in History of Art.'

'A third.'

Piers looked over at the girl who was laughing with a client. When she caught his eye, she smiled.

The Ukraine, Autumn 1941

1

Whistling to himself, Hans straightened up from the car engine and lifted his face to the sun. Every morning it was taking a little longer for the day to warm up. There had been a frost in the night. Although the oaks and ash trees remained summer green, the birches were already turning. The first snows of the year were not far away. Taking one last look under the bonnet, he replaced the dipstick: the dusty roads of the Ukraine played havoc with vehicles. He climbed into the car, and turned the ignition key. The engine hummed into life. 'Sweet oompah-pah!' he whispered gratefully to the healthy purr of the engine: the last thing he wanted was to risk breaking down. Although Ivan was in retreat everywhere, there were still pockets of resistance.

When Hans walked past the two young *Wehrmacht* conscripts detailed to the folkloric investigations, the boys saluted hastily. 'Heil Hitler!' one of them offered uncertainly. A rifle dropped to the ground.

Hans stopped; a wry grin on his face. 'A couple of real Wotans they've given us here. Have you ever actually fired this thing?' Picking up the rifle, he thrust it at the offending soldier. 'God help us all if the partisans do come sniffing around. Whatever you do, don't ever point that popgun at me.' With a wink to the other boy, Hans carried on.

He found Ernst sketching one of the farm buildings; the folklorist was barefoot, a long-time habit of his during warm weather. 'Make the most of it, boss,' Hans said pointing at the feet. 'The winter's not far off. Found what you wanted?'

Ernst continued drawing the barn for a while. His toes, brown with the sun, kneaded the dust rhythmically. Hans waited patiently; he was used to his friend's lengthy, almost other-worldly absorptions. 'It's certainly old enough,' Ernst replied at last. 'And the right shape. In fact, so is the whole homestead.' They'd been in the Ukraine for three weeks and for the first time Ernst felt a sense of excitement.

'Still, if I were you, boss, I'd probably put my boots back on. Never know when we might have to run.'

'The whole area's been cleared of hostile elements,' Ernst replied with half a grin. 'Don't you read the communiqués?'

'Even so, we're not in the Black Forest now.' Hans looked at Ernst's sketch then at the high apex of the barn. He nodded. 'Old enough, yes, but what I want to know is how Uncle Joe managed to miss it. This is the first farm we've found since we've been east that looks as though its stood here for longer than ten years.' The two friends peered up at the imposing façade. Hans pushed open the high doors and entered a tall, cool silence of dust motes and cobwebs. The rafters were half hidden in shadows.

'Remind you of somewhere?' Ernst asked, coming in after him.

'I could be at home. It's just like ours.'

'Have you any idea how old your barn is, Hans?'

'Older than me, boss.'

'I looked at the deeds when I was in Keilburg. Your barn is one of the oldest buildings in the area. It should be a monument.'

'You brought me a thousand miles east just to tell me that?' A twittering filled the barn. The friends looked up. A swallow was feeding young nested in the rafters. 'I hate it when that happens,' Hans said, spitting. 'A September swallow. Why haven't they flown away with all the other self-respecting summer visitors? As if this is the kind of place to hang about in.' He sniffed the air. 'It's been a long time since there was any livestock in here.'

'They were probably kulaks,' Ernst said, his toes exploring the cold beaten earth beneath them.

'You're getting a nose for the lingo as well, boss?'

'The wealthy peasants. Stalin killed millions of them. No wonder the poor bastards have been cheering us. By wealthy he meant owning your own cow. A barn like this would make you a tsar among kulaks.'

'Thank the gods for Hitler.' Instinctively the two men looked over their shoulders. Hans shrugged. 'Say what you like, at least he's

433

standing up to Stalin. Who else would? Without him Uncle Joe would be free to go kulak-fishing all over Europe. He'd have cast his fly right into Keilburg by now.'

'Let's just hope we don't all get flattened while the two giants slug it out.'

'Slug it out? Something tells me the Russkis are finished. I mean, why else leave the door open to the Ukraine like this?'

After the darkness of the barn, the sun dazzled Ernst as he emerged. 'More clues, boss?' Hans asked.

The folklorist nodded. 'Hawthorns. Can you see them? Planted in a perimeter circle. That's an ancient Nordic trait all right. I've found something else too.' Ernst led Hans through a bed of dying nettles, the tines on their stalks like the points of the harrow left to rust there. Ernst's feet had long since grown inured to most thorns and stings.

'The nettles are clearly Slavic,' Hans quipped. 'Too degenerate to sting.' Ernst kicked aside a tangle of nettles and blackberries. Hans found himself looking down at a circle of darkness. 'Ah yes, boss, the pure fountain, the spring of Germanic blood.'

'Maybe,' returned Ernst.

'I'm afraid it just looks like a dirty old well to me. What is it, a nixie's dacha?' Squatting over the well, Hans's voice boomed into the fern-fringed cavity: 'Hello, will all kobolds, pixies and sprites with Teutonic blood show yourself now?' Just as the echo of Hans's voice died, the sound of marching boots pounded the silence of the birch forest into submission: another long double column of soldiers was passing down the road, dust hanging over them like clouds. The two men waited. After the troops rolled a seemingly endless line of tanks. The dust drifted from the road, settled on the barn and the yellowing nettle leaves. At last, when silence was restored and the road temporarily empty, Ernst picked up a piece of wood and handed it to Hans. 'A piece of kindling, boss?'

'A well handle. Can't you see the carving?'

'Can't say I can.'

'I would have thought with your skill at clockmaking . . . '

'Let me see. Well, there's something. Or is that just a slug? Yeah, I can see; some kind of decoration.'

'An ear of wheat?'

'Could be.'

'What kind of wood?'

Hans stroked the wood, it was surprisingly smooth. 'Ash.'

'Sacred to Nordic culture. Yggdrasil: the tree of life on which the god of war Wotan hung himself so that he could find out about death. Slavs use chestnut or yew. I'd guess that that handle is as old as the barn.'

'What is this place; a museum?'

'In a manner of speaking.' Ernst allowed his excitement to show for a moment. 'Hans, this has all the hallmarks of being a Nordic island!'

'You don't say.'

'One of the places where Germans settled when they came east hundreds of years ago.'

'So we've finally done it,' said Hans, munching a late blackberry. '*A heimat* among the Slavs; a bulwark against the Asian hordes. Can we go home now?' He spat out the blackberry with a grimace. 'Should have known better: *God's before St Thomas's day, then in the Devil's pay.*'

'Of course, we won't be able to prove anything until we find the owners. Often the speech in areas like this, if the line hasn't been broken, will retain certain Germanic linguistic features; but it's the stories that will clinch it. Nothing proves a people like their stories.'

'Which is where you come in, boss. I can just see it now: *The Musicians of Tsarograd.* But I wouldn't build my hopes up.' Looking about the overgrown yard Hans fingered the blackberry seeds from his gum. 'As you say, Uncle Joe has killed millions, and you can bet he took the German ones first. An island? All right, but it's had one or two tidal waves to contend with in its time.' More soldiers were marching by; and the sky darkened as plane after plane passed overhead. Hans nodded. 'The Valkyries are riding again.'

'Your knowledge of German mythology is most gratifying.'

'Stukas, Valkyries, they smell the same. We're living in mythic times; just wish we could go and live them a bit more safely. We're too near the front line for my liking. When can we go home, boss? You said yourself there are enough stories waiting to be collected in the Black Forest to take us a hundred years — ' Hans broke off and studied his friend closely. 'What's the matter now?'

Ernst sighed. 'Sometimes I wonder.'

'Just sometimes?'

'Hans, why are they so keen to have us out here?'

'Would you rather they sent us here in a marching column, carrying a soldier's pack?'

'But I'm a folklorist . . . '

'Fine, then go and enlist.'

'Don't you worry, Hans?'

'I worry about bullets. I don't want to fire them and I don't want anyone to fire them at me. Now all *you* should be worrying about is how to keep us as far away from enemy lines as possible; and if that means drawing farms in notebooks then so be it. We could bake pies in the sky if they wanted us to.'

Ernst looked back over his shoulder at the barn. 'I'm almost entirely convinced this is German.'

'That's better.'

'My notes, I need — '

'I'll get them.' Leaving his friend by the barn, Hans went back to the car. The sun was well above the birch line now; it was growing hot. The two conscripts saluted him. Once more a rifle fell to the ground, this time dropped by the other. 'You're really going to have to practise that, Wotan,' said Hans, bending down to pick up the weapon.

'Sorry, sir,' the two youths repeated wretchedly.

'There are only two things I want you to do.

Firstly, don't point a gun at me; secondly, stop calling us *sir*. We're civilians. University staff if you must know.'

Hans walked to the road. Another column of troops was coming. He could hear them singing. He shook his head; give him mountains and fir trees, not this flat land of yellowing birches. It was claustrophobic. Although everything was silent on the partisan front and seemingly safe, somehow it didn't feel right: the cheese on a baited trap doesn't shout its head off either; but if you have a pair of nostrils . . . Even if Ernst kept his head buried in his notes as they drove along, Hans had seen the wreckage on the roadside, the piles of bodies. Yes, the war was getting altogether too near, and if the partisans chose to attack, then Laurel and Hardy assigned to the folkloric fieldwork would be about as much use as one of these wretched birch trees.

Humming uneasily, he reached into the car and opened Ernst's briefcase to leaf through the folders. He quickly found what he was looking for: 'Nordic Peasant Building Styles'. It was the best thing he had ever done, organising Ernst's notes into folders and files. The thought of partisans coming at them while his friend was endlessly rifling through a back seat strewn with loose papers had been more than enough incentive for Hans. As Ernst scribbled and sketched, he often found himself with whole days on his hands and nothing to do but wipe the Ukrainian dust from carburettor and lens cap, or watch the birch leaves yellowing. He had never really understood his friend's work. Why get so excited about a well handle or a version of *Hansel and Gretel* ending with the witch eating the children? What possible significance could there be if the old wives of one village told a story featuring a donkey, a dog, a cat and a rooster and those in the next told the same tale with a mule, a pig, a goat and a rat? He himself often changed stories to suit the audience. Hans breathed in; autumn lay on the air. All he cared about was getting home before the best mushrooms were over. He had a clock to finish too. Hans pictured his workshop; although he would never be as good a craftsman as his grandfather, that clock he had left unfinished on his workbench was the best he had ever done. No, for the life of him, he simply couldn't understand why grown men should bother themselves with fairy stories. Still, it was a hell of a lot better than invading foreign countries. Putting the folder under his arm, he headed back to Ernst.

But Hans didn't get as far as the barn. The conscripts were pointing their guns at something in terrified confusion. He looked over his shoulder and saw two men in bathing trunks walking an elderly peasant towards him. 'Where do you want him?' one of the men in trunks demanded.

'Me?' Hans replied.

'He's all yours,' the other shot back.

'What are we supposed to do with him?'

'Do what the fuck you like. You're the ones who requisitioned him. He's an ethnic German. Our boss got your boss's communiqué.' The man in trunks turned to the conscripts. 'Don't piss your pants, boys, we're the SS.'

Hans looked at the peasant. He had a long, sallow-grey beard; blood pooled in one of his eyes. 'How did he get that?'

'We thought he was a Yid.'

When the two in bathing costumes had gone, the old man sank to his knees. Hans gave him some water. 'Hello, Dad, seems they've been treating you a bit rough.' The peasant stared at the dust. 'So you're a German?' The clockmaker knitted his brow. 'Christ, I only speak Alemannic, you two boys have a go. Where are you from, Wotan?'

'Saxony, sir,' replied one of the conscripts for them both.

'Well, they speak German there, don't they?'

In turn the conscripts spoke to him, but the old peasant didn't seem to understand.

'Doesn't look particularly Nordic, does he?' Hans mused. 'More like a good old Ivan. Still, I suppose we'd all go native after a few centuries. The boss is going to be over the moon with him.' Hans tried the old man one last time. 'Home?' he shouted pointing at the barn. 'Is this your home?' Eyes averted, and still kneeling, the peasant nodded. Hans turned to the boys. 'Go and inform the boss we've caught him his fish.'

'Fish, sir?'

'A German fish swimming in strange waters. He'll understand.'

Having worked out the garbled message, Ernst set off at a run. If this really was a descendant of the original German settlers then he was on the cusp of the biggest coup of his career. There was every chance that the stories this man had been told in his childhood would pre-date the Grimm collection by centuries. Especially if he was illiterate. *Please*, Ernst whispered fervently, *please make him illiterate*. Unadulterated by literacy, such tales would be as near to the original narrative structures as it was possible to get. A Rosetta Stone lying in the Ukrainian dust! Listening to this old man would be like dipping into the very fountain of human storytelling; leaning back into a firelight far older than that bathing the Grimm brothers, it would be to glimpse the very shadows of the human soul. For many years Ernst Mann had dreamt of this moment.

At first sight nothing disappointed the folklorist. The old man's Cossack-style belt and long Ukrainian tunic were inevitable: clothes were the first features of an enclosed culture to rot, like the skin shrivelling from a corpse. Language lasted longer, especially in the nooks and crannies: curses, superstitions, sex; but it was a people's stories that were always the oldest: they lasted even longer than the gods; just like the teeth of an archaeological find.

With the speed of long practice, Hans assembled the camera and the Magnetophone Sound-writer. 'Here, you hold this, Wotan,' he said, handing one of the conscripts the recording machine and the other the microphone. 'Keep it close to the professor but don't get in the shot. I'll be filming. And don't so much as fart, it picks everything up.'

441

He looked across the weed-strewn space to where Ernst had taken the old man. He was showing him the well. 'Background shot,' Hans said to himself. 'Kulak den becomes proud Nordic cultural museum.' He panned round the homestead. What did the film boys call it? Getting a context. Well, here was one hell of a context. The huge old barn, a palisade of hawthorns, the clapped-out well, an ancient ethnic German, a barefoot folklorist and the serried ranks of never-ending autumnal birches. A worthless tree, the birch; its wood was no good for anything. Smiling, Hans pointed the lens at the Saxons. 'Hey, Wotan, want to show us your drilling skills?' It wasn't often that his duties as a folkloric cameraman allowed him to add humour to the record but he couldn't resist filming the boys; their calf faces were entranced as though the camera and Sound-writer were the bones of a shaman. 'Say something then, lads.'

'Heil Hitler,' they offered miserably.

'Christ, somebody wipe the blood from his eyes at least,' Hans said.

Having tried some of the German-influenced Russian phrases that had been collected in other German-speech islands, Ernst was just beginning to wonder about the provenance of the peasant when the old man started to talk. The folklorist's excitement surged as he realised that he was not speaking Russian but something far closer to German. He tried to work out what it might be. Yes; there was no mistaking it. The descendant of the Teutonic knights was speaking something recognisably Germanic! The Slavic content seemed limited to his accent. It was much better than he could ever have dreamt. If his tongue was this pure, what would his stories be like? Then he recognised the language the old man was mumbling.

'Smile, boss,' said Hans, filming as he came over. 'Smile, Nordic remnant. I'm capturing the magic moment for posterity. What's the long face for, boss?'

As Ernst turned to the two conscripts, Hans could tell how hard he was trying to control his voice. 'Will you lads take the recording equipment back to the car?'

Turning the camera off, Hans waited until the conscripts were out of earshot. 'What's the story, Ernst?'

'Hans, this man is speaking Yiddish.'

'Holy shit.' The two friends looked at each other. Hans puffed out his cheeks. On the road another column of tanks rolled by. The autumn day had turned hot. The old man's beard was clotted with gloops of blood and dust.

2

Ernst walked through the forest until his nerve gave way. What the hell was he doing? Everybody knew what happened to people who helped Jews. He looked at the figure limping ahead of him; how much longer would such an old man have left to live anyway? He'd been beaten so badly the poor bastard could barely walk. The Jew looked over his shoulder, terror on his creased features. Their eyes met. 'Go, run!' Ernst spat. The old man looked at him in disbelief. 'Look, just piss off!' the folklorist hissed. Stumbling in his eagerness to escape, the Jew dragged himself up with a whimper and thrashed through a thicket of blackberries. A doomed Rip Van Winkle, Ernst mused, then cold panic seized him. He bolted in the opposite direction.

The camera, which he had brought with him as an alibi should they be stopped, banged against his thigh as he ran. Heedless of the branches slashing his face, Ernst tore through the trees until a lifted root sent him somersaulting. He was still on the ground when he heard the voices. Peering through the wands of a hazel bush into which he'd crashed, he saw figures moving in what seemed to be a clearing. A tick-ticking was coming from somewhere even closer. Somehow the camera had been switched on. Were they partisans? His fingers fumbled with the camera mechanism but it was jammed. Tick-tick-tick-tick like a death-watch beetle. From somewhere there was a shriek of gunfire. A dog began to bark. He had been spotted. The voices were even clearer now. But they weren't Russian. They were speaking German. Never before had his own language sounded so sweet in his ears.

3

The first thing that the folklorist sees on entering the clearing is a bottle. It appears to be shimmering in mid-air; and it takes him a few seconds to realise that it is not floating but standing on a table. But this is hardly less incongruous: a table with a crisp white cloth set in a woodland clearing in the middle of a war zone. Only when he has fully assimilated the table with its bottle of schnapps and tower of glasses does Ernst take in what the camera, held at his thigh, is already recording for posterity: a group of men gathered in the clearing. A distinctly motley crew, some of them wear the wolf grey of the Waffen SS, others are stripped to the waist; a number sport swimming trunks in honour of the last warm day of the year. Laughing and joking they are being served the schnapps by a steward whose jacket is as starchily white as his tablecloth. 'So you've decided to come to the party after all,' a man dressed more fully than the others greets Ernst. 'We were wondering when you would show up.' Despite the heat, not only is his uniform buttoned up to the chin but he is also wearing his hat on whose crown the Nazi death's head glints in the sun. 'Your reputation precedes you. Gentlemen, I give you a personal friend of our esteemed Reichsführer. Apparently he's here to collect stories; isn't that right?' Ernst grins weakly. The other men toast him, tossing back their champagne goblets with bravado. 'Have you come to tread some grapes as well?' he smiles at

445

Ernst's bare feet. The steward hands the folklorist a glass. Under all those eyes, he drinks. His heart races as he looks about. There is no sign of the Jew; all he sees is the deep pit that has been dug right across the clearing. 'Did you get our present by the way?' the man with the death's-head hat asks. 'The lads thought it might tickle you. We'll have to have the old fellow back when you're finished with him though.'

'You can't,' Ernst says, his voice breaking.

'What do you mean?'

'He's dead already.'

'Saves us a job, I suppose.' Another drink is poured for him. As Ernst stares at it Deathshead grips his wrist and forces the spirit down his throat. 'Believe me,' he says not unkindly, 'it's the only way. You're just in time for our team talk.' The others gather round. 'Men,' he says expansively, 'I want you to toast yourselves. What else can I say? You know how important your work is; each and every one of you is a hero. I salute you. And today, even the film cameras have come. Don't try and hide the camera, Mr Barefoot Story-catcher, film to your heart's content. None of us are ashamed of what we do. And later tonight we'll all watch the movie together.' The men drink again. 'Now, kick off!' Taking a whistle from his pocket, the officer blows it. Shouts and savage barking echo through the trees. A feeling of vertigo assails Ernst as he pretends to film. The steward fusses over the little spills of schnapps on his tablecloth. The wood seems to have come alive; its trees appear to be rushing towards the clearing. So closely does the bark of young birches resemble European skin tone that Ernst only realises that it is humans and not trees when the first woman stumbles into the clearing. She is utterly naked. 'As ever,' the officer is telling the others, 'there is a prize for the top scorer.'

More and more women are arriving in the clearing; they stand huddled at the edge of the pit. The desperate momentum knocks one of them into the gaping earth. Some of those standing above the hole reach down for her. The whistle is blown. 'Offside!' Deathshead shouts. Plucking a birch branch from a tree, he waves it like a linesman's flag. Dogs leap at the would-be rescuers. Ernst rests his cheek against the side of the jammed camera. The Arri will capture forever this cold-blooded, drunken massacre, but it will miss the details to which only the human eye or ear is privy: the goosebumps on the women's arms held folded over their breasts; the bees plying the patch of foxgloves just in front of the pit; the sudden silence in which the suckling of a newborn baby can be heard. 'Take a seat in the stands, things are likely to get a little messy on the field of play,' Deathshead whispers to Ernst. 'You'll get a better camera angle from there too.' He winks at the folklorist then turns to the women. 'Enemies of humanity, you are being shot in reprisal for yesterday's partisan murder of a German soldier. And because Moses has to have his beard cut.' A flurry of titters from the men is silenced by two short sharp blows on the whistle, followed by a volley of firing. The first row of women fall into the pit. A second volley brings down the next line and so on until all the women in the clearing have fallen in the mass grave, and the clump of foxgloves has been shredded. Already the steward is refilling glasses, handing out cigarettes. The film jams in the camera. 'One-nil to us,' Deathshead pronounces. He comes over to Ernst. 'I hope we're giving you a good show.' The folklorist cannot reply. A bumblebee searches for the foxgloves; flies are gathering in the pit. 'Well, that's what you're here for, isn't it?' There's an edge to his voice. 'To check we're doing our job properly? All the other special units in the area have been in touch. Do you really think we buy this stuff about collecting stories? I mean, what kind of freak comes to a war to collect stories?' Deathshead stalks over to the pit. Someone is groaning down there. 'Not bad,' he grins. 'Our left wing needs to concentrate a little more.' He takes out a grenade, and his men laughingly dive for cover. He tosses the grenade onto the layer of bodies below. When the explosion has died down, the groaning has stopped. A second crowd of women are driven through the trees; a third wave, a fourth, then: 'Half-time, gentlemen.'

Meticulous as ever, the steward cleans spots of blood from one of his plates as he dishes up luncheon: chicken legs, sausage, pork; somehow he has managed to serve the potatoes hot. Ernst takes the plate he is handed, but the food piled on it slides to the ground. Later it will be devoured by ants. He staggers to the periphery of the gathering, but clearly he is too important a visitor to be left unattended. Skull and crossbones glinting in the hot sun, Deathshead bears down on him once more. 'So do I get a good report? I use the humour just to lighten the men's load a little. Like sending you old Grandfather Abraham. No hard feelings? It can get grim otherwise. Funny thing is,' he grins, 'my men *are* a good football team. You're never seen this before, have you? I can tell; your face is white as a miller's. Don't worry; none of us were born butchers. I was just like you. Two months ago I had never even shot a rabbit. I'm a lawyer.'

The waves of women come and go. The banter wears thin. Grim-faced, the men fire. Exhausted by the trials and tribulations of catering in such adverse conditions, the steward naps under a tree. 'Are there more to come?' Deathshead demands. He is told yes there are more. For the first time he seems to lose control. 'But the pit's almost full. Jesus Christ, who the fuck dug this scrape? Bring me the jokers who built this scratch.'

'They're in it already,' one of his men replies.

This time the laughter is forced.

When the next wave of women have been dealt with, the pit is full to capacity. Deathshead's brow wrinkles: yet another of his many logistical problems. For a moment he closes his eyes as though allowing himself to dream of the quiet farmer's life which will be his to enjoy one day. No more pettifogging over the law back in his native Cologne, no more butchering women: the simple life of the farmer. 'More schnapps,' he orders. Some of the men are flexing bad backs, others gingerly kneading shoulders enflamed by the repetitive action of prolonged firing; a number are lying propped up against trees like resting harvesters. An accordion tests itself on the silence with a few notes of a popular song. Nobody seems to have noticed the woman standing by the edge of the pit; somehow she has been missed by the guns. 'What the fuck is she doing?' Deathshead demands. He goes over to her. What will he do, the men wonder, punch, kick or shoot? 'It's Lili Marlene!' some wag cried. To a barrack of hilarity, the accordion obliges, wheezing out the introduction to the well-known ditty. When Deathshead takes hold of the startled woman and begins to dance with her round the clearing, the screams of laughter are almost as loud as the gunfire had been. When they dance past Ernst, the folklorist looks down at his feet.

'What's the matter, darling?' the dancer asks his unwilling partner, stiff as wood in his arms. 'Don't you love me any more?' He rolls his eyes in mockery of forlorn lovesickness. The men are hysterical. He dances her to the edge of the pit with mincing little steps. 'After you, my dear,' he says as he gallantly hands her onto the bodies. Now they are dancing on a floor of heads, bellies, breasts, and feet. The men sing:

> 'We will create a world for two
> I'll wait for you
> The whole night through
> For you, Lili Marlene
> For you, Lili Marlene.'

With a chivalrous bow, Deathshead relinquishes his partner to one of the grinning men waiting in a queue for their turn. The beautiful melody is marred with hoofed arpeggios and Siamese-twinned notes as the accordionist shakes with mirth. 'I see what you're going through,' Ernst hears Deathshead say to him. 'Your first time? We all have first times. I will let you into a secret. He's been out here, you know; your boss, Herr Himmler. He wanted to see with his own eyes what he was asking us to do. Admirable, admirable. Here, take my advice, drink.' The bottle is too heavy for Ernst; it is held steady for him like a mother feeding her baby. 'What's he like, our ReichsFührer?'

'Glasses.' Ernst's voice is mechanical. 'Short hair, shaved tightly at the back.'

Laughter: the folklorist is clapped on the back. 'I can see you aren't giving much away. *He* got upset too, you know. A friend of mine was there. Little H didn't like the blood either. Who does? *Are you sure they're all Jews?* That's what he asked them. You see, he wanted to save them, if it was possible. Christ, but don't we all feel that way? He even went up to the prisoners. *If you're not Jewish let me know.*' For a whole minute Deathhead's hilarity renders him incapable. 'None of them moved. Can you believe that? Not one said a word. Mind, you could tell by looking they were all friends of Moses. A real shtetl full of Yids. You know the saying: *hooked nose and hooked chin, a living devil lives therein.*'

At a sudden shattering noise, the accordion breaks off. The steward flinches; has someone

451

smashed another of his champagne glasses? What trouble he takes to keep these goblets intact! Not to worry, it's only the woman screaming. Having pinioned her down two men are rifling her orifices. Ernst cannot avoid seeing one of them penetrate her with his gun. The trigger is pulled. The shot meets with gusts of laughter, but Deathshead is furious. He rushes over and punches the perpetrators to the ground; they try to explain but it seems he is going to shoot them both until at the last moment something mollifies him. He comes straight over to Ernst. 'It's all right,' he smooths. 'They were looking for contraband. They had it on good authority that she had hidden the jewellery she should have given up to the Reich. They often do that, you know; they — there's no delicate way of putting this! — ram things up their cunts.' He smiles ingratiatingly, his teeth glinting like the silver skull and crossbones on his hat. 'I don't want you to get the idea that I allow cruelty to fester among my men! We all know how it can flare up in work of this nature. But these lads mean too much to me; I will not allow anyone in my squad to become brutal; and I hope you tell the ReichsFührer as much.' Deathshead looks about the grove. 'What a lovely spot, so peaceful. You know, some of us have been talking about settling here after the war. Once we get the birch trees up it'll be good land. I want you to know that you'll always be welcome. When all of this is over, this will be a haven of tranquillity. By the way, you may want to film this next bit for our friends in Berlin so they can see how I look after the welfare of my boys. Actually, it's an innovation of mine.' Mechanically Ernst raises the camera to his eye. It is a relief to have the horror reduced to the restrictions of the viewfinder. Even looking through the camera he can see that the light is at its most beautiful; the setting sun suffuses the grove with a honeyed topaz. 'Gentlemen,' Deathshead's voice echoes through the sylvan dell, 'I apologise but I must ask you for one final spurt. Yes; I'm afraid it's that time again when the men will be separated from the boys. Anyone who doesn't want to do this can be excused now — we'll fit you up with a dress and send you to a retirement home for exhausted ladies.' A strained titter runs through the men. 'Now, lads, I know it's been a hard day and you've been heroic, but you know as well as I do that we must finish the job. The little group. How could I be justified in asking you to kill the parents if I let you leave the next generation free to spawn? Now, we've got to be particularly careful. Other groups have lost men here. No bullets; this is bayonet work.' Turning to the camera he adds proudly: 'You see, I've found there's not enough flesh on baby bones; the bullets just ricochet.' Again the whistle is blown.

As though forming the long tail of an English folk dance, the men make two lines facing each other over a second, much smaller pit. It's cooler now and those who were wearing swimming trunks are fully dressed. A group of children are led from the trees. A pair of women are carrying two babies each; other infants are carried by members of the Ukrainian militia; some of them

453

are sleeping, their heads resting against coarse-clothed shoulders. One of the militia totes a sack over his shoulder which bulges with a number of fontanels and a hoarse infantile cry. A toddler makes a dash for it. A dog streaks after her. From the undergrowth come the dog's snarls and the child's squeals. The men on the near side of the pit take a child each which they then throw across to their partner's waiting bayonet. Some are cleanly spitted and have to be pulled off the blade; others have their internal organs severed by slashing blows; one is neatly decapitated. The slaughter is so quiet that the sleeping babies do not wake until they are in mid-air. The sack is swung against a tree trunk three times then emptied into the pit.

When the children are all dead, Ernst hears a rasping groan behind him. A woman, black with flies, has crawled from the first pit; she is trying to get to where the children are lying. The men watch her in silence. No one moves. 'You do it,' a voice suddenly commands Ernst. 'You've seen us at work; now it's your turn. Put your camera down and finish her off.' Relinquishing the camera, the folklorist feels the cold press of metal in his hand. It is a Pistole 08. 'Believe me,' advises Deathshead in considerate tones, 'the best thing is not to think about it. Just pull the trigger.' Ernst is given another drink and then escorted to the woman. 'What's the matter, bigshot friend of the Reichsführer; more of a Gretel than a Hansel? How can you be so heartless? She's just seen her child chopped in two like a log, and you're going to leave her in agony? What are you, some kind of sadist?' Under a lash of laughter, the folklorist shuffles forward and kneels down beside the woman who continues to edge forward through her aura of flies. Eternity passes in a single swallow of his throat. He feels something settle on the back of his neck just where the spinal cord enters the skull: one of the flies. Instinctively he reaches up to brush it away. His fingers encounter gunmetal. 'You fire or I will,' says Deathshead, crouching over him, 'Either way, it's going to be a skull-shot. I'll count to three. One, two . . . '

Auvers-sur-Oise, July 1890

I'm wondering how to show you the funeral procession that is winding through the narrow streets of Auvers-sur-Oise under a fierce July sun. If I place you in the garden of the white house with Monsieur Leblaine and his grandson, then you would hear the hard rattle of grief and wheels as the coffin cart passes up the lane. Running down to the knothole in the fence you might snatch a quick glimpse of the box which has been draped in a white sheet and drenched in sunflowers, or even see a face clenched with pain among the dark-clad bodies of the mourners, but to gain a real sense of the sorrow binding the tight group of funeral followers I'd have to move you into the cortège itself. There, standing near the back alongside Georgiana Fairbanks and James Dalrymple, you will be able to see the way Theo Van Gogh stumbles every twenty paces or so, a lurch that passes like a shock wave through the procession; from the rear you would also be able to see the manner in which Dr Gachet keeps lifting his head to gulp back a sob. 'Did you know,' you'll hear Georgiana whisper, 'the priest wouldn't even allow him the hearse?' Yet from this perspective, although you would be well placed to see how at each jolt of the uneven road a handful of flowers falls to the ground, you would miss the full agony on the bereaved brother's face. Neither would you be able to hear the gurgling of the deceased body's juices, as though inside the box Vincent is still smoking his pipe.

But perhaps I ought to let you see the whole thing earlier, as the mourners gather in the little room above the cafe, say. Since we can, why not rewind the cortège back through the streets sweltering under the midsummer heat to Vincent Van Gogh's last earthly bedroom. There is the box still open as he lies in state. At his foot stands his easel, beneath which his brushes are fanned on the floor. Watch the lid being nailed on, and the sunflowers, dahlias and ranunculi thrown over the white sheet now covering the casket. Hear the church bell striking; on the third peal the coffin is raised. Pause a moment before following it down the stairs and look at the walls. Every single inch of their space is covered with the artist's work. Here, with thirty or forty of his Auvers oeuvre before you, you will see the full blaze of this man's genius; a dazzling explosion of light as though the sun itself has come down to linger in that little room.

Yet maybe I should place you with Chip Coakley, who is on his way to the station when he puts down his suitcase to check the time and catches sight of the cortège winding up the hill to the cemetery. Then, like him, you would hear the mourners' sorrow reverberating in the bowl of Auvers, its ragged glissandos of grief reaching you like the tatter of wind chimes. From there you would be able to see how richly the white cloth and yellow flowers glint in the bright sun:

an eye-gold that reminds even millionaires of the unbankable riches of art's alchemy. Standing there, you can do as the Californian does now and stoop to pick up one of the sunflowers that fell from the coffin cart earlier. It's up to you whether you keep it or toss it aside like Chip Coakley as he heads for the train a disappointed man.

After all, maybe the best view would be provided if I bequeath you a pair of crow's wings. Flying with the flock drifting above the town, you can then follow the whole procession to the cemetery. Perching on one of the nearby gravestones you will see the unbridled grief of Theo Van Gogh, and Dr Gachet faltering as he addresses the gathering: 'This was an honest man who cared for nothing but humanity and art. In his art he will live forever, blazing for us like one of his own sunflowers . . . ' As a crow you might then lift and, rising, see how beyond the green grass of the cemetery, the wheat fields of Auvers seem to stretch forever. Flying back for one last view of the village with its church, town hall, chestnut trees, green river and cafe, you might spot two figures walking down the main street, an old man and a boy: the gardener and his grandson. Swoop closer and see them disappearing into the cafe. I have left the skylight open so that you can see them entering Van Gogh's room and watch them gathering up the flowerpots. Looking at the pictures on the wall, the gardener smiles. One of the canvases had been put there by the young English woman as a tribute; it's her version of the white house garden in spring. 'I've got your mate,' the old man says. 'So you might as well come too.' And easing out the lightly hammered nails he takes down Georgiana Fairbanks's picture, and rolls it under his arm. 'Now, lad,' he says, putting his arm round the boy's shoulder, 'let's go home and see what your mother's got for lunch.'

Acknowledgements

Mr P D Hodgkinson, Consultant Cleft and Plastic Surgeon, RVI Newcastle
Gertrud Mistry
Pamela Smith
Alistair Hicks
Ringo

We do hope that you have enjoyed reading
this large print book.

Did you know that all of our titles
are available for purchase?

We publish a wide range of high quality
large print books including:

Romances, Mysteries, Classics
General Fiction
Non Fiction and Westerns

Special interest titles available in
large print are:

The Little Oxford Dictionary
Music Book
Song Book
Hymn Book
Service Book

Also available from us courtesy of Oxford
University Press:

Young Readers' Dictionary
(large print edition)
Young Readers' Thesaurus
(large print edition)

For further information or a free
brochure, please contact us at:

Ulverscroft Large Print Books Ltd.,
The Green, Bradgate Road, Anstey,
Leicester, LE7 7FU, England.
Tel: (00 44) 0116 236 4325
Fax: (00 44) 0116 234 0205

THE GHOST LOVER

Gillian Greenwood

Josie Price has given up much of her life for the wealthy Haddeley family. Working and living with them, she knows their secrets. So when a young man, Luke, appears and claims, shockingly, to be the son of Kit Haddeley's late wife Alice, Josie helps the family come to terms with ghosts they hoped had been laid to rest. But Luke's arrival casts shadows on both the past and the future, and the ghost of Alice Haddeley hangs heavily over the family. Through Luke, she seems to demand to be both mourned and revenged. It is Josie who holds the key to the mystery of Alice, and it is Josie, beset by guilt, who must resolve the destructive inheritance that Luke brings in his wake.